THE CHILDREN OF DARKNESS AND LIGHT

Centrillio Publishing

THE CHILDREN OF DARKNESS AND LIGHT

Paul T Liversidge

The Bloodline War Chronicles

Book 1

FOR MY FAMILY AND ESPECIALLY MY DOGS....BOBBY,
BRONTE AND OF COURSE BEAR

Northlands of Erestor

Chapter 1 – The Children of the New World

Talis Quicksilver walked down the bumpy dirt track inside the forest as he returned from his hunting trip. He did this most days, as hunting was his favourite pastime and the inn needed a constant supply of meat. Unfortunately, he was pretty tired, and the wild boar he was pulling on his sledge was starting to get heavier by the minute. In addition, the track was being overly unforgiving on his legs, and it wasn't easy to navigate at the best of times. But Talis was generally in a good mood. It was the end of the season, and all the people in his village, Keros, was caught up in the throws of excitement. Everyone was running around preparing for the closing of the summer solstice and getting ready for the autumn equinox celebrations.

Talis redoubled his effort to get home as quickly as possible to show his sister what he had caught and see if he had bettered her hunt. Lauren had set off at the same time this morning, but they had gone their separate ways. They didn't want to see each other as they hunted, as this spoiled the fun of the near-daily competition they held with each other if their paths crossed. Talis always wanted the bragging rights that he had caught more when they were hunting. Lauren was a good hunter, no doubt about it. But he wanted everyone to know he was the best hunter in the area.

Talis and his sister Lauren were twins, and they were as inseparable as they were different. The only thing that showed them as kin was their father's eyes. A deep sky blue set against an auburn rim. Edged with fire, people used to say, a gaze that could penetrate the soul and make people feel as if their soul was being laid bare. Talis had rich golden hair, whilst Lauren's hair was a very unusual colouring of platinum and gold. Both were physically well-defined and athletic in appearance, but Talis had become a giant of a man, standing at just over six feet tall, and he was as strong as anyone in the area. On the other hand, Lauren was a good six inches smaller and was known for her great beauty, something he had never managed to pull off.

Their personalities were also polar opposites. Talis was more the severe and self-righteous individual who, some would say, was quite cold and lacked little warmth. He knew people thought this, and it did trouble him at times. However, he also knew that he must be strong of mind and tone if he was to become the man his father was and inherit his father's position as a community leader.

His heart only lightened when his damn infuriating sister was with him, and he grinned to himself as he pondered this. Lauren was beyond playful. She was a nightmare. Lauren talked non-stop if you let her. She was always in trouble and causing chaos wherever she went. Lauren took great joy in bringing laughter, and her constant practical jokes were his nightmares, but Talis and the village people loved her for it. She was not only a carefree spirit; she looked after the weak and the poor with the dedication of one of the old god's healers. If Lauren wasn't hunting or working in the inn, you would find her keeping company or running errands for the aged and infirm. She gave everybody something to lighten their day, no matter the form her kindness came in.

As he wanted to make the village before sundown, he pushed on as he watched the skies begin to redden and darken. He knew the chill of the valley would soon be on him, and the dampness would quickly be creeping into his bones. Gathering his cloak tighter over his head, Talis reflected on the simple life he was leading, a life he loved with every beat of his heart. Yet he longed to see more of the world. His father had taught his children much lore and shared a great deal of knowledge, creating a deep longing to go on a great adventure and discover new things.

After their mother had died young, the twins had spent much of their childhood with their father, Loran. Their father was not only the proprietor of the inn. Some would say he was a highly regarded community leader and a protector of the surrounding land and its people. However, he had also heard stories from the older folk that his father had come to settle in the village a long time ago. He had come from another land and was born of an age forgotten. They whispered that Loran possessed great powers of some kind in their stories. Still, Talis had seen nothing of this. Some years ago, when he had broached this subject with his father, Loran had just laughed at the idea and chided Talis for believing there was any reality to these child stories.

Their father had trained them in great detail about the power of life and death, and they had delved deeply into their surroundings and the many different hearts that beat in the skies, land and seas. Much of the knowledge he shared intertwined with the everlasting strength of the sun, moon and stars.

They had spent hours studying and discussing the old forgotten gods and the powerful elemental forces of Water, Fire, Earth and Air that come together to make the whole. He also taught them many of the laws of the natural world and gave them both a keen understanding of the land. But unfortunately, Loran had also made both of his children work in the inn, and the chores at times were hard going and never-ending.

Talis knew he resented the tasks at times, as they stopped him from going out hunting, which was his favourite pastime. Occasionally Talis would remind himself and Lauren that the inn didn't run itself and their father needed the help. But, on the whole, when he considered everything, the life he had, it did feel full and rewarding. However, he couldn't help himself wanting a little more adventure and to travel in the broader world.

Yawning as he came through the forest clearing into the glade, in the distance, Talis could now see the smoke of the village rising through the surrounding trees. As he got closer, he could hear the familiar sounds of the inn and the smell of some of the finest fare in the area. With one final push, dragging the sledge as fast as he could towards the inn, Talis made his way towards the store and the kitchen entrance at the back of the inn.

Opening the kitchen door and entering, the greeting was with a missile deftly aimed at his head, and he guessed who as he started wiping the tomato juice from his face and heard the light laughter; Lauren.

Chapter 2 – The Twins

Lauren couldn't help herself. As much as she loved her brother, he needed to be reminded that he was an obstinate stiff-necked pain. Seeing him return from the hunt through the inn window, noting by the size of the boar, he had a haul that was more significant than hers. Talis would gloat when he compared his boar to her pheasants and hares. Lauren knew she had to get to him as soon as he entered with something to lighten the mood, grinning she knew what to do. Rushing past her father, who was coming out of the kitchen with a massive platter piled high with steaming spicy meats and potatoes, she nearly knocked him flying in her haste.

"Lauren will you watch what you are doing, girl," he shouted after her as she entered the kitchen, where she grabbed the first thing that came to hand, a large beef tomato, which she let fly with skilful accuracy as soon as Talis's head appeared in the doorway.

"God damn it, shortcake," shouted Talis. "I will kill you one of these days."

Talis started to wipe the tomato residue off his face and broke into a grin. Talis knew she hated the nickname he had given her when he began to tower over her as a child. Lauren leapt at him, knocking half the kitchen utensils and prepared food onto the floor as she wrestled him to the ground and placed him in a headlock.

"Get off me", grimaced Talis as they fought and grabbled across the floor, becoming covered in various pieces of the savoury dishes Lauren had scattered everywhere.

"Stop," came a commanding and booming voice that could only belong to their father, Loran.

"How can I run the inn with you two running wild," Loran scowled at them as they slowly unravelled and got to their feet. "Look at the mess you made and the waste you have caused."

Talis started protesting his innocence, but their father was having none of it.

"Both of you will get this mess cleared up at once, and you will work in the kitchen all night now preparing food that you have ruined," shouted Loran as he glared at them.

Lauren was shocked.

"Father, please, everyone is getting ready for tomorrow's celebrations," cried Lauren. Their father just shook his head and walked back out of the kitchen.

"Great, well done, Lauren, you have done it again, I've been out all day, and now I have to do this all night," moaned Talis. "Then we will have to be up early helping with the food preparations."

"Shut up moaning all the time, Talis. Let's get tidied up, and I will work on father," grinned Lauren as she pushed Talis playfully.

Within the hour, the kitchen was clean and looking well-loved again, and Lauren had convinced Loran that they would be better out of the kitchen than within it.

They made their way out to the bar. Talis looked around and saw the inn was very full tonight. The inn was a well-loved, wooden building where most patrons were the locals, but occasionally they would house travellers, and their horses would be stabled at the rear. Everything about the inn was quaint. The chairs, tables and furnishings were as old as Lauren and Talis. Their father spent hours each week repairing and polishing all the wood to maintain the high standard he liked the inn to be in.

As they grabbed a couple of mugs of the inn's finest mead that their father brewed from their hives of honey bees in the adjacent field. They noted a group of friends sitting in the corner. They grabbed some stools and flopped down beside them. Soon they were deep in conversation about tomorrow's celebrations, what was happening throughout the day, and the different types of festivities they each enjoyed.

Later in the evening, Gerard came in and joined them. He had been working in the northern territories of the dales in Ascalon.

"I've returned this evening, partly because I wanted to be at tomorrow's celebrations, but I am also starting to feel uneasy being away from home," divulged Gerard as he drank some of the inn's mead heavily.

"Why?" Lauren asked. "Everything is the same as usual."

"But, haven't you heard all the rumours?" Gerard asked incredulously. "There is war in the northlands, they say. There are rumours from many voices, rumours of goblin armies pouring out of Jeliah sweeping away any resistance as they march south. I have heard many tales of great battles being fought, battles with the dwarves in the mountain ranges. The dwarves held for some time, or so they say. However, they failed because of the darkness in the end."

Gerard exaggerated the word darkness greatly and looked around his audience in excitement.

"They also whisper more of this darkness, an evil untold, a swarm of monstrous beings, they say, terror and fire in one, others say. What are they? No one knows, but they are giving certain victory to the goblin hordes, sweeping away all before them."

Everyone in their small group stared at Gerard before Talis broke the silence.

"Come, Gerard, you do not believe in ghost stories and fairy tales for children? Have you put him up to this, Lauren, one of your jokes?" Asked Talis.

Before Lauren could retort, Gerard hissed, "Talis, believe what you want. I saw the fear in the eyes of those telling the tale. I think we all should take heed and pray that the rumours do not come down into the valley."

They all went silent for a while and sipped their drinks. Lauren was bored of all this chatter of death and doom. The celebration day was just around the corner, and Gerard was depressing everyone with his fairytales. Still, boys seem to like stories of war and battle, no matter how gruesome. Men were strange, she thought.

Lauren suddenly got up and shouted to the now full inn.

"A song." Lauren hollered. "C'mon, everyone."

Lauren jumped onto a table and started singing a crowd favourite about drinking too much. Soon everyone was joining in with her singing, the mead began to flow quicker and not before long, her group had quickly forgotten the stories they had just heard.

The next day, Talis, Lauren and their friends had long forgotten the night before and the words of Gerard. They were all up at the breaking of the rising dawn. The whole village, especially the inn, was busy preparing the food for the celebrations and getting the final touches ready for the midday pageant, which would end in congregation around the stage for the rest of the festivities. Loran was running around like a madman cooking meats and loaves of bread in the big stone kiln oven. He was baulking orders at Talis and Lauren every few minutes. Even Lauren was doing exactly as she was told. Not only was Lauren really excited. She wanted to get everything done as soon as possible so she could make her way to the Equinox festival.

The food fayre was extraordinary when Lauren arrived thirty minutes after their father and Talis, who had already set off with all the goods the inn was providing. She had wanted to change into her best clothes, and it took time to do her hair. Lauren liked to have her hair platted for special occasions as she thought it made her look prettier and wanted to catch the eye of everyone. When she was ready, Lauren rushed down the street to be hit by the finest selections of meats, cheese, vegetables, fruits, and desserts on stalls and tables everywhere. A large variety of different drinks was available. Loran, who was well-travelled, had imported goods from many foreign places and ensured the village had the best he could find.

Entertainment was plentiful. You had children playing with toy swords, weaving in and out of the street entertainers. There was acting, singing and dancing on the stage constructed in the centre of the village. Everyone in the community had a wonderful time, and all agreed that it was one of the best equinox festivals in recent times. Lauren would freely admit she had a spectacular time, and her singing antics later in the evening became legendary for a few months. Even Talis would readily omit that he had enjoyed himself as he woke from the night before with a sore head.

Chapter 3 – The Awakening

Talis stirred from a restless sleep, filled with broken dreams and nightmares that had not entirely formed into any meaning. Yet, though they were constant each night, and he was sure they had some inner message of pending doom, he struggled to piece them together.

The dreams had started three days ago after the attack on his village Keros, where the marauding army from Jeliah had scattered his people. His people knew of the ghoulish scavengers from this region and the rumours they were under the sway of some new power that had arisen. It had been said in the inn many times that this mysterious power came into battle with armies shrouded in unholy darkness, and some said the host contained large hideous creatures cloaked in black. Horrors born from another world, destroying all that stood in the way. Moreover, the constant flow of strangers and refugees that passed through the village spoke of burning, looting, rape, murder, slavery, and suffering. If the rumours were true, it was also apparent that these soldiers were moving further south and getting closer each day. Talis wasn't sure about the truth of what he had heard over the last few months, and he couldn't get his head around the whole story, a story that had started on the eve of the autumn equinox celebration. But there was something very wrong happening in the world; he was sure of that.

Then the day had come, just as autumn was passing into winter. It was early morning, and darkness still held the daylight at bay. Drums and horns sounded from deep within the forest. Then the skies were alight with a greenish-red haze, and then the armies descended from the trees and through the surrounding meadows, and there was fire, screams and death as the marauders raised the village to the ground.

The battle had not lasted long. His people were not a warrior race and lived by working the surrounding land. There were too many of the goblins, and these devils, large, fast, strong, cloaked in blackness, drove through his people, though they had fought with courage. The darkness tore them down as if they were just petals being pulled from flowers.

Talis had initially fought alongside his father and sister, but the masses split them as the battle raged. In the distant melee, he saw the darkness surrounding his father. He remembered how his father's sword glowed, and his body was bathed in an unnatural silver-white light. It was intense, as if lightning was striking him as a crackling ringing sound broke through the thunderous noise of the battle. He was unsure how many it took to take his father down as Talis was fighting for his life, but his father, the village's protector, was struck down and fell out of sight as the screams of delight from the dark creatures could be heard. He knew he had tried hard to reach him. But the fighting in front of him had blocked his path, and no matter how he tried to push through the crowd of bodies, he couldn't reach him or get there to save him. Then there was pain, a blinding light, and he descended into darkness.

He had not seen any further killing of his people, friends, or family. Talis had slept in this world of darkness. Then, when, he did not know, he awoke in the deep wet undergrowth within the edge of the forest on his village's outskirts, and he saw that the village was no more. Talis saw the burnt, charred remains of what was left of anything that resembled buildings. As the tears rolled down his face, Talis saw bodies strewn everywhere, and the surrounding land was shaded in a deep rich brown, the blood of his people.

Talis moved gingerly towards the village, expecting to be captured or slain by some remnant of the enemy he expected to still be there. But he saw no one.

Finally, after some searching, he found his beloved father. It was funny looking down on him. His face was still how he remembered it, a face full of wisdom and calmness. Talis still saw the man he had followed and worshipped for twenty-one years. Kneeling beside him, he slowly closed his father's eyes and spoke to him, laying down a promise born of love and pain—a promise of revenge for his people.

Talis gently removed the unusual pendant hidden from sight from around his father's neck. Loran always kept the pendant with him, which was well hidden from view. He had told Talis and Lauren it was one of his most treasured items, and when the time came, it would pass to one of them. However, it was ancient and from another time, and they must ensure this family heirloom remained well hidden at all times as its value was immense.

Looking around, Talis recovered his father's antique longsword from the mud and bid him farewell. Then, slowly moving away, he continued his search for his sister. Talis looked through the strewn mounds of dead bodies and what was left of the buildings. Finally, he went to the inn, hoping she would be there. The inn was in ruins, but somehow, it still stood and was still recognisable as a building made for food and drink.

Talis stumbled through the front entrance and called for

Lauren many times, but she was nowhere to be seen. His head raced. Has she survived, he wondered, had she been taken prisoner or maybe Lauren had taken flight as she saw the battle was lost and only had one outcome. Talis knew he must find her, yet he did not know how. If Lauren had been captured, she would have been taken north towards the strongholds of Jeliah. If Lauren had escaped, indeed, she would have gone south towards the unknown realms of southern Ascalon. He made his way to his room and found that it was nearly completely intact and had survived the destruction of much of the inn. Talis grabbed his favourite hunting knife, longbow and quiver. He then exited through what had been the kitchen.

Talis decided in an instance that if she had gone south, she was safe. Therefore, he must go north towards Jeliah and try to catch up with what he expected to be slave caravans. He would hopefully find Lauren or at least more of his people.

Chapter 4 – The Meeting

The destruction of his village had been three days ago. Since leaving, Talis had moved through the forest, though it made his progress north slower. He decided this was the best way to avoid detection. Talis was well trained in forest lore and strong and athletic. Yet, he still moved at a pace that would challenge much less hardy folk. He travelled without rest as the pain of not knowing where Lauren was, became all-consuming.

Talis was cold to the bone, wet from the constant winter showers and was starting to feel the pangs of hunger as he survived, eating only the forest berries he found and drinking from the little streams that twined their way through the trees. Talis was tiring badly, and he was still in pain from whatever had hit his head in the attack. He knew he must rest soon, or he would lack the energy to free Lauren.

Talis continued for a few more hours when he came across a small stone hut in a small tree clearing. It had been abandoned some time ago as the door was hanging on for its dear life by a solitary hinge and the thatched roof had holes of various sizes in many places. Talis drew his father's sword and slowly walked towards the doorway. With the point of his sword, he pushed the door inwards and peered in. With relief, he saw it was desolate.

The hut was a solitary circular room of no size. There were remnants of what would have been a table, and there were broken chairs around it. Broken pottery and what might have been prized possessions were scattered all over the room. As Talis surveyed the room, Talis noted a bed in the corner and a small fireplace. Though damp inside, all things considered, it was good enough. Talis needed rest and to remove the chill from his bones.

Grabbing some of the smaller pieces of wood from the broken chairs, he started to build up the fireplace. Taking his knife, he shaved thin pieces of wood as kindling material and found two spigots which he vigorously rubbed together over the next few minutes to create a spark for the kindling. Before long, Talis had the fire alight, and the heat started to cut through the cold, even though the outside wind and rain that entered the hut tried to fight the heat it irradiated. Talis then dropped onto the bed and immediately plunged into a restless sleep.

As Talis awoke sometime later, his head ached with a consistent pounding that was as regular as a heartbeat, and to compound this, a fair majority of his body was in various forms of pain. Squeezing his eyes as tight as possible, Talis tried desperately to return to sleep. But the focus of attempted sleep was stolen by pain, the coldness that still lay deep within his bones and the most annoying and repetitive tapping sound.

Gingerly opening his eyes, Talis surveyed the surrounding environment. Where was he? How did he get here? Laid on what appeared to be a small bed that could have been made of granite, he clung for warmth with a makeshift blanket of nothing more than rags. Then it all came rushing back, and it dawned on him how he got here and the past events that had started this journey.

The room gave off an eerie glow channelled from broken moonlight through torn and mouldy drapes and the smouldering remains of the fire that tried to break through the silver-lined darkness.

The rain was coming down heavily. It dripped and flowed with meticulous ease down the inner walls, creating an array of puddles in the room. It felt pretty funny and unusual to lie in this environment as Talis remembered the warmth of his life several days ago.

As he cleared his eyes, he suddenly saw a dark form sitting on a chair in the corner next to the fire. Talis bolted upright and made an attempted grab for his sword.

"Peace, Talis Quicksilver," a robust and commanding voice said. "I come to speak to you, and I bring you no harm. My name is Berolarn. I was once your father's friend".

The man seemed to pause, and beneath his hood, his veiled face was studying Talis as the light flicked it in and out of the shadows. His presence brought a cold chill to Talis's blood.

"Who are you? What do you want?" Talis asked with unease.

"The name I have given you, as for what I want, is quite a long tale. I suspect you are hungry, Talis," replied Berolarn. Which came as a statement rather than a question, and the stranger was right as the hunger pangs hit him hard. Talis had not eaten in three days and felt exhausted and fragile.

"And you have slept for several hours as I have sat here. So let us build up the fire and eat before I start the tale," continued Berolarn.

Talis started to rise from the bed and protested that he must leave.

"My village destroyed, people dead or scattered. I must find my sister", blurted Talis.

The stranger pulled down his hood.

"Talis, you must learn to be calm, even in the most pressured situations. Your sister is safe for the time being. Lauren is a prize that the dark lord sought. Still, she escaped with the help of the elves," said Berolarn.

Tanis had no idea what Berolarn was talking about; who or what is the dark lord, and then what was this with elves? Finally, it dawned on him that this Berolarn also knew his name and Lauren's. He had never met him before, he was sure. Was it because he was indeed his father's friend, and their names had been mentioned in passing?

"Elves?" he asked. Berolarn turned and walked out of the hut.

"I will get some wood for the fire," stated Berolarn as he exited.

Talis paced around the hut, thoughts spinning around his head. Lauren, elves, dark lord, monsters. A friend of his father.

Berolarn returned with spigots of wet wood within a few minutes.

"You will not be able to make a fire with that wood," Talis stated as he studied the man.

Although this Berolarn was of similar age as his father, his face was weathered and had the appearance of tanned leather. His hair was a rich grey that fell to his shoulders. He carried a short beard, which was also grey though speckled a little with black. He stood at a similar height as Talis and was as broad, which was unusual, but it was his eyes. They were bright sky blue rimmed with the fiery red of his family. He had the same eyes as him! No one had ever seen his family's eyes anywhere else, and there was a stranger in front of him with the same eyes. His head started to scramble again, and he thought he would be sick.

"Sit down, Talis, the fire will start for me, and I will prepare the food," said Berolarn.

Talis slumped back down on the bed and watched the stranger intently. Somehow he managed to start the fire, and it roared with anger, spitting at the wet wood as it took hold. Talis tried to continue to ask the stranger more questions, but he was waved off.

"Peace for a moment longer, Talis. I will answer your questions soon enough," rebuked Berolarn.

Berolarn recovered some scattered cooking pots. Then, he left the hut again and fetched some water from a nearby stream. On his return, he closed the door and wedged it shut with some broken wood before being busy in front of the fire. Adding various ingredients to the water from a backpack at the side of the hearth, Talis saw meats and herbs dropping into the water as Berolarn stirred the contents over the fire. Before long, a wonderful smell filled the hut, and with it, Talis felt not only the coldness starting to subside but also an unbearable hunger.

Within the hour, they sat at the righted table on makeshift chairs, eating the meat broth Berolarn had cooked, accompanied by some small bread loaves, cheeses, and some wine that had also been recovered from Berolarn's backpack.

They both sat in silence as they ate. Talis longed to ask Berolarn questions, but it had been made clear to him that he would answer his questions later after they had eaten and not before. Soon they were finished, and Talis felt his strength and confidence returning. Talis looked deep into the eyes of this strange man. He hoped to see something that gave a picture of who he was. But his eyes were blank and filled with nothing that Talis could read. Finally, Berolarn went to his pack and pulled out a pipe and a pouch of weed. He filled his pipe with the weed and lit it with an ember from the fire. Berolarn drew on the pipe and breathed out large flumes of smoke that filled the room with a strange smell that Talis had never encountered.

Sitting back down, Berolarn looked at Talis and wondered where to start. He never expected to be doing this and telling this story. He also had not anticipated that Talis's father had never told him of the twin's true heritage. But it was apparent, by the look of surprise on his face, that Talis had no idea.

Berolarn had come to find Loran, explain what he saw from the north, that the evil forces had arisen again and a great storm from legends past was coming to consume all. But, unfortunately, he was too late. The servants of darkness had somehow known of the whereabouts of Loran as they had the others. They had got to Loran before he had arrived. Now it was up to him to tell Talis of his origins. He needed to explain the history of the world through the ages and some of what he knew of the dark powers. Berolarn returned Talis's stare and wondered how much Talis could cope with it.

"Talis, what I am about to tell you, is a brief history of the world, a history of who you are and where you come from. I will also try and explain the age we live in, and as much as I know of the darkness that comes to consume us all," said Berolarn, and then he stopped and pondered his following words as Talis shifted in his chair.

"The world we live in has changed many times, and many

ages have come and gone, long forgotten to most. Yet, the laws of nature decree that changes must be made. It needs to evolve and change for life to survive. But, the world must be with balance. Goodness and evil must strike this balance. If the scales tip too much one way, the world starts to collapse on itself," continued Berolarn.

Berolarn pulled something out of his pocket and, with sweeping movements of his arms, slowly whispered,

"sharla dafala ced undomin flam, undomain flam un ler delartu."

It was a weird language that Talis had never heard before. Much to Talis's amazement, Berolarn somehow conjured up a sizeable flaming ring that filled the room, which displayed images as he spoke in its centre.

"What you must understand, Talis, is that the world has seen many ages over millions of years since its birth. What I am about to show you is not a complete history of our world, as that would take a lifetime. What I will show you, though, is the most relevant period's that pertains to what happened in your village.

"At the beginning, before the dawn of man, many wonderous yet monstrous creatures walked the lands, controlled the sea and mastered the air, and the world was theirs. All other animals quaked and ran from their path. Chief amongst these were the great wyrms, legendary reptilian beasts as large as a mountain, scales as hard and strong as steel, wings beating with a sound of clapping thunder, and a breath that was death to all as flame and lightning were brought forth on their enemies. They were also highly evolved and intelligent, and they ruled supreme. They were the most blessed and were the firstborn of the gods. Our legends call them Dragons," continued Berolarn.

Talis stared open-mouthed at the ring as images of the majestic beasts flashed across the sky. Dragons of different sizes, colours and shapes. The scenes showed that the different colours of the dragons fought for supremacy in the skies, using bite, flame and claw, and the battles were deadly.

"Dragons were real?" whispered Talis questionably, to which Berolarn nodded.

"Dragons were of ancient lineage and fearsome power, longest-lived of all the children of the lands, and the gods gifted them the power of what you call magic, which was innate in all. Some were highly feared for their selfish, evil ways, born with sadistic natures, effective predatory skills, exceptional cunning levels, and unparalleled greed. They terrified their foes. Others were noble, good and wise and sought to protect all, seeing themselves as no more than a powerful race amongst many others. What happened to all that lived in this age is unknown. The forgotten histories give many theories, but all, including the dragons, disappeared, and the world was barren of most life. I suspect the balance had swung too far one way, and the gods and nature were readjusting to bring order, but that is a wild guess," said Berolarn, who went quiet as he puffed on his pipe.

"I just cannot believe dragons are real," said Talis with awe.

"Most things whispered in legends and stories have a hidden truth, Talis. So never be dismissive of what you think are fables," replied Berolarn.

"Continuing, we have the second age. In the second age, we saw the dawning of manlike people. As they evolved, one group lusted for knowledge and wisdom. They studied deep into the earth's foundations, the power of the seas, the winds' strength and the fire's uncontrollable chaos. They called to the gods as they looked to the stars and drew influence from the moon and the sun. Through their search for understanding, they brought forth forces of the most extraordinary power, powers not seen since the dragons. Once again, magic dominated the lands. The people were called Atlanteans, and for thousands of years, they flourished. There was peace across the lands, and the world was wondrous," smiled Berolarn, who seemed to drift off and appeared to be considering his words.

"As the world flourished under the Atlanteans, the world was also out of balance, and this cannot be. So the balance had to be restored. It came in a new form of man, the Vampiri, or as the legends call them, the race of vampires," said Berolarn.

He was about to continue when Talis broke in with a hearty laugh.

"Stories to scare children, vampires, what is this," he scoffed.

"Do not tell me my stories are for children," Berolan hissed. "What did I tell you, Talis, about the truths of legends? Do you think I would waste my time telling you child stories? Your life, your sister's, and everyone else's depend on what I tell you. Now be quiet whilst I speak," berated Berolarn.

The child had got under Berolan's skin, and he felt the anger rise inside him. How could he explain the knowledge he needed to someone so young of mind to know? Talis was so young, as was his sister. They had no training. He knew, though, that they were all he had; sighing and letting the anger dissipate, he continued with his tale.

"I am sorry, Berolarn, but it is hard to believe what you say. I have never heard such stories before. Please forgive me, do continue," said Talis.

Talis hoped he had not upset the strange man. He wanted to keep on his good side for the moment, as he seemed to have information about Lauren.

"As I was saying, a new breed of man came forth, and they were called the Vampiri. Where they came from it is unknown. Maybe they formed from Atlanteans who had dabbled with magics they should have left alone? Anyway, a great war was fought across the continents over the next century, scattering all other forms of man as both sides strived for victory. They unleashed magical forces not seen since. Neither side managed to better the other for many a century. Small gains were made by enduring massive losses. Then, in one final battle, the Atlanteans ended up victorious, though, at a great loss, the Vampiri were nearly driven into extinction. In the end, they both retreated from this world, and it is said they disappeared across the sea and, over time, became legends or fables you speak of. So closed the second age," continued Berolarn.

Berolarn paused and sipped his wine. "So begins the third age, the time of man, men similar to the people of your village. They evolved over tens of thousands of years from the low-level form of man that existed in the Atlantean time," said Berolarn.

"Man developed into a highly evolved race that spread to all corners of the world. Unfortunately, they became a curse on the land, a parasite, killing off other life forms and consuming everything they found. Over the latter centuries, many wars were fought across the globe as they vied with each other for control. They created many machines of destruction and power so great that, for a time, it nearly stopped the warmongering as all sides were scared of losing control.

But the world started to die as they consumed all of its resources in their relentless search for new things and power. Where they had cured most illnesses, the planet became saturated with humans. New diseases started to appear, and the ability to power their machines began to fail. People started suffering and dying, and humanity was on the brink of starvation as food shortages became common. The scholars of that time reached out to the power of the stars in the vain hope of capturing enough energy to support their machines. Through a colossal error of judgement, these scholars brought about a cataclysm that nearly destroyed the world; continents disappeared, new continents were torn from the seabed, and the race of man was taken to near extinction. So ended the third age," continued Berolarn.

Talis watched in awe at all the wonderous machines in the images, then the explosions of fire destroying life, lifting vast pieces of land, sucking seas dry, making others. Forming mountains where there were none and collapsing mountains that should have stood tall and strong for eternity.

"Now, the race of man is very resilient and has spread to every corner of the planet. More by the volume of people than by luck, there were pockets of people who managed to escape the cataclysm. They scrambled for life and survival in the new post-cataclysm world. The power unleashed and the unique environments created changed man into several different species," continued Berolarn.

"We have a man as we see today. Next, we have the dwarves who became dwellers under the earth as they looked to escape the hardships of life above ground. Next, we have the goblins, evil creatures in the shape of men, becoming animals, ravaged and changed beyond recognition by the disaster that closed the third age. Then we have the ogres, monstrous in size and strength, born of a similar history to the goblins, which evolved from a mutation that saw them become evil giants walking the land. Each settled in different areas of the continent of Restor and made their homes," said Berolarn as he rose from his chair and started pacing around the room as he considered his following words.

"At the same time, the Atlanteans reappeared. They also suffered from the power unleashed in the third age and returned from across the sea, as they now know they cannot survive in a world of separation from the new races, and you will now know them as elves. If you have seen them, they are a darker-skinned race and have made their home in the great forests of Aslandure. Together for thousands of years, each race has fought for survival. Unfortunately, neither race has much love for the other now, and though trade routes between the nations of elves, dwarves, and man exist, a severe distrust is present."

Talis decided he needed to interrupt the spellbinding imagery and the words Berolarn was speaking as his brain was starting to spin out of control as he tried to digest everything.

"Berolarn, what you have shown me, and your words are confusing. Are you saying that the world nearly ended due to man, and now all the races are descended from that time?" asked Talis.

"Yes, but do not forget the elves, Talis. They have transcended two ages, though much of what they were is now lost. But they are not of man as we know them now, and in some, their magic still exists, though much of the real power has been lost. This is important, as the Vampiri who had dwindled greatly in number also came out of hiding and returned and have now mingled with the races," replied Berolarn.

Again, Berolarn stopped, and with a swipe of his hand, he closed the magic fire circle and sat back down.

"The Vampiri or vampires as you know them originally were not precisely the evil as portrayed in legend. Although they were neither good nor the darkest of evil, they suffered from hunger, a thirst that drove them mad. This hunger made them predators of man, as they thirsted for his blood. This made them evil in the eyes of all others," said Berolarn as he stared at Talis.

"However, they also developed an overwhelming lust for the Atlanteans' power, similar to the dwarves for gold and precious rocks, and that quest nearly destroyed them in the second age. On their return after the cataclysm, some continued their pursuit of power, and the scales started to tip them towards evil as their actions became more unholy."

"But a small number of the Vampiri broke away and wanted no part of these evil undertakings. Instead, they roamed the lands and worked across nations to broker relationships and peace. These Vampiri holding some of their forefathers' powers became known as the Solarian Knights, an antediluvian holy order for good. They became ingrained across the nations, including the elves, and for many centuries, the nations of man, dwarves and elves prospered. The clans of the goblins and ogres shunned the outside world and lived in small communities in the northlands," finished Berolarn.

Berolarn stopped and poured more wine.

"Does everything make sense so far, Talis?" asked Berolarn as the old man rose from his seat again and chucked more wood on the fire. Talis nodded and thought, not really. First, he would have thought he was in the hands of a charlatan or a madman if Berolarn hadn't known his name and his family's names. But then, the magical conjuring of the fire ring and the vivid images brought the story to life.

"Good, let us rest and pick up the story after a few hours of sleep."

Chapter 5 – The Dawning

Berolarn awoke Talis as the sun rose from the east, and the day started to break. A meagre breakfast of berries and water awaited this morning. However, Talis was keen to continue with the story and had no qualms about the breakfast as he ate and stoked the fire back to ablaze to remove the chill.

"Talis, yesterday we understood that we have the five races, the race of man, elves, dwarves, goblins and ogres. Then we have the Vampiri split into two factions: those seeking power and the Solarian Knights, who tried to bring harmony between the races. Do you remember," asked Berolarn.

Talis nodded, and Berolarn continued,

"For many years, the order of Solarian Knights worked with the kingdoms to bring solidarity and at times engaged in wars to bring about this and maintain some form of order. In some ways, the Solarians were trying to control the destinies of the races. Whilst interfering, albeit with the greatest of intentions, in the affairs of the races. They left the remaining Vampiri to their own devices."

"This turned out to be a fatal mistake on the Solarian Knight's part. One within the Vampiri they left behind was an arrogant, skilled young man named Olgrich Validorol. He delved deeper than any before him, deeper into magics so dark and unforgivable that he rose above all other Vampiri elders and set himself apart as their lord and master. An evil overlord who became known to the Vampiri as the blood prince or, more commonly to all others, as the dark lord. He became mighty in both his abilities and his temporal domain. The world he rules now shakes at his will. It is not enough to simply control his kingdom or to have lived for centuries. The dark lord wants to own all and be the true master by dominating all minds, life, and death. He wants all to fall and bow before him. So he started the great wars, and all were within his grasp," said Berolarn.

Berolarn came and sat at the table and looked over at Talis.

"Over the years of the great wars, he had hunted down the Solarians, and one by one, the dark lord's forces started to eliminate them. Then, finally, the Solarian Knights that were left gathered together and marched on the dark lord," said Berolarn as he lit his pipe before continuing.

"Both sides fought with steel, and the sky over the continent was alight with magic unleashed. When all seemed lost for the Solarians as the dark lord's power had grown great and could not be defeated, a solitary knight, as if guided by the gods for this one purpose, managed to reach the dark lord and dealt him a terrible blow that would have killed any other."

"The dark lord was defeated, mortally wounded, carried away from the field by his winged servants, and the Vampiri disappeared as the Knights took the victory. But, though they had won, the victory was hollow as many of their kind were dead, and they were now very few in number. As the years passed, the dark lord had gone from sight and mind, the remaining Solarians drifted apart over time, and the knights were no more. Nearly eight hundred years ago to the day this occurred."

"Talis, this brings us to current events. Armies are marching from the north, as you know, and this army is slowly taking over much of the northland territories. Kingdoms are starting to fall and being laid to waste, and their people are scattered, murdered or enslaved. At first, I suspected it was a new powerful lord flexing his might. With an old friend, Luthur, who knows as much as anyone about the northlands, We spent many days of travel over hazardous terrains scouting in the northern territories for any sign of who or what was behind the darkness arising. Finally, on the ninth day, as I was becoming increasingly fatigued and was giving up hope of finding evidence of these armies, we stumbled on lights in the distance. We headed in the direction of these lights, and as we drew closer, we could hear the noise of many voices. We had come across a large host on the western side of the Milnmor Mountain range, just off the Great Northern Plains. There were hundreds of campfires set in the middle of makeshift shelters. There were thousands of goblin soldiers everywhere we looked for as far as the eye could see."

"I also could sense a great evil in the surrounding area, a power I had never felt before. Trying to find the source of this feeling, we moved with great stealth and gave no sound away in the pitch of darkness as the campfires started to die. We moved closer and closer, travelling along the camp outskirts just out of sight, looking for something unknown."

"It was not long before we stumbled on something that filled us with apprehension and chilled us to our core. An intense initial fear hit Luther. But the terror didn't consume him as, luckily, he is powerful of mind. I personally had not felt such an experience in all the years my feet have been on this earth. Nevertheless, even for those of us who have long studied the histories of the Vampiri and the past accounts of the world forgotten, darkness and a sense of dread opened doors to our hearts and filled us with foreboding."

"We saw two individuals walking together, talking as equals, which was strange. A female dressed all in black leather, with a blood-red corset of the finest chain-mail and a cloak of black velvet fluttered behind her where there was no wind. It carried the mark of darkness, a red cross with legs of equal length, each end finishing in a sharp point. With a ring cutting halfway from its centre and halfway from its end. I had no doubt it was one of the Vampiri that I knew. She is one of great importance and close to the dark lord."

"I am sure the other was a male, but not of this world. Muscular and lean of frame, he was dressed in rich dark red robes and was not in attire for war. I sensed his power and knew the initial feeling of despair that had hit us came from his presence. It was his eyes, though. They shined through the night with a yellow glow with pupils of red. What manner of man he was, I cannot say, and I have given this much consideration. I know the Vampiri walk with no one as equal, yet this was not the case from what we saw. We could not hear the words they spoke as we could not get close enough, and I suspected they knew someone was nearby, for the man had turned and looked in our direction before being brought away by something the woman said. This was an opportune time for us to leave, and we quickly made off and left that place," finished Berolarn.

Berolarn tapped the dying embers from his pipe and refilled it with more weed. He relit his pipe and then looked again at Talis.

Talis was shocked by what the older man had relayed. This was not what he had expected when he woke to see the stranger.

Legends and stories from the inn now come to life in the lands he walked.

"Who are you, Berolarn? You speak like a great sage who understands things that no normal man would. Yet, you talk of vampires, dragons and dark lords and imply that somehow all of this involves Lauren and me?" Talis asked.

"Bear with me a little longer, Talis. I will complete the story as it is laid out in front of us soon, you will know as much as I can tell you, and then we must discuss a way forward," responded Berolarn, who poured some water into a cup and took a hearty mouthful. Berolarn then stretched, wiped his beard and puffed on his pipe for a few seconds.

Chapter 6 – The Birth

"It is said that the Solarians died out over the years after being hunted down to nearly the last of their kind. Only a tiny remnant had survived those battles, dispersing at the end. Although they lived many years longer than their human counterparts, they and the Vampiri have fewer children than other races. Yes, the Solarians declined, and with each year passing, fewer were left among the races. Until all appeared to be gone, I have looked over recent years for others who have survived, though I have found nor seen any for many a year. Though I cannot be sure, I am perhaps one of the last Solarians Talis, as was your father. Now you and your sister are probably the last of our kind on this continent," continued Berolarn.

"But, that ….." started Talis.

Berolarn reached forward and grabbed his arm in a vice-tight grip.

"Before you pull away and speak words of denial, look at our eyes, Talis. Look deep into my eyes and inwards towards your heart, and you will know that I speak the truth," posited Berolarn.

Talis tried to process what Berolarn had said, the eyes, the rumours of his father that his father Loran had dismissed, certain things that Lauren and he could do that no other in the village could do. How they would jump with ease across the stream to the other side, scaling large trees in seconds, feeling the heartbeat of the prey they hunted, always knowing their next steps. There were many little oddities about the pair of them.

But how could their father do this to them and keep their identity from them? It made it hard to believe, as he was sure his father would have told Lauren and him of their ancestry and the history of their people.

Berolarn could sense the chaos in Talis's mind; he needed Talis to feel the rush and the maddening burn of the hunger, the lust for the kill, the power, the blood. Could Talis control it without the training? How Loran had stopped the hunger in both of his children when they attained adulthood, he did not know. He didn't have time to spend the many years training them, and this was only the first part of the journey he foretold they must make. Of course, Berolarn had lied by omission on the Vampiri traits of a Solarian and the hunger; At first, he had not thought of taking them through the hunger, but as the story unfolded in front of Talis. Finally, he realised this was a mistake, and they needed to do this in preparation for what lay ahead of them.

Berolarn grabbed Talis's arms by the wrists and painfully slammed them down on the table.

"Talis look deep into my eyes and listen to me," commanded Berolarn.

"What are you doing," shouted Talis as he tried to pull away from a grip intense and painful.

The grip should be coming from an ogre rather than the wizened old man in front of him. Instead, the room around him was suddenly wrapped inside a vortex of wind as if he had walked out into a storm. A great heat pulsed through his body as his arms were crushed in the vice-like grip.

"You are going on a journey of discovery, a rebirth", shouted

Berolarn as the wind howled within the small hut.

Berolarn squeezed even harder as he started to chant strange words. A white flame erupted from Berolarn's hands and began to creep up Talis's arms, and within seconds the cold heat of the white flame was engulfing his whole body. Talis's entire body was bathed in a heat that brought no pain to his skin but burned from inside outwards. He could feel his body convulsing in a surreal out-of-body experience, he was there, but Talis could see what was happening as if he was a spectator looking in.

As Talis threw his head back with his mouth open wide as if to scream, his arms were suddenly freed, and they pushed outwards to form a cross with force so great his arms felt as if they were about to be ripped from his torso. The table was pulled from in front of him as an unholy force snapped him upright. It gave Talis the look of someone who had been nailed to a crucifix. The pain was unbearable, his body trying to convulse as it was held firm in the white flame wrapped in the spinning vortex. Berolarn muffled chants started to get louder, and Talis's earthly body rose upwards as he smashed through the hut's roof, taking him to the outside world. As he levitated upwards away from the ground, reaching some forty feet, a great pillar of stone which had torn free from the earth wrapped around his legs like a coiled snake and held him.

Berolarn walked outside, still chanting. Then, with a forceful movement, he brought both his arms together, the amulets on his arms colliding with a loud ring. Red flames burst from his arms and hit Talis at full force. As the burning heat of this new flame smashed into Talis, the flames arched upwards and then down, spinning into a large ring of molten red fire that revolved around the inner white flame.

Talis, in unbearable pain, sweating profusely as his body attempted to free itself from the elements of wind, stone and flame. Talis's eyes burned as they became filled with red fire. He could feel the blood pulsating through his veins like a colossal river unleashed from the sea. The thumping beat of his heart was a volcano about to erupt from his body at any moment.

Just when Talis could take the pain no more and wanted to kneel before any god that would listen and pray for death to come swiftly. The pain suddenly started to subside, and his mind was nearly torn from him with a wave of anger so great, burdened with an unquenchable thirst, a hunger for something unnatural. He needed to hunt, yearned to kill, and longed to feast. The world around him was turning dark. No joy or happiness would ever be his, and nothing had any meaning now. Talis must escape this prison and bring death to all.

As Berolarn watched from below, he saw the white flames consuming the pulsating body of Talis; he knew the hunger had begun. He knew that Talis would walk this earth filled with a lust for blood as it was for all of their kind. Berolarn also knew that the Solinarian blood flowed in his veins, and the other half of what he was could not only control the hunger but become its master. This half would work for the good of all that walked this earth. Talis would need to discover that path as part of the journey of attaining the wisdom of his kind. If he unleashed the knowledge and full powers of what still remained inside, at this moment in time, when he was just learning of the hunger, it would probably tear him apart. No, that would come, Berolarn thought. Let Talis control the burning rage of the hunger and start to embrace some of the power of the Vampiri.

"Talis," Berolarn shouted, "listen to me, look inside yourself, go deep inside, delve down into your mind."

Talis looked downwards, making out the man's silhouette shouting upwards towards him. The longing to get to this man burned deep inside, and he wanted to rip him slowly apart and feast on his blood.

"Fight the thirst, Talis. Go deep inside yourself. You know that this can not be who you are. The hunger is not what you are. It is born of Hel's spawn and has no place in your life. Come back to me, Talis. Your sister Lauren needs you whole again. Come back now," screamed Berolarn over the deafening noise of the vortex that held Talis.

Berolarn brought his arms back together with force, amulets ringing as his arms collided. Then, another blast of blue-tinted white energy drove upward through the white flames and hit Talis full force.

Talis had heard the fool's words from below, and they had no meaning to him. All that mattered was the kill. Then he had heard the words "sister Lauren", and yes, he had Lauren, a twin by birth, a sister born of goodness. He loved her dearly, and they were connected like no other, kindred spirits bonded together by more than blood.

As his mind turned over thoughts of his sister. The words spoken by Berolarn started to take hold, and he fought back against the lust to kill, the hunger that had burned inside and slowly, the urges of death dissipated into nothing, and he was back to being Talis and was whole again. As the transformation back from the hunger began, the stone holding him fast started to uncoil from his feet, and the burning red flame receded into nothingness as he moved back to being himself. Slowly the white flamed circle descended to the ground and was gone as Talis felt the earth once again beneath his feet. Talis dropped to his knees, tears rolling down his face from the pain, the hunger and the realisation of a legend living inside of him. The dark plane of existence he had travelled to brought an excruciating reality to everything Berolarn had told him last night and this morning.

Berolarn walked over to Talis and kneeled beside him.

"Talis, perhaps I should have warned you of what myself, your father, sister, and you are. The Vampiri and the Solarians are as much vampires depicted in fables and legends as they are anything else," soothed Berolarn as he held Talis.

"However, it would help if you realised that much of what the legends say omits much of the real history, and our kind's power is hardly mentioned. You have felt the hunger once, and it nearly drove you insane. But quickly, you brought it under control with little training. The Solarians mastered keeping the thirst at bay long ago, and the training usually takes years to complete, but you managed to control the craving within minutes."

Berolarn lifted Talis's head upwards slowly, and as their eyes met, he continued speaking,

"I did not expect my words to take hold immediately and you to come back to me quickly. It shows that you are strong of mind and destined to walk the Solarian path, not the Vampiri path. Do not be dismayed that you felt the evil flow through your veins. It comes to all of our kind. You have much to learn, and with learning comes great power and, therefore, great responsibility. I will guide you and your sister where I can, yet you will need to focus on yourself at all times."

Talis looked deep into Berolarn's face, trying to garner some form of understanding.

"I am scared of what has happened, what you have made me into and what is happening around us. I am scared for my sister. I am afraid of what I am and what you say I must be. It is so dark and clouded to me at the moment. I am terrified of what our futures will hold, Berolarn. But you should know I will fight by whatever means to ensure the survival of what matters most to me, my sister Lauren.

The conviction in Talis's face gave Berolarn hope that between them and perhaps with help along the way, then just maybe, they might have a slight chance of being successful and banishing the dark lord and his minions back to the hell they belonged from.

"Good Talis, we must have hope and have the inner strength to lead us forward on our quest. We may not know the way or what path we might end up taking, yet with heart and wisdom, we will overcome what is put in front of us," Berolarn stated as he clasped Talis's shoulder.

"Let us be on our way Talis. We need to be off from this place. As unfortunately, we have now just told the whole world where we are from the use of magic, it is like a beacon to all who understand the arts, and soon they will come looking for us. So let's grab our things and head out."

With that, Berolarn rose and marched towards the hut with Talis scrambling after him.

"Where will we go?" asked Talis.

"There is a need first to go towards the kingdom of Lorevich and find Luther. We will need a guide, and no one is better across all the lands. He has travelled far and wide, and he understands the wilderness as good as anyone alive," answered Berolarn.

Chapter 7 – Lauren

The party finished late, and the mead was hitting her hard. Lauren didn't do anything half-heartedly. She could hardly stand up and probably would have slumbered in some village gutter if her father Loren and brother Talis had not found her as they stumbled back towards the inn. Laughing and falling over themselves, they picked an arm each and threw Lauren about like a rag doll, positioning her between them as they dragged her home. Yes, they dropped her a few times. But she awoke early in the afternoon the following day fully dressed, hanging out of her bed, rocking, ready for the fall.

"Please save me," whispered Lauren.

Another wave of alcohol-induced nausea hit her. Lauren rolled onto her back and looked upwards as she took deep breaths. The ceiling was moving up and down, and the room was spinning faster and faster. Finally, she flew to the side window, ramming it open and nearly smashing it with the force she hit it with. With then no effort at all, Lauren parted company with the contents of yesterday's festivities.

Lauren lay on the bed for the rest of the afternoon, not feeling well enough to venture out. But finally, by early evening, the waves of nausea and the room's spinning subsided. As Lauren gingerly exited her room, she walked down the hallway towards the inn's main room. As she passed Talis's room, Lauren peered through the doorway. She caught Talis's eye as she squinted in.

"Well, look who is up," Talis laughed. "I can honestly say,

shortcake, you were totally out of it by early evening. I have never seen anyone drink so much."

"Don't you remember that you were trying to marry Dougal, the ugliest man you could find, and he didn't want you? Then you jumped on stage and started serenading him with love songs. I thought you would offer to sleep with him in front of everyone. Finally, father had to drag you off. After that, you were the laughingstock of the village," Talis roared with laughter as tears started to stream down his face.

"Talis, I swear you are lying. Dougal would marry the oldest ugliest sow in the village," she tenderly grinned back.

"I suppose I am in trouble with father again!" Lauren exclaimed with a sigh.

"Where is he, in the kitchens, or is he tending the bar this evening? If I am honest, I want to get something to eat. Pretty hungry, even though my stomach feels as bad as my head. All things considered, perhaps today's best option is to keep my head down and generally avoid father!"

Talis jumped to his feet, stretched and headed past his sickly-looking sister.

"What do you want to eat, shortcake? Then, with the stealth of a hawk, I will breeze past the old man and return with wares to fill your stomach with delight," grinned Talis.

"Anything!" moaned Lauren.

Lauren didn't care at this moment in time. She would literally eat anything to take away the hunger pangs.

"Bring a skin full of water back too, Talis," Lauren called out as he turned the hallway's corner.

She entered Talis's bedroom and slumped down on his bed. She looked around the room with boredom, noting that his room had never changed. Instead, various hunting garbs were strewn over multiple pieces of furniture as usual.

Talis never changed. He was so messy. Hunting knives were scattered across his small table, and Lauren could see Talis's pride and joy in the corner next to the bed. The archery gear, a gift from his father belonging to their mother's side, a longbow made of the finest yew and an ancient odd-looking leather quiver marked with runes or symbols of some kind. To complete the set, the quiver was filled with arrows, made of Tulipwood and turkey feathers and the arrowheads were honed of tempered steel, sharp and true, deftly made by Talis to a level as good as any fletcher she knew.

Lauren was ok with a bow but was as good with a knife as anyone. She could hit and kill any animal within striking distance with a knife, and Lauren was also really good with a sling, a weapon that Talis sneered at. On many a hunting trip, when in competition with Talis, she would beat him to the target with her sling, much to his annoyance.

The room held nothing further of interest. Lauren lay there staring at the ceiling as she tried to recall what had happened the evening before as she awaited Talis's return. Finally, after some time had passed, Talis returned with his arms full of food and a waterskin over his shoulder.

"Father knows you are awake, but neither of us has to work today. I think he knows you are in no fit state to do anything," smirked Talis.

Talis threw the food onto his table and sat down. Lauren got up with some effort, walked to the small table, and plonked herself down opposite Talis.

Lauren was starting to feel better as she tucked into some of the bread, meats and cheeses and took some hearty mouthfuls of water from the skin to quench her thirst. As she dropped the skin back down, Lauren opened up conversations about the night before, and soon, they were both lost in discussions that lasted the rest of the day.

Over the next few months, Lauren's life was no different to any other time in her life. She and Talis worked in the inn serving drinks or helping out in the kitchen. They went out most days and hunted in the surrounding woodland and fields to keep the inn fully stocked with an assortment of meats. Lauren also often drank at the other side of the bar, would break into song when the mood took her and made merriment whenever she could. Lauren was still enjoying life to its fullest.

Whenever she had free time, Lauren would also run errands for the old and sick in the village; in general, she had an entirely happy life. The only distraction to this routine had been the constant stream of strangers coming through the village as they made their way south. They brought stories of war. A great cloud had descended in the north, armies, they said, filled with goblins, men and monsters and were creeping southwards by the day. At first, she took no heed, but it was starting to play on her mind.

Then the day came. The family was always up early, getting the inn ready for opening. The inn had to be cleaned, food had to be prepared, and casks of ale and mead had to be moved in and out of the bar. They had just been getting ready to make a start when Loran stopped speaking in mid-sentence. He slowly turned his head and appeared to be sniffing the air.

"Something is wrong. I feel a presence I have not felt since times long forgotten," mused Loran as if sniffing the air. He walked to one of the inn's windows and stared for a few seconds before suddenly turning towards Talis and Lauren.

"Quickly, Talis, Lauren, go fetch your weapons," shouted Loran with real urgency.

Loran turned before they could question him and moved with haste to the back of the building. Talis and Lauren ran to their rooms and returned to the bar area with their hunting weapons. Loran was waiting for them and had already unsheathed his ancient longsword.

"What is it, father," cried Lauren in fear. Loran never carried his sword in public. Then there was a thunderous boom, which continued as they ran to the door and made their way outside.

"The drums of war," shouted Loran over the loud noise.

Lauren could see a green mist rising out of the treetops and the sound of many feet marching toward the village.

"To the market square," called Loran as they ran to the edge of the village.

"War! Get out! Out I say and fight for your lives," bellowed Loran as they ran through the streets. Lauren could hear doors opening behind her and people running around in chaos. She did not know whether they ran away in fear or ran to join them. They reached the market square just as the soldiers entered the village.

Ranks of hideous, deformed goblins and giants that must have been ogres came towards the few standing in the village's defence. As they immediately engaged in combat of life or death, her father pushed Lauren out of the way of the goblin blade that narrowly now missed its target. Then, with her knife in hand, Lauren deftly rolled with her father's push and stuck the pig-faced goblin in its chest, and it collapsed dead as soon as the blade hit.

Lauren looked up to see her father running forward into the goblin hordes. He was surrounded by a whitish glow that flickered like a flame. The longsword Loran carried glowed blue in contrast as the blade rang as the steel cut down all in his path. Lauren just stared, not understanding what she was seeing. Loran was a warrior like no other. So many lay dead at his feet, and none survived his deadly skill with the blade. She looked around for her brother. Talis was nowhere to be seen.

Lauren suddenly felt darkness grip her insides, intense fear. She couldn't understand its source at that moment, even in the raging battle. But then, she suddenly saw the reason for her anxiety. Out of the night sky, to the jeers of the goblins who parted, winged demons dropped around Loran, garbed in red as dark as blood with black robes marked with silver runes.

She heard one giggling and say, "Hello Loran, it's been a long time. We have been looking for you and your foul offspring. But, unfortunately, the blood prince requires the girl and the boy. Where are they?" she demanded with sickly sweet innocence in her tone.

"Tarani," spat Loran. "Olgrich has sent out his playthings. It is interesting, is it not that he dared not come himself? Perhaps your master now has fear running through his veins. The bite of the blade was too much for him?" he said as he watched the circling enemies.

"Now, now Loran, be nice! Tell me where the children are, and I will ensure your death will be as painless as possible," grinned Tarini.

Lauren heard her father utter some words. He looked Lauren in the eyes, and she thought he smiled as he turned and attempted to cut down the one who had spoken. She narrowly avoided his death blow with great dexterity. But as his sword swung in an arc, Loran managed to drive his blade deep into one of the demons.

The fight was ferocious as Loran cut down several of his foes, his sword ringing as it spouted out blue energy as the demons screamed with unholy anger and pain. But then, as the intensity of the battle raged, Loran finally succumbed to the overwhelming numbers, and he was down as the demons flew at him from all sides. Lauren was blinded from looking further as intense white energy erupted from the core of the melee.

"Come girl, quickly," a voice said in her ear, "there is nothing you can do for your father now, we must run and avenge him some another time, or we will also suffer his fate."

Lauren was pulled up to her feet and dragged away by someone. Who was dragging her through the streets, she didn't know, and she didn't care. Numb from the loss of her father, Lauren was in total shock.

Lauren suddenly came around as they ran through the forest after stumbling in the undergrowth. Grabbing the arm and spinning the hooded stranger around.

"Who are you? What part did you play in this?" snarled Lauren as she pulled the hood off the stranger with a jerk. In front of her was a beautiful woman, one of the most angelic women Lauren had ever seen.

"I am Elisha, from the kingdom of elves and privy of the king's council. I was sent looking for you," she whispered to Lauren. "Please keep your voice down. The trees have ears, and we are being hunted, even as we speak."

Lauren had never seen a girl like this, lithe in frame, garbed in green and brown hunting attire. She was of similar height as Lauren, dark-skinned and had delicate features, young-looking with eyes of green and long flowing locks of golden brown. But her beauty was extraordinary and breathtaking, yet somehow lined with maturing years of wisdom.

"Come, we must hurry away from here. Make haste Lauren," whispered Elisha with insistence in her tone.

Although Lauren didn't make the connection that the girl knew her name, she read the urgency in the stranger's voice, and though confused and not full of trust, Lauren dutifully followed the stranger further into the forest.

They had been walking for some time as they took an untravelled route through paths unfamiliar to Lauren. It was now drizzling with rain, and the forest canopy had long given way. Water rolled gracefully along the branches and glistened on the leaves as if it fell into the ferns, grasses and weeds that covered the forest floor. The undergrowth lashed against the legs, and Lauren's legs were as heavy and wet to the bone as if they had been wading through a stream. Lauren had no cloak and only had a light blouse and leggings on. Not before long, the drizzle had conquered what little protection her clothes had given, and she was shivering down through her core.

Lauren began to cry as the misery of her predicament took

hold. She had seen her father killed by a hatred she did not understand. Talis was missing. Lauren was tired, wet through, freezing cold, and being led with unsure footing by a stranger to who knows where. She had tried a few times to question Elisha more, but the answers were the same; "Be quiet, please, Lauren," ….. "now is not the time," ….. "we are being hunted," ….. " we must gather pace," ….. "not long, keep going, soon we can rest and speak".

The morning passed into the afternoon, and Lauren could shed no more tears. The coldness was now complete, and she was totally numb to everything around her. However, she did note that the forest was starting to thin, and the undergrowth was lessening with every step they took. Finally, the drizzle stopped, and some sunlight broke through the canopy.

"Come, Lauren, we are nearly there," Elisha whispered. "We will be safe for a time, very soon."

"Stop, standstill. Some of my brethren are coming," Elisha said.

Lauren could not hear anything even as keen-eared as she was from her years of hunting. Immediately and instantaneously, three individuals dressed as Elisha appeared from behind some of the great trees of the forest. They all stepped forward and bowed to Elisha. The tallest of the three spoke.

"Well met, Princess Elisha, in these troubled times, I am glad you made it here. Your father, the King, will seek the glad tidings of your safety and hear of your mission. We had sent small parties of the royal guard to several areas in the surrounding area in search of information on your whereabouts.

It makes my heart fill with joy that you are safe." He then turned and looked at Lauren.

"Princess Elisha, is this the child you seek?" he asked inquisitively as he turned back to Elisha.

Lauren looked intently at the four of them. Not only were they dressed the same, but they all had similar characteristics. They all have a timeless look as if the summers and winters pass them by without interfering with them. She couldn't work it out. Like Elisha, they looked young but carried a look of age and wisdom that you would only see in the old of her kind.

"She is the daughter of Loran, Treldor. Her name is Lauren. Since I left you, I travelled for a few weeks hoping to reach their home before the armed forces of the dark lord, but I did not come quickly enough to warn Loran of the pending doom," said Elisha.

"Where is Loran?" asked Treldor.

"The village has been destroyed, hundreds slaughtered, and Loran has fallen at the hands of the dark lord's evil spawn. His son, Talis, may have also have been lost. Of this, I am not sure," sighed Elisha.

"I grabbed Lauren mid-battle just as her father fell. It was too much of a risk to search for Talis. We had to flee. Too much power had come to Keros in the form of the Vampiri."

"Vampiri!" exclaimed Treldor.

Seeing the shock on Treldor face, Elisha continued.

"Yes, the council we received from Berolarn has come to pass. The Vampiri are now walking the lands. They must have known that Loran and his family were there and attacked with this certainty, judging that the Vampiri came in such numbers. There was at least a dozen, maybe more," explained Elisha.

"Princess Elisha, you bring tales of great sorrow and grief that all of our kin will feel at the passing of the great Lord Loran and the village of man where he made his home. A dark day for all of us, and a shadow now lays heavily on our hearts," replied Treldor with great sadness in his voice.

With tears rolling down Lauren's face again as the pain of her loss was brought sharply back, she couldn't help but ponder the conversation. The Vampiri are walking the lands? Her father a great lord? She had no idea what they were talking about, Vampiri had no meaning to her, and her father was a simple innkeeper. She stood silent, as confused as hell, as the words came out of their mouths. Then suddenly, she was hit in waves; the vision of the battle came like someone had opened a tap in her head, truths she did not see at the time.

Loran's speed was as fast as the quickest of hawks dancing in the sky as it hunted its prey. Her father's form shimmered in a white heavenly flame, his sword glowing with a faint blue aura. Loran, ploughing down all who stood in front of him, either by steel, and she was sure, by bolts of white energy that erupted from his hands cutting down his foe. The memories flooded back, showing a simple man, an older man, suddenly reborn with great power, like a warrior king of forgotten legends. Then the demons came, he showed no fear, and though he fell in battle, he fell, still with a sword in hand, and he had looked over at her in those final moments as a true master of his destiny.

Lauren came back around to the ongoing conversation with the elves.

"What news have we of the conquests across the land, Treldor," asked Elisha.

"The dwarves brought news that the goblins have control of most northern territories, all the land above the great Mountains of Crelodine. The dwarves hold the goblin's movement further south at most mountain passes. But they have broken through at the largest if rumours are true, Heavens Gateway has fallen. They now march on man's lands, but this seems to be more targeted skirmishes," Treldor said.

"What does our intelligence think is the reason for this," asked Elisha.

"From the dark lord's search for Loran, as foretold by Berolarn, we can only believe that he is looking for any Solarians that may survive in this age rather than an all-out attack," stated Treldor without any emotion.

Elisha knew from Berolarn that the children were vital. But, though her father, King Ethera, had pressed him hard, he would not speak of why the children of Loren were crucial to the efforts to thwart the domination of the land by this renewed evil. He feared spies may exist even amid elves, and all could be lost if the story was revealed. Moreover, the Vampiri finding out such news would bring grave peril to the success of any plans to defeat the dark lord.

In a private meeting, Elisha recalled all she had heard and what Berolarn had told her and the King.

"The dark lord's eyes will be turning directly towards the elves. His hate for you is all-consuming," said Berolarn as he looked at Elisha.

"Long ago, it destroyed his mind, and deep into his body, it burned. It ruined whatever little of a soul such a foul creature of the darkness could have; he attempted to be master of the darkest of the arts as he looked to gain the power to become master of all. Your kind always thwarted the Vampiri, and he despises the name of elf and all you are. He fears you and will not stop until he wipes the name of elves off this world. You must be ready to act, King Ethera. You and your kind must be prepared for war. Put aside your differences with men and dwarves and come together and fight. It is our only chance to have any hope of survival."

"You ask much, Berolarn," said King Ethera as he considered the news from the council and the words he heard in his private chambers.

Ethera was no fool, and he knew the manipulations of the Solarians in gaining what they believed would be the solidarity of all peoples. So Elisha watched the two men play out the mind games of risk with each other, as often they did when they met.

"Why are the children of Loren vital that you ask for my daughter Elisha, beloved Princess of the royal household of Celestar, heir to the throne of elves, to seek them out? Come, we are alone if you cannot trust the royal household in such troublesome times. Then none are now trustworthy, and the world is lost," stated Ethera

Berolarn knew the game, and he knew he must give a bit more. The King was wise and long been a master of people, and there was politics one must submit to.

"My King, you know I trust your family like no other, and I would not ask for Princess Elisha to go on this quest if she wasn't already a queen in waiting. We know she has all the skills necessary to lead the elves in your place. Yet you are here, and still, your line burns strongly in your blood. I need your strength, the strength of your people, to help the children of Loran, guide them where they might fail, and steady them as they walk the lands. I know no one better in all the lands than your daughter," replied Berolarn.

Elisha could feel herself burn under the scrutiny of both men and the unfounded praise of Berolarn.

The King laughed.

"Berolarn, you continue to say all the right words to penetrate an old man's heart. To break down the barriers of being a father. I agree my daughter Princess Elisha is ready," smiled Ethera.

Looking over at her with the love of a father. King Ethera changed his tone back to being stern and commanding.

"But come now, if I give you my daughter and risk the flower of her people, what of the children of Loren?" questioned Ethera, looking back at Berolarn and raising himself out of his chair.

"Please tell me, why do we search for the Solarians? In what guise will they enable us to defeat the evil that is upon us," persisted Ethera as he walked.

"I cannot answer this with any certainty King Ethera, when I searched through time in the lost libraries of the Solarians, looking for the hidden key that could bring down the Vampiri and the dark lord. I struggled to understand all that was shown and all of what could be," replied Berolarn.

"I am sure you know more than you wish to say, Berolarn. What is special to him about these Solarians outside of kinship," asked Ethera as he sat back down.

"What I can tell you, King Ethera, it was clear that two children, brother and sister of Solarian decent, locked together by their spirits, more so than their blood. They need to search for the lost Dragonheart Stone to gain the knowledge and power to throw down the evil that walks the lands. Only they would have the right to free it onto this world again. I do not know what power the stone has. I just do not know," shrugged Berolarn.

"But I do know of it. I found reference to it in the most ancient tomes the Solarians held. The books said that a rock was thrown down from the skies and sat deep in the earth's bowels while it was still young. In its centre sits the starstone, burning red with an everlasting flame set perfectly inside a massive flawless diamond. The histories say it disappeared during the age of dreams in the second age. However, I think I know roughly where it now resides, but not only am I not positively sure, I cannot be more specific than saying we need to go to Caledonia," said Berolarn.

Ethera rose and walked over to the fireplace. He stoked the fire, watching the fire licking upwards as it tried to escape.

"Caledonia is no place for any to walk, we search for the fire to bring about victory, but you understand the perils of walking in that land. It is a land of ice, right on the goblin's doorstep, filled with barbarians. So you go to knock on the side door of Validorol, the lands of the dark lord himself," muttered Ethera.

Then Ethera pointed his finger at Berolarn.

"Heed my words Berolarn. Death is a distinct possibility to all who go there. However, it appears to me to be a fool's quest, we have fought him once before, and we can fight him again without falling headlong into the snake's pit," said Ethera positioning himself directly in front of Berolarn.

Berolarn banged his fist on the table.

"You cannot win this war Ethera by steel and your magic alone, he has arisen once more, and I am telling you that his strength has increased to a level no one could have foretold. If we do not walk this path, then all will be lost, and the world will plummet into a barren waste filled with darkness. This must not be," shouted Berolarn angrily.

The King looked at his daughter.

"What say, you, Elisha? Princess of your people, child of the morning light, your name is called to action, and your wisdom as heir apparent should be heard," asked Ethera calmly as he looked at Elisha and ignored Berolarn's anger.

Elisha knew deep down Berolarn was right. The elves relied too much on the strengths of their army and what magic from their forefathers they still possessed. However, she did not think it would be enough, as Berolarn had said it would not be.

"Father, though I cannot see the path in front of us, and I fear that we might lose our way. We must do everything to bring about the end of the dark lord and his war machine. All possible roads must be travelled. I will go find the children of Loran and give them whatever help I can. If this is what Berolarn advises," replied Elisha.

Berolarn looked over to Elisha, and he was pleased with his

decision about her. She had the inner strength and the wisdom to help Lauren and Talis.

"It is what I advise," stated Berolarn bluntly as he nodded.

"So be it", sighed the King," looking over to his daughter. "You must quickly prepare to leave and find these children of Loran, I would go rest Elisha, and I will get Captain Belpin to prepare everything for the morning."

The conversation had been some months ago. Elisha had looked in many places, and it was only by luck that she was with Lauren now.

Elisha looked at Lauren and her three companions.

"Let's quickly be gone from this place and make way to the Morallis outpost. Treldor, do you have horses?" asked Elisha.

"We only have four Princess Elisha, hidden in a clearing, not two minutes away," replied Treldor.

"The girl can ride with me. But, I would advise before we set off that the girl needs to change out of those wet clothes before death catches her," said Treldor looking over at the shivering Lauren. "We have some spare garb and a cloak she can wear. They should fit well enough," continued Treldor. Who then motioned for them to follow.

Elisha then came closer to Lauren.

"I am so sorry, Lauren. I did not note the state you were in. Let's get you warm, and as soon as we get to the outpost, we can further discuss our plans," said Elisha.

She then pointed at the other two elves, "here are Calion and Brish, royal guards of the King. They will protect you with their lives. Whatever happens, you can trust them," continued Elisha. Both the soldiers nodded toward Lauren.

Within minutes they had reached the horses. They were mottled white with colouring like the breaking of waves. Standing with heads held high, they had an appearance of nobility and wisdom, born free to the plains. The Holinari horses were the steads of elves and would not be ridden by any other. Lauren was taken aback by how majestic they looked. Being the smaller of the elves and closest to Lauren's size, Brish went to his horse and passed Lauren a set of elven clothes.

"Hopefully, these will fit you, Lauren. You will find them warm and light. They should suit you well," said Brish, smiling at her.

Thanking him, Lauren went behind the nearest bush. Then, with Elisha standing guard, she undressed out of her sodden clothes and quickly changed into the elven clothing whilst the soldiers prepared the horses for travel. Lauren was amazed at how light the garb was, the rich green woollen breaches were like velvet, and the more delicate light-green blouse and tunic were like silk. The thin tunic and hood were of the finest leather, also tanned green but far darker than the rest of the clothing. Moreover, it was embroidered with markings that Elisha said symbolised the royal household and gave everyone a measure of the person's importance in court. Surprised, Lauren was amazed at how warm she felt, yet the clothes had no weight that usually could bring one warmth.

"Wait there, Lauren," said Elisha, walking towards her horse. She rummaged in one of the horses' packs and returned with small elven brown leather boots.

"We have similar-sized feet. These are made for someone of my size, I think. See if these fit you as you will struggle in your wet boots. These will keep the weather at bay," said Elisha as she passed the elven boots to Lauren. She slipped them on and tied them tight, walking forward. They were a perfect fit, as if they moulded themselves around her feet.

"Thank you, Princess Elisha, they fit well, and the clothes are wonderful," smiled Lauren.

Lauren's heart had somehow been lifted since she got changed, and it felt like some of the burden of her loss had subsided.

"Please call me Elisha. The title of Princess is not fitting if we are to travel on the road together as friends," smiled Elisha.

Lauren continued to smile and nodded.

"Treldor", Elisha called the captain, "Lauren will ride with me, as it would be good to talk. Also, it will put less strain on your horse, as the two of us together will be similar to you on your own."

Captain Treldor nodded to the Princess and made an upward gesture to Calion and Brish. All three, in unison, mounted their steeds and waited for Elisha and Lauren to climb Elisha's horse. Elisha quickly grabbed the horse's mane, elegantly rising through the air as she swung her leg over the great horse's back. Lauren, following her lead, grabbed Elisha's arm, and, with one motion, she sat behind her with her arm lightly around Elisha's waist.

Chapter 8 – The Ride to Morallis

Elisha told Lauren as they started their journey that the ride to Morallis would take several days by horse at a steady pace. Once there, they would meet more of the royal guard and hear news from the scouts travelling the lands. Lauren felt warm and comfortable dressed in her elven gear as they travelled and galloped through the countryside. She found that Elisha was an exceptionally skilled rider who easily controlled the majestic animal they rode. After a few hours of quiet, Lauren's shock and initial bewilderment at the day's activities started to wane, and she began bombarding Elisha with questions about her homelands and people. As they talked, Elisha discussed the origins of the elves.

"You may have heard in legends of the cataclysm brought down on this earth by the forefathers of this land?" asked Elisha.

"Only a little, from my father. Everyone nearly died, is as much as I can remember. But some managed to survive," said Lauren as she searched her brain for the histories Loran had told her and Talis.

Elisha nodded.

"The scattered people who remained started to come out of the shadows, and civilisation restarted as part of the need to survive. The elves returned to the lands once again too. We had been hidden, awaiting a time for our return. Finally, as the race of man had nearly destroyed the world, we saw that the time was right for us to come forth and bring healing back to the lands and help man understand their errors. I think we were naive in this, as man had changed in many ways, as had we over the millenniums. Man had become distinctly different races, man, dwarf, goblin and ogre, and we had lost some of our powers of old. However, the truth was that we had become similar to the races we had come to help, and this is a path that continues," explained Elisha.

Elisha went quiet for a while as she pondered her following words.

"As the lands healed, the nations of the races expanded and grew stronger with each passing century. Then the wars began again between the four strains of man, fuelled by the evil that runs through the goblins and ogres. And perhaps the thirst for more that comes with greed, which has always blighted the lives of the dwarves and those we now call man. We became embroiled in these wars. Great sorrow and grief were felt for the elves that fell. Dismayed at these events, the elves closed the doors and pushed away, for the most part, outsiders, letting few have safe passage through our lands."

"Why then did you come to help me?" asked Lauren as she was drawn in by the stories of the elven princess.

"Over several decades, my father Ethera, king of the elves, has shown great wisdom and has slowly brokered peace with the dwarves and some of the nations of man. He understood that no nation could stand alone and forget the outside world," replied Elisha.

"What you must understand, Lauren, is our ancestors of another age had done this before, letting the world become a place of suffering, sickness and war. It had nearly destroyed every living thing, including the elves," said Elisha.

"You came to stop that happening again?" asked Lauren, slightly confused.

"Yes. Now we come forth because the elves look to help the nations maintain peace and heal the lands. We struggle with this sometimes and must break down our resistance in not getting involved. However, the dark lord rising again has pushed down our walls and seen some of the resistance disappear, and now we will help all who call for our aid," replied Elisha as she turned her head and smiled at Lauren. "We shall travel for a few more hours and then make camp for the evening."

The small company stopped near some woodland at the great river Tarth and set up camp. Lauren felt much better and light-hearted being with the elves after eating. The five of them talked about various trivial things. Lauren was back to her old self. She was asking the elves many questions, prying into their lives, asking about their families and constantly making jokes, much to the amusement of the rest of the party. Finally, as the fire started to die, they all made for their beds and slept, with the three elven warriors taking turns to guard against any lurking dangers that might stumble upon them during the night.

They had a small breakfast when dawn broke and set off again towards their destination.

As they travelled over several days toward the outpost. Elisha and Lauren continued to talk. Elisha taught Lauren about the elves' closeness to nature and how they were a protector of the greatest gift, the gift of life.

"The environment is all around and stretches further or smaller than the eye can see. It's the air we breathe, the land we live on and the seas we sail. We must look after the environment as it looks after us," explained Elisha.

Their ethos was very similar to her father's, she thought. Elisha showed Lauren through her words how all is connected, from tiny insects to the tallest of trees. They discussed different types of trees, bushes, ferns and flowers. They visualised through words the many variants of animals in the world and the lives they lead.

Elisha explained that the elves felt bonded with nature, and to the elves, life was sacred. They celebrated life and the celebrated death if it had been full and had served its purpose. However, if life had been lost before it had fulfilled its destiny, the elves mourned with great sorrow as it was a life unfulfilled.

The two girls got closer and closer as the days rolled on, and soon, they were discussing their own lives in depth. Lauren discussed her own life with her father and Talis. How they lived in an inn that her father had owned, and how he had brought her up with Talis, her twin. She wasn't sure, but her mother had died when she was very young, and her father had never remarried. A vague memory of beauty, a soft voice, and a smile were all she could remember of her mother.

Lauren spoke much of Talis and their relationship on the pressing of Elisha. She discussed how both loved being out in the wild, that they were trackers and hunters most of the time or if not, they would be helping their father with work in the inn. Some would say how close she was with Talis, that they had a strange bond, but others said it was just because they were twins. They always knew what was on the other's mind, whatever it was. They shared thoughts and understood the pains of the other. Sometimes, Lauren felt their minds were joined as if they were the same person.

However, she also explained how different their personalities were with many humorous interludes and antidotes. Talis was the more serious of the two, and she was the lighter-hearted one and, with a grin, laughed about how she was most likely to be in trouble out of the two.

Elisha discussed being the only child of the King. Like Lauren, her mother had died young, and a male heir would not ascend to the throne for the first time in a millennium. This made it more difficult for Elisha, she felt. She was concerned about how she was viewed for not being male and thought she had a lot of expectations on her shoulders. Elisha always had a nagging feeling that her people looked for any signs of her failing, even though she readily admitted that the love from her people was unwavering. Therefore, Elisha always went out of her way to prove herself to her people and father. To prove that their trust in her was well-founded and that she would be worthy of being the queen of the elves one day.

As they were entering the sixth day of travel, Lauren enquired why she had been at Keros on the morning of the attack. It had been playing on Lauren's mind for the last few days. She had never seen an elf before, as none had ever walked the village's streets as far as she was aware. But on the day when the armies attacked, when she lost her father, her brother, and her friends, a princess from the land of elves had appeared and helped her flee, helped her survive. Elisha had not answered any of her questions when they were on the run from her village.

"It is a difficult question to answer, Lauren", hesitated Elisha. "For I do not know the full story myself. But I will try to explain."

"A great sage walks the land called Berolarn. He is well known to the kings of men, dwarves and elves. Where he comes from and where he goes, no one knows. His life is as long as the elves, and he has been walking the land for many centuries. Berolarn is mighty in mind. His intelligence and wisdom are probably unsurpassed now within this world. However, some think his advice is dangerous, but the royal house of elves has always found his advice comes in times of great need and always gives the races a path to follow. My journey started with such a visit to my father."

"What did he say?" asked Lauren.

"Berolarn spoke of a great evil coming, which can plunge the world into darkness. At the end of his conversation with the King, he asked that we search for Loran and his family and bring them to our lands. I am sure my father knew more of this, but neither explained why in more detail. Then, Berolarn specifically asked me to lead the hunt across the lands for you, though I do not know why. So, my royal guard and I went out across the wilderness. First, we separated for speed and stealth. Then, individually, we went hunting across all the villages and towns we could find for anyone who might know the whereabouts of Loran," answered Elisha.

"By chance, I had come upon your village the evening before the attack. I needed to find a room to rest. I discovered your inn and took a room. One of your workers had shown me to my quarters, and it was only during the evening when I came to the bar area for food that I heard the name Loran," continued Elisha.

"You were in one of the rooms at the inn? I cannot believe I didn't see you. How strange," said Lauren.

"I couldn't believe my luck as I looked over and saw Loran, and he was talking to you and your brother as you walked across the bar area. I thought about speaking to him there and then. I am sure he would have remembered me," said Elisha.

"But the bar was busy with life and full of travellers, I decided to wait until morning by misfortune. If I had spoken earlier, would it have changed the outcome? I do not know. But I awoke to your father's cries. I dressed as quickly as possible and followed to where I heard the fighting. I grabbed you when your father went down. I saw your brother fall as we made our escape. He was being dragged away from the fighting by others. Hopefully, he survived, and the royal guards will find him as they continue to search the lands, unbeknownst to them what has already transpired."

Elisha stopped and, after much thought, continued, "Lauren, many things are going on in the world which I do not understand, and I feel the path is uncertain for us both. We know the world is now in great peril from the hosts of the dark lord, and it was his forces who attacked. Therefore, we must gather as much strength and courage as possible and fight the evil upon us. When we get to the outpost, maybe we will find out more. I think, though, we must make our way back to the house of the king, my father Ethera, and hope that Berolarn will be there. Hopefully, the path will become clearer through the wisdom of the king's council and that of Berolarn," finished Elisha.

She looked at the skies and saw it was beginning to darken as the clouds became overcast.

"Treldor, it seems like the skies will open soon. We should head to the caves next to the forge and take shelter before the evening sets in and before the rain comes. It is not a massive detour. What do you think?" enquired Elisha.

"Yes, princess, I think this is a good idea. Come, let us turn slightly and head there now," answered Treldor.

Within a small number of minutes, they arrived at their destination.

"Look, Lauren, you are now at the Hills of the Dorals, ancient hills with caves cut from the rocks by the dwarves long ago. The elves now use this for shelter if there is a need," smiled Elisha.

Lauren saw an extensive set of tree-covered hills only. They dismounted. Brish led the way with the horses up what can only be considered a cleverly concealed track, with Calion coming up the rear. After a climb of one hundred metres, a small opening in the cliff wall was reached. They squeezed the horses through the entrance into a small corridor that opened into a large antechamber.

Brish and the others tied the horses to hooks set in the walls and walked into a massive room through the chamber. There were beds in the room. A large stone cooking fire took centre stage in the middle of the room, with some tables and chairs. The room had a fusty smell, probably coming from the slightly damp stone and some bales of hay that rested in the corner, ready for visitors.

"This cave is used now by the elves, and we keep it stocked with provisions. Over here, Lauren, come help me," asked Brish, who smiled at Lauren.

He took Lauren to one of the beds, knelt, and rummaged

under the bed. Then, he pulled a large chest and a sack from underneath with a grunt.

"Here, Lauren, grab a handle and help me take it to the table near the fire," said Brish.

Lauren helped Brish with the chest. They carried it to the fire, where Brish flung the lid upwards. Lauren could see various beets at different stages of ageing, pots of powders and herbs, dried fruit and various items she had never seen before, which she guessed were foods of some description. There was also a good supply of wine bottles, which she assumed was why the chest was so heavy.

"Shall we go into the woods and see if we can find anything to hunt Lauren?" asked Brish as he motioned towards the doorway.

She nodded with a smile. She was surprised at how excited she was to go out into the woods and find food for the table.

"Brish, do not stray far, and even the smallest signs of anything unusual come back straight away," said Elisha.

"Of course, we will stay close by and be on our guard," answered Brish.

Elisha glanced at Lauren before pressing home firmly to the young elven soldier with an air of responsibility to keep Lauren safe. Lauren noticed this, and she mused over how the woods were as much her domain as it was the elves. She would be fine. Elisha worries too much, and she could evade or hunt anything in this environment.

"We will be fine, Elisha. I promise I will not let Brish get into trouble," said Lauren as she laughed at the princess, who smiled back in return.

"I hope you are good with your promises, Lauren. Ask Treldor; Brish is a wayward spirit! If any form of trouble can be found, he will be in the middle of it," said Elisha smiling.

Brish and the others started laughing.

"Thank you, Princess Elisha. Your words continue to make my heart light and full of joy," Brish said. He bowed and walked towards the doorway that led to the outside woods, motioning for Lauren to follow.

As they walked outside, they noted that the rain was in full flow and by how wet the forest floor was, it must have started not long after entering the caves. It was working its way through the canopy of the great trees and was consistently falling on them as they moved away from the caves. The air was fresh and cool, with the evening closing in fast. It was ideal weather for hunting. Brish and Lauren started moving sidewards, maintaining five to ten metres apart. Both had their bows ready, and an arrow notched as they silently walked through the undergrowth.

They had been hunting for twenty to thirty minutes when suddenly Lauren heard the breaking of a twig and heavy breathing. She raised her hand firmly upwards and motioned to Brish, who stopped dead and squinted towards where Lauren was looking. Within seconds Lauren saw her prey and let the arrow fly. Then, with a big thumping sound, Lauren knew her hand had found its mark. Stealthy, they both walked over to the dead animal. It was a young Ibex, a wild goat of the mountains and hills.

"Well done, Lauren," Brish said, smiling as he pulled the

arrow out of the goat's chest. He grabbed its legs, and with a grunt, he threw the animal over his shoulders. "Come, let us return to the caves. We have a hearty beast here who will give us much nourishment for the days ahead."

When they arrived back at the cave, the fire had taken hold, and the whole place was now full of warmth, if not filled with a haze of smoke and a charcoal smell. First, the elves all congratulated Lauren on her hunt. Then, they all set about getting the meal ready, drawing water from the little well positioned on the cave floor, preparing vegetables and butchering the meat. An assortment of ingredients was in a large pot on the fire not before long, and a fine-smelling stew was underway. When the smell of the food hit Lauren, she realised how hungry she was for a substantial meal. Lauren was bored with the traveller's rations. She longed to be back at the inn with her family, eating one of the inn's finest meals. As she thought about good food, she drifted off in thought about her father as she sat on her bed waiting for the food to cook.

She mused over the strange powers he had wielded in battle. Who was he, really? Where did such power come from? Was this the truth of the rumours they heard about their father being of another age? Then her heart went dark as she saw images in her mind of him falling. How did the demons know him by name? She just couldn't understand that.

Lauren then thought of her brother, seeing images of him smiling at her as he teased her with the name shortcake. Was he dead? Could Talis have survived? She didn't think it was possible, the enemy soldiers were too many, and there was nowhere to run, but then she escaped with help; maybe he had escaped like her. It drove her insane, not knowing where Talis was or his fate. Perhaps she needed to leave the elves and go searching for him. She was grateful to Elisha and understood some mystic had told the elves to find her. But Talis would need her as she needed him. So perhaps leaving is the best course of action.

"Lauren, the food is ready," Elisha called over as the others filled their bowls with the contents of the stewing pot.

Startled out of deep thought, Lauren jumped up, made her way over to the pot, and filled her bowl. Then, joining the elves around the table, Lauren forgot her dark thoughts and made small talk with her companions as they ate. Over the next few hours, with the wine flowing freely, they all laughed and joked without a care in the world. Treldor finally made a move away from the table, speaking to Calion and Brish.

"It is time for us to stop drinking and prepare for bed. I will take the first watch, followed by Calion and then you, Brish," said Treldor. They both nodded and rose from the table.

"I suppose we should sleep, Lauren. We have a long day tomorrow as we make a final push to reach the outpost," stated Elisha as she rose from the table.

Lauren made her way over to the bed she had claimed, laid down and made herself as comfortable as possible. But, as she lay there, Lauren realised she was exhausted, the past few days' events were starting to take their toll, and with thoughts of the battle and her brother, Lauren drifted off to sleep.

Chapter 9 – The Run for the Gate

Lauren was in a deep sleep when she was awoken by Calion shaking her.

"It is time, Lauren, you need to be up, and we need to leave in the next five minutes. There is something wrong, and we need to go," Calion announced urgently.

Lauren jumped up, a bit lightheaded from the wine the night before and the haste of the awakening.

"What's going off," Lauren asked Elisha as she saw the princess strapping on her boots and reaching for her short sword.

"Brish can smell evil in the air, and he fears the creoch, great grey wolves from the Mountains of Credoline, can be heard in the distance. This means that there will be goblins too. I suspect the hunt is for us. There will be no safety until we reach the outpost. We must move with haste, Lauren. We mustn't be trapped in these caves when they come, or that will be our end," answered Elisha.

The hurriedness and foreboding of Elisha's comments made Lauren hastily grab all her gear and rush towards the opening, where Elisha and Calion now waited.

"Treldor and Brish have already untethered the horses. They have led them down and await us," said Calion swiftly.

All three rushed down the hillside and broke out of the trees to see the other two elves already mounted on their horses and holding the other horses ready for them. Brish and Elisha mounted their horses, and Lauren jumped on behind the princess, grabbing hold of Elisha's outstretched arm.

"Ride!" shouted Treldor as the howls of the wolves sounded too close for comfort.

The companions rode at breathtaking speed as they gave the Holinari horses the freedom of their kind. They glided through the landscape as the horses pounded across it with no foot wrong did they set over rock, grassland or stream. They had been riding for a few hours, and still, the howls of the wolves were with them. Once they smell blood, the creoch do not give up the hunt; the elves knew this, and they knew they would be in trouble if these creatures of the mountains were to catch up with them.

"We must make for the valley pass before midday as our marker for the day. If not, we will not make the closing of the Brendal Gate and reach the outpost before sundown," shouted Treldor as he looked backwards at his companions.

"What is the Brendal Gate?" shouted Lauren over the noise of the galloping horses.

"It is a small opening in the mountains just before we reach the other side where the crossing over the river lies in the Brendal valley. It is a strange place. There is a great stone wall that closes the access just before nightfall. How it came to this place or for what purpose, we do not know. But it appears each evening, and none can pass this place until the sun rises the next day. If we do not make it, we will be cornered in the valley with little hope of escape from the creoch and goblins that hunt us, so we must not be late," Brish shouted back.

Lauren was beginning to feel despair creeping into her. As if

Elisha sensed this, she gave encouragement to Lauren.

"We will make it. Do not worry. The horses are the fastest of their kind, and they will sense that they are hunted," said Elisha positively.

As time flew by, Lauren surveyed the passing landscape. They were riding over undulating grasslands and small hills that were furnishing groupings of small trees and bushes. The land was, in general, relatively sparse and grey. The path they followed offered no real vantage point to see the pursuers, though Lauren did keep casting a glance backwards to see if she could see the creatures that pursued them. The rolling landscape continued to fly past them at speed, and she wondered how long before they reached the valley pass as midday was approaching. Thirty minutes later, they came upon the valley pass without incident.

Treldor commented, "we have hit our mark just in time as it must be around midday looking at the sun's position. We must continue to push on as we have no time to lose."

They galloped through and emerged on the other side. Before them, the landscape changed into a trail that cut through a forest covering the valley hills, dense with various small and large trees fighting for the sunlight.

Lauren was spellbound by the variety of hues and colours as they entered. They were significantly different to the trees back home. The forest floor was damp from the rain of the night before and covered in leaves of various sizes of green, red, brown, orange, greys, and purples. All along the trail's edge, white and blue snowdrops glistened in the sunlight that followed the path. She could hear the birds singing and the thrum of many insects that made their homes in and around these great trees. There was not the faintest echo of evil in this place as they galloped down the trail under the forest's eaves.

"Elisha, I have never seen trees like these before. But, of course, there are mighty oaks, that is one there," said Lauren as she pointed across at a large reddish barked tree as they raced past, "but even they look different."

Elisha glanced at Lauren.

"You are now entering the lands of my kind Lauren. The trees here differ from any other in the lands of other races. This is because they have been blessed with the attention and love of my people. The forest is one of the oldest in all the lands and predates the elves' arrival. Our forefathers were drawn to this land by the natural beauty you see before you. Yet, much of our lands differ from the lands of man and the other races. This will become clearer when you come to my home, the city of Solanstar," replied Elisha.

As soon as she spoke, a sensation of impending doom hit Lauren as Brish approached the rear.

"Ride, ride, the enemy is upon us," screamed Brish.

Lauren looked back to see how very close five of the biggest wolves she had ever seen, mammoth in size, a lot larger and bigger girthed than a horse. Howling as they got closer with each step, bellowing hate coming from their mouths. Mouths filled with massive teeth that could tear an animal apart in one bite. On their backs, riding in spiked war saddles, sat creatures of horror, deformed faces with protruding fangs and green and grey leather skin. They had great muscular arms, so long that they didn't belong to their bodies. Goblins! Lauren had heard tales of these creatures before seeing them at the attack on her village. Evil men deformed by the gods for their sins, consumers of man's flesh and the carriers of death. Lauren pulled close to the back of Elisha, her hair raising on her arms and the nape of her neck. Then, with a racing heartbeat, she whispered in Elisha's ear.

"We are doomed. Goblins on great wolves are upon us," shouted Lauren.

"We are not doomed yet!" shouted Elisha as she urged their horse on.

As they raced forward, the creoch and goblins were closing with each step. Maybe no more than one hundred yards away, Lauren was sure she could feel the heat of the creoch's breath on the back of her skin.

"Brish, Calion", shouted Treldor, "our race is up, they are too close, it is time," Treldor then shouted words in a language Lauren did not understand. Then all three elven soldiers pulled their horses to a standstill and turned as Elisha and Lauren raced on. As Lauren turned her head, she could see the three elves racing towards the enemy, swords raised above their heads as they engaged the creoch and goblins.

"No" screamed Lauren as she gripped Elisha hard that her knuckles turned white. "Elisha, we must go back to help. They cannot win," she cried with tremors in her voice.

"It is their destiny, Lauren, to protect us. We must go on," said Elisha in an emotionless, flat voice.

Lauren shut her eyes for a moment, and burning hate for Elisha coursed through her mind as battle cries dissipated. How could she do this and have a nonchalant attitude about their inevitable death? As the guilt and hatred worked through Lauren, they raced on.

She paused long before responding as she gathered herself.

"I do not understand you, Elisha. Your guard turned to certain doom, and perhaps with our help, they could have survived. Yet you do not seem to care. You only cared for your own skin," snarled Lauren, who finished speaking as the heat in her mind started to rise.

"Lauren, do not speak to me about caring. You know nothing of the loss in my heart, how I am overwhelmed with mourning the loss of my people, guard, and friends. The feeling of powerlessness knowing that you must be saved over all other costs, a hope for us all against the dark lord Berolarn said, but I know not why. I have no satisfaction from their deaths, just pain, be quiet!" Elisha snapped, carrying a certain sadness and anger in her retort.

They continued at pace into late afternoon with no more exchanges of words. Neither uttered any further comment after the shock of losing their companions and their heated words. Then, finally, Lauren plucked up the courage to break the silence.

"I'm sorry, Elisha. I didn't mean to blame or offend you. My words came from the shock and disbelief of losing our friends. It brought back the loss of my father and my brother. It hurts so much and tears at my insides, and at times, the pain causes a mist that strangles my thoughts and brings so much anger that it courses through my body until I am ready to explode," explained Lauren.

Lauren halted speaking, giving thought to what she wanted to say. She couldn't quite find the words. She asked the only thing that really had any meaning at the moment.

"Do you think there is a chance they would have got away?" Asked Lauren with apprehension.

Elisha turned, and Lauren could see much sorrow in Elisha's eyes. She shook her head.

"I hold on to hope, Lauren, where perhaps no hope should be given. But the royal guard is the best trained of the elven army, and Treldor, Calion and Brish are some of the most skilled in the arts of battle. Even though against creochs, the chances are slim, yes, I do have hope," replied Elisha as she smiled at Lauren, and her eyes gleamed as she held back the tears.

"I was angry at the loss we suffered and your words. When I lashed out, I was as angry at myself for not helping as anything you said. But my words were valid, their sacrifice is just a tiny cog in this war, and we must not lose sight of what we are trying to achieve. I do not blame you for your words, and as much as I wish what happened could not have been, we cannot rewind time to gain another outcome." Elisha continued with a sigh, "we will arrive at the outpost soon. We are probably about twenty minutes away from Brendal Gate and just over an hour away from arriving at the outpost."

It seemed minutes before Elisha announced, "Here, Lauren, you behold Brendal Gate, the doorway to the valley we have just travelled."

Lauren was transfixed by the two giant warriors carved out of the rock face, one on either side of the valley, reaching the heights of the skies. They looked like kings of old facing each other ready to do battle.

"At sunset, the great stone wall appears between the two warriors, and none can pass through the valley or over the wall. They protect the valley from the night. We are not sure of their origin or what magic controls the wall. But no one travels this road at night after the path is closed," commented Elisha as they passed the two sentries, moving on to the next step in their journey.

"Not long now," continued Elisha, and she motioned forward to Lauren.

Lauren looked into the distance, and she could just make out a keep and a large tower on the side of a cliff face.

Chapter 10 - Morallis Outpost

As they galloped up the steep craggy stone road up to the keep, they heard the shout from inside, a giant mechanical grinding noise, and the front gate opened. They rode in at a gallop, and their horses reared up in the small courtyard, nearly throwing Lauren off. But, instead, she pushed off backwards and landed on her feet in a crouching position. Elisha calmed the horse and dismounted and then flung her arms open, seeing an elf running towards her, she embraced the man.

"Well, met cousin," said the male elf in an exciting bubbly voice. "It's been a long time Elisha. So what brings you out to Morallis? And with a friend too," looking over at Lauren, "and no guard?" he said slowly, looking confused.

He looked over to Lauren again, trying to ascertain who or what she was and why she was travelling on the back of a horse with the princess.

"Well, met Jerrel," said Elisha warmly. "I have missed my childhood friend, Jerrel. This is Lauren. Lauren, please meet Jerrel, my beloved foolish cousin. Close the gate Jerrel and have the guard stand ready. Then, we can go inside and discuss further."

"Hello, Jerrel," said Lauren. Jerrel nodded in return.

Jerrel shouted swift commands, and the outpost was a hive of movement as the gates started to close. Lauren saw at least twenty men moving around the keep. They began to man the walls as the gate slammed too. Jerrel led their way into the keep, walking down a small, dimly lit hallway towards his personal chambers. Jerrel opened the door, and he waved them in.

"Come, please be seated, and I will get you food and drink," said Jerrel.

Jerrel shouted down the hallway for refreshments to be brought.

As they both took a chair, Jerrel sat opposite them.

"Please tell me, Elisha, why are you here? And where is your guard?" he asked inquisitively. "I have not seen you in a few years, and you arrive, visit unannounced and in the company of a human girl? Then immediately, you are telling us to close the gates? And indicate we are at risk?" questioned Jerrel.

"Jerrel, a lot of the story, I do not know and much remains to be answered. But you must have heard the rumours of war and the spreading darkness across the lands? Lauren," Elisha nodded towards her companion, "is being hunted by the dark lord, and we were chased by creoch and goblins soon after I found her."

"Why are you with the girl, Elisha?" asked Jerrel.

"I am here because of the advice of Berolarn and by command of the King. I was sent, as were others of the royal guard, to search for the family of Loran. Lauren is the daughter of Loran, and at great risk, she was rescued as the dark lord's armies consumed her village and killed Loran," answered Elisha.

At the mention of Loran's death, Jerrel looked aghast. Then, in sadness, he shook his head, looking toward Lauren and reaching for her hand.

"Though you do not know me, I have much sorrow for your loss. I knew of your father for what it is worth and speak only highly of him and his legacy," said Jerrel. Then turning back to Elisha. "These are indeed dark times, and you bring news that chills the heart. What of your guards Elisha?"

Elisha shook her head.

"We were hunted by these creoch and goblins from this morning's dawn. Lauren had counted at least five creoch with riders. They caught up to us as we entered the forest on the path toward Brendal's Gate. As they gained on us every second, the three guards who came with me as my escort turned and engaged. We could hear the cries of battle as we galloped on, but the noise faded quickly, and the outcome of the fight we do not know. But it is a massive task to take on one creoch, never mind five. I live in hope as the three guards were Treldor, Calion and Brish. Some of the finest warriors of the elven army and royal guard" answered Elisha.

"This is grievous news indeed, Elisha, and as for the enemy, their daring is great to travel into the land of elves. But, as far as I'm aware, creoch or goblin entering our lands has not been seen before," muttered Jerrel, who had turned ashen in shock.

There was a knock on the door.

"Enter," called out Jerrel, and two elven soldiers entered with an array of refreshments and placed them on the table. They all thanked the soldiers, who nodded as they left the room.

The companions and Jerrel talked for the next few hours as they ate. Recounting what had happened to the two women since leaving the village and how it had turned into a flight for life in the final hours. Jerrel relayed what news of the outside world he had picked up from visitors to the outpost.

"Many goblin raiding parties are coming down from the north, that much is accurate, and they have laid waste to many villages and towns. They have killed many and enslaved others, it appears. However, our spies tell us that we have not seen more than a fraction of their forces in the southern lands. They are still amassing their army and machines of war in the great plains, that much is true, but they appear to be waiting for something. Perhaps the search for Lauren and her family was part of this. Who can tell what the answer to this riddle may be? But, they have not come yet in force, and neither have they made any direct attack on the larger cities and towns. War has not officially begun in any of the countries. How long have you been left, Elisha?" asked Jerrel.

"A few months", pondered Elisha, "maybe more, we left around the closing of summer, and we have spent much of the time searching for Lauren and her family before we could locate them."

Suddenly the whole keep shuddered as if hit by a massive earthquake. The room occupants were nearly thrown from their chairs. The room was filled with dust as another tremor hit. There was a colossal sound of the keeps' structure falling to the ground. They heard shouts and screams as the door was flung open.

"You need to leave. We are under attack from unknown forces in the sky. I fear the walls will not last long. They are being torn down by flame and darkness. We can see goblins coming at speed out of the forest in the distance, where they should not have been able to walk," shouted the elven soldier through the doorway.

Jerrel motioned for them to follow him as the soldier left the room, he pushed against a part of the wall, and a well-concealed section swung back.

"Quickly, Elisha, down the passageway, it stretches for several miles, keep going and do not turn around. It will eventually bring you out at Niars Rock next to the temple of Sol. Then, the priests will have horses, head down the causeway and make for the city," shouted Jerrel as another thunderous boom shook the keep.

Jerrel pushed Elisha and Lauren through the doorway and slammed the door shut. Expecting darkness, Lauren could see that the tunnel had a faint light not much of the way down. Running, they passed little alcoves set in the walls that carried a strange light within them. As they ran, these well-placed cavities continued to light their way.

Chapter 11 – The Ranger Luther

Berolarn and Talis had left the hut nearly two weeks ago, and they had headed east on foot towards the lands of Lorevitch and the town of Lowedom, where Berolarn said Luther would be. It had been a pretty miserable time for Talis. He found Berolarn poor company for a lot of the journey. He would not offer many conversations himself, and when Talis asked him questions, he would answer with a mundane short response. However, if Talis dug deeper into anything about the war, his ancestry and the experience of the hunger, then Berolarn would not speak any tales. Instead, he would tell Talis to be quiet. The subjects were not for the road; all will become apparent.

"How much further is Lowedom? Berolarn, we have been walking for weeks now," enquired Talis. He thought about how fed up he was with the trip's monotony, and he wished for better food and better company.

"We will be there soon, Talis, maybe another day or two. We will look for Luther at the Devil's Punchbowl inn, an unusual tavern full of half-goblins, mercenaries and thieves," replied Berolarn, who turned and smiled. "You need to be on your best behaviour there, Talis, if you want to stay out of harm's way."

Talis's head scrambled. Who on earth was this Luther? As usual, Berolarn had spoken little of him or the reasons behind why they searched for him rather than going after Lauren.

"Please, Berolarn, will you tell me who this Luther is? And why do we go looking for him? Especially if he inhabits such a place," asked Talis.

Turning to his companion, Berolarn felt quite appreciative to be drawn out of his dark thoughts

"This is a long story, Talis, worthy of its own book. But nevertheless, I will attempt to tell you what I know. As I can see, you will not be at rest until you hear of the tales of Luther. It would be good, actually, for you to have an understanding of Luther as he is one for you to always trust no matter what he tells you to do," said Berolarn.

"Where do you start with Luther? He is a conundrum, a puzzle that is difficult to solve. As far as I am aware, no one knows where he came from, and he does not share any information about his past. He is known to some as a mighty warrior, to others, a highly skilled tracker and a ranger who leads the way where others would fail. But many mistrust him as he is generally sullen and difficult to approach," mused Berolarn.

Talis grinned to himself at this. It seemed the story could have been about Berolarn himself. He wished some god would help him. But, unfortunately, he could see it now. Having two defensive antisocial people in his company would be a worsening nightmare.

Berolarn continued as he looked back to the road.

"It is said he was a man child, a youth of thirteen or fourteen years of age when he was enlisted into or joined an army of mercenaries in one of the far-off regions in the south. He was with these mercenaries for years as they sold their swords and allegiance to the highest bidder. Luther started out as a tracker with this band. He learnt his trade so well that soon he had no rival. Luther understands the surrounding landscapes and how nature works on the land. Soon he could track any living thing over miles of land and water, read any signs left on the trail, no matter how small, and read the wind and the smells left behind, like a wolf hunting its prey. But his most incredible skill is when Luther is tracking. It is how he understands the thinking of man and beast. Luther understands each turn they will take and the path they are going down."

"As he grew and matured. Luther soon became renowned amongst them over the years as one with an iron hand who could strike down his enemies with one crushing blow. He is also highly skilled with all forms of weapons. Luther is perhaps the most complete soldier you will find."

"I think Luther became disillusioned with the mercenary way of life as the years passed. Or maybe something happened. I do not know. But he left the mercenaries and came north. Since then, he has travelled the full breadth of the lands. Sometimes Luther has worked as a ranger, other times as a hired soldier for some just cause, and he has walked dangerous paths with me as we have sought to protect the lands."

"Now, this has happened over many years, but when you meet him, he looks to be of an age," Berolarn stopped and pondered, "no more than thirty to thirty-five." Then, continuing to walk on, "I suspect that he is half-elven, hence his long years. But he is very human in appearance and build," finished Berolarn.

"He seems like he is quite a character," commented Talis. "Why does he make his home in Lowedom and frequent such a place as this Devil's Punchbowl? It sounds like an evil place!"

Berolarn looked amused.

"I would say more that it is unsavoury rather than evil.

However, there is no doubt that some form of sin is in the place with the half-goblins taking up residence, and I am sure some thieves will have murdered plying their trade," answered Berolarn.

Berolarn turned more serious again, "There is a level of uncertainty in my mind as to why he chose Lowedom as his home. Lowedom is central in man's land, which could be part of his thinking. It is also a town without much steer from any centralised government, being part of the small kingdom of Lorevitch, whose ruler cares little for his lands and people. It is run by a town council, and generally, there is little control. This would suit someone of Luther's personality, where he can come and go as he pleases, with no one being particularly interested in his movements."

"As for the Devil's Punchbowl, it will be a great source of information. One thing is sure: a host of vagabonds and thieves will know as much of what is happening in the world as any other. Talk becomes much freer as the wine flows. It loosens the tongue of its most stubborn adversary," grinned Berolarn. "It will aid Luther to know such things."

"Why do we need to fetch Luther to help us? He seems like he has a lot of uses, that is for sure," questioned Talis.

Berolarn laughed. "I knew I should be careful talking to you about such things. I had no doubt that the questions on the why's would start," replied Berolarn as Talis grinned back.

"But a fair question, I suppose," continued Berolarn. "You have gathered that Luther has skills that perhaps no one we know has. I would say he is the best at what he does. Luther is focused, adaptable and calm while chaos rages all around him. I know that Luther is no friend of anyone with evil designs for the most part. However, he has great compassion and is merciful, where perhaps it is unwarranted. Which I think comes from elven heritage, perhaps. He works for the greater good of all people, making him a great ally." Berolarn lowered his voice and leaned closer, "the most significant reason is that we will travel into lands that no one travels. Maybe Luther has. Perhaps he hasn't. But either way, he will be our guide if all goes to plan. Our very success, my heart says, will rely heavily on his talent."

"Do you think then he will come?" enquired Talis.

"I have no doubt that he already knows part of the story once we have discussed the situation, as I mentioned back at the hut. It was he who messaged me that your family had been found. It was Luther who had another ranger watching your village and waiting for my return. It was he who sent the message of the battle at Keros and that your sister Lauren had gone with the elves, and you had not been among the dead," returned Berolarn. "His message indicated that he would be at Lowedom for a month after the date of the message, and I was to send word or meet him at Lowedom if and when I needed him further. But unfortunately, I do not have Luther's hawks for sending messages. So we make our way on foot to find him."

Talis was quite excited to meet him and was ecstatic to hear further about his sister, wondering why Berolarn had omitted this part of the story. A ranger, he thought. I bet he really is a brilliant tracker and hunter. Hopefully, I can learn more skills on the journey. You always have to improve your hunting skills as you never know when they will come in handy, he was always telling Lauren this in part of getting her to go with him on his own hunting trips.

"Where are we going after we have seen Luther, Berolarn? I wish to find Lauren," asked Talis.

"We will make for Solanstar, the wonderful city of the elves. I hope to find Lauren there waiting for us by the time we arrive, and before you ask, we will go in front of the king and discuss our plans further. He is wise and indeed powerful. We will need his support along the way." Berolarn stated as he surveyed the landscape. "I think we will arrive mid-morning if I have my bearings right."

Talis hesitated before he continued, "Can I ask you another question?"

Berolarn looked at Talis and could see something was on his mind. He nodded.

"The hunger played on my mind since we left the hut. I am unsure how to describe it. I haven't mentioned it again. I felt I was losing myself. The thirst for blood to murder you was all-consuming. An evil flowed through me, which was horrific and terrifying," Talis shuddered as the memory returned, "and it was only you calling Lauren that broke down the wall that was building inside me," stated Talis.

"How will I control this again, Berolarn and what about Lauren? Will she have to go through the same fire and the same tests? I fear for her, and I fear myself as well as anyone around me. Or perhaps it will never come again?" questioned Talis.

"It is difficult to know the full outcomes of the thirst for you and your sister Talis," sighed Berolarn.

"We discussed that the Solarians have years of training before adulthood to tailor the thirst and hunger into something else. But, how, and I do not know why your father not only did not train you, but why he also stopped it from coming to life. Which makes me wonder what is different about both of you and why the histories of old foretold your coming, was it the god Sol interfering in the world? This is a wonder in itself," stated Berolarn.

Berolarn sounded objective in his thoughts as he continued, "I considered the risks of taking you into the hunger and thought about all the trials that will come your way. I could not risk you releasing the hunger under pressure and letting the chaos of the thirst loose on the world. It had to be. You had to live through the chaos as long as possible, which I could help control. But you calmed it down quicker than any of our kind would have expected. This means you have the power to control it, and with the control, you will start to call on it and with it comes great responsibility, strength and power. You will need to call on it at times as we move forwards with our quest. Of this, I am sure," said Berolarn.

"What of Lauren? Will she have this power?" asked Talis.

"On Lauren, materially, she has the same problem as you, and the hunger and thirst will be buried deep inside, waiting to explode. But for Lauren, it differs. She is female, generally the more powerful of the Solarians and holds the seed of the future generations," answered Berolarn.

"However, she will pull more from your mother's side as you do from your father's side, and your mother's ancestry will determine much of what is to be. It is difficult to know what Lauren's destiny will be at this juncture." Berolarn cut short as if he was saying too much.

"Please let us rest from talking for a while", and with that, he finished the conversation, and Talis sensibly let matters drop, if not slightly annoyed, that he had many more unanswered questions.

Berolarn mused about what would happen with Talis and Lauren for some time. He had long been a scholar of the Solarians. For hundreds of years, he had visited the ancient castle of Kin-Kathenel and delved into the troves of various pieces of literature from the ancient worlds that laid out the evolution of their kind. Many ancient tomes documented the world's history and recalled elements of the world of science. But the ones of most tremendous significance and value, laid deep in a secret chamber within the bowels of the earth under the castle, were the three books of power. One bound in white leather, one in black leather, and one in blue leather. The three are closed and locked with unbreakable clasps of precious metals that can only be opened with a unique key.

After the gods brought life to the earth as they looked down from their planer worlds. So started the eternal conflict between good and evil, mortals prayed to their gods, taking sides, and all things eventually fell on one side or the other of their religious conflicts. The saying goes that if a day is good, then the night is evil. It is said that the gods listen to their call, urging through their priests for mortals to take a stand, and the wars between evil and good began.

It is said in other tomes that the deities created these books to aid their worshippers, the white book called Hopenal, the book of life. Dealhanal, the black book, the book of death and sat between these warring factions is Neutar, the blue book, the book of balance. All magics seen throughout the ages were born from these books.

It was the black book that Olgrich had delved too deep into, and it had taken him, consumed him, and transformed him into the dark lord. At the war's end, they brought the book to Kin-Kathenel and locked it away with the other books the Solarians had also recovered.

Berolarn had learned within an ancient scripture that it had been foretold by the priests of yesteryear that a great pestilence would come to the world in the form of a dark lord. Who, like a disease, would spread across the lands, and all would fall in his path. This fate could be stopped, but only through the greatest of sacrifices by a sister and a brother, twins by birth, children of a line once formed of darkness. Whose forefathers long ago transformed to the paths of light and came from the age of dreams. The texts had shown him many other things, and some were lost on him. The true meanings maybe never be discovered.

He wasn't sure if the books of power would be needed again, but they must never fall into the dark lord's hands, and he was tempted to see their destruction. But held back because the need in the war for them might be great, and he knew not how to destroy them. The children of Loran were the twins that the histories spoke of. This he had no doubt of due to their heritage. A heritage Loran had implied the last time they had spoken when the children were young. A legacy that seemed impossible, but then Loran's wife Gabrielle had an aura of strange power that he could not read.

Berolarn's mind constantly considered the merits of how much he should let Talis and then his sister Lauren know and how much of the path they needed to follow on their own as part of self-discovery. He was sincere, open and honest in most things. But the world was a game of politics and manipulations, and he had to join this game to ensure that the outcomes were the right ones. It was one of those times. So he would tell Talis and Lauren no more than what had already been said.

Chapter 12 – Chaos at the Devils Punchbowl

They reached the walled town of Lowedom at around midday, and large crowds went in and out of the town gates. Talis had never visited a town of such size, and as they entered, he gazed at the various races and people milling about the entrance. There were men, dwarves, maybe some elves, and more than likely, looking at the faces of some. Half-goblins.

Peasants and beggars were accosting those in fine clothing with entourages or servants in tow. They looked down on the beggars with horror as the filth of their unclean hands came near them for money. They also watched with great satisfaction as their servants hurried the poor away to allow their master to continue their business. Next, Talis saw people taking their wares into the town to sell, with a steady stream of carts carrying various goods and commodities. There were also long lines of animals being herded into the town. You then had soldiers and others with a myriad of armour and weaponry milling about. All in all, Talis realised this was a hectic town.

As they walked through the streets, Talis looked intently at the various types of buildings. It was an odd assortment of businesses and homes. All of different sizes and ages. Berolarn had told Talis that it had been a small village that had grown and grown over the years and now was a thriving town and one of the central places in Lorevitch. He had indicated that they would find the Devil's Punchbowl at the far side of the town after they had been through the market area, which was about a twenty-minute walk.

As they arrived in the marketplace, Talis was spellbound by the noise, the enormous waves of wondrous colours from a massive variety of different things to buy. There were all sorts of things, wool, pieces of woven cotton and silks, beddings, knives and tools, swords and various weapons, pots and pans, baskets and animals. There were also some delightful foods that offered a multitude of tantalising smells that made Talis really hungry. His stomach turned, and he yearned for something more than the traveller's rations he had become accustomed to over the last few weeks.

As they walked past the bazaar and the stalls started to thin out, Talis found that the crowds also started to disappear and soon, they were walking down streets with little sign of any occupants. The buildings were far less well kept, the area smelled of sewage, and the whole neighbourhood gave him an uncomfortable feeling against an air of poverty and danger. Finally, they walked to the end of a long road and turned right, not far from where they turned on the right-hand side. Talis saw a sign swinging gently in the wind out of a large ramshackle three-story building. Devils Punchbowl.

As they were about to enter, the door flew open as two projectiles flew past them, missiles that looked like goblins. Then, a voice growled,

"Next time dogs, ya wi be duped in the ewers with ta gut rats wi dem throats cut ear t ear."

The speaker was a massive man who stood in the doorway. He stood maybe eight feet tall, arms and legs like tree trunks and where his belly finished, his thighs joined his knees. He was huge!

"Ah Mster Berolarn, g'day to ya sir, it's bin a bit a time sin I see ya," he growled as he smiled with a mouth full of missing and broken teeth.

"Good day to you, Biggy. I see business is as good as ever," smiled Berolarn. "Biggy, have you seen Luther? I am expecting to meet him here."

"Cum's in ery nite, all nite, pect to see hide t-nite." Biggy snarled, which amused Talis, as it was a slightly more modified form of his initial growl. Talis thought he had practised this as part of being an innkeeper, to become the perfect host. He must have ogre in him. Talis grinned to himself.

"What ginning at peasant," said Biggy. The half-ogre started moving towards Talis as he stared at him menacingly.

"Now, now, Biggy, the young man means you no harm, and I am sure he is not attempting to create any offence. On the contrary, I suspect he is new to town life and somewhat in awe of you." Berolarn spoke smoothly as he stepped slightly in front of Talis. Luckily for Talis, Biggy had no idea what words such as offence and awe meant, but it sounded good to the half-ogres ears, and he looked wary of Berolarn.

"Good, this is good, as I sorry yung mster, tis sum tink tis fun t' laugh at Biggy, I get a bit u no, bit angry fast," snarled Biggy "cum, cum side, get Lilla t get drinks. He bellowed "Lilla" as he escorted them into a massive room full of patrons. "Lilla, where r u? God dmn it".

"I'm coming, you big oath, shut your hole. I only have one set of hands," said a beautiful girl as she pushed through the melee of bodies.

Talis noted she was no more than twenty years of age. She was dressed in a very revealing blouse and skirt, which showed too much leg and probably more cleavage than she knew. She really didn't look like she belonged here.

"Ah, Berolarn, what brought you to town and with a good-looking young man," she said, smiling and winking at Talis.

"This way," Lilla said as she guided them through doors at the other side of the taproom and led them down a small hallway.

"I presume you will want one of the side rooms, Berolarn", she continued as she opened one of the doors along the corridor and showed them in as Berolarn nodded.

"Ah, Lillaanthisil, this is perfect, thank you," Berolarn commented as he surveyed the small room, which by the inn's standard was well kept, clean, and one would say well-loved as it was apparent a lot of spit and polish was used on well-worn timbers around the room. The room was well-lit, with a good-sized table and several chairs in the middle.

"Ah, god damn it, Berolarn, how often do I ask Luther and you not to call me that? It makes me sound like a damn elf. You'll get my throat cut. Call me Lilla if you must speak to me," moaned Lilla.

Smiling, Berolarn sat down, looking up at the girl.

"I am sorry, Lilla, but your birth name is your name, and it is a lovely name. It marks you for who you are, not what you are. Talis, this is Lilla. Lilla, this is Talis. Lilla is an old friend of both Luther and mine; we have known her since she was a child. She is in Biggy's care. He is her protector. She is as loveable yet as mean and quick to anger as Biggy," grinned Berolarn.

He laughed as she looked at him with venom, and Talis was sure she was about to hit him with something.

"Well, met Talis", Lilla finally responded. "You always drive me insane, Berolarn. So what do you want to drink and eat?"

"Hello, Lilla," smiled Talis.

"Wine and whatever the house special is, please, Lilla. Also, do you have two rooms? I think we will stay the night. Perhaps if I ask Biggy, you could take my friend back towards the markets to get some new clothes, as he has only what he is wearing. Would that be ok, Lilla?" asked Berolarn of the young woman.

Talis suddenly became very self-conscious about how he must look to the young girl.

She smiled broadly at Talis and turned towards Berolarn.

"If you can get Biggy to agree, it will be my pleasure to help such a good-looking young man get dressed," laughed Lilla.

Talis was sure he was going red. He was already very uncomfortable in front of this girl.

"Good, in fact, if you ask him, Lilla, and if he gives you any bother, you can tell me when you bring the food and the keys to our rooms, and I will go and speak to him," Berolarn said, and with that, she smiled at Talis, nodded and left the room.

"Who is she? How come she works for Biggy in this place?" Talis asked with a mix of wonder, scorn and sorrow.

"Ah, that is an interesting story, but it can wait as she might return at any time. Plus, it would probably be better for her to tell her story rather than me or maybe ask of it from Luther, as he knows the tale far better than I do. However, she is a really good girl, trustworthy and someone you can count on. Yes, she is fiery and sometimes loses her head, but she has a heart of gold. It is also worth noting that Biggy is devoted to her, and she loves him like a father or brother as much as they curse each other. So watch what you say to either," answered Berolarn.

As Berolarn had just finished. Lilla walked in with another girl carrying drinks and plates of hot food.

"You should have heard the big idiot moan, Berolarn, how busy we were. You're not paying for me to go shopping. It was non-stop moaning and snarling," Lilla laughed. "But he said yes, I can take your little friend out to the market in a few hours when the bar is less busy".

"That is fine, thank you, Lilla. By the time we have eaten, got to our rooms and washed, it should be about time," smiled Berolarn.

"Talis, I will come to your room when no one is watching and get you," Lilla laughed as she poked Talis in the side and walked out of the room.

"These town folk are all crazy, and the sooner we are done and gone, the better," muttered Talis, much to the apparent amusement of Berolarn.

For the rest of the afternoon, Talis and Berolarn ate undisturbed and made small talk. The food was delicious, which you would not have thought by looking at the inn.

"Biggy and his crew are renowned chefs in the area, and their food is highly regarded. I know, I know," grinned Berolarn as he could see Talis was about to comment as he shook his head.

"If his inn was in a better area, and he had a slightly better approach to his patrons, I am sure Biggy would be acclaimed across the whole of Lorevitch, not just Lowedom". He pushed his plate forward and finished his wine. "I'm finished. How about you, Talis?" asked Berolarn.

"Yes, I'm all done, and I must agree, that matched anything we used to make back home," Talis sighed with contentment as he shoved his plate forward. He gulped down the rest of his drink, rising as Berolarn did.

"Follow me. I know the way," stated Berolarn as he grabbed their room keys off the side table and passed a set of keys to Talis.

Berolarn opened the door and walked down to the staircase at the end of the corridor. "Next floor," as he walked upstairs with Talis following. Near the end of the hallway on the second floor, Berolarn stopped and pointed to a door.

"This one is yours, and mine is that one at the end," said Berolarn, pointing to the last door on the right.

Talis unlocked the door entered the room and closed the door behind him. The room was actually quite neat and tidy. It had a good size bed and side table, a small fireplace, mirror, washbowl & jug and a place for his clothes. He looked in the mirror. Talis grimaced as he looked at himself. He looked as if he belonged on the street. He found himself thinking about what Lilla must have thought as there was a knock on the door.

"Are you decent, Talis?" called Lilla as she opened the door and peered in with a big smile.

"Come now, you haven't even washed the grime off your face. I am not taking you down to the markets looking like that," laughed Lilla.

She came in, and Talis saw she had changed and dressed in clothing similar to what Lauren would wear: leather trousers and a white blouse under a fine-quality tunic. She completed her outfit with a brown leather belt with a wicked-looking knife at her side and a winter cloak. Lilla went to the bowl and filled it with water from the jug.

"Come here, Talis", ordered Lilla, "and remove your shirt. Let's get some of this grime off."

He gingerly approached, pulling his shirt over his head and dropping it on the table. He watched Lilla as she dipped a towel in the water. She came to him deftly and grabbed him by the jaw.

"Do not move," whispered Lilla seductively as she looked into his eyes and with a full smile, she gently wiped his face, removing the grime that had accumulated over a few weeks. She then scrubbed his back and front with more force.

"Hmm, I suppose you will do. I think it's the hot tub for you tonight. You cannot be putting new clothes on without a proper bath." Lilla said, looking at him teasingly.

"I'm fine," muttered Talis, lightly trying to pull away.

Talis was angry with himself. This girl was already in his head, making him feel like a teenager who had never been around girls.

"What is wrong, Talis? Have you lost your tongue? You seem confused!" she pressed on, laughing.

"Er, well, er, we have a problem. I have no money for clothes. So we will have to go shopping maybe tomorrow," sighed Talis, relieved that he now had an excuse to get himself out of the girl's company.

"Luckily, Talis, Berolarn had thought of this, and as I was about to knock on your door, he came out of his room, called me over and passed me a large amount of gold. Not only are we good for the money, but I also need a protector with this amount of gold," Lilla said flirtatiously. Talis had enough. She was driving him to distraction.

"Ok, that's great, let's be off," said Talis, putting his mucky clothes back on. "You're really nice, Lilla. But I will be leaving tomorrow. We can never be more than friends." The words came out of his mouth before he could stop himself.

Lilla laughed as Talis went red. Lilla loved joking and flirting with the villager and seeing him squirm in embarrassment. Though she did admit to herself on reflection that this one was slightly different to other men she had met. He had something special about him that was intriguing, but she couldn't quite figure it out, which was frustrating.

"Well, I am glad I am making an impression on you. That was the plan. But anyone in Berolarn company usually leaves very quickly. So I guessed as much, do not take my words and teasing as anything bad, Talis," said Lilla, turning serious.

"As much as I love Biggy, I hate this place and the creeps who come here. So it is nice to see a regular, young, and, if you don't mind me saying, good-looking man, dirt and filth aside. But, of course, what you are doing with Berolarn begs the question. But anyway, I will stop now, promise," said Lilla as she gave a big sincere smile that took his breath away.

They arrived at the market, and for the next two hours, as she dragged him around all the stalls, Lilla had chatted with him, asking about who he was, his hunting, where he was from, and his inn and his town. She was especially interested in Lauren, what she looked like, her work at the inn and her charitable work around town. She asked about what things Lauren was interested in and what she wore. The questions were endless. Talis found he could talk openly with Lilla and the words came freely as they discussed his life. Finally, he asked her how she ended up working at the Devil's Punchbowl with Biggy. Once Talis started to get to know her, he really didn't see her working at that place.

She laughed.

"Has no one told you the tale? It is an odd one," inquired Lilla.

"The story goes that Luther found Biggy carrying this baby in some far-off woods. They fought as Luther thought Biggy would eat me. But, as you have probably worked out, he is a half-ogre, and Luther demanded that the fiend put me down and leave. Biggy thought Luther would hurt me, so he put me down and ran at Luther. Not the cleverest thing Biggy has ever done! Luther is a master of combat."

"Anyway, they fought, Biggy was incapacitated, and Luther was about to end his life. Biggy starts pleading for the baby's life, begging Luther not to hurt her. If you know Luther, you know he has a lot of empathy and forgiveness in that solid heart. When you crack that hard exterior. He can be virtually saintly. Luther saw what he considered a beast pleading for the child.

He lowered his sword and let Biggy go free as such. He brought Biggy and me to this town, placed Biggy in this inn and left me with him as my guardian. Luther looks after Biggy. Biggy looks after me. The inn belongs to Luther."

"Why on earth were you with Biggy?" asked Talis.

"As the years rolled by and I grew, we discovered much about my story between Luther and me. Supposedly, I was part of a caravan of somebody powerful or wealthy, and it was attacked by a notorious group of thieves who operated in the area. Biggy was part of that crew and probably knew no better. There was a big fight, and everyone in the caravan died but me. Most of the thieves were killed. Biggy being what he is, was generally unmarked," answered Lilla.

Lilla smiled as she continued.

"The remaining thieves were loading up the spoils, and they came across me. They had no use for a baby. They wanted to kill me, but Biggy looked at me, fell in love and wouldn't let them. They fought, they died, and Biggy has been with me ever since. He is like a stupid big brother with Luther, the visiting father. Honestly, I don't remember much until I hit my teens. Luther said I banged my head and forgot my childhood."

"But it has been good for Biggy too. Over the years, his love for me and my constant kicking taught him right from wrong and good from evil. It is not what he is that made him bad. It is how he was brought up. Ogres and goblins kill for fun. How could he have turned out any different?" finished Lilla.

Over the hours they walked around the stalls, Talis picked up an array of new hunting garb, cloaks, stockings, gloves and boots. When he finally thought they were done and was commenting as such, Lilla laughed;

"Not so fast, Talis. Berolarn requested that we go to the armourers and get you kitted out. Come this way," and she led him down a narrow street to a large shop with an adjacent blacksmith.

Talis had never seen so many different types of armour and arms on display. Lilla went and spoke to the owner and disappeared through a doorway at the rear. When she returned, she told Talis that the armourer had just what he needed. "He has the most delicate tunic of chainmail that money can buy, unearthly light in weight yet as strong as any plate of armour. He wants one hundred gold coins for it. Ten times the cost of regular mail. I managed to get him down to fifty coins. We don't have enough for it, but he knows me. I also dropped in that you are a companion of Berolarn and Luther. That did the trick. He is letting me take it on payment trust. I am sure it is special in some way. I have never seen the like before. He probably bought it from some goblin or vagabond for a fraction of the cost. Anyway, come it's out back. Let's see if it fits," said Lilla.

Talis followed and tried on the mail. As soon as he slipped it over his head, it seemed to fit perfectly, and it was so light he couldn't feel any weight in it. All he could think to say was, "it's perfect," and he smiled boyishly at Lilla.

They returned to the inn and made their way to Talis's room. Berolarn was waiting on the landing as they returned.

"Ah, the wanderer's return. I see you have many packages and presume you have everything you need for the long journey ahead," asked Berolarn.

Talis opened the door to his room, and as they entered, both told Berolarn about the chainmail.

"Please let me see it," requested Berolarn.

"Have you anything so fine," asked Lilla as she opened one of the packages and held up the chainmail as if it was made of paper.

"Here, Lilla, lay it out of the table for me," asked Berolarn.

Berolarn walked around the table, moved his hand, and uttered some words that neither Talis nor Lilla understood. The chainmail slowly gave off a faint blue glow, which died after several seconds.

"Curious, it is imbued with some magic. I do not sense any evil in the magic it is infused with. I wonder how it comes to be in the hands of a small town armourer," reflected Berolarn.

Giving it some more thought, Berolarn turned to the pair of them.

"Yes, it is interesting, and it might be a great find. I think it will do you no harm to wear it under your tunic. However, I would err on the side of caution and let us show it to Luther, as his knowledge might be more significant in such magical artefacts. I understand that he usually arrives within an hour or two of sunset. Is that correct, Lilla?" asked Berolarn.

"Yes, Berolarn, it is usually around that time," answered Lilla.

"Good, I would suggest you get some rest, Talis, for an hour or so, and I will send word when he arrives," said Berolarn, and with those parting words, Berolarn turned and exited the room.

Lilla looked over to Talis,

"As much as I like you, Talis, you still stink! You are going nowhere else but to have a bath in one of the tubs in the bathhouse downstairs, come with me right now," said Lilla in a commanding voice.

Talis realised it was going to be futile, so he just nodded.

"Good," said Lilla as she picked up a smattering of his new clothes and the chainmail and exited the room with Talis. Talis turned and locked the door and followed her downstairs.

The room was stifling and steamy as Lilla filled one of the three sizeable old wine barrels with hot water in the small room. That will do, Lilla thought, and she walked over to the door and locked it.

"Ok, Talis, the bath is ready," said Lilla grinning from ear to ear. "Get undressed and jump in."

Talis feeling much more comfortable now with Lilla, responded and laughed, "When you unlock the door and leave."

"I'm not going anywhere, we have much more to discuss, and Biggy has given me the rest of the day off," said Lilla, smiling now with a twinkle. Talis had never met such a persistent and adventurous woman in all his life. At times, he had thought that Lauren had the devil in her. There was no comparison.

"Turn round whilst I undress and do not move until I tell you," chortled Talis in what he hoped was a witty manner.

"You are so mean…..you are not impressing me as a skilled hunter," laughed Lilla as she turned her back to him.

He quickly undressed, jumped into the barrel, and regretted his haste to fully submerge. It was sweltering, and he was sure you could cook food in such heat. He motioned to Lilla, seeing her eyes wandering in his direction, that she could turn round as he spluttered the water out of his mouth. He grabbed some of the liquid tallow and started to scrub his body.

"So Talis, you are meeting Luther tonight. As strange as Berolarn is that one," muttered Lilla as she tried to help Talis with his washing activities. "What are you discussing tonight, and why did Berolarn want you to get armour and clothing for travel? Do you know what you are getting into, Talis?"

"I do not really know, Lilla," Talis said as he pushed her hands away, trying to retain as much dignity as possible. "If I am honest, there is talk of war, and Lauren and I are being hunted for some reason. In fact, I have seen war. I didn't tell you earlier, but my home has been destroyed, and my father is dead. After our village was attacked, the only news of my sister was that Lauren was with the elves. Berolarn is the keeper of the whole tale, and he says we need to take Luther with us as part of some quest to stop the war." Talis told her with as much honesty as he could afford.

"Just remember, Talis, you don't have to do everything Berolarn or Luther says. You are your own person. As much as I love Berolarn and Luther, they have always been there for me….." replied Lilla.

Pausing as she considered how to phrase her words, she cautiously continued.

"I know of them, and I know some of their tales, and nothing they do comes without risks that if they were told to you beforehand, you wouldn't think twice about following them," urged Lilla.

"I know Lilla, the movements of the wise and powerful look to the greater good, and they will sacrifice," said Talis as he thought of his father's words. "I don't know anything of Luther, but Berolarn saved me probably from certain death if he had left me. He also told me things about the wars that were and what is to come, I think for now I must follow, and I also must trust he will take me to Lauren. But, amusingly, he told me to trust you, yet you give me the opposite advice," grinned Talis. "Perhaps we should all trust each other for now."

"You trust my words. No good can come from following Berolarn. But, still, I can see you are resigned to this fate, be safe, hunter," stated Lilla.

As she finished, and before Talis could react. Lilla had her arms around his shoulders, and Talis could feel Lilla's lips on his and the taste of her mouth on his. Within seconds she pulled away and unlocked the door.

"Remember Talis, I have warned you. However, I could offer you much if you stayed," purred Lilla, and with those parting words, she was gone, and the door closed.

Talis found this whole day bizarre as he sighed and submerged his head under the water. He had only been with Lilla for several hours, and she appeared to have taken a real likening for him within that time! How could that be? Making matters even stranger, there were feelings he had for her. Talis wasn't sure what it was, but there was already a warmth deep inside when he was with her. He flew up out of the water and shaking his head, all he could think was she was dangerous to him. When she spoke or came near him, it clouded his brain.

Talis relocked the door, dried himself on some of the towels, and slowly dressed as he continued to mull over the day's events and what had happened over the last few weeks. His life had been thrown around in a vicious chain of events. He just couldn't think straight. Talis longed to see Lauren again and speak to his twin. She would have been able to answer some of the riddles that were constantly running in his mind. But, unfortunately, she was not there. It was the time that he needed to rely on himself, and at the moment, he felt like he was on the road to nowhere. As he considered this, his yearning to see Lauren blended with a desire for Lilla to return.

He left the washhouse and made his way back to his room. Talis continued to pace his room for several minutes when a knock on the door broke his thoughts.

"Hello, who is it?" asked Talis as he moved towards the door.

"Time to go, Talis. It is time for us to meet Luther," he heard Berolarn respond as he opened the door to his room. He saw Berolarn was now moving down the hallway towards the stairs. Quickly closing and locking his room door, he chased after him.

They entered the main bar area. Talis could see through the inn's windows that night had fallen, and the bar was in full swing with the evening's clientele. He looked around as Berolarn pointed to a table in a corner alcove.

"Sit over there," motioned Berolarn as he called over to the red-faced pot-bellied barkeeper to have wine brought over.

"Will have it brought over as soon as I can. We're swamped, you know!" commented the barkeeper as he turned away to another customer. Talis heard him continue muttering, "outsiders…..busy….. too good…..fetch your own."

Talis pulled a chair out and sat down facing the crowd as Berolarn joined him. The crowd was similar to what he had seen earlier. It was packed full of armed men and, without a doubt, wastrels, vagabonds and thieves. The drink was flowing freely, as was the merriment and arguing. The patrons of the Devil's Punchbowl came in all sizes. Some men and even a smattering of the women who freely displayed a vast array of weaponry looked mean and intimidating.

Talis suspected some of the patrons were dwarves or some other form of a halfling, smaller, stockier, all with a full face of large braided beards. There also looked to be a variety of half-breeds, ugly individuals with deformities on their faces. He was sure some had small tusks protruding from their mouths. Those in the central area were in full swing of drink, laughter and partying. Though, he noted, others preferred the shaded areas of the room, huddled in corners, cloaked and shaded from viewing eyes, whispering in the candlelit darkness.

He suddenly saw Lilla walking towards them with a tray of drinks.

"I thought you weren't working the evening," greeted Talis as Lilla dropped the glasses and the bottle on the table.

"We're busy, and I have nothing better to do," snapped Lilla, looking at Talis meaningfully. Lilla had been musing over her earlier encounter with Talis and was now annoyed that he had rejected her offer to stay longer and was going to continue following Berolarn. She hoped he could read that in her eyes! "Anything else, Berolarn?"

"No, thank you, Lilla. Though, please point Luther in our direction when he comes in," requested Berolarn

Lilla nodded and turned back towards the bar, pushing various ruffians out of her way. Berolarn took his gaze off Lilla and turned his attention back to Talis.

"It appears that you have upset Lilla?" Berolarn asked quizzically. "You are on a dangerous path Talis. If you anger that young lady, she has a fire you do not want to turn in your direction. So please be careful," he smiled.

"Ah, here comes Luther" he looked towards a towering man making his way through the crowd. Massive in size, probably a good foot taller than most men and twice as wide at the shoulders. Clad in leather armour with a gigantic sword at his side, Talis could see the firelight gleaming on huge scarred biceps, and his legs looked as big as Biggy's.

"My friend, welcome" Berolarn stood up, grinning broadly, as he hugged Luther in welcome. "I am glad to see you safe. Please be seated. This young man," pointing towards Talis, "Is the one we sought, Talis." Looking then at Talis, "this is Luther."

"Well, met Talis, son of Loren, brother of Lauren. It is a pleasure to finally make your acquaintance. I am glad you are safe," said Luther in a deep, commanding voice as he nodded toward Talis. Then, turning towards the bar, he caught the barkeep's eye and raised a finger.

"Will send over in a minute," shouted the Barkeeper.

"Berolarn, you made it out of Ascalon. I hear on the winds that Keros has been burned to the ground. So the forces of darkness have finally arrived with the goblin hunting parties?" enquired Luther.

"Yes," answered Berolarn, "the dark times as foretold are now upon us, I was too late on arrival, but I saw the village and could see the mark of the one."

"I expected as much when I heard that the goblin scum had come deep into Ascalon unchecked and raised the village to the ground. This without any sign or threat from any of the Ascalon armies," uttered Luther as he looked over his shoulder at Lilla coming over. "Ah, here comes Lilla, the bane of my life," he declared, knowing Lilla could hear him full well.

"Well, if it is not the great churl himself, welcome back to the greatest hovel on earth. I hoped I would find you in the gutter dung collector with your throat slashed when I went out this morning. But, unfortunately, the gods do not smile upon me, and I continue to be cursed by your presence, dog." Lilla smiled at him with a reddened, agitated face as she hit him with her venom.

"Ah, I see someone has rattled your cage today," grinned Luther.

Then, smiling at his companions, "It is rare for Lilla to greet me with such pleasant words."

With that, Lilla hit Luther on the back of his head with her tray and stormed off. Then, rubbing the back of his head, Luther smiled again, this time more softly.

"She has such a temper. I am sure she is the daughter of a banshee!" Luther laughed, "My not by choice daughter is pig-headed, stubborn, and generally hates me passionately. But she is a good girl," reassured Luther nodding his head. "I find my love for her amusing as much as a nightmare," jested Luther rolling his eyes as he smiled towards Berolarn.

Talis was taken aback by that exchange. First, he witnessed the temper of Lilla and then the quite jovial and what appeared to be a loving side of the massive ranger in front of him.

"What of Lauren," asked Berolarn taking his attention away from Lilla, "have you had any more news, Luther?"

"My hawk Torken that flies the wind saw many things from the skies. The girl was alive and in the company of four elves. They made their way from Ascalon, making for Morallis. They were ambushed near the Dorals and took flight. The elven warriors fought with the assailants as Lauren and another made their escape. Lauren reached Morallis, but it was under siege the same evening as they arrived. Torken left due to the darkness that arrived as the goblins began the siege. When Torken returned the morning after, he found that the keep was smashed asunder, and the bodies of many fallen were scattered over the cliff face. He couldn't see anything of Lauren; she was hidden from sight as he scoured the lands. Torken still searches for her now," answered Luther as he mulled over his mead.

"How can you know this," blurted Talis.

"I was born with, let us say, a gift," offered Luther as he considered his response.

"Certain animals I can bond with. When I focus my mind on them. I can feel the beating of their heart, can sense their thoughts, and visualise what they see. It takes time and effort. I have had Torken since he was an eyas."

Seeing the confused look on Talis's face, Luther explained, "Eyas is a baby or a chick, perhaps you would call it."

"Luther, what was the darkness at Morallis," Berolarn asked

quickly.

"I could not tell. My eyes were closed to it," responded Luther. "Whatever it was, Berolarn, I sensed a great power, and when the hawk returned, the damage I saw was beyond anything a goblin could do against elves."

"Yes, this is all very well, but what about Lauren?" said Talis in a loud voice as he couldn't help himself.

Luther turned and looked at Talis and then pointed at him.

"For one of such youth, you should open your ears, use what is between them, and listen to what I said. Lauren was not among the dead, and Torken searches for her," scolded Luther. He then turned towards the older man.

"Berolarn, have you been to Morallis? I presume there are escape routes from the keep?" asked Luther.

"I have, and yes, I understand that secret passages lead through the mountain out to the other side," answered Berolarn. Then, looking at Talis, "I think we should be thankful, Talis, that Lauren appears still to be alive and is making her way towards the city of elves if she has taken the passage."

Berolarn started to stroke and pull on his beard. Then growing unusually silent for a moment, looking deep in thought with a fixed look of concentration.

"However, what concerns me is how the goblins managed to amass an attack on Morallis in the evening. The laws that govern Luther. The potent magic of old has protected the Doral's from entry for thousands of years," stated Berolarn quizzically.

"Maybe the darkness broke down the barrier?" offered

Luther. "Who knows what was behind it, but Torken could sense that the power was great. I agree that the wall across the Dorals protects that area of the elven border. It has not been breached for as long as can be remembered."

"Berolarn, what are you to do with this boy? Have you decided your plans?" Queried Luther.

"Yes, I think so. But, first, we need to go to Solanstar, the city of the elves and take an audience with the king of the elves, King Ethera. It makes sense. He will reach out to the dwarves and the kingdoms of men to decide the actions to take against the dark lord, goblin and ogre nations. Next, we must hope that Lauren makes her way safely through the lands of Aslandure and will also arrive at Solanstar," answered Berolarn.

"What are you expecting from this audience? I can see that the dwarves will answer the call. They hate the goblins with a passion as great as they have for their own great halls. Some of the kingdoms of man will also answer a call from the elves. I suspect they will see the dangers of being overrun by the goblin and ogre forces and will even be making plans for war and of defence. However, we saw the scale of some of these forces and the hands that guide them, even if the dark lord's whereabouts are unknown." Luther asked, questioning Berolarn's comments.

"We go to present what we know of the dark lord, the history of Olgrich Validoral and his kind. And the mission that a small group must undertake to bring about the beginning of his demise and removal of his power," replied Berolarn.

"And of the twins?" questioned Luther, much to Talis's frustration that they were talking not only now as if he was not there but also specifically about Lauren and himself.

"Well, no decision has been made. However, when we discuss the quest and take counsel from others, a decision will be made on their fate," answered Berolarn.

Berolarn looked over to Talis.

"Do not worry, Talis. You and Lauren will also make hard choices and decide your own destiny. But I suspect you will be asked to be part of this small group," stated Berolarn as he attempted to ease the conversation for Talis's sake.

"Luther, this brings me to you. The group will need a guide and now is when many people will need to fulfil their destinies. So I wish you to come with me to Solanstar and offer your services," requested Berolarn. "What are your thoughts?"

"I suspect you are not telling me much, Berolarn. I know you too well. What are my thoughts outside of this? I will come. You knew that before you asked. However, I think Talis and Lauren need to be forewarned of the dangers you and others will ask of them. They are obviously crucial to the defeat of the dark lord. We have searched for Loran and his children, as did the dark lord's forces, then we raced to reach them first," contended Luther, pointing out to Berolarn the need for more information.

Luther turned and looked at Talis, "Why are you and your sister so important, Talis? Has Berolarn told you? What power do children have against the might of the dark powers? As he unleashes his will on the land, do you know? Look, Berolarn, look at his face. It is full of self-doubt, no understanding, and there is fear, fear he will fail of what you are to ask of him, though he has no idea what this will be. Luther's said scornfully. "He will go. Of this, there is no doubt. But, nevertheless, they must be told more, Berolarn."

Talis wanted to speak, but he was in the presence of two titans doing battle, and he felt it was best to keep out of the discussion as Luther was right; he had no idea of his role. Berolarn had shown him his ancestry and, of course, the hunger that Berolarn had brought to life. He had said great power comes with it, but what was that? Talis had absolutely no idea, and it scared him. However, he had already decided that the best way to control it was to forget about it and its uses.

"Luther, you know as well as anybody that you cannot define which path you must walk to get to the end. Life is not that simple. You must walk with eyes wide open and change direction as the wind blows. What do I know? I know many things, and my friend, I could share such knowledge with you over the many years it would take. Will all have value? I do not see that far in the future, as it depends on which paths you go down. You know this," answered Berolarn, pointing his finger at Luther.

"Also, Luther, you know the direction you walk down sometimes has to be discovered. If you go down a path too quickly, you might take a wrong turn or do not become aware of the dangers before you until it's too late," argued Berolarn.

His response was measured and calming. Talis had no idea what his riddle meant, but Luther appeared in thought and then nodded his head. This seemed to be the end of the discussion on the value of more knowledge being given to Talis and his sister. They moved on to how they would get to the city of Solanstar as quickly as possible.

"For speed, let's take a straight line to the Alion River, cross where it is shallow, follow its line to the great forest of Tellingwood and enter Aslandure near the Korallis outpost. We should be able to pick up the road for Solanstar from there. The route should be simple enough, and like most of the area around the river into the elven lands, there will be trees and cover," said Luther.

"You are proposing we go by foot?" asked Berolarn.

"No, by horse until we reach the thick of the forest, where it will be difficult for the horses to travel. Then we dismount and let the horses return. They will find their way back home. It will indeed be watched if we take the direct road into Aslandure. I do not think that road will be safe until inside the elven lands. When inside Aslandure, we will pick up the same route as mentioned. It is a danger to enter the elven lands any other way. The elves will expect everyone to present themselves down this road as a friend, not skulk in the undergrowth," answered Luther.

Chapter 13 – Unlucky for Some

Luther and Berolarn continue talking late into the night. Talis switched off sometime earlier as the conversation had moved on from his pending doom. However, he spent the rest of the night trying to see Lilla and catch her eye. Unfortunately, no matter how much he tried, she totally ignored the table and Talis.

Talis was drawn back to the discussion as he caught the tail end of Luther and Berolarn arranging to leave at dawn.

"What?" Talis looked around at the pair.

"Talis, you must pay attention," Luther snapped at him. "We leave just as the sun breaks at dawn. Hopefully, our leaving will be missed by many."

"Oh," Talis replied as he surveyed the room, suddenly noticing it was considerably emptier than earlier. The crowds had started to disperse, and he hadn't seen any sign of Lilla in the last fifteen minutes.

Berolarn rose and motioned for Talis to do the same.

"Let's get some rest, Talis. We have a long journey ahead," said Berolarn.

"Morning, be ready," Luther said to Talis as they started to leave, and Luther also rose and walked across the bar to what, Talis presumed were the kitchen doors. They exited the alehouse and made their way up to their rooms. Talis unlocked his room, entered, dropped on his bed, and was gone. He was so tired that sleep came to him when his head hit the pillow.

Talis awoke in chaos as his room exploded with debris, and pieces of the room landed heavily on top of him. He scrambled off the bed onto the floor in a daze, and in half running, half stumbling motion, he slid across the floor to the doorway. He grappled with the lock and pulled the door open as Berolarn had just reached the door.

"Quick, they have found us," shouted Berolarn over the noise and shaking of the inn. Then, grabbing Talis by the back of his tunic, he dragged Talis onto his feet and a few steps down the hallway in one sweeping motion.

Talis suddenly came to his senses.

"Wait," he shouted as he slipped Berolarn's grip, jumped back to the doorway of his room, and disappeared back inside.

"Talis, damn your fool hide, get back here," demanded Berolarn.

Berolarn was about to chase back for him as Talis emerged, running out of the room with his gear, long sword, bow & quiver.

Talis grinned at Berolarn.

"Not going to win a war without them," shouted Talis over the din of the inn being ripped apart as they ran towards the stairs. As they reached the end of the landing, they looked down to see Lilla screaming at Biggy to let her go. As she pulled desperately towards the stairs, she saw Talis.

"I'm comi..........." Talis never finished his words.

The building shook violently, and a massive explosion plunged what remained of the inn into darkness and dust. Talis felt momentary that he was in the middle of a slow-motion dream as he was flung spinning downstairs. He looked up to see Berolarn dropping through the floor and what had been the ceiling disappearing with the roof in the grip of massive, hideous claws with talons of blood. Then it went dark.

Talis awoke to being shaken violently by Lilla.

"Get up, damn your hide, you will get us killed," she screamed at him as she violently kicked out at Biggy. At the same time, Lilla was holding onto Talis. Biggy was trying to drag the screaming girl to safety, and unbeknown to Lilla, he was seriously considering knocking her over the head as Talis came around. Talis was just getting to his feet when he heard laughter, chilling laughter that turned his heart to ice and stopped him dead in his tracks.

They looked up to where the roof had once been to see a beautiful yet slightly pale woman with long obsidian black hair, clad in red and black attire, floating down at speed while fire danced around her. She landed gracefully just at the top of the stairs.

"Ah, there you are, my boy, my Talis. I have been searching far and wide for you," she smiled, but the look hidden behind this was the most horrific of sickly smiles, it was one of death and murder, yet Talis could see nothing but a powerful, beautiful woman who wanted him. He was totally entranced by the spell of her voice.

Talis felt something big barge past him with a deep-throated shout of battle. He saw Biggy flying through the air at the woman. She stepped forward, and with unnatural strength, she caught Biggy mid-air with a strike of the back of her hand. As soon as she connected with Biggy's face, he disappeared as he flew sidewards through the staircase and the bar wall. She laughed again, which chilled Talis to the bone.

"I'm sorry about that," she smiled as she reached the bottom of the stairs and stroked Talis on the face. "So beautiful," she whispered in his ear, and he felt her tongue running along the side of his neck. Then she pulled away and looked at Lilla, who was shaken with as much fear as Talis felt.

"Why, Talis, who is this, another one who is so beautiful," she said as she looked deep into Talis's eyes whilst grabbing Lilla by her hair and dragging her towards herself. Then, pulling harder on Lilla's hair, she yanked Lilla's head back as Lilla tried to struggle. The woman grabbed Lilla by the throat to stop her struggling and slowly ran her hand down to her chest with her other hand.

"So, pretty Talis, is she yours? She smells familiar?" she said seductively, yet slightly confused as if she was trying to place Lilla. She rolled her tongue around her lips and laughed as her front canines started to grow before the horrified Talis.

"Let her go, Selene," he heard Berolarn's voice command the woman.

"Well, Talis, I thought you might be socialising with this one. Hello Berolarn, my love. It is no wonder that when I come out to play, why the gutter rat has lifted himself out of the excrement he usually lives in and decides to play with my prize. It has been a long time since you stood before me, Berolarn, begging for forgiveness, begging for me not to go." She laughed as she pushed Lilla with a force that took her flying off her feet and through the inn door.

"Berolarn, are you still playing in the affairs of the races, trying to save them from their self-inflicted destiny? You should know their destiny is set, and a new world order arises. You cannot stop it, no one can, and soon all will submit to our will!" shouted Selene.

Selene suddenly flew at Berolarn as if gliding in a storm through the air, hands burning with red fire. Berolarn met her midair with white fire coursing through his body. As they collided, the spell of her voice was broken on Talis, and he immediately came to his senses. The battle raged between the two powers as they grappled, neither giving up ground. The air crackled with the intensity of the magical forces both combatants unleashed. Each time they engaged or circled each other, they looked for a weakness to take advantage of. He was about to go to the aid of Berolarn, drawing his father's long sword, when he was knocked flying as the giant Luther deftly went past him to attack the woman.

Selene saw the man coming toward her from the corner of her eye, his steel glinting brightly in the magic she unleashed. She knew of this one. He was as dangerous as Berolarn. What was she to do? Selene cursed herself for not just grabbing the boy. Straining with great effort, she broke down Berolarn's flame and flung Berolarn backwards with all her force. Selene would deal with him in a minute. She flew at Luther.

Luther knew as he always knew. He saw her coming and deftly sidestepped and caught her arm with his long knife. She hissed at him as she recircled. What is this, she thought. How did he catch her and bring her pain? It felt unnatural to her. It had been too long.

"That was naughty, Luther," giggled Selene.

Selene then flew at him again. Luther ducked and shifted his weight to strike again, but she had learned the art of war through the centuries, and this time, Selene read this giant bastard of a man, she fluidly disarmed him, and now Selene had him. Selene knew what she needed to do. Her mouth opened, her fangs sharp. Selene moved slowly towards his throat as she prepared to take his life by ripping into the pulsing veins in his neck and letting the warmth of his blood bathe her soulless spirit.

"Say goodbye," she whispered in the man's ear as she strained against his phenomenal strength to hold his arms. Then, as Selene continued playing with her kill, it was her undoing. With a massive will stretching every fibre of his colossal biceps, Luther started to break free. As she battled this man's strength and started to call on her magic, suddenly, an enormous bolt of brilliant white flame grabbed her from behind and lifted her upwards. The magical flame was intense, it started to consume her, throwing her left and right, and she battled with all her will to escape the burning, the pain. Selene tried desperately to call her magic, her flame, to bring her power to life, but the intense white heat kept her in check. Then, finally, she screamed a cry not heard by her kind for centuries. Was it the final cries of a desperate fight for survival, revenge or murder? And then she was gone in an explosive crack. The night consumed her as quick as she came.

Berolarn dropped to his knees in obvious pain as Luther scrambled to his feet and ran over to him.

"Talis, help me quickly," called Luther. Talis rushed over to them both. "Come help me get him up."

"I will be fine. Give me a minute," coughed Berolarn as he closed his eyes and flopped forward.

"Talis, come over here. We must go. I will take Berolarn, quickly go to Lilla, make sure she is ok, and then meet me at the stables. We need to go now," urged Luther.

Biggy tumbled back through the wall. Seeing Luther with the old man on his shoulders and the further devastation to the inn really confused him. Luther slapped Biggy across the face to wake him from confusion.

"Grab the old man and take him to the stables. We will be there in a minute," shouted Luther.

Biggy grabbed hold of Berolarn from Luther's shoulder, and they all piled out of the inn. They found Lilla out cold in the middle of the road, blood pouring profusely from a wound to the head. The side of her face swelled grotesquely.

"Talis, carry her. I will protect the way. She is breathing. This way," shouted Luther as he pushed Talis towards Lilla.

Talis looked at her momentarily, skillfully picking her up, and slung her over his own shoulder. After that, he carried her at pace. Luckily, he was used to having to take such a burden at speed, a skill learnt whilst hunting. They ran as best as they could down the street, turned down a side street, and returned to the rear of the half-demolished inn and the stables.

"Quickly untether the horses, Talis, you take Lilla with you, on that one over there, yes, the big brown one and ……." said Luther, who stopped mid-sentence by another voice.

"Put me down, Biggy. I am fine," came the voice that was Berolarn's.

Luther moved and grasped Berolarn's arm as Biggy ungraciously dropped him.

"Come, Berolarn, we must go," urged Luther. "You take the white stead, and I will take the black one."

Then seeing the confused half-ogre, Luther walked over to Biggy.

"Biggy, now listen to me, you cannot come where we go, I will take care of Lilla, and she will return soon. Go back to the inn, get it repaired, and open again," soothed Luther.

"Biggy, not cum," Biggy said as he stroked Lilla's hair, as Talis held her in his arms. "You horse, Biggy hold," he lifted Lilla out of Talis's arms.

With that, he walked over to the horse for Talis.

"Cum," Biggy said, beckoning Talis.

Talis jumped onto the horse, and Biggy lifted the lifeless body of Lilla on the back of the saddle. He found some rope and tied Lilla to Talis. Luther and Berolarn were also ready to ride.

"Goodbye, my friend," said Luther as his horse came towards Biggy. He reached out and grasped Biggy's arm, "we will look after her and keep her safe." He turned to Talis and Berolarn. "Ride now. Let us be off."

With tears streaming down his face, Biggy watched the companions ride off into the distance before turning and returning to the inn.

Chapter 14 – They Take Flight

They rode through the gates of Lowedom at a gallop. They took no note of the guard who shouted at them to halt. Instead, with Luther leading, Berolarn in the middle and Talis coming up the rear, they rode hard through the gatehouse. They flew down the dirt track road, and soon Lowedom was out of sight, and they were deep into the countryside.

Once a couple of hours had passed, the horses had dropped their speed to a canter as the immediate danger Luther felt had gone.

"We should conserve the horse's energy, or they will tire fast and be no good to us in the hunt," commented Luther.

Talis could hear the groans of Lilla and beckoned Luther to slow down. They pulled over to the side of the road. Luther dismounted and came over to Talis and Lilla. Luther held her steady as Talis undid the rope and gently dismounted. Her eyes were still closed as they gingerly lifted her down and laid her on the ground. Talis got down beside her. Stroking her hair away from her forehead, he started gently calling her name as he tried to bring her around.

Berolarn slid off his horse.

"Let us rest for no more than fifteen minutes," said Berolarn as he reached them.

He knelt alongside Talis, rubbed his thumb under Lilla's nose, and muttered something. Her eyes shot open, and she struggled to get up as shock and fear hit her despite not knowing what was happening or who was around her. As Talis tried to hold on to her, Berolarn intervened.

"Calm, child, calm. Lilla, you are safe," Berolarn said gently, and Talis felt her go limp in his arms.

She groaned as she realised who the three faces were.

"My head is killing me. I feel like my whole body has been beaten by a club. Please let me die," whispered Lilla.

"You are fortunate. The demon woman Selene or whatever her name was, threw you as if you were just a feather in her hand. You smashed through the inn's door, took it clean off," exclaimed Talis, "and landed in the street, several metres from the doorway."

Lilla just closed her eyes and moaned again.

"Here, Talis give Lilla some water," said Luther as he passed him a waterskin.

Talis unstopped the skin and brought it to Lilla's mouth as he lifted her head.

"Here you are, Lilla. Come on, drink a little," beckoned Talis. She opened her eyes, and Talis proceeded to give her small mouthfuls of water.

"That's enough," Lilla said in-between mouthfuls and, with the help of Talis, pushed herself up.

"I cannot remember anything. What happened? We were in the inn and had closed up for the night, and then everything went dark, and I remember no more," grimaced Lilla as her hand went to her head in obvious distress and pain.

"We will discuss it later, Lilla. Let's get back on our journey. We must be off," ordered Luther. He came over and helped

Talis get Lilla to her feet.

"Talis, jump on, and I will lift Lilla up." Talis mounted his horse, and Luther lifted Lilla up behind him. Luther looked into Lilla's eyes, "you ok to ride?" enquired Luther, "we can tie you to Talis's waist again if you wish?"

"No, I am fine. I will be able to hold on," replied Lilla as she wrapped her arms tightly around Talis's waist and laid her head sidewards on the back of Talis's shoulder.

Luther and Berolarn mounted their horses and started to move off again.

"How long until we make the river?" asked Berolarn looking over to Luther.

"I would say we should make the river by late afternoon or early evening if we keep up a moderate pace," replied Luther. "Then we will cross the river and make camp. A few small clearings dotted around the woodland will be appropriate for us to get some sleep, yet still affording us some cover from spying eyes."

"Good. I wonder if there was a spy in the inn last night?" Berolarn commented questioningly. "One that informed the enemy that we were there. I cannot see how Selene would have explicitly known that we were in the inn and had rooms for the night," said Berolarn, shrugging as he returned from deep thought. "The roof was torn away exactly above where we were, and she entered right on top of Talis." He looked at Luther and then moved his gaze to Lilla, "did either of you see any unusual strangers in the inn last night?"

"Berolarn, we live on the scum of the earth entering the inn," replied Lilla in obvious pain. "Yes, there were plenty of strangers last night. Did I note anyone paying specific attention to your table? No!" she grumbled.

"I agree with Lilla. There were plenty of strangers at the inn last night as there always is, Berolarn," returned Luther. "However, there was an unusual amount of half-goblins in last night. It is hard to tell whether that was salient and whether they were spies sent by the dark lord."

They continued on in silence as the rolling countryside went by. Talis saw the odd stranger or caravan on the road moving towards Lowedom. But nothing untoward as the afternoon came along with a light winter drizzle of rain.

Lilla started to come round more, though the side of her badly bruised and swollen face was causing her significant discomfort. She began to question Talis on the night's events as she had little recollection still.

"Talis, what is happening? What happened last night? I recall the three of you in deep conversation, we were swamped, and I didn't see much of you after initially serving you. Then Biggy made me go down to the cellar and tidy up. When I returned, the bar room had started to empty, and the three of you were gone. So I went to the kitchen, and Luther was there talking to the kitchen staff and Biggy," recollected Lilla.

"We talked for quite a while, I seem to remember, and then I had a massive argument with Luther about wanting to leave and do something more than working in that shit hole. So I left the kitchen and was making my way across what was now an empty bar, and then it was dark for me," mused Lilla as she gazed into the distance and reflected on what had happened.

"I am not sure where my story starts against when yours went dark," said Talis as he also tried to recall the night's events.

"However, I had gone to my room, just dropping and going straight to sleep. There was a massive crash against the building as something significant hit it at full force. My room was collapsing around me, I managed to run out, Berolarn too, and we were making our way down. I saw you, Biggy and then boom, the roof disappeared, torn away by some unnatural force. Berolarn disappeared. I was thrown downstairs where you were shouting for me to come," replied Talis.

Talis took a deep breath.

"Then, the woman Berolarn called Selene came out of the dark sky from where the roof once was. She floated down, and her feet never touched the floor. Biggy attacked her, and she swatted him away like a fly. She hovered there using strange magic as she levitated just before us. She grabbed my arm and you by the throat and then spoke to us, and I was in some unnatural trance as if she had cast a spell on me, and I think your death was imminent. She was going to kill you!" continued Talis.

Lilla gripped him tighter as if the memories had started to come back.

"Then Berolarn appeared out of the wreckage of what had been the floor, and he told her to let you go and used her name. Selene. As I said, he knew her. How I have no idea. She threw you away like a pebble, and then she and Berolarn fought. It was a battle of what could only have been magic. Neither gave any ground, though. I thought she looked like she was going to win, and suddenly Luther appeared, and she threw Berolarn away with a blast of magic. After that, she and Luther started battling. Berolarn, recovering, caught her in his white magic, and she tried to battle it. That much was obvious. She couldn't call her magic, though, as if she couldn't break down the white flame of Berolarn, and he held her fast until she was gone with a final scream. Then we found you in the street, got you to the stables, and fled, " said Talis.

Sounding shocked at Talis's story, Lilla asked, "and Berolarn knew this evil demon?"

"Yes, I do not know how, and she knew him too. I intend to ask him tonight when we make camp," replied Talis. "He knows a great deal, I think, and he needs to start sharing more of the dangers we are facing," he whispered back to her with a hint of anger. "I also think Luther knows far more than he has said too. Between us both, we need to get into them for more answers."

"Luther will definitely know more. There will be no doubt of that, damn his hide," Lilla grumbled with annoyance in her voice. "He always keeps everything from me, yet he calls me daughter. Still, I know him better than he thinks. I can read the truth and lies and generally know when he's keeping things from me." Lilla grimaced a bit at the last words.

"You ok?" asked Talis hearing the discomfort in her voice.

"Talis, you're not showing signs of caring for me, are you?" joked Lilla through the pain.

"Of course, I care, damn it," snapped Talis without thinking.

"Well, I am sorry for asking Talis Quicksilver!" she snapped back.

"I'm sorry, Lilla, are you ok," asked Talis with a more comforting tone.

Lilla sighed. "Not really. I have no idea what is happening. First, my home is destroyed by some evil magic witch. Second, I am riding on a horse with you to god knows where. Thinking about it, no one has told me anything, but I know it will be perilous if we go with this pair, that much I do know. Third, my face feels like it has been punched a hundred times, my whole body aches, and I want to be sick." whimpered Lilla as she finished. Talis thought she was crying but thought it was best not to mention it.

"I know, Lilla, it is all a mess, but I am sure we are doing the right thing. Being with Berolarn and Luther, I would say they are the best chance of safety at the moment. As for the where, we go to the elves. To the elven city of Solanstar. I hope to find my sister there, and Berolarn has said all will be discussed on the war, and it will be explained why we are wanted by this dark lord and what we will do about it," said Talis brightly, trying his best to soothe Lilla.

"You will see as soon as we get there. Then, I am sure we can get this mess sorted out and return to our normal lives," said Talis.

He finished more half-heartedly. It had suddenly dawned on him. He didn't think he would get back to everyday life, it was war, and he was in the thick of it. He became lost in thought, and Lilla didn't reply. Instead, she tightened her grip around his waist and laid her head back on him.

After a few hours, Luther started to slow down.

"We will be at the river soon. We will make for the ford,

where we can cross and go straight into the woods. As soon as we get a small distance from the ford, we will make camp, as I think we could all do with a rest," said Luther, looking meaningfully from Berolarn to Lilla. "Come on, a bit further," called Luther as he again urged the horse forward.

Within the hour, they arrived at the mighty river Alion. Talis thought the chances of them being able to cross anywhere were slim. Nevertheless, they followed the river for about five minutes, and Luther raised his hand for them to stop. The river was about fifty meters wide at the spot Luther had stopped at, Talis looking at the fast-flowing river as the rain lashed down, adding to the gushing surge of the water. We are going to drown, Talis thought miserably.

"We can cross here. It is not as deep as it looks, maybe just below shoulder height. It is fast flowing, but the horses are strong enough and sure of foot to travel across without losing their way." Luther told them. "We need to enter here."

Luther guided his horse to the bank and urged his horse into the water. They followed in single file on the path Luther was taking, and though the river churned and gurgled around them, Luther was right. It only touched the lower part of their legs, and the horses' somehow ploughed on through the currents to the other side, and they managed to escape onto the embankment without losing their footing.

They followed the river for perhaps twenty minutes before Luther motioned for them to stop and dismount.

"Let us leave the river now and find a place in the woods to rest. We need to get out of this rain and find as much shelter as the trees can afford us," said Luther as he motioned them forwards into the trees.

The companions walked the horses through the woodlands for several minutes before coming across a perfect spot. A small clearing with an overhanging ledge cut into the side of a small hill. It had a good amount of coverage from the dense large oak trees. In addition, the trees would afford them a reasonable amount of shelter from the rain.

"Ideal," muttered Luther. "Let us build whatever fire we can and see if we can get some warmth into our limbs. Talis, see if you can find some dry wood in the undergrowth. Lilla, come sit in the corner, here under this ledge, you too, Berolarn. I will tether the horses."

Talis walked off and, after several minutes, returned with some reasonably dry wood. Luther soon got a good fire burning. They all huddled around and let the fire spread its warmth toward them. They sat there for some time, each lost in thought. Finally, Luther got up and went to his saddlebags.

"Luckily, I had provisions prepared for the journey before we were attacked. So here you are, come on, eat," smiled Luther as he passed around jerky, hardtack, dried fruit and nuts. They all devoured the food quickly as hunger hit them.

"Lilla, let me look at your face," asked Luther when he finished eating.

He came and sat down next to Lilla and Talis. Luther gently put his hand on Lilla's face and turned the badly swollen side towards him.

"It looks far worse, luckily, than what it is. I will be back in a minute," said Luther.

Luther walked off into the woods and was soon back. He came up to Lilla again, knelt beside her and passed her some bark.

"Here, chew this. It will help with the pain," said Luther.

"What is it? Do I just chew it and spit it out?" asked Lilla.

"It is the bark of the black willow tree. No, chew it until you can swallow it. You will find the pain will ease. I will get you some water," replied Luther.

He went back to the horses and brought Lilla a waterskin.

"Here, have a drink," Luther said as he passed it to her. "You will find the pain will subside soon, and it should last you the night. Then eat some more in the morning." Lilla did as Luther told her and swallowed the bark mush in her mouth.

Grimacing, she half-heartedly smiled at Luther.

"I knew there was a kind soul somewhere in your dark hide," smirked Lilla.

"If that is a compliment, daughter, I will take it," Luther said as he smiled back.

For the first time, Talis actually saw a bond between them. It had been hidden all the time he had been in their company. He saw it now, a bond that was rooted deeply. It was as deep as anyone who walked as father and daughter. But, as Talis noted all this, Luther's and Lilla's faces hardened simultaneously, and the bond was gone.

Talis waited until Luther had turned away.

"Lilla, how are you really doing?" asked Talis.

Lilla smiled, the best she could through her swollen mouth, though her face hurt like mad.

"I will be ok, I think. A hell of a night, Talis," replied Lilla. "I would kill for a drink from the bar now. How are you? It must have been as strange for you as it was painful for me. That girl thing, actually knowing you by name?" questioned Lilla as she looked at Talis inquisitively.

"Honestly, I have no idea how she knew my name. It must be part of why Lauren and I are hunted. I guess something to do with the war," said Talis with a shrug. "I hope to get more out of Berolarn or the elves when we arrive at their homeland. I do miss my home too. I wish we could go back to how it was, a land in peace. I would love to be travelling the woods and hunting with Lauren."

"And me?" questioned Lilla.

"I am glad I have met you, Lilla, no doubt about that. The only thing that has been of any good on this trip," smiled Talis as he gave her a gentle hug and pulled back.

She attempted to smile back.

"I'm also glad, Talis. Please tell me more of your homelands and stories of Lauren and your life. Let's talk of happier times," whispered Lilla.

Soon the pair of them were lost in conversations about their lives. Luther watched the young couple with interest, and he felt concerned about the closeness Lilla quickly gained towards the young man. He did feel warm, though, to see them joking and laughing. But would this relationship end in tears? This was highly likely, but he knew he would need to let it play out, and whatever their destiny was to be, he would not interfere.

"How are you, Berolarn?" asked Luther as he turned to the older man.

"I'm ok, Luther, but the events of last night, have drained me. I gave more of myself when we were attacked than I wished to," said Berolarn, who sounded quite discouraged when he spoke.

"There is always a price you have to pay to the gods, Talis," Berolarn said sadly as he noted Talis looking in his direction. "You should know that when you call deeply on the magic of the white flame. It is a gift, and there is a cost to having such power. The gods demand a part of you is paid to them. It has been a long time since I called on such magic to do battle, and it hit me hard. Harder than ever. Perhaps it is a passing of an era that is being foretold, as all things must come to pass."

"You will live forever, old man. So stop being melodramatic and foretelling pending doom for yourself. It is not healthy for one's mind to do so," grinned Luther as he berated Berolarn.

Berolarn laughed as he spoke and smiled. "As I act as the advisor to the races of the land. Luther stands above me always, my trusted advisor and friend." He turned and looked at Talis and Lilla again.

"Sometimes, I forget myself and get lost in being old and frail, yes frailer than you think, Talis. I have walked the land for centuries and am now ancient, even for one of our kind. With this comes aches and pains," grinned Berolarn. "Luther is right. Take no notice of me. I will be fine once the warmth of the fire has finally filled my bones."

Talis was quite surprised to see some of the walls around Berolarn coming down and to find fragility in this powerful man. It felt like a perfect time to question Berolarn on the events of the night before and his knowledge of the demon Selene.

"Berolarn, can I ask about last night?" asked Talis nervously.

Berolarn searched Talis's face and then the faces of Luther and Lilla. Finally, he sighed.

"What would you like to know, Talis?" asked Berolarn.

"In the inn, The girl who attacked us knew who I was and knew you by name," Talis asked questionably. "Not only did she know you, you knew her by name too, and she talked to you with a familiarity of not just a foe. She spoke to you as if you had a friendship, maybe, one formed long ago?"

"Ah, Selene, named after the goddess of the moon," mused Berolarn as he fumbled in his clothing and pulled out his pipe and weed pouch. He slowly filled his pipe and was deep in thought.

"Be a good lad, Talis and bring me a light off the fire," requested Berolarn clearing his throat,

"and then we will talk of Selene," continued Berolarn.

Talis jumped to his feet eagerly and walked over to the fire. He grabbed a small stick and lit it. He let the flame take hold and took it over to Berolarn.

"Thank you, Talis," smiled Berolarn.

He took the burning stick off Talis and proceeded to light the weed in his pipe. He drew deeply on the pipe, inhaled, and savoured the taste as the cloud of smoke left his mouth. Then, after much pondering, which was evident on Berolarn's face, he spoke.

"Yes, I have known Selene for hundreds of years, though perhaps to your eyes, she looked no older than someone of thirty-odd winters. She is actually over one thousand years of age. She was one of the surviving younger children of Olgrich Validorol," sighed Berolarn.

Talis was shocked at this news, a child of the dark lord, thousands of years old. Hunting for him. He shook his head.

"I don't understand Berolarn," said Talis overwhelmed.

"Of course, you don't, Talis," smiled Berolarn. "It is hard to understand why a villager is hunted by a thousand-year-old Vampiri, a child of the dark lord! But I have just started my story. Be patient whilst I continue."

"Sorry," Talis grinned sheepishly.

"Please continue, Berolarn," Lilla piped up. "I, for one, want to know who that devil witch is."

Berolarn continued, "Here we have Selene, who has walked this world for hundreds of years, born of evil and magic. The child of the dark lord, who no doubt would be privy to some of his council. One who was sent looking for you, Talis. Who is she?" He looked at each of them in turn. "Yes, I knew not only of Selene as she stood before us. I knew a Selene who walked outside the shadow, devoid of the influence of her father and her people," Berolarn finished the last comment with great sadness.

As Talis watched, it seemed to him that Berolarn was reliving memories as he stopped talking for a minute and puffed on his pipe. Berolarn then coughed and continued.

"I have told you already of the great wars when the dark lord hit the lands like a plague. One by one, the kingdoms fell to his power and kneeled before him. Then, finally, the Solarians marched on his lands, the deathlands and banged on his gates. The dark lord and his host answered this call, and they rode down onto the battlefield, and great power from both sides was unleashed. Power so great that it had not been seen since the end of the third age. Both sides suffered heavily, but the dark lord was too powerful, and against him, none should have been able to stand," declared Berolarn.

"But in the darkness, one Solarian knight came forth, and through the melee, he broke his way through to the dark lord, and he struck him down with a deadly blow. Such a blow would have killed an ordinary mortal, but long had Oglrich dabbled in the dark magic arts, and I surmise he was carried away from the field by his servants, and he survived. The Solarians should have continued to his castle, found him, and ended his life. It is apparent on reflection that he would arise again when you consider his defeat was not the final defeat of death. Also, the malevolence within his soul cannot be stopped if any element of life still exists. I curse the day we didn't push to attack his home," concluded Berolarn.

"You were there!" a shocked Talis exclaimed aloud. "But that would make you over a thousand years old too."

"Think a moment, Talis. I have already spoken to you at some length of our kind. We are not of man but come from another age when Atlanteans and Vampiri ruled this earth. Yes, I was there and was not young even then. I fought alongside your father, Talis. It was he, yes, your father that mortally wounded the dark lord," divulged Berolarn.

"What are you talking about, Berolarn?" Talis shouted as he jumped to his feet. He started pacing. "This cannot be. My father was not a thousand years old. He was a simple man, a villager."

"Talis, firstly, be quiet and stop shouting. Then, I will answer your questions, but you already know some of this. We have already started the journey for you at the hut near your village. I am sure this is partly why he hunts you and your sister," defended Berolarn in response.

Lilla seemed to awaken to the conversation as she learned Talis was the son of a vampire killing clan alive thousands of years ago.

"What is all this nonsense? Were you wounded on your head, Berolarn? Talis is as normal a man as I am a woman. He is not a creature of the night," shouted Lilla in dismay.

"Hush, Lilla, let them speak," commanded Luther as he looked at her sternly. "It is not the time for you or me to enter this conversation."

Lilla looked aghast at Luther's comments. As she looked at him and he stared at her. She thought he knew what lived in her heart, even though it had just been born. Curse his hide.

"The battle was won, and we were now few in number, our race nearly wiped from the earth. We turned and went to leave the battlefield. Our hearts were filled with great sorrow and pain. We mourned the devastation that the dark lord and his kind had wrought upon the world and the losses of my people," continued Berolarn.

"As we were leaving, I saw Selene. Just a child of her kind, a young Vampiri woman, beautiful and sad. She appeared to be looking at me. I went to her, and she was alive, though life was flowing away from her. I was spellbound. I could see a certain innocence in her face and purity that evil had not touched. Maybe it was on a whim, or perhaps divine intervention. Whichever it was, I carried her away from the battlefield with me. The others, including your father, questioned my wisdom in taking in one of the enemies, and it was clear she was of their royal blood by her clothing. As mentioned, a child of Olgrich Validoral."

"I nursed her and brought her back to health. I helped her learn to push back the evil that laid heavy on her heart and control the lust for the kill. For hundreds of years, we were happy." He shrugged, "I was naïve to think that I cured her of the sickness of her kind. Then began a period where I noticed she became more withdrawn, and though I pressed her on what was wrong. She would not say. Then she was gone. One night, she just disappeared. Finally, I think her father called for her, and she had no choice but to obey his command. Such is the control of the dark lord on his children."

"Since then, Selene and I have played cat and mouse. Sometimes she hunts for me as I walk amongst the races interfering with their plans. Sometimes I search for her as she walks this world, bringing death and destruction. But, when we met at the inn, this was the first time our paths had crossed in many years," finished Berolarn as he then pulled some more weed out of his pouch for his pipe.

"She is dead now, though. So she fulfilled her destiny at the inn?" asked Luther.

"I am not sure, my friend", responded Berolarn. "My magic consumed her, but I am not sure whether it was the magic that took her into nothingness. I have been pondering this as we rode. It was an unexpected conclusion to the battle; instead, I had a small nagging feeling that something else was involved." Berolarn shrugged as he was lost in thought. "I do believe she died, but I could be wrong. Needless to say, if she is alive, she will have lost favour with her father by not returning with you, Talis, and his punishments might be worse than death."

The companions remained quiet for some time as they stared at the fire and considered the words of Berolarn. Talis was struggling with everything that had happened over the last few weeks, and the more knowledge he was passed, the more his mind raced with turmoil. Talis felt beaten down with emotion. He longed for his sister, he longed for his father to come and make sense of all this for him, the stories of his heritage and the dark lord, and for the first time in a long time, Talis longed to hear his mother's angelic voice and the comfort Talis believed it used to bring when he was a child.

On the other hand, Lilla struggled because Talis was not an average man. Lilla had no idea what a Solarian was, but the tales of lives of hundreds of years, evil and magic, were not something she had any understanding of, and Lilla felt like she was being cursed with nothing more than bad luck. She would have to learn to live with it. Lilla looked at Luther, now lost in thought. He caught her eye.

"I will take first watch," Luther said as Berolarn started to lay down.

Lilla's mind was made up. She turned to Talis.

"Come, Talis, let us sleep. I am starting to feel drowsy, and you look tired," said Lilla, and she then whispered, "there is nothing more that can be discussed tonight. Hold me and keep me warm."

Talis looked at Lilla and saw the beauty of her face hiding behind the swelling and bruising. He smiled at her, laid down and opened his arms for her to lay with him. She lowered herself and put her head on his chest, and he wrapped his arms around her. Soon they were both asleep, as was Berolarn.

Luther looked at his companions as they rested. He hoped that Berolarn knew what he was doing. Berolarn was not usually as open as he was tonight. Berolarn was generally quite reserved with the information to be shared, and this was the first time he had heard the story of Selene. He knew from Berolarn that he had indeed once been married. But, he had always been under the illusion that Berolarn's wife had died. This is why the decision was taken on the child. His wife had supposedly been killed in an attack orchestrated by the dark lord, and their child had to be hidden.

This obviously was a half-truth. But then Luther was used to half-truths, or should he say omissions to the truth by Berolarn. His way was to let the stories unfold as people made their own discoveries. It was unusual that Berolarn spoke freely. Still, he had never told anyone the truth about himself and his origins. Not even Berolarn knew who he was, of his birth line. It did trouble him with Lilla that she did not know. Perhaps he should tell her, but then perhaps not. Why burden her? Luther pulled his cloak tighter around his neck and stared deep into the fire's dying embers as he chucked another log onto it.

Talis awoke. It was early morning by the look of things. He

slowly looked around and saw Berolarn standing near the newly made fire warming his hands. He slowly unwrapped himself from Lilla and lowered her head to the ground. Luther was nowhere to be seen. Talis got up and walked over to Berolarn.

"Morning, Where is Luther?" Talis asked Berolarn.

"Ah, good morning Talis. Luther is out scouting. He has been gone for thirty minutes, so I expect he will be back soon. Why don't you wake up, Lilla? You two need to eat breakfast as we will be off as soon as he returns," said Berolarn.

Talis went back over to Lilla. He knelt down and slowly shook her.

"Lilla, Lilla, it is time to wake up, Lilla, wake up," Talis said quietly to Lilla.

She opened her eyes and undertook a slight stretching movement.

"What time is it, Talis?" asked Lilla.

"Early, Berolarn says we will be off as soon as Luther returns from scouting. Come, you need to eat before we leave," answered Talis.

He helped Lilla to her feet. They then made their way back to the fire, where Berolarn was busy preparing something.

"Morning, Lilla," said Berolarn as he passed her a large leaf with some form of cooked fish on it. "Luther was up very early and had fish ready when I woke", he continued as he passed another to Talis. "How are you feeling today, Lilla? The swelling looks to be going down slightly."

"I feel much better if I am honest, and I have some more of

the bark that Luther gave me, which eased the pain. I'm chewing on some more of this, and I think I will be fine for the rest of the day," replied Lilla.

"Good, come eat…..eat, we have a long day ahead. I hope for us to reach the Korallis Outpost as soon as possible. Unfortunately, I doubt that our flight has gone unnoticed. The sooner we are out of these lands, the better. I am sure the hunt for us continues," said Berolarn.

Talis was beginning to note that Berolarn was always the bringer of doom. So he made a mental note that he would take a wide birth of any future interactions with Berolarn or anyone else involved if he ever got out of this alive. Then looking at Lilla, he made a mental amendment…..not including Lilla.

They finished, drank some water, and started packing their things and preparing to leave. When they heard faint steps in the undergrowth, Luther appeared immediately out of the woodlands.

"Good, you are all awake," commented Luther, "and I see we are fed. It is time for us to go, I see nothing close by that should concern us, but there is a quietness in the woods. This should not be so. We should leave this place now in case danger is looming."

Within minutes, they left and followed the river along its bank again.

Chapter 15 – The Race for Korrallis

Over several days the companions continued towards Korrallis without incident. The worst conflict they experienced was against the constant rain and winds. The river was now beginning to encroach onto the embankment. It started to become evident that the side of the river was becoming slippery and unstable under the horse's weight, and soon if there was no let-up, they might have to abandon the horses and go on foot through the woodlands.

Talis and Lilla were generally feeling miserable as they rode together. Though they occasionally chatted with each other and their companions throughout each day, the constant chill in their bones dampened their spirits, which led to lengthy periods of silence.

The rain started to ease on the eighth day since Berolarn had spoken of Selene. Then, finally, some sun broke through the clouds and took some of the chills out of the winter air. Luther told them this was a good sign, as soon they would need to leave the horses and go on foot through the trees, deep into Tellingwood forest.

As the day progressed, Talis began to feel more cheery and relaxed. Soon Lilla and Talis were deeply conversing about what they knew of the elves. Apparently, their knowledge was sparse as neither of them had ever met an elf. However, they had a general consensus that the elves were a secretive race that kept out of the affairs of others. They were strong and feared by the other races, so all the other races left the elves to whatever elves did. Talis had heard that their lands were like no other. His father had told him that the land of elves was full of fantastic trees of enormous size. There were fauna, plants, and even animals that lived in Aslandure, that did not live anywhere but in the lands of elves.

As Talis said to Lilla, not only was he excited to see the elves, he was actually quite excited to see if all these rumours were true and what wondrous animals might live there. He loved woodlands and their occupants, perhaps not as much as Lauren. But it did run deep within his family. On the other hand, Lilla had no knowledge of the elven lands and had very little understanding of the world of nature. Yet she was fascinated by what Talis was telling her, and she admitted to Talis that she was also very excited to see the land of elves.

As the day started to pass and the night was beginning to draw in. Luther motioned for them to stop.

"It is time for us to go into the woods. We will look for shelter, make camp, and make a big push for the outpost tomorrow. Now let us try and unpack everything we can carry, and then we must let the horses try to make their way home as the passage will become too dense for the horses to travel in," said Luther as he looked around the woods.

They unpacked everything they could from their trusted steads and spent time repacking things to maximise what they could take. Luther then went up to his horse.

"You must return home, Delfair. It is up to you to lead the others. We go now where you cannot pass. Be safe, my friend," whispered Luther.

As he turned and walked away, his horse seemed to understand and trotted off, and the other two horses followed.

"They should be ok," Luther said to the companions as he came towards the forest's edge where they stood.

"They are trained for this and have travelled far across the lands, knowing them well. They know their way back to their home and how to navigate the dangers of the lands. Right we must enter and get undercover. Now we are bereft of the horses. It now makes us more vulnerable to being seen and captured. I still see no sign of pursuers, but I still feel unease in these lands."

"Yes, let's go quickly," said Berolarn entering the woods. "If we bring a ranger such as Luther, we would pay well to heed his words." Then, turning to Luther, "we haven't discussed this unease you have had since we met the river, Luther. I have been too preoccupied with my own thoughts to ask. Do you have any idea what it is that you sense?"

"It is strange, Berolarn, I sense no one is watching us, and there is no sign of any other trails or smell of any ambush. But I know these lands, haven't you noticed how little of the animal world we have seen or the absence of birds in song or flight?" replied Luther, and he shook his head. "I do not like it, Berolarn. I feel there must be evil afoot."

"Well, whatever it may or may not be that is causing the quietness, we must be prepared for the worse and keep a close eye on all around us," Berolarn shrugged. "Talis, Lilla, keep your eyes open and wits about you."

They both nodded.

As they walked through the forest, Talis whispered to Lilla.

"Are you trained with any weapons, Lilla? Luther and Berolarn are making me nervous, if I am honest, and it would be good to know that you would be ok if a fight broke out?" Talis asked.

Lilla smiled at him.

"I am ok with most weapons. Luther saw to it. I wouldn't say I was skilled, though. It was just child play when I was taught," replied Lilla.

Talis reached into his scabbard.

"Here is my hunting knife," Talis said as he passed her a long sharp-bladed knife. "When we get to the land of elves, we can spend more time with the bow and sword. I think it would be good for you to train again," he smiled at her.

They continued walking deeper into the forest for quite some time. The trees were large and old by the width of their trunks and height, all densely packed together as they reached for the skies, fighting each other for the sunlight. The floor was heavy underfoot. It had a deep canopy of various shrubs, lianas with long, flexible climbing stems rooted into the ground, with long dangling branches. There was a good amount of foliage, such as leaves, branches, bark, and limbs, existing in various stages of decomposition with copious amounts of fungi feeding on them. The whole place had a very musky smell about it.

"It doesn't look like anyone travels this way, Luther?" asked Lilla, which was the question that had been on Talis's mind.

"No, Lilla, you are right. Everyone walks the roads to the elven lands in a more peaceful time. Even the elves who are at one with nature and love walking in the world's green forests and woods would rarely come through here as they find it strange, and some say it is dangerous," replied Luther.

"It is said that the forest is born of another age. They say that the trees were planted to honour the deity Arweln-Sol, Sol, Dagda, Sol Invictus, a deity of many names, the creator, the sun god or goddess, but as the gods were forgotten by many, so was the forest." chipped in Berolarn.

"Who is Arweln-Sol?" asked Lilla.

"That is a good question, Lilla. One that would take many a year to answer. Let us wait until we make camp, and I will talk some about the gods," smiled Berolarn.

"How long before we do that, Luther," asked Talis.

"I am not sure, Talis, I was hoping we would find a clearing somewhere, but the forest seems to have swallowed all. I think we should continue looking for at most fifteen minutes. That will just give us enough time before darkness takes hold," replied Luther.

Luckily after ten minutes of searching, they found an area without what you would call a clearing. However, it did have little in the way of decomposing foliage, and it would be big enough for them to rest comfortably and make a small fire. So Talis got to work making a fire whilst Lilla prepared food for each from the meagre rations they had left. It was not long before the fire was burning, and each was sat eating the dry meats, hardtack, and fruits. As they were eating, Berolarn started speaking of the gods.

"As I mentioned to Talis, there have been many ages, Lilla. You would say that we are currently in the fourth primary age. This age is more unique to the other ages. The races, besides small cults, have forgotten their gods for the first time, and no one calls them. However, there have always been deities or gods over the last ages. These deities or gods would be at the head of what they call a religion. Religion was a system of worshipping a divine supernatural being, an all-powerful force that controlled nature, the world around us and our very being," explained Berolarn.

"It is said that the gods looked down on the world and watched the affairs of the races from afar. However, they also listened to the call of their followers, and the gods spoke. The followers listened and believed in their god's teachings and divinity as part of following their chosen religion. It is also said that these deities would even interact physically with mortals and interfere with the natural workings of the world."

"Now, for some races, there was only one all-powerful god, who ruled supreme, and all other gods were false gods belonging to cult worshippers. Whereas for others, there were pantheons. A group of gods. Gods who were masters of some aspects of the physical plane, such as the sun, the moon, fire and air. Then there were the gods of actions or feelings, such as war and love. Yes, followers of such religions might worship a particular god within the pantheon, but they believed in all the gods and wished to anger none with their actions. Does that make sense?" asked Berolarn.

Lilla was nodding her head.

"I have heard of such gods, Berolarn. I wouldn't say they were forgotten. Not worshipped perhaps is a better comment," suggested Lilla.

"Forgive me, Lilla. You are quite right. They are not worshipped anymore, though people occasionally refer to or sing of them in their songs," said Berolarn with a smile of recognition.

"Well, I have never heard of such gods," said Talis. "I am surprised that my father never gave us any teachings of such things."

"Yes, it is surprising, Talis, perhaps Loren saw little value, or maybe there was an ideology with his thinking," remarked Berolarn as he shrugged. "I suspect we will never find the answer to that one, Talis. Your father would have had his reasons, I am sure."

"You must understand that there is always a common theme when looking at the mythology of particular pantheons. Most religions had the same gods but under different names, and they held greater or lesser prominence, depending on the religion. For example, in other faiths, Arweln-Sol, the sun goddess, could have been called Ra, Inti, El, Sol or Belenos. The list goes on. Interestingly, the nature of gods is all about the power they hold and the control they exert on this world. Many deities rule the various aspects of mortal existence, cooperating with and competing in administering the affairs of this world and the universe," continued Berolarn.

"Why is that so, do you think, Berolarn?" asked Lilla, who was fascinated by the words of Berolarn. He is probably the wisest man I have ever met, she thought.

"It is essential to understand this, where there is good, there is evil. Where there is light, there is darkness. Where there is war, there is peace. Where there is love, there is hate. Where there is health, there is sickness. The list goes on," defined Berolarn.

"By its very nature, religion looks to answer the questions of everything that happens in the mortal world. It gives the races something to hold on to; a set of beliefs and practices that supports them to cope with the chaos around them. The teachings are continuously moulded in a similar fashion so they can be understood," clarified Berolarn as he attempted to answer Lilla's question.

"You know a lot about different gods then?" questioned Lilla.

"I have studied long the histories of this world, Lilla, and yes, I have a good understanding of the gods and how they will relate to us," answered Berolarn. "I foresee as events unfold during the war, we will see the gods again walking among the races."

"I would like to know more of the true gods, Berolarn. How do I learn more about such things?" asked Lilla.

"Once we arrive in the elven homelands, they will have ancient tomes within their great libraries that you can read, Lilla. These will outline much of what I just told you and give you a perspective of deities as viewed by the elves of yesteryear," answered Berolarn.

"You talk as if these gods are real, Berolarn?" stated Talis.

"That is the question, Talis, were they? Or are they real? This perhaps is not the time to answer that fully, but yes, they are real," declared Berolarn with certainty, giving Talis the impression that Berolarn believed it to be true.

Why does Berolarn always talk in riddles, thought Talis. He never answers anything fully and always leaves something open to discussion.

"Well, whatever the case may be, we should look to rest now. Lilla, will you take first watch, Berolarn, me, and then you, Talis," interjected Luther as he went around the group. Luther noted each one, nodding in turn. "Good, let's get settled down."

As her companions slept, Lilla kept vigil. She gazed at the fire, transfixed by the flickering flame as her mind wandered back and forth on Talis, the war, the inn and its destruction, and the stories of gods. Finally, Lilla looked over at Talis and thought about the confusion in her mind, which had become a constant battle as they got closer each day. What started out as a joke with a villager was part of the overbearing boredom she had constantly whilst she worked at the inn had now become an overwhelming fondness that had turned into what Lilla thought was love. She had never been in love with a man before and was scared that Talis didn't have her feelings or mistook her feelings.

Lilla sighed and threw another spigot of wood onto the fire. She had toyed with telling him her real feelings, but he had enough to worry about and might not have any feelings for her in that way. So yes, she would let it play out and see where it took her. That would be best. It would give Luther time to accept him if they were meant to be. She knew that Luther was constantly watching them like a hawk, and she didn't want Talis on the wrong side of Luther. Stretching, she was just about to wake Berolarn for his turn to take watch.

Suddenly Lilla heard a faint but distinct noise in a thicket close by. It was definitely not her imagination as she listened to another twig snap.

"Luther," hissed Lilla.

Luther immediately and instinctively jumped up. He put his

finger to his mouth for silence and motioned for her to wake the others. Luther was surveying around the campsite as the others came over towards him.

"What is it, Luther?" asked Berolarn as he rose, as did Talis.

"I have only had the unpleasant experience of them once before. They walk only where great evil and death have once occurred. Deathwalker's by the stench, arisen from the dead." whispered Luther.

Luther looked at Talis and Lilla

"What an evil fate this is when we are so close to our destination. Quickly, Talis, Lilla. You must not look into their gaze or listen to the words that enter your minds," whispered Luther.

"How many are there, Luther?" whispered Berolarn.

"At least three or four, they are slowly making their way towards us from all directions," replied Luther.

Berolarn suddenly raised his arm and shouted an incantation which lit the sky and their camp with brilliant sunlight as the deathwalker's came crashing through the trees. Five of them. Lilla or Talis had never seen such monsters before. Human in shape, blue and purple of skin, with heads that were demonic in appearance. Their heads had large jagged horns protruding on each side, and smaller spikes covered their upper backs and shoulders. They were heavily muscled across their legs, torso and arms. Each hand had massive claws on each finger. Then there were their faces, horrifying. They had neither eyes nor a mouth. Yet all could hear the scream of anger from mouths that did not exist.

Luther engaged the two that ran at him. This left the other three all running toward his companions. From the corner of his eye, Talis saw a bolt of fire coming from Berolarn hands as he tried desperately to use his long sword against his foe. The deathwalker was too quick for Talis and easily dodged the blade. It started to circle Talis as it looked for an opening. Talis heard voices telling him to lay down his sword that he could not win. He momentarily lost his concentration as he heard the voices, and the deathwalker struck and jumped at Talis, taking both to the ground.

Luther had killed one, taking its head clean off with a single blow from his sword, and was fighting with the other, who was now warier of the enormous human in front of it. Berolarn was hanging onto the arms of his combatant, and flames coursed from his body over the screaming faceless deathwalker. Lilla could see all this occurring like it was happening in slow-motion. Lilla had not engaged the deathwalker who had come for her, she was too fast for it, and it could not grab hold of her. Lilla had caught it a few times in passing with her knife, and they continued to circle each other.

Suddenly she heard the screams of Talis, the deathwalker he was fighting had pinned him down and had struck him a raking blow across the face and neck with its muscular clawed hand. Lilla saw the badly burned deathwalker lift Berolarn off his feet and throw him backwards. Without thinking, she ran at her deathwalker in a few steps and, with the momentum from pushing off a raised rock, somersaulted over the creature of the night, leaving her blade in its head with only its hilt showing. Then, as she saw it falling down, in one motion, she yanked the knife out of the creature's head and flew into the side of the deathwalker who was holding down Talis. As they both flew sidewards and landed on the ground, Talis started to get up to help Lilla. Only to see Lilla rising, with the knife he had given her, firmly logged in the chest of the deathwalker who had attacked him. It was dead. They quickly looked around to see Luther had killed the two who had been attacking him and helping Berolarn to his feet as his deathwalker lay motionless.

"Well, daughter, the training was obviously successful. Is everyone ok?" smiled Luther as he came over to Lilla.

Berolarn nodded, but Lilla was already helping Talis sit back down and trying to stem the blood from his facial wounds with one of her vests.

"Talis is hurt. He has taken a blow across his face and neck. The wounds are deep, Luther," stated Lilla in answer. Talis closed his eyes and tried not to think of the pain.

"Let me look," said Berolarn as he came and crouched next to Talis.

He gently pulled away Lilla's vest, which she had used to stem the blood flow. The wound was superficial along the neck but quite deep across the face. Berolarn rubbed his hand, which glowed lightly across Talis's face. To the wonder of Lilla and Luther, the blood flow slowed and then stopped. Talis's grimacing face eased, and he looked at Berolarn with surprise.

"The pain has gone, Berolarn. How did you do that? This is staggering," expressed Talis in amazement. Berolarn smiled.

"Unfortunately or fortunately, depending on how you see it. I didn't do anything but help your body react to the wound. By tomorrow the injury will have closed," said Berolarn.

"How is that possible?" Questioned Lilla jumping in.

Berolarn Turning to Lilla.

"I explained to you some of Talis heritage. As part of that heritage, Talis acquires certain benefits. One is regeneration, where normal wounds will heal to a point where the damage never happened. However, Talis has just started his journey, and there is much for him to learn," replied Berolarn.

Then, turning back to Talis.

"Talis, when you were under attack, did you feel any rage or hunger, no burning desire like when we first met at the hut?" asked Berolarn.

"No, I didn't, to be honest. It was more just fear! Did you expect me to turn or to do something else unexpected?" answered Talis.

"I wasn't sure, but perhaps I did expect you to call upon it. Yes, I was convinced that when danger loomed, it would happen. It is like it has been locked away and is now guarded," said Berolarn, peering deep into Talis's eyes. "No matter, it is what will be. We can find out more later. Luther, what do you think?"

"It is time to go. Unfortunately, we should push on and not stop now until we have reached safety. I know we are tired, and this will only get worse. But I think the risks now outweigh the rest needed for our aching limbs and heads. Come, let's pack up and begone before more of the enemy find us," replied Luther as he looked around. "I think if we march hard, we should reach the outpost sooner than we think, maybe twelve to fifteen hours."

"Then it is decided, Lilla, please help Talis, quickly redress his wound. I will pack up all of our gear whilst you stand watch, Luther," stated Berolarn.

They were soon off again through the woodland, carrying a small lantern and relying on what moonlight cut through the treetops to guide their way.

"Berolarn, what were those creatures? These deathwalker's?" asked Lilla.

"I would like to understand where you got those fighting skills from, Lilla?" smirked Talis.

Lilla smirked in return.

"You should be in too much pain to be asking such questions of a lady," giggled Lilla.

Even Luther and Berolarn laughed at her response.

"Fortunately, you have Luther to thank for anything I did today. Though I must admit, I cannot remember you showing me the somersault trick I did, Luther," continued Lilla.

"It was because I never showed you that," said Luther, smiling and shaking his head. "It must be already a skill you were born with but haven't had the call to use it. I must start watching my words with you, daughter. You are more dangerous than I thought," he said, now grinning.

Berolarn was thinking similar. But it was good to see them all smiling after nearly meeting an end in the deathwalker's attack, as many more such incidents would likely occur. The dark lord's arm reaches far if he has deathwalker's hunting in the sacred woods, so close to the elven outpost.

Clearing his throat Berolarn responded to the question of deathwalker's.

"Deathwalker's are shadows of what once was alive. Some call them or their state; the undead. They are shadows of evil mortals of some great power, full of malice and strength of will to survive. They must have bargained with the long-forgotten deity Hel for some form of life after death. They are intelligent and do not follow others usually as they do not bow to any master. Deathwalker's kill and hunt for a form of pleasure. Yet they do this independently and not together in packs. I can only surmise the obvious: they were sent, and it can only be by the dark lord if they were sent," stated Berolarn.

"The dark lord controls such creatures?" asked Lilla.

"How he gained their allegiance is again of interest and a riddle to which I do not have an answer," conceded Berolarn as he nodded.

"Do you think more lie ahead then?" asked Luther.

"I'm not sure. Yet I think not. For five to be in one place simultaneously is unheard of. Being an unholy abomination, they are scarce worldwide and encounters with one usually means death. He would not have expected us to survive such an encounter, never mind us walking away intact," replied Berolarn.

They continued to walk through the forest, and the minutes turned into hours; before they knew it, the darkness had turned into daylight. There had not been any further encounters, and the tiredness they had expected had not hit them yet. In fact, Talis was feeling better by the hour and was chatting freely to Lilla as they walked, and the pain in his face had gone.

"We are very close now," said Luther as the day was just passing through midday. "We would come out along the southwest face of the outpost wall. It is best to avoid coming up to the outpost totally unannounced. I would suggest going to the road now instead and approaching in full view. I would sooner not have elven arrows being fired down on my head if I could help it."

"I agree," said Berolarn. "The elves will be warier of folk coming towards their lands under the current circumstances."

"Good, let us cut across here. We should make the road within ten minutes and just before the area where we would normally be spotted from the watchtower," said Luther

Luther turned in direction. Moving towards the east, and carried on through the forest. They had gone no further than a few hundred metres.

"Don't move, drop your weapons and place your hands on your head unless you want certain death," said a commanding voice.

Suddenly, many elven soldiers came out of the trees from all directions. The companions all did as they were told and dropped their weapons.

"Bind their hands, collect their weapons and take them to the keep," ordered the soldier, who was obviously the commander. As they were about to be bound, Berolarn asked one of the soldiers to mention his name to the one in charge and asked if he could have an audience. The soldier looked at Berolarn, nodded, went to the commander, and started whispering and pointing at Berolarn. The commander looking up said something to the young soldier and came towards the companions.

"Well, met Berolarn. I am Captain Ular. I am second in charge at the outpost. You come back to our lands at a time of war and mistrust. By order of the king, no one is to enter Aslandure unless invited. Anyone found entering our lands will discover that their lives are forfeit. You are lucky that we are patrolling the surrounding areas for the enemy and came across you before you attempted to enter. However, it is not my decision whether to let you go or not. First, I must take you to my commander and see if she is happy for you to enter our lands," said the elven officer.

"Thank you, Captain Ular. Please tell me whilst we walk to see the commander what news of the outside world has reached the ears of the King," enquired Berolarn.

"I cannot speak of what the king does or doesn't know. However, it is common knowledge that the war is spreading, and attacks on populated areas around the kingdoms have become more common," answered Captain Ular.

"And what of the elves? Have you engaged in battle?" persisted Berolarn.

The elven commander surveyed Berolarn before answering.

"I can only tell you what I have learned as rumours. We have lost the outpost at Morallis, which is why the borders are now closed. Morallis was attacked in the darkness of night by goblins and a massive force of darkness that came with fire and tore down with ease the walls that had stood for thousands of years. How the goblin breached the pass, we do not know. A large section of the elven army rode swiftly to the keep when the wind voiced news of the attack. They arrived to find none of the enemies remained, the keep was in ruins, and all of our brothers and sisters there were found dead save a few survivors who had escaped down a secret passage that led them to safety," answered Captain Ular.

"Is there any news of the dwarves?" asked Berolarn.

"I hear rumours that they are hard-pressed in certain parts of their lands, but then I hear the same for the kingdoms of men. So who knows," stated Captain Ular.

"Thank you, Captain Ular," said Berolarn as they walked up the giant gates at the entrance to the outpost, which was now opening on their approach.

As they entered the courtyard, he spoke to one of the soldiers and then turned back to the companions.

"If you can follow Julaan," said Captain Ular, motioning towards the soldier to whom the captain had just spoken. "He will escort you to a waiting room, you will be unbound, and food and drink will be brought. But, while you are waiting for the commander's decision, it would be foolish to attempt to leave this room. I will speak to the commander now."

The companions were escorted to a waiting room in the keep. Food and drink were brought to them, and they sat to eat while awaiting news on the commander's decision. They had not been sat long when the door opened, and a middle-aged woman entered in the form of army ceremonial clothing. So this must be the commander, thought Talis.

"Berolarn, it has been a long time," the woman called over to Berolarn as she broke into a big grin.

"Eleran," smiled Berolarn with evident joy. "I had wondered

where you have been over the last few years. The king has moved you out of the court, has he? You must have been causing your usual chaos," he started laughing.

"You know me, I can never keep my mouth shut when it comes to Elisha. My brother is overbearing and too protective of the child. How will she ever be the queen her father has been as the king if she is not allowed out of court? Anyway, that was then. This is now. My brother yielded sometime ago and did start to let her live life," laughed Eleran.

"Where is Princess Elisha now, Eleran?" asked Berolarn. "She went in search of Loran's family some time ago. I was here when the King agreed with her to lead the search."

"So it was you. I might have guessed it was you, Berolarn, who had convinced the king to let her leave the kingdom on a mad chase with no idea what the riddle was about. Some things never change, my old friend," laughed Eleran.

"I try very hard to meet expectations," laughed Berolarn. "You was saying, ….. Elisha?" he asked quizically.

"She returned from the south to the palace only a few nights ago. Or so I hear, and the King was overjoyed to have his daughter return home," replied Eleran.

"Did she have a human girl with her? A girl called Lauren?" asked Berolarn with a more urgent tone.

"I hear that is the case, though I do not know the girl's name. Only the Princess and the girl returned. The princess guard was not with her. Outside of that, I know no more," answered Eleran. "What is happening, Berolarn?"

Before Berolarn could answer, Talis excitedly jumped in.

"It must be Lauren, Berolarn. You said she was with the princess. This is such good news," said Talis, sighing and smiling simultaneously.

"Sorry, Eleran, this is Talis, the girl's brother. Who we believe was with your niece. Luther, you know, and this is his daughter Lilla," said Berolarn.

Motioning toward the girl and then looking at his companions.

"This is Eleran Celestar, King's sister and second in command of the elven army," turning back to Eleran, "The boy has not seen his sister since his village was destroyed by raiders from the north. He searches for news. They are the children of Loran. Unfortunately, he was killed in battle, trying to save the village."

"Elisha was sent by the King on my request to find Loran and his children. I wished for them to be brought to your lands for immediate safety as the enemy searches for them," revealed Berolarn.

"This is grievous news you bring, Berolarn," sighed Eleran. Then, turning to Talis, "I am so sorry, Talis, I knew your father well, and over the years, he has been a great man, a great servant to the lands. All that knew him will mourn his passing."

Talis could do no more than nod his thanks as the memory of the loss came rushing back.

"We need to go to see the King on your leave, Eleran," stated Berolarn.

"Yes, yes, of course, I will arrange for some horses and a few of my troops to escort you to the palace," replied Eleran. "We must speak again, Berolarn, when time is more favourable to you". She turned and left the waiting room.

Soon after, the captain they had seen earlier returned and informed them that all was ready for their departure and that they would be escorted by several guards.

They set off not long after the meeting with Eleran and were travelling through the rich countryside of the elven kingdom. There was a chill in the air, and sporadic winter rain splashed around them as they crossed the lands. There was, however, a certain warmth they felt. An inner feeling of happiness seemed to come from the lands around them. The tiredness that should have been with them after the exertions of the battle with the deathwalker's and the lack of sleep had passed them by. The companions all were in good spirits as they talked and laughed.

As the day moved on and the hours passed, it was not long before the companions could see the palace looming. A magnificent domed tower dominated a large building that they could see peering over the walled city.

"Welcome to Solanstar," said the Captain as they neared the city gates.

Chapter 16 – Together

As they entered the palace, they were greeted by an elven woman. Their escort all bowed, turned and left them. She smiled at them.

"Well, met again Berolarn and you, Luther," said the woman.

Berolarn and Luther both bowed.

"Welcome, Talis, son of Loren, brother of Lauren. I have heard much about you from your sister. "I am Elisha Celestar, daughter of King Ethera Celestar. I bid you all welcome," said Elisha.

Seeing the look on Talis's face, the elven woman smiled again, making direct eye contact with Talis.

"Do not worry, Talis, she is well. I will take you to see her soon enough," soothed Elisha.

"Errr, hello, Princess Elisha," replied Talis, who was confused about what to say.

Turning towards Lilla, she gently smiled again with a friendly, warm face.

"Lillaanthisil, the child in exile, daughter of Luther, I have not seen you since you were a baby," smiled Elisha.

Lilla going red, looked at Luther, who stared back expressionless. Lilla had no idea why the woman had greeted her like that. But she felt really frumpy and dirty in front of the elegant beautiful princess.

"Hello, Princess Elisha. Please call me Lilla," replied Lilla quietly, feeling highly embarrassed.

"Princess Elisha, I am very encouraged to see you returned safely and to hear that Lauren is safe. I would like Luther and myself to take your leave and see the King," said Berolarn.

"That is fine, Berolarn. I am sure the King will make time for you, even though I should warn you, he will be feeling challenged at this time, and bearers of ill tidings will perhaps not lessen his mood," smiled Elisha.

Berolarn took her smile and words as a gentle warning with firm honesty. He knew Ethera well and knew that though he was a very wise old elf, he could be quick to anger. He thought something must have happened recently for Elisha to give this warning.

"Thank you, Princess Elisha. Your words are noted. Please do excuse me, Luther, please follow me," replied Berolan as he and Luther walked away.

"Why don't you two come with me, Talis, Lilla? I will show you to your rooms. We will have baths ready for you, and I will have new clothing brought," said Elisha as she looked at them both. "I think I will have healers come to see you both and check your head wounds."

"We are both fine," replied Talis, as he tore off the head dressing to reveal to a shocked Lilla that there was no wound and his face looked as it did before the attack.

"I'm fine too, the swelling has gone, and the bruising is fading," said Lilla.

"I need to see Lauren," requested Talis with a hint of frustration.

"I know, Talis. Lauren wishes to see you too. But she sleeps now as she recovers from a head wound. So it would be sensible to let her rest a while longer, and it is a perfect time for you to bathe and change your clothing," soothed Elisha.

"How is she?" asked Talis glumly as they started to walk.

"She is on the mend, and soon she will be back to full health. But, unfortunately, she received a significant blow from a creoch which found us," replied Elisha.

Noting the confused look on their faces, she went on to explain.

"A creoch is a mindless wolf-like creature that attacked and caused her horse to fall. Lauren banged her head on a rock when she landed. Luckily I managed to kill the beast and help her onto my horse. After that, we rode like the wind and managed to get to Solanstar without further incident. But her head wound was deep and caused a long sleep without Lauren waking up. She finally woke last night, and the healers say she needs to rest for a few more days before being allowed out of bed," explained Elisha.

"You were with her?" asked a confused Talis, who was again thinking why was an elven princess with Lauren.

"I was Talis, but that story is for another day. Perhaps one that Lauren can tell you both, as we are now here. So, please, this room is yours, Lilla, and this is yours, Talis," said Elisha.

Elisha took them through an archway to a small anteroom with two opposing doors.

"I or another will come and fetch you both later and take you to the hospital, where you can visit Lauren. But, for now, please enter," Elisha said, opening her arms and motioning to the two doors. "Someone will be with you shortly with new clothes and some food." Elisha turned and walked away, back down the corridor.

Lilla shrugged. "Well, I suppose we had better do as she told us unless you want me to come and help you bathe again," teased Lilla as she gave Talis a wicked, mischievous grin.

Talis smiled wearily as tiredness started to take hold.

"Ask me again another day, and I am sure I will answer yes, but I think I will decline your offer today," sighed Talis.

"Please yourself. You know where I am!" Lilla flirtatiously responded.

Lilla turned and opened her door. As she entered and started closing the door, she called out to Talis, who was entering his room.

"Come and get me when you are ready," said Lilla, closing her door.

Lilla had never been in a room like this before. The walls and floor were all made of grey marble. They were inlaid with various patterns of gold and silver. The bed was as significant in size as was the bathing tub near a balcony area. There was a large mirror, settees, tables, and chairs. It was like a house all in one giant room.

She walked over to the balcony and noted that the bathing tub was already filled with warm water with light steam rising. She wondered how they managed to fill it when they had just arrived. Lilla opened the balcony doors and looked down into the courtyard to see many different people coming and going from the palace. Lilla looked out across the city. It was bigger than any place she could have imagined. Sighing, she would love to live in a place like here.

Lilla walked back to the tub, closing the balcony doors behind her. She quickly removed her clothes and dipped her toe into the tub. So perfect, Lilla thought as she gently lowered herself and fully submerged her whole body and head. Dreamily lying fully immersed for some time before she realised she had no air left, Lilla lifted herself upwards as she coughed and gasped for air.

"That was a bit stupid," Lilla laughed at herself.

Lilla proceeded to get washed, scrubbing ferociously at the grime and ground-in dirt from her hands, face and body. This was no mean feat, looking at her hands and the colour of the water as it was turning a murky brown. She was filthy.

Lilla started to reflect on the past events and what lay in store for her next. Lilla knew she had already decided to go with Talis wherever he was going and face whatever dangers they would encounter. But she still couldn't get her head around that he was something different, not human. Lilla had constantly been thinking about this on and off since Berolarn had let it slip. It was more important to her than any dangers they had faced or were to face. But, the more Lilla tried to work it out, the more confused she became. Perhaps she should ask Luther or Berolarn about it in private. But Lilla soon dispelled that idea, they wouldn't understand the purpose of my questioning, or maybe Luther would, which might cause me problems. No, she would have to figure it out herself.

Lilla lay there for maybe forty minutes as she let the tiredness take hold when Lilla suddenly awoke from her dreams, and she heard the click of the door to her room as it closed. Turning around wildly, she saw the room was empty. Instead, there was steaming hot food on the table and what looked like a dress laid out on the bed.

"How did they do that? I heard nothing until the door closed," marvelled Lilla to herself.

Lilla grabbed one of the towels and started to get dry. Then, she moved across to look at the clothes that had been provided. It was a beautiful gown of green silk ribbed with light blue and gold edging.

Lilla slipped it over her head, and it fitted perfectly. She felt like a princess. This was much better than working for Luther in the inn and having Biggy ordering her about. She wondered if Biggy was ok. Lilla was actually missing the big fool. She went to the table and quickly ate some food, eager to leave and find Talis.

Lilla left her room and silently opened the door to the room belonging to Talis. She decided she would creep up on him and catch him unawares. Lilla found this was far simpler than she expected. Talis was lying asleep on the bed. He had obviously bathed as he was nice and clean, wrapped in a towel around his waist. Lilla marvelled again at how muscular he was and good-looking she found him. There was also a certain innocence in his face, highlighted more so as he slept, that she found appealing from the day she first met him.

Lilla slowly approached closer to Talis and gently climbed onto the bed. As she gingerly moved closer, she lay beside him, and he turned in his sleep to face her. Lilla could feel the warmth of his breath on her skin. It gave her goosebumps as she fought the urge to kiss, touch, and make love to him. Lilla suddenly realised she was falling in love with him. Lilla had no idea how this had happened. Yet Lilla knew it was true. She would feel warm when they talked or even just caught his eye. It was all very strange to her.

Lilla slowly ran her fingers along his chest, delicately moving up and stroking his face.

"Talis," Lilla whispered. "Talis, wake up."

"Hello, sleepyhead," said Lilla with a smile as his eyes slowly opened. "You must have fallen asleep after your bath."

Talis smiled back, "Hello you," he whispered.

Lilla moved closer, and he put his arm around her. That was all it took, Lilla couldn't resist, and she suddenly pressed her lips to his and kissed him passionately. Lilla felt the moisture of his mouth, the strength of his embrace and his increasing passion. Then she went cold. No, she couldn't, not here, not now. It wasn't the right time. Lilla had decided this and knew this. There were too many problems to sort out without adding another. As she worked things out, she knew someone could come anytime. She lightly pushed him away and smiled at him as he looked confused.

"Soon, Talis, but for now, you need to eat. Come get dressed and have some food. You must be hungry. I suspect someone will fetch us to go and see your sister as soon as we have eaten," smiled Lilla.

"Ok, coming," smiled Talis.

Talis jumped off the bed and started to get dressed into the new clothes as Lilla looked on. He's definitely more comfortable around me now, thought Lilla. Simultaneously, Talis was trying hard to hide his confusion. Lilla was driving him crazy, she looked highly desirable in the dress, and the warmth of her body next to his had clouded his mind. He wanted her madly but didn't want to get attached as he suspected he would be dead before the war had been completed. Talis, to that mind, didn't want Lilla coming with him and risking any more danger to herself over what she had already done. Which was enough. He would feel more comfortable if she were thousands of miles away from the wars.

"What's to eat?" inquired Talis as he buttoned up his shirt.

"Well, some of it is now colder than it was, but there is a full assortment of meats, pieces of bread, vegetables and fruits," replied Lilla as she started to eat an apple.

"You better hurry," continued Lilla between bites.

Talis joined her at the table and ferociously attacked the meats and vegetables with the vigour of someone who hadn't eaten for days. But, as he told Lilla, the food was excellent and was too good to waste a morsel, as was the wine he drank heartedly.

After an hour, both of them had eaten until they could eat no more. Lilla had to fetch some food from her room as Talis had eaten non-stop as they talked. Talis was desperate to see and speak to Lauren and find out exactly what had happened to her after their father had been killed. Talis wanted to tell her about their adventures to get to Solanstar.

"Plus," Talis said excitedly, "Lauren will get to meet you, she will love you to bits, and you will love her too. You are very similar. I think I told you that before. Both of you are beautiful inside and out, yet full of mischief and fight," laughed Talis.

Lilla laughed whilst thinking this was high praise indeed for me. Talis thinks Lauren is the best, and him comparing her to me can only be a good thing.

"I will take that as a compliment, I think," giggled Lilla.

"I hope they come soon. I am getting restless, even though we have only been here a few hours," muttered Talis.

"I should suspect that they will arrive soon, Talis. But, hey, did you not note that the baths were filled when we entered, and when we were not looking, the clothes appeared, as did the food? I suspect they know when everything should happen, though I do not know how. It's all bizarre," exclaimed Lilla.

"To be honest, Lilla. I stripped, got in the bath, scrubbed, and dropped on the bed. Was so tired that I took no notice of anything. As soon as my head hit the pillows, I was gone. The next thing I knew was you were next to me," smiled Talis.

Not long after they had finished, there was a knock on the door, and an old elf entered.

"Good evening, my name is Hamil. I am sorry to disturb you. But, if you are ready, I have been requested to take you to where the healers have your sister, the young woman by the name of Lauren. She is awake and asks for you, Talis, son of Loren. The girl, Lilla, is also welcome to come, I am informed," the old elf said in a rather officious and disinterested formal tone.

"Yes, please, Hamil," said Talis eagerly.

"Come, Lilla, I think Lauren would love to meet you," he

continued to Lilla as he quickly rose from the table.

Lilla was suddenly filled with nerves and dread as soon as he spoke. What if Lauren doesn't like me? I know how close they are. Lauren could spoil everything. What am I to say to her to make her like me? The thoughts kept tumbling around Lilla's head as they followed Hamil to where the healers looked after Lauren. By the time they reached the door where Hamil had implied Lauren was, Lilla was a bag of nerves.

Talis over-zealously burst through the door. He ran across the room as Lauren's tearful face smiled in greeting. He flew into her arms, and both held each other for a long time as they laughed and cried simultaneously as they let all the emotions of the last month flood out. Lilla stayed in the doorway as she watched the twins embrace and share that bond only ones of a family could have, probably more as twins, as Talis had implied it was so with him and Lauren. What did he say? They shared the same spirit and thoughts, or something like that. Lilla felt a great well of happiness for them and a slight nagging feeling of envy.

"Wow, shortcake, you look like you've been in the wars," gasped Talis with concern.

Talis couldn't believe how pale Lauren looked. She was covered in scrapes and bruises up her arms, chest, and face and had a large laceration across her forehead. She looked worse than Lilla had when Selene attacked her.

"What happened? Come on, tell me all. I want all the gory details," asked Talis, speaking in a funny voice and pulling comical faces.

"I see you could have done with a bang on the head, fool,"

smiled Lauren weakly.

Then she looked over with a stronger smile at Lilla.

"I am sorry you have to spend time with this one. Talis, you are still the dumbest person I have ever met. Where are your manners? Please introduce your friend! Hello, I am Lauren," called out Lauren as she peered over Talis's shoulder with a cheerful voice.

"Hello Lauren, I'm Lilla", said Lilla as she smiled back.

"I am sorry, Lilla, come, come," beckoned Talis to Lilla.

Lilla came towards the bed.

"Lauren, my twin sister, Lilla......." he suddenly stuttered. Lilla suddenly realised Talis didn't know how to introduce her "…..a close friend," Talis finished uncomfortably.

Lauren looked at Talis and Lilla looking at each other as he spoke the introduction. Lauren had a good idea straight away of what was going off. He is such an idiot, she thought, feeling amused.

"Please, Talis, I know you are desperate for me to tell you what has happened since I left the village, and I am the same for what has happened to you. However, " she paused with a very flamboyant roll of her eyes. "I will speak of nothing else until both of you explain how you met and how long you have been together!" Lauren laughed heartedly, though she grimaced in pain.

Talis and Lilla looked at each other. Lilla blushed and laughed slightly nervously.

"Come on, Talis, I am not stupid," smiled Lauren.

Lilla felt straight away that she could bond with Lauren. Lauren seemed lovely.

"Ok, ok, shortcake, you win," replied Talis as he grinned.

They both went on to tell Lauren how they met and what had happened since leaving the inn. Lauren asked many questions and was particularly interested in their battle with Selene, the deathwalker's, and everything about Lilla's life at the inn and the story of her childhood. Lauren asked about his time before meeting Lilla after the attack on the village. How he had got involved with Berolarn.

Talis decided that now was not the best time to discuss their ancestry and what Berolarn had done with him regarding the hunger. It was frightening. Talis didn't really understand it, and he thought he might tell her with Berolarn present. Otherwise, Talis knew he could cause big trouble if he tried to explain himself. Lauren had a tendency to do the unexpected, and the truth about their heritage could cause the unexpected. So instead, Talis told her that Berolarn had been searching for both of them. That Berolarn had arrived at their village too late. He continued to search and found Talis in an abandoned hut. Talis left it at that.

They spoke for hours about Talis's adventures. When they had finished, Talis asked her to tell her story. Lilla then jumped in

"Talis, it can wait until morning. Look, Lauren is tired," said Lilla as she looked at Lauren's pale face, now looking drained.

"But I want to know," started Talis.

"No, Talis, she is too tired," said Lilla firmly. Lauren knew she really liked Lilla, an excellent ally to boss around Talis.

She took Talis's hand.

"Lilla is right, Talis. I am exhausted. It can wait until tomorrow. I am going nowhere," said Lauren as she assured Talis.

"Ok, both of you win", replied Talis. "However, I do want the full story tomorrow Lauren, no buts," he smiled. He had missed his twin more than he could put into words.

"Come, Talis, let's go," beckoned Lilla, and she took his hand. "It has been great to meet you, Lauren. We will be back tomorrow," she continued as she pulled Talis hard. Lauren couldn't help but snigger.

"Good night, Talis, Lilla," Lauren smiled as Lilla continued pulling on Talis.

Finally, Talis wished his sister good night, as did Lilla, as she finally got Talis to leave. As the pair walked towards their rooms, they carried on their conversation.

"I really like Lauren. She is nice and has a bit of a wicked side, I think," said Lilla grinning.

Joyfully, Talis replied, "Yeah, she is brilliant, and she definitely has a devil's side. I think she likes you a lot, too, not that Lauren dislikes anybody. But the way she looked at you and talked to you, it was like you were her sister. We talked freely."

Talis doesn't get it, does he? Thought Lilla.

Of course, Lilla had already got a good inkling of what Lauren was doing, which was fine. Lilla noted how Lauren looked at them and how when she listened, her facial expressions gave an impression that she was working out what I meant to Talis and what he meant to me. Lilla was sure of it. Lilla hoped that Lauren had gotten the right messages. She appeared to have. Lilla mulled over the last few hours. She really liked Lauren, which was true, and she was convinced Lauren liked her.

"I think we will become terrific friends, Talis. Hopefully, Lauren will be out of the hospital soon, and we can spend more time with her," said Lilla as they walked down the palace corridors.

"Ah, here we are," said Talis as they found their rooms. There was a moment of uncomfortableness as they entered the alcove area leading to their room doors. "I suppose we should get some sleep. We haven't really slept now for two days."

Hesitating momentarily before replying.

"Yes, you are right. Goodnight, Talis." Lilla said and then quickly kissed Talis.

She turned and entered her room, closing the door behind her as Talis wished her goodnight as the door closed. Talis entered his room and got undressed, lying on the bed. He quickly fell asleep.

It was late in the morning when Lilla entered Talis's room. She had slept well and was eager to wake Talis. She wanted to go see Lauren. Lilla also wanted both of them to look around and explore the courts of the elves. She was intrigued by the place. What Lilla had seen of the palace so far was spellbinding. So many different people as well. Everywhere people were walking about, singing and playing, laughing and eating. It looked as if there was much more to discover. Lilla also supposed she should go find Luther and see what he was up to.

Lilla saw Talis was still asleep. Excited and eager to make a grand entrance, she tiptoed to the edge of the bed and mustered as much effort as possible. Lilla jumped through the air and landed perfectly on a stricken Talis whose face was a picture as he abruptly woke up.

"God damn it, Lilla! You scared me to death," Talis said, smiling in disbelief, as he grabbed Lilla, threw her sidewards and rolled on top of her. Lilla was laughing uncontrollably at the look on his face when she woke him. As her laughter subsided, they looked at each other, and their eyes sparkled mischievously. Finally, Lilla raised her head, kissed him in one fluid motion, and kicked him off her.

"Come on, lazy head, get up and get changed. The day is already late, and we have lots to do," Lilla berated him as she walked across the room, sat down, and looked at the breakfast on the table.

Damn, she thought. Was it there when she came in? I wish I knew how they did that. She wasn't sure if breakfast had been in her room as she had rushed to see Talis. Lilla considered that it must be a form of magic as she picked at the food.

"Are you coming for breakfast or not," Lilla called over to Talis, who was still lying in bed.

Talis sat up and stretched.

"Yes, on my way," yawned Talis as he got up.

Then, he got dressed, walked over and sat opposite Lilla. Talis looked at the array of food in front of them, followed Lilla's lead, and started eating some of the delicate exotic meats and cheeses.

"I wonder if Lauren is awake? Perhaps we should go to the hospital wing first off," Talis asked questionably to Lilla as he ate.

"I think she should be awake. We left quite early last night and then slept in until late," answered Lilla. "If we go and spend a few hours with Lauren, but no longer Talis if she gets tired again. Then we can go and have a look around. Who knows, perhaps Lauren might be able to come for a little walk. We didn't actually ask how long she was to stay in the hospital or how long it would take for her to be well enough to leave. I think we should also seek out Luther and Berolarn. Let's see what they know and what we are doing next."

"Agreed, all good ideas," Talis replied. "Let's finish up and get moving."

Within ten minutes, they were walking toward the hospital wing. When they arrived, they were escorted to Lauren's room, where they found Berolarn talking to Lauren. Lauren smiled as she saw them both at the door's entrance.

"Ah, Talis and Lilla, come in. I am just about to leave," said Berolarn, beckoning them in. Berolarn turned back to Lauren, and he held her hand. "We will talk later when you have gained your full strength." Berolarn rose, "I will talk to you two later today. I will come and find you." He nodded and left.

"Morning," smiled Lauren.

They both replied their greetings to Lauren and commented how much better she looked as they came over and sat at the side of the bed.

"I feel a lot better, hate to say it, but seeing your ugly face, Talis, seemed to brighten the world and aid my recovery," laughed Lauren.

"Err … thanks … Lauren," said Talis as he and Lilla laughed.

"What does Berolarn have to say? Anything interesting?" inquired Talis.

"Not really. It was more us just catching up on the events after leaving the village. You know, what I did and things like that. I did try and ask a few questions, but Berolarn kind of brushed them off. Said all will be answered in good time. Something about a big discussion to happen, a council or meeting of everyone. All got a bit boring, to be honest," smiled Lauren as she rolled her eyes humorously as she answered.

"He is a strange one," laughed Talis. "I am never quite sure if he is telling you everything he knows, what he thinks you should know, or even what you want to hear. I don't quite trust him, though ..... He has always appeared to have our safety at heart," finished Talis as he looked towards Lilla.

"I agree," nodded Lilla. "But you will also find the same with Luther when you meet him. They are made of the same material. So you are never quite sure where you stand," she replied.

"Luther, that's your father, didn't you say" asked Lauren.

Lilla nodded, "I would say he is more my guardian and a serious annoyance," she laughed, "and definitely not by choice."

"Ah yes, you touched on your life at the inn and how you ended up there yesterday. Sorry," Lauren said sheepishly.

"No, don't worry, it's fine, and to be honest, it is quite a boring story," said Lilla as she mocked a yawn and chuckled.

"We are more interested in what happened to you and how you got here?" asked Lilla.

"That's right, shortcake," grinned Talis, "Come on, let's have it. What happened?"

Lauren blurted out all that had transpired since the attack on the village by the dark lord's forces. How she had been saved by the elven Princess Elisha after their father had fallen. That she and Elisha travelled in secret with three of her elven royal guard from the woodland near their village Keros. How they had set off towards the outpost at Morallis, part of the elven lands. She explained with great sorrow that as they neared the outpost, they had been hunted by these massive wolves called creoch, each with a goblin rider. That the elven royal guard, who she had befriended, had left her and Elisha, attacking the hunters. She presumed they must have died as they were outnumbered. Though through their sacrifice, they had reached the outpost.

She explained that the outpost had been attacked whilst they were inside. It was by what she could only presume was a tremendous force as the whole mountainside had shaken. They had run for their lives, making their way through a secret passage in the mountain. When they had come out, Elisha went to the priests her cousin had told her about and acquired horses.

"We then rid like the wind was behind us. We hadn't been riding for more than a few hours when we were being chased again. You could hear it in the darkness, It wasn't long before I could feel the enemy's hot breath on my neck, and then I remember a huge force ramming into the horse, and everything went dark." Lauren said to them as she explained how she became injured.

"Elisha told me a lone creoch had brought the horse down. Elisha wasn't sure if it was the initial fall that made me blackout and not awaken or if it was from the creoch throwing me. It had picked me up, shaking me probably just before the kill. Where this had given Elisha time to turn and hit the beast with a mighty blow. It threw me some considerable distance when Elisha dealt the blow, and I might have banged my head then. Anyway, my understanding was as it turned to face Elisha, she hit it with a death blow."

Lauren then shrugged as she thought back.

"My horse was dead, and Elisha somehow managed to get me on her horse and rode unhindered back to Solanstar. When I arrived, they rushed me straight to the healers, and here I am." But, Lauren laughed, "the enemy will need to try a lot harder to keep me down."

"It is interesting that we were chased by the vampire Selene and the deathwalker's and you by creochs and goblins. I wonder if they knew we were with Berolarn," commented Talis as he considered everything Lauren told them.

"When you think about it, no offence, shortcake, but we had the harder enemies to deal with," said Talis, laughing as Lauren tried desperately to hit the ducking Talis.

"I am not sure that's right, idiot. The enemies chasing me destroyed a keep that had stood for thousands of years," hissed Lauren in her usual droll manner," think about it, the woman Selene only destroyed the roof at the inn from what you said".

"To be fair, Talis, Lauren has an excellent point. However, I think I declare this a draw," argued Lilla. "Can you both stop now, or I might die laughing at you two fighting, over which has the best enemy," she giggled.

"Ok, ok, a draw," smiled Lauren.

Talis nodded and smiled in agreement.

"Lauren, do you think the healers would allow you to come for a walk in the palace gardens?" asked Lilla. "I think some fresh air would be good for you."

"Not only is that a great idea, Lilla. I don't need anyone's permission!" said Lauren, who winked. "There are clothes over there. Talis, get out while Lilla helps me dress" Lauren looked at him menacingly. Talis obliged and left the room as the girls got Lauren ready to sneak out.

They managed to move Lauren out of the hospital area without anyone noticing. It was only when they arrived back a few hours later that trouble was brewing. Berolarn was there with the Master Healer. After a severe telling-off and some arguing, the Master Healer finally agreed to allow Lauren to leave under Lilla's care. However, she was to stay with Lilla on this proviso, and Lauren was her responsibility. They readily agreed, helping Lauren collect her things as Berolarn talked to them.

"I was going to talk to you this evening, but it might as well be now. I spoke to King Ethera, who informed me a council meeting will be held the day after tomorrow. Now Lauren is as fit as she can be. All three of you are ordered to attend. Please feel free to do as you please tomorrow, but ensure you are not late for the council. It starts just after breakfast time. Be up and ready. The king is a stickler for punctuality," stated Berolarn.

Chapter 17 – The Kings Council

Lauren awoke early on the day of the council meeting. She stretched and glanced at Lilla, who was still sleeping peacefully. Lauren gently swung her legs out of bed and rose as carefully as possible, not wanting to wake Lilla. Then, grabbing a robe off the chair at the side of the bed, she put on the robe as she walked towards the double doors leading to the balcony.

On opening the doors, cold air rushed into the room. Quickly moving onto the balcony, Lauren pulled the doors shut behind her and pulled her robe tightly around her neck. She looked across the city, silhouetted in the rising morning sun that was breaking through the haze of the morning's winter clouds. Lauren stood there for some time, watching the hustle and bustle of a city beginning to wake and take its first tentative footsteps. Then, she felt the first drops of rain. Suddenly, the downpour came, and she dived through the doors with a crash and slammed them shut. Lilla nearly jumped out of bed in shock at the noise of the doors slamming and seeing a grinning, slightly wet Lauren.

"God damn you, Lauren! You scared me half to death," moaned Lilla as she slumped back down and buried her head into the pillow. Lilla berated Lauren in a muffled voice, "I was having such a lovely dream as well. I will not know what happens in the end." Finally, Lilla sat up again, "You have ruined it," she cried as she tried to hit Lauren with a well-aimed throw of her pillow.

Lauren ducked laughing.

"Come on, sleepyhead, it is time you were up anyway. It's the big day, council day," said an excited Lauren.

Lilla just scowled at Lauren and reattempted to lose herself in the bed. As Lauren started to quickly get dressed.

"I will go and wake Talis. You better be up and ready for breakfast by the time we are back," said Lauren as she pulled her boots on and left the room, shouting, "get up!"

Lilla lay there for a few minutes, thinking of many unsavoury things she would do to Lauren as payback. But, finally, she relented and climbed out of bed. After wiping the sleep from her eyes, Lilla hastily washed and got dressed. Surprisingly Lauren and Talis came in nearly immediately as she finished putting on her boots. She wondered how she got him out of bed and dressed so quickly.

"Morning, Talis," smiled Lilla.

"Hello, you," smiled Talis in return. "I presume by the time of day and that this one woke me up." he nodded towards Lauren. "That you suffered the same fate."

"She's a nightmare, Talis. She is non-stop. It's like having a child in the room," laughed Lilla.

"You pair needed to be up. Look, breakfast is ready as well," cried Lauren as she protested her innocence with a giggle.

Lilla looked over at the table. How do they do that? She must ask one of the elves. It was really annoying to her how food just appeared.

Lauren, Lilla and Talis sat down to breakfast. They started chatting about what would be discussed at the council. They went through what might be the options for them and the war that was coming. Going through the pros and cons of each as they ate.

"I wonder how we will know when the council is to start? Berolarn said it starts not long after breakfast, and well, we are done on that one," said Talis, looking down at the near-empty food platters. "Hopefully, it will be soon. I cannot stand waiting and hanging about."

"Shall we go see if we can find where it is held? We don't actually know," asked Lauren.

"I think that is ….." Talis started to say, breaking off as there was a knock on the door.

"Hello?" called Lauren.

The door opened, and Hamil, the old elf who had escorted them on their arrival, entered the room.

"I have come to escort you to the council room for today's meeting. It starts soon. Are you ready to go?" asked Hamil with a tone of disengagement and possibly resentment of having to take the three of them to the council, noted Talis.

As Hamil started to leave, they all jumped up and grabbed what they could as they ran out of the room and chased Hamil down. Hamil led them through a maze of hallways and large chambers of areas in the palace they had not seen. The splendour of the halls and rooms was not lost on them. Everything was furnished with the most extraordinary items they had ever seen. The windows were draped in silk, and the walls were decorated in scenes of woodlands, seas and mountains climbing into the sky. Exotic wooden furniture and vases were highly decorated with precious metals and stones inlaid into their surfaces. They walked on spellbound by its beauty.

Hamil told them they had arrived as they walked into a reasonably sized room that was sparse, with only a few chairs in each corner and a pair of large ornate doors at one end.

"You wait here until you are called," growled Hamil as he turned and left.

"Friendly sort is Hamil," laughed Lilla.

"He must be the only unfriendly elf here," grinned Talis. "He's definitely a bit strange!"

"They must select him for odd jobs, Talis, and your certainly odd," laughed Lauren.

Talis and Lilla both laughed.

"Hilarious, Lauren," grinned Talis.

The large double doors opened, and Berolarn beckoned them to follow.

"Ah, you are here. Good, everyone else has arrived, and the meeting is about to start. You will sit next to me," said Berolarn.

They walked down the corridor to another set of identical large ornate doors. As they approached the end of the passage, the large doors opened, and the companions could see a room full of people sitting around a massive round table. As they entered, Berolarn again motioned for them to follow him. He made his way around the table to four empty seats and pointed at the chairs for them to sit.

The companions all felt nervous as they started looking around the room. Every seat was taken by an assortment of elves, men and dwarves. They were either dressed in uniforms and armour belonging to soldiers and warriors or in garments only those of importance or nobility would wear. Finally, six elven soldiers bowed toward an older elf and left the room, closing the doors behind them.

Lauren, noticing Elisha next to an older elf, presumed he must be the king. Lauren wanted to crawl into a hole, as she had never felt so uncomfortable in her life. She just didn't belong here. Talis and Lilla were also having similar thoughts as the elf Lauren thought was the king stood up and spoke.

"Welcome, Welcome friends to those of us who are well met again and those who are new to the table of the king of elves. All of you are indeed welcome in these troubled times. I am King Ethera, and I thank all of you for making this meeting," said King Ethera, who nodded his head slightly in return as everyone nodded in homage to the king.

He then went around the room, pointing everyone out.

"My daughter, Princess Elisha Celestar, heir apparent to the throne of elves. Lady Ardith, Advisor to the king. Lord Guthrum, commander of the elven army. King's sister, Commander Eleran Celestar, is second in command of the elven army. Captain Aetherhard of the elven royal guard. Lord Strang, an emissary from the lands of Lara. Princess Cwen and Lord Guncar of the lands of Ellion. Then our good friends from the dwarven lands of Widdell. Lords Ballor, Heard, Helm and Bron. We have Berolarn, advisor to all the lands, the ranger Luther, and his ward Lillaanthisil. Finally, we have the children of Loran, Talis and Lauren," said Ethera as he acknowledged everyone in the room.

Talis and Lauren had never seen dwarves up close before. Studying them, they were shorter than men, maybe by a good head. Each one was stout in body, broad in girth. Lauren suspected they were powerful, looking at their arms. Their skin looked like well-tanned leather, and they all had extremely long beards braided in various styles.

"Where is Loran?" asked one of the dwarven lords.

King Ethera turned toward Talis and Lauren with a sad smile and then to the dwarves.

"It is with much sorrow I must inform the council that Loran fell to the dark lord's forces," replied Ethera.

"This is grievous news, King Ethera. How?" asked Princess Cwen.

"It is not for me to tell the tale or give much advice on Loran to this council Princess Cwen. I must pass this dubious honour to Berolarn, who is chief in understanding the enemy and all those who defy him. Berolarn, will you now speak," asked Ethera. "It seems fitting that you tell your tale first."

"Princess Cwen," said Berolarn, looking to Talis and then Lauren.

"Let us discuss Loran later in the story. I deem that much of what we will discuss on the events happening in the north and the wider outside world will be defined by what we consider. Loran is only part of this story."

Princess Cwen nodded in acceptance.

"We need to go back in time and discuss the history of our world. Much of what I will tell you has not been heard for thousands of years and is long forgotten. A significant amount of what I tell you will seem irrelevant, but I assure you that it will become relevant by the end. Where you might have heard of some aspects of these histories, I will surmise that you will probably liken them to legends, fables or fools speak. Therefore, I urge caution in dismissing anything I tell you. These are the histories of our world and all peoples," said Berolarn.

Talis saw Berolarn conjure up the flaming circle, visualising the stories he told just like he had when they first met. Much of what Berolarn discussed about the first three ages was the same as he had described to Talis already, though perhaps in more detail. This time, he briefly addressed that the gods had created life and given power to their firstborns, the dragons, in the form of magic. He detailed the gods giving birth to the Atlanteans and the Vampiri. The great war between these powers, and they're falling out of favour with the gods. How it had left them on the verge of extinction.

Berolarn discussed how the Atlanteans and the Vampiri withdrew to allow man's time, becoming the lost civilisations. Then men had nearly destroyed all, not with any magic or help from any gods. But with their thirst for science and natural resources. Berolarn detailed how they starved the world.

Using their machines, it was man who had finally torn the world as it was known apart, nearly killing all life. However, a new world was formed in the aftermath, and new life rose from the ashes. At the same time, the Atlanteans returned from their self-imposed exile in the form of elves and what remained of the Vampiri also returned.

"We reached our age, the fourth age," said Berolarn.

"Alongside the return of the elves and the Vampiri, the new

races were formed, dwarves, men, goblins and ogres. Each race claimed land areas and formed kingdoms and clans. They all struggled with the hardships brought down upon their heads by the sins of the third age. But slowly, over the centuries, each race to varying degrees started to thrive and began to look at their neighbours with greed, envy or fear. This led to occasional wars and disagreements. But the land began to heal, and the world slowly started to prosper," continued Berolarn.

"However, one of the races, the Vampiri, still had a burning hunger for blood and the lust for power. They never forgot the defeat by the Atlanteans, the elves. So much hate and malice had been eating away over thousands of years. They wanted to rule all and destroy the elves. They rediscovered what had long been forgotten by all as they searched for power, the gods. The Vampiri uncovered through much searching a vessel, an ark containing the three books of power. These were the scriptures of the gods."

"The white book, Hopenal. It is of the light, the sun, day and goodness and belongs to the god Sol. It is the book of life. The black book, Dealhanal. It is of darkness, the moon, night and evil and belongs to the god Hel. It is the book of death. Finally, there is the blue book, Neutar. This is the book of balance, belonging to the god Scalel. Neither good nor evil, it holds the world together as the night and day struggle for superiority," concluded Berolarn as he paused to take a sip of water.

"What is so special about these books," asked Ethera.

"They are a gateway to the gods, it is said," replied Berolarn as he put his glass down.

"They hold power so great that no one can stand against the

power that the knowledge can unleash. These books contain the keys to all magic in the world. This was the power they wanted. Once released, they believed the book's magic would make them the masters of all life. But they couldn't unlock the secrets of the books. Those who read the books were driven into insanity."

"For a long time, the books were locked away again. The Vampiri deemed the scriptures were too dangerous. Remember Talis, I told you that the Vampiri were neither exactly good nor evil at the start. They were just like men. However, they were born as a special kind of predator, a predator that craved blood. Hence the legend of the vampire was born. This carnivorous trait with a superior intelligence took them down evil paths and drove them to lust for power and control."

"Anyway, one among them, a young, ambitious Vampiri, full of hate, greed and a burning lust for power, found where the elders had locked them. His heart, already dark, was blackened beyond description as he slowly discovered the keys to unlock the words of the black book. His mind was destroyed, and his soul began to empty. This was Olgrich Validoral, the one who became known as the dark lord or the blood prince to his kind."

"Though it took time, finally, he mastered the black book, Dealhanal or the book overpowered him. Whichever it was, the elders of his kind could not now stand in his way. He took the throne of the Vampiri, and all of his kind paid homage. Great darkness would have spread across the land unchecked. Yet, there was a twin brother who had feared what his brother was becoming. He knew his brother's secrets and of the three books. In his fear of his brother and the dark book. Through great toil and persistence, he managed to break into the secrets of the white book and studied the text in secret from his brother. Not only could he read the scriptures. He embraced its words and shook off the shackles of the Vampiri and their lust for power."

"In secret, he gathered others around him of similar dispositions who were against the darkness engulfing their people. Using the white book, they learned of goodness, the ability to control their hunger, and their thirst to kill. Then, when the timing was right, they left the Vampiri lands, much to the anger of the dark lord. The brother had stolen the three books, and the books once again passed into history. The ones who had left were now known as the Solarians, the brotherhood and sisterhood of the Solarian Knights."

"They hid the books, never for them to be returned to the lands. For hundreds of years, they travelled the lands helping the races and became friends with the Atlanteans, the eternal enemy of the Vampiri. The elves."

"The Solarians left the Vampiri alone, thinking without the books, they had stopped the world from another catastrophe and Olgrich and the Vampiri would be content in their own lands. Why we thought this is something I cannot answer. We felt that as strong as the dark lord had become, he would not concern himself with the rest of the races and risk all-out war. But unfortunately, the Solarians….. were wrong! The dark lord and his host spent centuries preparing for world domination. Then, they started hunting down the Solarians when the timing was right, and the dark lord was at the height of his power."

"The dark lord began the great wars, where the Vampiri waged conquest against all. Kingdom by kingdom, they fell. They pursued and massacred the widely dispersed Solarian Knights. Until the world was within his grasp. He wanted to recover the book and make his final assault on the elves."

"The final remnants of the Solarian Knights gathered together for the final battle with their kin. Heavily outnumbered, they marched on the death lands carrying their god Sol in their hearts and knocked on his door, and he answered the call. Magic never seen before was unleashed on the land that day. As powerful as the Solarian Knights had become, the dark lord was mightier, and against him, no one could stand."

"But there was one solitary Solarian Knight who managed to cut a way through the Vampiri and reach the dark lord with the blessing of Sol. It was time for the twins. Yes, the dark lord's brother was that lone Solarian Knight. Brother against brother, twin against twin. It was he who fought the dark lord. The lands stood still as they fought. Even time had no meaning as they threw each other down. It appeared that the Solarian Knights were weakening, the dark lord would finally throw down his brother, and the world would be his. But fate intervened, and there was another twist when he was gloating over his brother as he prepared for the death kill. The Solarian summed all his energy into his sword arm and called on Sol for deliverance, and with that, he thrust his sword upwards at the dark lord. The blade cut through the dark magical defences of the dark lord and smote him with a blow that should be the final death blow for any mortal, and he fell. However, he managed to cry out to Hel and his children in his last gasps, and he was gone."

"His hordes dispersed as quickly as they had come, and the Solarians that were left counted just a few. We mourned the loss of our people and left. It was the biggest of all mistakes that were made on that day. Though conquered, we should have known that the dark lord was not gone. We should have marched on his castle, found him in his weakened state and ensured we cast him down, so he could never rise again. But in our grief for the loss of our kind that weighed heavy on our minds, we argued against it, not foreseeing him ever rising again. We left."

"For hundreds of years, there was no sign of the dark lord or his kind in any lands. Eventually, he and the Vampiri became a myth, a legend. No one ever went to the deathlands, and no one came out. It became part of the same legends, a cursed land you do not return from if you enter. As for the remaining Solarians, they continued their work for many years, spreading the word of Sol and helping the races. But, over the years, they drifted apart, some died, some disappeared, and they moved towards becoming a myth."

"This brings us to the present day. All indications are that the dark lord did escape death and has arisen. He has brought together all clans of goblins and ogres. All in this room have felt his arm stretching outwards and seen his horned wheel of chaos brandished by the goblins and ogres that have attacked your lands. The Vampiri now walk openly through the lands, as do other creatures of the night," finished Berolarn.

Berolarn sat down. He had been talking without interruption for a few hours. He reached for his glass, poured himself some water and silently started sipping from the cup.

"Thank you, Berolarn. That was a long tale on the history of the world and the insight into what happened to the dark lord. I am sure that most in the room, including myself, are not only grateful for your words. We have many questions about the tales you have brought to the council. I would also like to learn what is happening in the other kingdoms," said King Ethera.

"However, I bid all of us retain any questions until we have had refreshments and have stretched our legs. We have much more to discuss, and I need a rest before starting the next session, as I am sure does Berolarn," grinned Ethera towards the nodding Berolarn.

The king rose from his chair and called for his house staff. The great doors opened, and the room from which the companions had entered now served as a banquet hall. A giant table was now centred in the room, surrounded by chairs laden with food and drinks.

The council made their way into the banquet hall to the food and started to pick at it. Then, breaking into smaller groups, Lauren, Lilla and Talis grabbed some food, opened the patio doors, and went into the garden area. It was fresh and had a cutting winter breeze. The chill hit them, but they were too pumped from this morning's session. As well as all that Berolarn had discussed. They strolled down the garden paths to the ornate fountain in its centre and sat down.

"What do you make of all that, Talis?" asked Lauren.

"Yes, Talis, you've had these conversations already with Berolarn," stated Lilla.

"To be honest, the initial history of the world was near the same. Though I am not sure even now about its overall relevance. But the accounts of the dark lord were in far more detail than what he told me. For example, he never mentioned anything about gods, books of power or how the Solarians were formed," replied Talis.

"Why are we relevant to the dark lord, Talis? What has this to do with our father? I presume that Berolarn must have given you some inkling of this Talis?" asked Lauren, beginning to sound frustrated.

Talis looked at Lilla and then back to Lauren.

"You both know something! I saw the way you stared at Lilla. I insist you tell me right now, Talis Quicksilver!" demanded Lauren.

"Ok, it's not easy this, Lauren. I do not know much myself, and even now, it challenges me as I don't understand," said Talis as he looked around the gardens.

"When I was found by Berolarn, as I told you, we discussed the histories of this world. He also addressed the relationship between the Vampiri and Solarians. As you heard, they are the same but split by the paths they walk. The good and the evil. What he hasn't mentioned yet, and I haven't dared to tell you more because I don't really understand it, is that our father was hunted, and we are hunted because," Talis hesitated, "we are Solarians just like Berolarn. We are supposedly the last of our kind." Talis finished speaking as he continued to think about today's events.

Lauren looked at Talis and then Lilla and then laughed.

"Oh, c'mon, Talis, what tale is this? We are not Solarians. What power do we have!" exclaimed Lauren, laughing still, though Talis could now see something dawning on her face.

"Think Laura to the attack on our village and the ease at which Father cut through the enemy," said Talis, grabbing hold of Lauren's arms and looking deep into her eyes.

"Think how he knew what was happening. Think about the rumours we used to hear about him and how he laughed them off."

"They came for him, the blinding light, winged demons," muttered Lauren as she drifted off in thought.

"You know, don't you, Lauren. That all this weird shit is true," stated Talis firmly.

"Yes, it has all started to click together. But we have no power, Talis. We are like everybody else. We are just ordinary Talis," Lauren hissed back at Talis in apparent confusion.

"I would think that too, Lauren. I was of little use when we were attacked on our journey. But, when I was with Berolarn, back at the start when we were in the hut, he told me all that stuff. He did something else that I haven't told you," said Talis with apparent reservation in his words.

"What, Talis, will you get to the point," demanded Lauren.

"He did something to me. I am not sure what, but he unleashed what he calls the hunger or sometimes the thirst in me. He grabbed my arms and engulfed me in white flame. As he did this, I was consumed by pain and anger. It hurt so badly that I thought my mind was going to explode. But instead, I started to levitate and smashed through the hut's roof. I was there, fifty feet or more above the ground, trapped in a vortex of wind of flame, and all I wanted was to kill, hurt, and drink the blood of Berolarn. I wanted to do it so badly. But, you must understand, nothing else mattered but getting to Berolarn and ripping his throat out. He was shouting at me to fight the hunger, control it. At first, his words had no meaning, but slowly, they penetrated the fog in my brain. Then he called your name out, it totally smashed the hunger from my mind, and I dropped. The hunger and pain were gone. Everything returned to normal," answered Talis.

"What are you talking about, Talis? This cannot be true. It cannot," gasped Lauren in disbelief.

"I didn't tell you, as I do not understand it myself. So I took the coward's way out and hoped Berolarn would tell you, or I would speak to him again about it. Make more sense of it, I guess," explained Talis.

Lauren looked at Lilla accusingly.

"You knew?" trembled Lauren.

"I knew both of you were Solarian. What that really meant has no meaning to me," answered Lilla, who looked at Talis in slight horror. "But this thirst for blood and the need to kill is new to me."

Lilla shook her head in shock, looking pale as if the world had been torn from under her feet. Then, she turned and started to make her way back to the palace.

"It's time. We should return. I should suspect the council will be starting soon," croaked Lilla.

They saw a few stragglers in the banquet hall as they entered the palace. But most had returned to the council chamber and were now seated. So they made their way back to their seats. As they sat, Berolarn, who had been talking to the King, looked over and came across.

"Is everything ok?" asked Berolarn, seeing anger and confusion in their faces.

"I should have been told, Berolarn," spat Lauren venomously at Berolarn. "So should Lilla. Who knows? I could have killed her in her sleep!" she said sarcastically.

"Ahh, ok. It is good that Talis has told you; yes, you are right. I should have ensured you were told. But your brother should have told you somehow. That was always the plan I had in mind," replied Berolarn as he smiled. "I am pleased in that respect. Anyway, I was waiting until you regained more strength, and before I knew it, the king had called the council, and the opportunity had been lost on me."

"Well, I am really pleased that your plan has worked out," snapped Lauren.

"I know you are angry, Lauren, and it is partially justified. We will need to discuss more after the council. Please hold your anger until then. Remember, we are here for a greater purpose, and you sit in front of the king in his home," urged Berolarn.

"Don't worry, I am sure I will behave myself and not kill anyone yet," answered Lauren with sarcasm, and she folded her arms and looked directly at the king.

Elisha looked over at Lauren with concern. She saw that Lauren had a heated exchange with Berolarn and was upset. She must speak to her later, noting that everyone was now taking their places. The meeting was about to start again. First, she would check if Lauren was ok. Plus, as much as Elisha hated to admit it, she missed Lauren quite a lot. They had become very friendly on their flight from Lauren's village, and she wanted to see her anyway. Elisha's attention was drawn back to the meeting when her father started talking.

"Welcome back, everyone. Let us start. I have a question for you, Berolarn, and I am sure everyone would like to know more about many things. My question is about the dark lord. Where has he been, and why now?" said Ethera.

"Where has he been is an interesting question," said Berolarn looking deep in thought.

"The blow he received would have killed any mortal, of that, I am sure. Yet it is obvious he did not die. Instead, something about his being or the magic he harnessed continued to breathe life into his body. I surmise that he needed to spend centuries recovering, rebuilding himself into the force he once was. Perhaps he cried out to the gods, who aided his survival, or he had gained the knowledge to live through the black book, but again, this is just another hypothesis," confessed Berolarn.

Berolarn got up and made his way to the centre of the floor as he continued to talk and look around the council.

"Why now, indeed, why now. Is it because the dark lord has finally gathered his strength to openly proclaim his survival and continue with the conquest of the free world? You would argue that he is stronger in terms of numbers than he was in the last great wars. In the last wars, he scavenged the plains of the land with just his kin and, relatively speaking, a smaller host of servants. This time he has realised perhaps a mistake he made in arrogance, thinking he could defeat all with his power. This time he will not make the same mistake. He has brought all the goblin and ogre clans together for the first time under his banner. We had witnessed some of his demon hordes first-hand when we were en route to Solanstar. The deathwalker's, creatures of the night, created through the death of the evilest, lured only by the promise of more death, and they are willing to serve only ones of the highest intelligence and power."

"Is it due to the beginning of the end of the Solarians? He would remember the time he was mortally wounded. He would remember how close he was to winning and annihilating the Solarians. The dark lord appears to have been planning the erasure of the Solarians since then, and to me, at least, it is now clear as the sun dawns that he has slowly been assassinating any Solarian his agents of death found. I didn't see it at first. The Solarians were widely travelled and dispersed. It only became apparent when I realised he was hunting Loran and his children. He nearly succeeded, and he now feels he has nothing to fear. Once many took arms against the Vampiri. Now there is none."

"Or perhaps, is it that he searches for the black book of Hel. One of the three books of the gods, this book gave him all his power and opened a portal to the gods. His tome studies would have been incomplete, and he would crave this book over all other things. It would give him more strength. If he mastered all its content, a power that has never been seen walking in these lands would be unleashed. Or maybe something else? I am sure these are all very salient reasons, and there is probably more," concluded Berolarn.

King Ethera noted that Berolarn did not speak directly of the children of Loren or of Loren himself. Though he had been asked to do so. This was quite interesting to the king, who now wondered what Berolarn was up to. But, of course, you could never entirely trust a Solarian and their decisions.

Their hearts were true and always in the right place, but the paths they guided others on and what they hid were always made for the greater good. In doing so, they missed the point that sacrifice and decisions were the choices of the free and only fate could decide a destiny. It was not something that should be manipulated to try and create the desired ending. You should never contradict and attempt to change the given path.

Even as great as Berolarn was, no matter how much knowledge he had acquired or how much he worked for the benefit of all the races. He really missed this vital point. The Solarians are not gods. His ancestors, the Atlanteans, had fallen into this trap and meddled with nature's forces. Thinking that they equalled gods. The result was they were cursed with the Vampiri walking the land.

Ethera decided he would wait right until the end of the council before any decision was made by himself. Ethera knew he could be rash and would be stubborn.

"This is good and full of maybe's, my Lord Berolarn," said one of the dwarves. Talis thought it was Lord Ballor as Berolarn nodded toward one of the dwarves.

"However, as much as I understand the magic and how great it lives within the dark lord and ones such as yourselves. We, the dwarves, see nothing but blood made by steel," continued the dwarf.

"Forgive us, Lord Bellor and to all of you," said Ethera as he looked apologetically around the room.

"Unfortunately, you suffer even in these hours of need, the conversations of two old men, who constantly forget themselves and all around them and battle in debate."

Lord Bellor nodded towards the king.

"We will now hear the fate of others around the table before continuing with the specifics of the dark lords' design. The elves understand the loss of lives by steel and fire. We lost the ancient outpost at Morrallis to the enemy, and all who stood within perished, including king's sister Eleran Celestar's son Jerrel," revealed Ethera, who nodded to his sister.

The dwarf lords all stood up and bowed toward Princess Eleran.

"We are sorry for your loss, as we mourn all who have lost their lives to this evil," said Lord Bellor.

"Thank you, Lord Bellor, and your words mean much to me. Even though I mourn their passing. They had full lives, and they now travel on to the next stages as they walk in the halls of Sol," said Princess Eleran. "Please, though, tell us what is happening in your lands.

"Thank you, Princess Eleran…..King Ethera," said Lord Bellor nodding to each.

"It is true that we have had many years of conflict with the goblins as they attempt to raid our lands out of Jeliah and the deathlands. However, we have guarded the rest of the races and haven't begrudged this. No, we have seen it as an honour for all dwarves, and I ask, what more incredible honour can there be? Than to be protecting the lands from the scum of the goblin race. For centuries, we have spent many years guarding the passes and our home in the Milnmor Mountains. To this end, the lands have had relative peace. We have ensured that the goblins and ogres have not walked freely in other lands and have asked for no gratitude."

"Over the last few years, the situation has changed quite dramatically. We initially saw more skirmishes, more probing at our defences. Perhaps we took little heed to this change as we easily repelled the invaders. In retrospect, we feel they looked at the dwarves with intelligence not usually seen in goblin scum. They were actually looking for and working out our weaknesses. Yes, the probing of our defences was no more than gathering intelligence. With this newfound knowledge, they understood how we moved troops between passes and the type of defences we deployed.

In the summer, we were surprised by a sudden attack. It came on all fronts, but the most fierce fighting was at the Gates of Duldor. We believe that concentrating their attack here allowed them to cut off any support to our forces at Heavens Gateway. We lost many numbers holding the passes and repelling them from the Gates of Duldor. But we lost Heavens Gateway, the largest of the passes. Now the goblins can have free run of the lands. Great numbers can march through the pass at once with ease. We are looking to retake it as we speak, but it will not be easy. The thing about the gateway is that it is easy to defend when held with numbers. It is at the highest point in that part of the range, and it looks down on all around it."

"We are hard-pressed on all fronts, and it is only through the bravery and might of the dwarves that the dark lord's forces are not flooding into the land. However, we fear that soon we might be overrun, as the goblins outnumber us by at least twenty to one. Therefore, we come to request aid where possible….." continued Lord Ballor, who didn't manage to complete his last sentence.

The dwarf was interrupted by Berolarn.

"Lord Ballor, I think the forces you have seen are just a smaller part of the dark lord's forces. When the time is right, I feel he will unleash his full force on the lands. I fear it will not be long before his plans are set in motion," said Berolarn.

There was muttering around the room after Berolarn comments.

"I think he will march on all the lands soon," added Berolarn.

"This is grievous news," answered Lord Bellor. "What is to be done? We cannot protect all the lands at once if the forces are as great as what you imply. What of the lands of Man," he said, looking at Princess Cwen, Lord Guncar and Lord Strang in turn.

Lord Strand was the first to speak.

"I cannot speak for anyone but Lara, but our exposure to war has been limited. But we have engaged with goblin forces, and we answered the call. Goblins have not entered our lands in centuries. We understand the tide is changing. All I can offer on hearing everything that has been put forward in this council is that you will have the full support of Lara," said Lord Strand.

"We voice similar experiences in Ellion, though I wonder why Ascalon and Jalhorn have not answered the call," said Princess Cwen. "As always, Ellion will support all actions recommended by Berolarn. Our history with the Solarians is long, and often did they aid us." Then, nodding to Berolarn, "What is your advice, Berolarn?"

"Before you answer that question, Berolarn, can I ask more of the fate of Loran and why his children are here? I think everyone needs you to answer this," interrupted King Ethera.

"As for Ascalon and Jalhorn, Princess Cwen. I should think they are busy battling with their own inner politics. But, is it not true that both areas are always slow to act as they debate for years what actions to take," shrugged Ethera. "Please, Berolarn, I am keen for everyone to know the tale around Loran as he was a leading light in our battles with the darkness."

"You are right, King Ethera," said Berolarn. "Loran, as many of the lands know, was a Solarian Knight of the highest order. So long did he lead the Solarians across the land, bringing peace and the word of Sol. Loran walked many paths that none have walked as he went about his life's quest. Over hundreds of years, he followed his quest, and the years started to sit heavy on his heart. Though he had begun to move into his senior years, he met a girl and fell in love. He then disappeared out of sight and out of mind for most."

"I came across Loran once by chance on my travels. Much to my shock, Loran, the greatest of the Solarian Knights, was in a town in Ascalon. We spent most of the night and the following day in discussions and discussed many great things. Evidently, Loran had found peace in life, and though he had much sorrow of losing the girl, who had become his wife, he was happy with his new purpose. He had decided he was dedicating himself to looking after their children. Loran would interfere no more in the lives of the races. He felt he had fulfilled that part of his destiny. Hence, no one has seen anything of Loran across the lands for thirty years."

"When it was clear that the dark lord had arisen again, I searched out the histories of our world kept at Kin-Kathenal, the hidden home of the Solarians, and I spent much time looking for clues on how the evil could be stopped. Eventually, I found ancient scriptures of a long-forgotten prophet, and much of the tomes were hard to understand. But reading between the lines, they wrote of a plague on the land. A dark mind and hand that destroyed all in his path. The prophet foretold that there would be those born as twins, who are split by birth, by sex and by race, that would arise out of the flame of night, and if they came through their trials, they could bring about the fall of the dark lord. It talked of ancient mystical power, a stone called the Dragonheart and that it must be found before the darkness takes it. Otherwise, all will be lost."

"It wasn't clear to me straight away what this meant. Then by chance, I met Luther on the way to Solanstar, and he had heard rumours that the dark lord's hosts were searching for Solarians and were keen to find the one called Loran and his children. I knew where Loran had been but had no idea where he was now. So Luther and other rangers searched for him, and I appealed to King Ethera to send search parties out."

"Loran had actually reappeared sometime ago in Keros with twins, one a female and one a male. He had taken over an inn and made a new life as a simple innkeeper. His children, you see before you, had grown up and still were with their father. Luther sent word to me that they had been found. I raced towards the village of Keros, as did Princess Elisha, who had tracked them to the village. But unfortunately, we were moments too late. The goblins and a score of Vampiri attacked the village. In the heat of battle, Loran was smitten down by the Vampiri, and he was gone. Luckily Princess Elisha managed to get Lauren out, and I later found Talis. We then made our way to Solanstar, facing dangers, as you have heard along the way, such as the attack on Morallis and the deathwalker's."

Berolarn considered what to tell the council. Firstly, he must keep it a secret why the children of Loran were essential to defeating the dark lord. Neither this council nor Talis nor

Lauren should know why the dark lord searched for them; not all was clear to him. He had told them enough, of that he was sure. The children would need to walk the steps and let the truth find them at the right time. Yes, it was enough to know they needed to search for the Dragonheart stone. It was the first part of the quest to be completed. After all, if they were unsuccessful in this endeavour, then everything else would probably not matter.

Berolarn continued, "We have already discussed the dark lord and his quest to unleash the Vampiri as the dominant race and rule over all others. We have discussed that he would have been successful in the great wars if he had not been stopped by the Solarians. We have mentioned that Loran was a Solarian Knight of the highest order, and the dark lord would know if anyone could have stopped him, it would be under his leadership. The dark lord would have known of the children of Loren through his spies and would know of their Solarian heritage. This would have been of concern and driven his thought process and perhaps has caused him to show his hand and come out into the open. He is well versed in the histories of all races and perhaps is aware of the prophecy and has correlated it to the children of Loran."

"What say the children of Loran?" said Lord Gunthar, looking directly at Talis and Lauren, who looked at each other.

They turned back to face the question and saw everyone, including Berolarn staring at them. Lauren reached under the table and held Talis's hand.

"The words being spoken about our father are not the words we would speak about our father, and it is not the man we knew. This much is true. Both Talis and I have perhaps been very ignorant of what is happening in the world. Though both of us were well educated by our father."

"Yet, already, we have seen pain, suffering and death at the hands of this so-called dark lord, and we both have nightmares about what could be. We have no powers. I didn't even know of our Solarian heritage until today. We are as ordinary as the next person. But I think I can speak for myself and Talis." Lauren said, looking at Talis.

"We will have no peace, and our lives have changed forever. We will have no sense of normality whilst the dark lord walks the lands. If we must act and attempt to undertake a journey or quest as advised by Berolarn and this council. Then we will do so. We may not go with much hope. But we go with the knowledge we did everything we could," finished Lauren as she squeezed Talis's hand tighter.

Berolarn nodded approval towards Lauren and Talis and gave them a quick smile.

"King Ethera and all who are gathered in this room, what are your thoughts? It seems to me we have two paths to follow. Our first path will be to gather what armies we can and prepare for war across the lands. The second path is for a small group to go on a quest to find the Dragonheart stone and find the meaning of its riddle," said Berolarn looking around for agreement.

"Berolarn, forgive me for questioning you, but we do not know where the Dragonheart stone is. I have never heard any tale of it," said Elisha.

"I think I know where it is, Princess. Though much is dark to me, it resides in Caledonia. The scriptures show me as much," replied Berolarn.

"What foolishness is this" cried one of the dwarves. "No one goes to Caledonia. It has the same evil as the deathlands. The berserkers that reside there kill all who go to their lands."

"I have walked these lands, my good fellow," said Luther. "It is not for the faint-hearted. Indeed, it is from a world of another age and is a world of ice. But I can guide the way. I know of the inhabitants, too. Yes, they are a fierce collection of humans; you should not cross their path foolheartedly. But, the Celtic tribesmen are not wanton killers; if we are hard-pressed and walk towards them, arms open in peace, they will help."

"You will never get to it. The whole Jeliah will be there to meet you, and you must go through the goblin's lands," scoffed Lord Bellor.

Luther smiled, "We will not go by land. We would go by sea."

Talis was not liking the sound of this and was now cursing Lauren's offer. He had never been to the sea and had no wish to go on a boat. He heard the stories of ships sinking and people drowning.

"Good, we have a plan forming already. It seems clear to me that we should go to Caledonia," said Berolarn.

King Ethera stood up.

"It seems you have already decided your plan, my good friend," smiled Eleran, looking over to Berolarn.

"I find it difficult to argue, though the search of Caledonia seems foolhardy. I think we will need to discuss with more focus on the preparation for war than in today's meeting. If everyone is agreed in principle, do we all agree with Berolarn's proposals?" asked Ethera.

The whole room chorused "I" in return.

"Let us close today's session, as I feel tiredness creeping onto me for one. Then, Berolarn, we will also discuss the party to go with Talis and Lauren at a later date," said King Ethera.

"And me," shouted Lilla before she could stop herself. She put her hand over her mouth as soon as the words came out. Much to the amusement of the king, who smiled at her.

"Yes, and you, Lilla, will be considered," answered Ethera soothingly as he looked from her to the stern-faced Luther. "We will make plans for war in a separate council. I now close today's council."

On King Ethera's last words, the doors to the room opened, and the six royals' guards returned and escorted the elves, except for Princess Elisha, who spoke quickly to the King, who nodded. She then came over to the companions, followed by Berolarn.

"Well, that was a long meeting, and I could do with refreshments. Luther, would you like to come with me to eat? I am sure the others will either find their way back to their rooms or where ever they ask the princess to take them, speak soon," and then Luther and he were gone. Talis looked around the room and noticed that everyone else had dispersed.

Chapter 18 – Innocent Times

It had been two weeks since the council, and they had not seen much of Berolarn or Luther. Occasionally in passing, they would have ten minutes of conversation. Lauren had moved into her own room as she had improved immensely and, as she put it, didn't need babysitting anymore. This meant she sometimes spent time with Princess Elisha away from the others. But, in general, Lauren, Lilla and Talis spent all their time together and were left alone to do as they pleased within the palace walls and the surrounding city. They were called to no more meetings, and no one had given them any indication when they would be leaving. In that time, they had walked the whole length of the city.

Today they were visiting the Grand Bazaar. Standing alone in the middle of an ornately paved square, an enormous domed building sits in the middle with four significantly sized rectangular buildings feeding off the dome. Lauren thought it must be like a ginormous cross. Inside it was a labyrinth of passageways running back and forth like a giant comb. Each aisle was full of small shops and stalls. They were spellbound by the wares for sale as they wove their way through the halls.

There was every form of exotic clothing and materials you could think of at one store. Then, walking past another shop, they were hit by the most beautiful smells. As they entered, they saw it was wall to wall full of spices, teas and sweet treats. Another was full of ceramics, the next one cushions, pillows and small textiles and the next one metalware. Every place they went had something different. As they walked, Talis felt drawn towards a shop that caught his eye as the girls were just about to enter a clothing shop.

"Wait here, he said, back in a minute," he called as he turned and walked away.

"Where is he off to?" Lauren asked Lilla.

"No idea. Forget about Talis," said Lilla as she peered into the street and tried to see where he had gone.

They spent several minutes or more looking around the shop, picking up various clothes, remarking how pretty this item was or that it would look good on you this dress. When finally, Talis entered with a big grin on his face.

"You found anything you like," asked Talis.

He then grinned as he saw the shop owner running around bringing them various items and telling them he would do them a good deal and how it was made for them.

"You have to be kidding! I think it is more is there anything we don't like," laughed Lilla as Lauren explained to the shop owner that they would return later.

"Come on, let's go," grinned Lilla, pushing Talis back out the door with Lauren quickly following them.

"Where you been, Talis?" asked Lauren.

"Ah, I will tell you when we return to the palace. Got you both a surprise. You will be astounded when you see what I have for you," laughed Talis.

Rolling her eyes, Lauren humorously chided Talis to Lilla. "He has the sense of a goblin. It is bound to be stupid."

Talis pretended to feel hurt, clutching at his chest in mock pain.

"I have never been so offended, shortcake. But, you wait. You will be surprised how good it is," grimaced Talis sarcastically.

"The only surprise will be if I don't chuck what it is within the hour," muttered Lauren under her breath, just loud enough for both of them to hear.

All three of them laughed.

When they were finally done and left after a full day of walking around the Bazaar, Talis moaned how tiring walking around shopping with them two was. But, whereas Lilla and Lauren agreed they were tired, it was the best place they had ever visited, and the only downside was Talis following them around.

When they got back to the Palace, they all went to their rooms to get washed and changed and then they would meet at Talis's room to eat, knowing that food would be ready for them. An hour later, they sat in his room, around the dining table, discussing how brilliant their day had been and all the wonders they had seen.

"Talis, what have you bought us both? I am ready to be underwhelmed," mumbled Lauren as she sat eating a banana. Talis reached out and expertly pushed Lauren's feet off the table.

"Manners cost nothing, shortcake!" beamed Talis as Lilla laughed.

Lauren thought about attacking him. But she decided she

was more interested in what he had bought than causing him pain. She would sort the pain out later.

"Fool, what have you bought," demanded Lauren as Talis jumped up and walked over to his bedside table.

"This is for you," teased Talis as he walked back.

Talis passed Lauren a beautiful jewelled pendant. At its centre was a pear-cut sapphire gemstone held inside an ornate platinum three-claw surround with a halo of scintillating round-cut diamonds. The delicate stones enriched the blue hue of the sapphire, accentuating its eye-catching pear shape. Its brilliance shone in the candlelit room.

"It is like the one father had," cried Lauren in amazement, "except it is a sapphire, not an emerald …… but the surround is the same," she continued as she held it in her hand and looked closely at it.

"I have fathers. I forgot to tell you," said Talis as he pulled the pendant out from his pocket and passed it to her.

"I was right. The pendants are exactly the same," whispered Lauren excitedly. She was obviously amazed as she compared them. "It's only the stone that is different. How did you see this? How did you afford it?" she looked up at Talis quizzically.

"It was bizarre, to be honest. We were walking around, and as we passed the jewellery shop," said Talis pondering a few seconds, then grinned. "I felt like I was being drawn to the shop as if I was being called, cannot really tell you what it was. This sounds really weird, but everything has been strange for some time now. I had father's pendant around my neck, and it felt kind of warm and alive when I entered the shop."

"Once inside, the shop owner, a very old man, comes to me."

"Ah, young man, you have arrived. What can I do for you ….. come ….. come ….. over here, the old man says to me with a weird grin on his face."

"Then he bent down under the counter and pulled out two boxes."

"You have a sister and a very close friend, I hear? Yes ….. yes, you do, and I have some beautiful things for you, Talis ….. ah yes, here we go, he continues."

"Then he proceeded to open a small rosewood box with a golden sun inlaid on the lid. He pulled out the sapphire pendant and said,"

"This is for your sister. It is ancient and beautiful, to match what you already hold, he says,"

"and I didn't think anything of it. But the old man knew I had father's, I am sure of it. So then he passed me this and pulled out a pure platinum ring set with four sapphires and one diamond mounted inside the platinum, set perfectly at equal distances around the ring."

"He says this is for your special friend. They both must wear them all the time on their journeys, and you must wear yours."

"As you can imagine, I was baffled, holding these two immensely expensive items, and I told him I didn't have much money on me."

"The old man says not to worry. He is a friend of the king and Berolarn. That they will pay in kind later. Hurry, hurry; Lauren and Lilla will be waiting. As he finished speaking, the old man nearly pushed me out the door."

"It didn't even dawn on me that the old man knew our names. I was just excited to give you these," concluded Talis smiling as he passed the ring to Lilla.

Lilla looked at the ring with the similar curiosity that Lauren had shown. She was in love, it was the best thing she had ever seen, and she forgot everything Talis had just said about how he had acquired the pendant and just thought about how much Talis cared for her. She put it on, and it fitted perfectly, and she felt warm and at peace as soon as it slid onto her finger.

"Thank you," Lilla whispered to Talis as she welled up with emotion.

"Talis, how do we know they are safe?" asked Lauren. "It all seems a bit too much. You have even alluded to it yourself."

"I am sure they are. The pendant I wear called me in, I am sure of it. Yes, how the old man knew us, I don't know. But he said he's a friend of the king and Berolarn, and we are in the elven city. So you are probably worrying too much," said Talis.

"Put it on and see how you feel. How do you feel, Lilla?" Talis asked, looking excitedly at Lilla.

"I feel happy and weirdly warm," smiled Lilla.

Hesitantly Lauren slipped the pendant over her neck, and yes, she could feel its warmth as it fell down her front onto her chest and the heat spread over her body. It, funnily enough, started to calm her fears about it. Lauren actually found she was fighting this calming feeling.

Finally, she decided to wear it for the time being. Otherwise, there would be loads of grief from Talis. But first thing, however, I will go and find Berolarn and ask him to check what it is and if it's safe, she thought.

"It is really nice, Talis. Thank you, I guess. Though you didn't really pick it yourself," Lauren exclaimed and laughed.

"Well, I love mine, Talis," said Lilla as she leaned over and kissed him.

"Please, can you wait until I have gone," yawned Lauren and then smirked.

The three of them continued to discuss the day as they finished eating. Talis and Lilla had generally forgotten about the gifts. But Lauren was itching to leave and find Berolarn. So finally, after completing their meal and thirty minutes of small talk, Lauren feigned tiredness and excused herself.

Within ten minutes of asking various people, she found Berolarn in the Library.

"Lauren, what a pleasant surprise," said Berolarn, looking up from a book he was reading at one of the Library tables.

"All alone?" he inquired.

"Hello, Berolarn, yep, all alone. Can I discuss something with you?" asked Lauren.

"Of course, I was just reading a few things about Caledonia. Not sure if you are aware, it is mostly a desert of ice, bitterly cold and doesn't have many inhabitants except for the Celts. Lauren, it is worth noting that they are savage tribal warriors descended from the third age and retain much of what they are from that time. We will be looking to avoid them as they do not take kindly to any entering their lands unless you know the clan. Even the goblins avoid these lands," commented Berolarn.

"Nonetheless, Caledonia is where we go, and to most, it is usually called the icelands rather than Caledonia. Perhaps not the best of times to be going during winter," stated Berolarn.

He then realised Lauren was not overly interested in what he was saying.

"Anyway, how can I help? Is something troubling you," asked Berolarn.

She nodded as she sat down opposite Berolarn.

"Today, Talis, Lilla and I went to the Bazaar," Lauren continued, telling him the story Talis told them about the pendant, the ring and the old man. Berolarn passed no comment as she told her story.

"….. what do you think?" asked Lauren.

"Can I see the pendent?" asked Berolarn.

She pulled the pendant from under her blouse and passed it to Berolarn. She noticed the warm feeling disappear, which she relayed to Berolarn as he held the pendant up in front of his eyes and slowly rotated it.

"I sense no evil," Berolarn pondered for a moment.

"This is very rare, Lauren. Indeed the only one I knew that still existed belonged to your father. In all that had happened, I had forgotten about its existence. I am not overly sure what it does, but it is endowed with a very potent form of magic. That much is clear to me. It was a gift of the god Sol. They are called the Palantari Stones, given to the head priest and paladins, knights of the highest order. I believe there were four in total. Each one had a different gemstone that portrayed its own traits and empowered the user with unique capabilities specific to the owner's pendant. It also had a matching ring, making me wonder if the ring given to Lilla was one of these. How intriguing, you say it feels warm when you wear it," Berolarn finished off as he was lost in thought.

"Yes, it feels as if it is alive. Lilla implied the same with the ring, and Talis said it was the same with the pendant he got from our father," said Lauren. "Though he never really thought about it, he guessed it was just him, making a connection to our father."

"Yes, I am convinced that is what they are. You see the shape of the stone, cut similar to a pear. It represents a shield, shaped this way, as it acts as a protector of the wearer. I would have to look through the vaults of knowledge to see what gift each gemstone empowers the user with. But, you will be safe wearing these. In fact, I suggest you do, as they appear to have been gifted for that purpose," said Berolarn.

What was intriguing, Berolarn, was the old man who had given them to Talis. Lauren's pendant was definitely not showing any signs of an evil curse. Instead, it was imbued with ancient magic beyond his skill to understand. He was convinced that it was a Palantari Stone. It was the same as Loren's and radiated a similar aura.

Who was the old man who gave them to Talis? Who was he? It couldn't be, could it? Perhaps it was time for him to try and revisit the Solarian ancestral home. Did he have time? Probably not, he mused. He had some tough choices he would have to make, Berolarn thought as he bid Lauren farewell.

After Lauren left them both, Lilla and Talis remained and continued to talk about their day at the Bazaar. Lilla was excited by the ring Talis had given her. She had never really had any lovely gifts. Biggy had no idea, and Luther was just damn practical in everything. When her birthday came around, what was in question was if it was her actual birthday. It was just another day for her. No presents, no gifts, nothing. For the first time in her life, she felt special. Talis had made her think that, and she felt fierce love for him at that moment. Lilla knew she had met the right one here. He was kind and caring, funny in an awkward way and very unlike Lauren in that respect.

Talis was strong, muscular and quite handsome. He was unlike any man she had ever met. She had generally been repulsed for one reason or another by all her suitors back at Lowedom. Lilla knew she was good-looking, many people had even told her how pretty she was, and Lilla, therefore, had been given the benefit of many choices of would-be husbands and lovers, but she always rejected them all. However, the minute she met Talis, she was attracted to his village charm. Ok, she reasoned, this Solarian problem he had was something she couldn't work out, and his weird eyes were a strange part of the charm. Talis was pretty unique in this respect. But everyone has a problem, don't they? No point worrying about that. She smiled at him again. Yes, he was the one.

Talis was really happy with his gifts. Looking at Lilla's smiling face, she seemed pleased with her ring. He was actually glad that Lauren had left. As much as he loved having Lauren about, it did leave limited space to spend time alone with Lilla.

Lilla stopped smiling and looked deep into his eyes. She had been anticipating this moment for some time now.

"Talis," Lilla seductively spoke to him, "kiss me."

She placed her hand gently on his cheek, leaning forward. Lilla slowly brought her mouth to his. Then, slipping her hand round to the back of his head, she pulled him forwards as her tongue darted into his mouth, letting his tongue become entwined with hers.

Talis slowly started to move his right hand from her waist towards her breast, and reaching it, Talis felt Lilla shiver and her heart beating fastly. Then, pulling her up as he stood, Talis bent down slightly, and Lilla could feel him lifting her dress and running his hands up the back of her thighs, and he was lifting her. Lilla wrapped her legs around his waist. She continued to kiss him passionately as he carried her over to the bed and slowly lowered her down.

Talis slowly kneeled at her side and started unbuttoning her dress, teasing Lilla's flesh with his hand as he leaned forwards, giving small caressing kisses as he worked each button undone. When he reached her waist, she shivered in nervous excitement as he slowly worked his hand across her stomach and tenderly brought his right hand back up until he cupped her breast. Lila could feel the roughness of his fingers playing with the hardness of her nipple. Lilla then felt him remove his hand and pull her dress down to her waist. Talis was then back squeezing her breasts, tongue gliding back and forth across her skin. Then his hands were gone as he returned to directly looking into her eyes, and he continued to gently kiss her. Finally, Lilla felt his hand return to her legs, caressing and moving upwards, reaching her inner thigh and then sliding his fingers underneath her undergarments. Again, Lilla shivered as he gently caressed and moved inside her.

Lilla couldn't help herself any longer as she pushed him

backwards and began to help him pull off his clothing until he was naked. Lilla pulled Talis's back towards her as her hand caressed his manhood. Looking deep into his eyes again.

"Make love with me, Talis," Lilla whispered passionately.

Talis quickly helped Lilla take off her dress. He gently parted her ankles, and then she felt him draw apart her knees. Talis gently moved on top of her, and the kissing became more passionate. As she was in mid-kiss, Lilla felt him suddenly spreading deep inside her moving slowly deeper, giving her a wonderful throbbing feeling. She gritted her teeth as spasms rocked her body as he moved backwards and forwards. As their bodies entwined as they made love, the passion increased slowly, the pleasure they were experiencing continued to increase, and the excitement was now overwhelming for Lilla and Talis. The movement's rhythm and ferocity grew; Lilla suddenly felt a deep warmth inside her as he shuddered and slowed down. The hotness flowed back all around her. Talis then started to kiss her more tenderly now than passionately, and after some time of continued kissing, he slid off to her side, gasping for breath as she was.

Smiling to herself as Talis looked at her and ran his fingers through her hair. Lilla thought this was how she imagined it would happen and how it would feel with Talis. The girls in the village had said the first time with the right person would be so special.

She loved this man, she loved sharing her body with him, and she loved him sharing his body with her.

"You ok?" Talis asked, smiling.

"Well, I'm not sure," Lilla started, but saw the horror look on his face. "I'm fine silly," she giggled. "I think we need to practice that a bit more now," she laughed even more.

"Well, I am a busy man, you know, will have to fit you in with all this saving the world stuff," grinned Talis, pulling a face of I could be too busy.

"You will do as you are told," Lilla said, punching him on the arm.

"Ouch, hold on a minute," Talis grumbled with a smile as he rolled back on top of her and kissed her again.

They laughed and talked as they continued playing and kissing for several minutes before making love again. They lay there for some time after they had finished, talking and joking. Then suddenly, the door to Talis's room burst open.

Lauren had rushed back from the library. She didn't really understand what it meant as Berolarn didn't quite understand what the pendants were. Yet, they sounded extraordinary. A gift from the god Sol. Same as the white book that Berolarn had talked about, opposite to the dark lord's black book. Arriving at Talis's door, she burst in and was just about to relay everything. But all that came from her mouth was.....

"Oh, sorry," and as soon as the words left Lauren's mouth. She had worked out what is front of her. She burst out giggling.

"While I might have guessed you two would be at it, I give you five minutes alone and look at you both," Lauren said way too dramatically, and she knew pretty childishly.

But she was so happy she could burst, and anyway, it was always good to have a go at Talis, and if Lilla was going to have him, she might as well get in some ribbing.

"C'mon, don't just lay there if you have finished," Lauren looked at them quizzically, still smirking.

"Because if you have done, I've been to see Berolarn. Not quite as interesting as what you have been doing, but I got some exciting things to tell you. I will tell you in Lilla's room when you're ready," Lauren finished off shouting as she ran out of the room, closely followed by a large pillow Talis chucked in her direction.

Finally, thirty minutes later, Talis and Lilla entered the room to Lauren's amused grin.

"Well, look who has finally come," Lauren laughed as she tried to be witty in the situation. Then, seeing Lilla starting to flush a burning red and Talis looking less than amused, she hastily apologised. "Sorry, it was just a joke. I am thrilled that you two are together. Honestly."

"Thanks, Lauren," answered Lilla tentatively.

"Yes, thanks to Lauren," said Talis with his usual underlying tolerance when annoyed with her. Whoops, she thought, bet work a bit more on him. He will probably calm himself when I tell him what Berolarn knew of the pendants and the ring. The pair of them walked over to Lauren and sat down.

"What's up, Lauren," asked Talis. "What's all this talk about Berolarn and something to tell us."

"Well, as soon as you showed us the pendants and the ring and how you got them. To be honest, it all seemed a bit strange. As soon as I left you two alone to do whatever," said Lauren pausing slightly as she realised how she couldn't help making a comment again. But quickly observing their faces, they hadn't noticed. She continued,

"I rushed to see Berolarn and tell him the story of the pendants and ring. I found him not long after leaving. He was in the library studying stuff about where we had to go. This Caledonia place it's also called the icelands or Winterholm, you know. He said it was all snow and ice. Anyway, I told him what you told us and showed him the pendant you gave me. He was really interested and said he thought they were the Palantari Stones. It was fascinating that they were rare gifts from the god Sol to his chosen knights. He said there were four of each in total, and they had some magic power. Though he didn't know what. But, they are all different in power, and the stone in each pendant and ring is also different. He only knew of the one that our father had. He said he would need to research more about what they can do, but he said we should wear them," revealed Lauren looking at them to see if they were amazed as she had been.

"Ok," laughed Talis extending the word as he spoke. "All joking, aside, though. It is pretty cool that they are something special. I wonder what our fathers does," he said, taking out and peering at it.

They spent the next hour lazing about discussing all the wondrous possibilities that the pendants and Lilla's ring could bestow on them. Finally, they all agreed that they would keep them on all the time, as it appeared they would do them no harm and only benefit them. Finally, Lilla made her excuses telling them she was tired. Kissing Talis, she left and went to her room, leaving Talis and Lauren alone.

"Well, Talis, you have outdone yourself there," commented Lauren happily as Lilla closed the door.

"What is that supposed to mean," asked Talis.

"Lilla, stupid," Lauren replied, punching him.

"Oh, yeah," Talis grinned. "I do really like Lilla, if I am honest. Foul temper, though."

"I think she is brilliant, really like her too. Way too good for your ugly mug, Talis Quicksilver. Make sure you hang on to her and don't let her down." Lauren said, poking him.

"Alright, alright. Damn it," cried Talis. "Will you give over, punching and poking me."

"Making sure it registers in your thick head," replied Lauren.

"If I am honest, Lauren, I think I have totally fallen for her. I think she feels the same. But now I am concerned. We're in the middle of trying to save the world. I think we are going to die. She is coming with us, and I don't want that burden. I want Lilla to stay safe. But then I am concerned I might lose her. Then who knows what Luther will think? I think he might tear my head off!" fretted Talis.

"Damn it, Talis, why do you always overthink things? Though you did miss the fact, we could live well over a thousand years." Lauren laughed.

"You cannot think too far in the future. You have to deal with what you have now. Who knows what will happen? Yes, we might die, but we might not, which I am planning on. You have to live in this time, not the future. Lilla is here at this time, and she will go with us and be part of the future," reasoned Lauren optimistically with a smile.

Talis wasn't sure he understood that logic, but he nodded in agreement anyway.

"What about Luther and also Berolarn, come to think of it? Do we tell them we are together?" pondered Talis.

Lauren shook her head.

"I would say not. They probably already have an inkling of your closeness. Maybe it would be best to let that knowledge develop more on the journey. Let Luther get used to it over time. You know him better than I do, but I would be cautious with that one from everything Lilla has told me," argued Lauren.

"You're right, and Luther is probably the most dangerous man I have met outside Berolarn. We need to play this right. I had better see if Lilla agrees," surmised Talis.

"You mean, let her tell you exactly what you are going to do," laughed Lauren, rising from her chair.

"Right, I am off to bed too, brother." Playfully punching him again as she walked past him for the door. She turned as she opened the door.

"I am really happy for you," enunciated Lauren as she smiled lovingly, and with that, she was gone.

Talis rose and went out onto the balcony. He looked out across the moonlit city. Then, sighing to himself, how did life get so damn complicated? Talis stood there for some time, lost in his thoughts. Finally, he had to agree with Lauren. He couldn't pre-judge what was going to happen. He had to jump into the flow and let it play out to whatever fate decided his destiny to be. Leaving the balcony, he got undressed and climbed into bed. Within minutes he was in a restless sleep, lost in dreams of trying to save Lilla and Lauren from the clutches of unseen evil.

Chapter 19 – Time to leave

A few more weeks passed in the elven city. The three of them continued to spend time together. Though Lauren split time between Talis and Lilla and visits to Elisha, with who she was now very close. Lauren felt that though she had lost a father and thought about him daily as it continued to break her heart. Yet, Lauren had now gained two sisters, which eased the burden of losing her father. She loved both of them to bits, though Lilla was more like her, and Elisha was stiffer like Talis.

On one of those lazy days when Lauren had been out riding early morning with Elisha, who was showing her some of the elven lands. Berolarn had met them on their return. He said it was now time for them all to meet again. They were to make their way to the council chambers after lunch. He told Lauren that he had spoken to Talis and Lilla. Lauren decided to stay and have lunch with Elisha and go with the princess to the council.

They had a light lunch, and then Elisha led them to the council chambers. Not long after they arrived, Berolarn, Luther, Talis and Lilla came into the room. In the chambers were King Ethera, Captain Aetherhard from the royal guard, the dwarf Helm and a lithe woman they had never seen before. She was decked out as a warrior and carried a large scar across her face.

"Good, ….. Good, ….. we are all here," said the King as he surveyed the room.

"Please all be seated. Those of you who have not been part of the council meeting since our first meeting. We have discussed many different options for the wars we believe are coming. But unfortunately, we could not come to a general conclusion on the best course of action. We do not know when the dark lord will unleash his full might or where he will attack first. His mind is closed to us."

"We know that the dwarves," nodding towards Helm. "Are already at war. We considered the many factors, such as elves and men are not used to fighting within the rocks. But, we also need to support all in the fight against the dark lord, and we surmise if the dwarves fall, then the lands are open to his hordes. Lord Ballor was very accurate in his words about how the dwarves protect the lands. Therefore the council has agreed to send units in aid. What aid and how many will come from the lands of men is unknown. They need to hold their own counsel. But it will come. It is more the when."

"As for the elves, We cannot send the cavalry or our standard legions as we see at the moment they would have little scope to aid, and they make up a vast amount of our troops. However, we will send one thousand or so archers and a small selection of cavalry and foot soldiers with a supply train of goods and items of war. In addition, we have agreed to send healers to aid the wounded, as we are highly skilled in this area. They will march within the month, at the beginning of the new year."

"That now brings us to the quest for the Dragonheart stone, Berolarn?" Ethera finished by calling on Berolarn.

"Thank you, King Ethera," said Berolarn nodding to the King.

"As mentioned in the council meeting, I believe from my

studies that the most likely place for the Dragonheart stone is in Caledonia. Caledonia is a land of ice but burns deep inside with fire from the earth. In the ancient writings, I have found that there lies a once-mighty kingdom, now broken and gone. Within the fire encased in frosted ice stands a golden crossed sceptre of kings. The great star, the Dragonheart stone, constantly lies dormant in its head, always waiting to be awakened. From ancient maps of the third age and my studies, I believe Caledonia was once part of a place called Britannia, and I know of the sceptre and its place of keeping. We need to search out a tower, and there we will find it."

"We will set off from the elven city within seven days and make our way across Aslandure towards the elven port of Tristol, where we should arrive in about three weeks. Word has been sent ahead, and a ship should be prepared for our arrival. It will take us another few weeks to arrive in Caledonia. Then we will land and set off on foot. How long we will be in Caledonia is unknown, but the ship will wait for our return. Alongside Talis and Lauren, Luther will go as the guide. Our good friend, Helm, will go on behalf of the dwarves as a small act of repayment for the elven contribution towards the dwarven war effort." Berolarn nodded towards Helm, who nodded in return.

"To help us on our way, and by her own request, Princess Elisha will also go with a small company of elite royal guards counting ten in number. On behalf of the land of Ellion, I would like to introduce Garrett, the personal guard of Princess Cwen, who she has been left to aid the quest. Garrett was once in the company under the command of Luther. I believe Luther, you suggested her services to the princess many years ago?"

Luther curtly answered, "Yes, I can vouch for Garrett's sword."

"Finally, there is myself who will complete the group," concluded Berolarn.

Lilla jumped up, incensed that her name had not been called.

"You haven't called my name, I told you," looking at Luther like a snake raised to strike and full of venom. "They go nowhere without me. I am going, or he isn't." Lilla hissed as she started to reach boiling point.

"You forget yourself, girl. Please be seated," shouted the king.

"I wasn't talking to you, old man! I do not answer to you or anyone else," Lilla shouted back.

Jumping at Luther, attacking him with everything she could. Pandemonium broke out as Luther battled his enraged daughter, the king's guards rushing in. Talis grabbed her from behind, wrapping his strong arms around hers and pulling her backwards. Whispering soothing words in her ears, she went limp and burst into tears after seconds. Berolarn was calming the king whilst Elisha was dealing with the guards.

Finally, as everything had calmed down, Talis had spoken to Lilla in the corner of the room. They came back hand in hand.

"If she doesn't go, then I will not go either," said Talis to the room.

"Talis, please be reasonable. There is a good chance of death on our quest. I would not have Lilla punished with such a fate," said Berolarn urgently.

"Stop, Berolarn," ordered Ethera.

Looking at Berolarn and Luther penetrating deep with his eyes, he turned to Lilla.

"I have stood here for hundreds of years, Lilla. No one, and I mean no one, has called me an old man and effectively told me to shut up." Ethera then smiled. "I think we should not trust in the wisdom of old men! I think perhaps friendship and fire in the belly might be stronger. With Luther's agreement, the girl should be allowed to go where she will and with this company. Then so be it."

Luther looked at Lilla angrily as he spoke,

"If this is what you want, then fine. But remember, everything I did was for your safety up to this point. So you take the consequences if you wish to throw that away, Lilla. I have no time to prioritise your safety anymore. More important things now take precedence. So you stand and fall on your own. Do you understand?" Luther asked decisively, making sure she understood the consequences of her demand.

"I understand, and I have no fear. I will prove my worth as I have done before." Lilla snapped back at Luther.

"Then it is fine by me, King Ethera," returned Luther.

"So be it," said Berolarn tiredly.

Shaking his head, he wondered how something so simple had quickly fallen into such chaos. He didn't want Lilla with them and hadn't expected her reaction. He was concerned about how close Talis and Lilla were becoming, and it could not only be dangerous to both of them. It could have real catastrophic consequences. However, he had to give her credit for insulting the king though.

He gave a slight smile to himself. Perhaps Lilla's mother's blood runs stronger than he thought. Berolarn was sure no one had ever managed that one either. Perhaps her fire might be tempered as Ethera had implied. Well, it is what it is. Berolarn would just have to observe their blossoming relationship carefully and watch Luther as well. He needed Luther to remain onside.

"Follow me, you three. I want to talk to you, ….. My king," Berolarn nodded to Ethera and beckoned for Lilla, Talis and Lauren to follow him.

They arrived at the Library, and Berolarn guided them into a small drawing room leading from the king's library.

"Please do sit. I prefer to come here. The quietness allows me to think," Berolarn said quietly. "I commend your commitment Lilla, but you need to think sometimes before reacting." She started to retort, but Berolarn raised his hand.

"Please hush. I say this not only for your own good but for all of you. This is a quest not only for our potential deaths but for all of the races. Yes, we must show tenacity, the strength of will. But it must be controlled with a purpose. We will fail if you don't have a direct sense of what you are doing. Think Lilla, you have just insulted not only one of the greatest of his kind but probably the more important person in this war. His hand could well define our fate. Now by luck, you touched his heart or clouded his brain. I cannot say which, but think before you react, and the same for all of you. Can you achieve your goal in a better way? Thinking before you act is all I ask," reasoned Berolarn.

"Do you all understand?" he queried.

They all agreed and apologised. Lilla thought he was nuts, but she wouldn't annoy him further or Luther. She got what she wanted, which was enough. She would play their game. For now, that was fine.

"I am sorry, Berolarn. But I am old enough to make my own decisions. It was a shock that someone had made many decisions without discussing them with me. You can understand that?" asked Lilla.

"I understand, child. I am just saying, at times, try and control your temper," emphasised Berolarn, smiling sadly. "I know these trouble times do rattle our thoughts."

"We will be leaving soon. Make sure you have everything you need for the journey. The elves will provide clothing for the trip, including gear for the harsh winter environment and enough rations. But anything else you might need, ensure you have it. Talis, I know you have the chainmail shirt, but perhaps Lauren, Lilla, you should go to the elven armourers to have suitable lightweight leather armour fitted and maybe weapons of choice can be furnished. In fact, yes, I will ask Princess Elisha to arrange it. Right, does anyone have any questions?" Berolarn asked, looking around his audience. They all looked at each other and shook their heads. "Good, nice short discussion. I will bid you all goodnight then, and I will speak to you again, hopefully before we leave."

Over the next few days, good to his word, Princess Elisha sought them out and took them to the armourers. Lauren and Lilla both received wonderfully light full-body armour. It fitted like everyday clothing and felt no different to any other apparel.

Elven magic Lauren had declared to the amusement of Elisha. Talis already had his father's longsword, bow and favourite hunting knife. He just filled his quill with newly made arrows of the finest quality. Lauren and Lilla were both furnished with short swords and thin long knives. They also made Lauren a sling at her request. Lilla had jokingly thought about asking for a beer tray, then thought better of it.

They had been ready for a few days, and now everything was beginning to grate on them to different degrees. The fun of being together in the elven city was starting to wane as they lost interest in everything else but setting out on their journey.

Lauren couldn't stand the boredom and began to annoy Talis and Lilla. Even Elisha was too busy most of the time to spend real time with Lauren. She tried desperately hard to find something of interest to do. But, Lauren struggled to find anything of interest when she was alone, and it was evident that Talis and Lilla wanted time alone. Then, finally, she had a brilliant idea. Why Lauren hadn't thought of it earlier, Lauren had no idea. She would find the dwarves, specifically Helm, as he would be a new companion. It was a great idea, she thought. Lauren knew nothing of dwarves and would love to learn about their lives, history and ways.

"I'm off out," said Lauren as she jumped off Lilla's bed.

"Where you going?" asked Lilla, as Talis secretly smiled.

"I'm going to find Helm," grinned Lauren.

"Who?" asked Talis.

"The dwarf Helm," exclaimed Lauren.

She saw the confused look on Talis's face.

"The one who is coming with us, dunderhead," laughed Lauren. "Honestly, Talis, what is between your ears? Do you ever listen to anything you are told?"

"I will see you both later, don't do anything naughty whilst I am gone," grinned Lauren as she walked towards the door.

"See you later, Lauren," Talis said with a mock exasperated voice and gave a massive sigh of relief, to which Lilla giggled.

"Mark my words Talis Quicksilver. You will miss me when I am gone. I know it!" laughed Lauren as she left.

Lauren wandered aimlessly along the corridors of the ginormous palace for some time as she tried to find the dwarves. She asked various passers-by if they had any idea where they could be. Most looked at her strangely as they all gave multiple forms of no. Lauren was giving up hope as the frustration started to take hold. Then, she suddenly saw Elisha across an opposing corridor, deep in conversation with another woman in military attire.

"Elisha,….Elisha," shouted Lauren.

"Lauren," smiled Elisha as she turned her head, and the two women stopped. "What can I do for you?"

"Hi, Elisha, how are you doing? ….." replied Lauren as she looked at the other woman. The other woman was glaring at her. Lauren realised she hadn't called her princess. "I mean Princess Elisha," grinned Lauren. "I wondered if you could tell me where I can find the dwarf Helm. It seems I should get to know him better if we travel together," stated Lauren.

Elisha grinned at Lauren's childish excitement. She goes on another adventure, Elisha thought.

"You will find him in the workshops with the stonemasons and carvers. He is helping with new ways of working stone, I believe. Dwarves are master craftsmen. Word of warning ..... he is old even for a dwarf and has a certain manner, which is hard to get used to. So don't take his words to heart," smiled Elisha.

"I really must go now, go out to the left-hand side of the gardens and follow the path through the trees into the grounds. You will come to a large stone building with massive wooden doors. You should find Helm there," Elisha called back to Lauren as she walked off.

"Thanks, will come and see you soon," Lauren called back as she turned and nearly ran down the corridor.

Elisha turned to her companion.

"There goes one who is wonderfully innocent, kind, and light-hearted. Sometimes I think Lauren is more an elf than I am," laughed Elisha.

Lauren dashed as fast as she could through the gardens and followed the path indicated by Elisha. Soon she came upon the large stone building. As she entered, she could immediately hear the dwarf barking orders at the elves assembling a large item. Lauren had no idea what it was.

"Hello, Helm," shouted Lauren above the din. The dwarf turned round.

"What do you want?" asked Helm abruptly.

"I thought we could talk," offered Lauren, now nervous as she looked at the scowling dwarf.

"About what might I ask, I am busy...... No, no, no .....

don't you listen to me, Gilantar? How many times do I tell you the stone will not run true if the drive is not square," admonished Helm to an elf who was sitting pulling on a massive round bar with funny teeth on it. The elf nodded and pulled the other way as the dwarf walked closer to Lauren.

"What do you want,…. Lauren is it?" asked Helm.

"Well ….. err ….. I was thinking we are going to be travelling together, and I would like to no more about you and dwarves, I guess," stammered Lauren.

Helm broke into a grin.

"Do you know how many humans or elves have asked to know about me or my kind? I will tell you ….. None!" laughed Helm. "Why not," cooed Helm as he looked at Lauren and preened his beard. "Come with me," said Helm as he marched past Lauren, who scurried after him. "Let's leave this place, maybe have a walk in the gardens, and you can eat with me as it's nearly time for lunch."

"Lauren, what would you like to know about Helm and the dwarves, do tell," inquired Helm.

"Well, I have many questions. I'd never met a dwarf until I met you. I know nothing of the dwarves except the snippets I garnered of my father. But if I am honest, I don't remember much of what he said anyway," Lauren answered hastily.

"I see," interrupted Helm, laughing. "I will just take you to know exactly nothing. Then we have a good starting point. Agreed?"

"Err ….. yes, I know nothing really as I was saying, my father ….." continued Lauren as she was half running to keep up with the speed of the rapid short strides of the dwarf.

"Crikey, I can see you speak too much. Perhaps that is why you don't listen enough. I bet your father told you a full history of dwarves," laughed Helm again as he abruptly stopped and sat down on one of the garden benches.

Lauren grinned as she sat next to Helm. She pulled her jacket tighter around her neck as she realised it was pretty cold.

"Where do I start," mused Helm. "Let's, start with me. As you might have gathered, I am a lord in my homelands under the mountains. I am a Hammerhand. Helm Hammerhand, and I'm the second cousin of King Reuden. I am quite old for a dwarf to be on his travels," grinned Helm as he looked at Lauren. "I am widowed and have three sons who now fight in the goblin wars."

"Do you know why an old dwarf travels to the home of elves and has stupidly agreed to join you on your quest?" he continued.

"Well, to be fair, Helm. You don't look that old," smiled Lauren. To which Helm laughed. "I wouldn't have wondered such a question."

"I see you are already trying to get me to like you," beamed Helm.

"I came because I love my people dearly, but many of the young still carry the prejudices of our kind and the distrust of other races. However, I see past this, which is why my king asked me to come. You must understand that people have too many biases in their lives and struggle to shake them off," finished Helm as he leaned back and looked into the sky.

"I often wonder what it would be like to be a bird, flying high with the wind in your hair," yawned Helm. "Anyway," he said, looking back at Lauren with a shrug. "That is why I am here and why I will come with you, nothing more."

"What are you good at?" blurted Lauren.

Again causing the dwarf to laugh.

"What am I good at? What sort of question is that girl," chuckled Helm. "I am good at a great many things. I am a dwarf!"

"Sorry, I didn't mean it like that. But a king doesn't just send someone because of their wisdom, do they?" asked Lauren.

"Indeed they do," said the dwarf indignantly. "However, luckily for you, I am pretty good with a hammer or axe. I have survived many of the extremes you find around the lands and have participated in several battles. Do not worry about that."

"Oh, I didn't mean anything by it. But, you know, I was just wondering, that's all," mumbled Lauren.

"Let's go get some food," said Helm gruffly as he got up and started walking towards the palace. Lauren also rose and chased after him.

As they sat at the table, Helm told Lauren about the stronghold and subterranean realm of the dwarves' mountain home. How it is full of great halls held up by highly carved pillars of the very stone that had been removed to make their home. Helm described how the dwarves' cut their way through the mountains to join them together. He explained to Lauren the wonders of Iron and Steel created in the mountains and how they had used it in great mechanical devices for mining and weapons of war.

He also took great joy in describing how the dwarfs had brought light and life inside in the darkness of cut stone. Now even trees and flowers grow inside the halls of the dwarves.

"It is a wonderous site, Lauren. Although it is difficult to tell the tale properly, you would only have to look upon it once and feel your heart melt, and you would struggle to look at another place with the same affection as your mind would always drift back to the Milnmor Mountains," explained Helm.

"I would love to see it," said Lauren.

"Maybe one day, I will take you there," smiled Helm. "Right," he said, pushing his plate away. "I must get back to work. You have stolen much of the day from me, Lauren."

"It's been brilliant, Helm. Thank you so much," smiled Lauren in return. She watched Helm leave, and then Lauren got up and made her way back to find Talis and Lilla.

Lauren continued to be bored and was a general nuisance to anyone she could find. But, finally, six days after the council meeting. They had been sent word that they would be setting out tomorrow morning and to be ready to leave soon after breakfast.

Chapter 20 – Sea Sickness

Morning came, and as requested, they made their way down to the courtyard next to the palace stables. Everything was prepared, and the party was just waiting for everyone to arrive.

"Ah, good," said Aetherhard as he saw the companions arrive. "Your horses are those three over there." Aetherhard pointed at some magnificent-looking horses already saddled up and ready to ride.

"In the supply wagon, you can put any possessions you don't want to carry. We will probably be leaving within the next ten minutes. We are waiting for Berolarn and Princess Elisha to finish with the king."

Minutes later, Elisha and Berolarn entered the courtyard and, after brief conversations with Captain Aetherhard. Finally, the party left the palace grounds and made their way through the palace gates and out into the woodlands and fields of Aslandure.

The journey was largely uneventful, though generally miserable, as it became bitterly cold as winter finally took hold. It had been snowing on and off as they worked their way westward towards the elven port of Tristol, and the more they travelled northwards on the westward path, the heavier the snow began to fall. By the middle of the second week of travel, everywhere as far as the eye could see was covered in a soft blanket of snow. The woodland greenery became lost in the whiteness, and the wind whipped the snow into blizzards. As they got closer to Tristol, the party finally had no choice but to change into some of the clothing they had for use in Caledonia in an attempt to stave off the elements.

Lauren spent her time between Talis and Lilla or with Elisha most of the time, and the only time they ventured into others' company was at mealtimes when they made camp, except for Garrett. The royal guard generally reminded her of Brish. Most were relatively light-hearted and kind. Captain Aetherhard, on the other hand, could be the twin of Luther. He was very sullen and to the point most of the time. He generally offered little in the way of conversation.

What surprised Talis, Lilla, and her most was Garrett. She wasn't quite as she first appeared. Finally, after several days, before the snow hit hard. Lilla had made a play for them to sit with Garrett at the campfire. She wanted to delve a bit more into Luther's past. All three of them found her full of fun, hilarious at times and very easy to talk to.

After some time had passed, Lilla decided to ask more about Luther. Garrett explained how he had appeared as a child in the mercenary group and worked his way up quickly. Becoming the leader of the mercenaries they were with.

"We travelled the land as swords for hire, but Luther changed us into being righteous warriors for hire," Garrett chuckled, looking in Luther's direction to make sure he couldn't hear. "It was not what I had signed up for. But once he decided this, he refused to allow us to serve any unjust cause."

She told Lilla and the twins that no one had ever known him to lose in a battle with an enemy.

"That one is cursed with not knowing defeat and pain. Luther is a master with all weapons and any form of unarmed combat. His tracking ability is second to none. Yes, he was special, one of a kind." Garrett shrugged, "and then one day, he was gone. No goodbyes or anything. We all thought he had died or maybe an assassin sent by some irate lord or king, who we had somehow offended, had put an end to him," she laughed.

"Then, one day, maybe five years later, I walked into that Inn of his, The Devil's Punchbowl. Didn't give it much thought about who now owned it. You were just a young girl, maybe thirteen at the time, Lilla. Who was there? The great man himself. I was totally shocked. He would tell me nothing, but we had what you would call a polite conversation, and that was it. But, I have seen him periodically since, and he got me my current role with the Ellion princess." Garrett sighed. "What you do have to understand, anyone who walks with him is loyal to him, he has that skill, and I guess charm….. I know," she said, looking at Lilla's astounded face. "But he does. I would follow him anywhere. Not sure why, but I would."

"How did you end up with the mercenaries then, Garrett," asked Talis.

"Ah, well, that is a long story." Garrett grinned as they all looked at her scarred face. "I was a street urchin, no parents, you see."

Stopping, in apparent thought, she chucked what was left of her food into the fire. Then looking back at them, still smiling, Garrett teased with each word.

"Every bit of food was precious. I had to fight every day to survive. I would eat, fight and do anything to live. It burned inside that will to win against whatever the day threw at me. I became a very good pickpocket, and by the time I had reached my mid-teens, I was a battle-hardened master thief. I would break into anywhere and try to steal the richest people's jewels and gold. They were always very generous as well," she laughed.

"But then I cursed myself. I saw Luther enter the Inn," she said, motioning toward Luther.

"For all his swords, all I could see was the large money purse he appeared to be carrying. I watched and waited until I knew his room. Then, I entered the darkness, thinking he was asleep. I was ready to cut his throat if he awakened. Well, he did awake, didn't he? He easily overpowered me and was about to bring me a swift death. But he managed to look into my eyes in the darkness, so he told me. What did he see? A scared child, a girl who had known no better, trying to survive!" Garrett took a big mouthful of wine. "He stopped just before the death stroke took me. He then started talking to me instead. Asked me my name, told him it was Jenna…."

"What, Garrett isn't your name?" blurted out Lauren, who was fascinated by the story.

"God, no. My name is Jenna. I was given that name due to my tendency to kill people with a Garrote." Garrett answered and then looked at Lauren's confused face. She laughed. "I used to strangle people with silk scarves and the like. They call it using a Garrote to strangle someone. Anyway, yes, that's how I got the name."

"Where was I …… oh, yes, he talked to me and said I was coming with him, didn't have much choice, and he tied me up and dragged me off to his mercenary group. I was young. I was scared at first. A lot of big powerful men in this group, you see. But they trained me, looked after me, and soon I became not only one of their own. I became one of their best." Garrett finished before taking another big swig of wine.

"What I did learn, though, was his lordship's righteousness," She chuckled as she looked over at Luther. "He changed my path from evil to good. Well, kind of good, and you know, I learned I actually preferred helping people rather than killing people. I am now what I am. My past is forgotten in general, and happier for it."

"Can we call you Jenna? I prefer it to Garrett," asked Lilla.

"Yes, I agree," said Lauren. "It is a much nicer name than Garrett."

"Call me what you want. I can answer to either," laughed Garrett.

Then finishing off the last dregs of the wine from the skin, Garrett made her excuses and left. The companions also decided to leave the fire and went to their tents to sleep.

During the following day, they were getting close now to Tristol. Aetherhard had said they would be there before nightfall. He explained it was a small fishing village, and there was not much to it. So they would go straight to the ship and, hopefully, set sail the following morning, weather permitting.

As the sun started to drop below the horizon and the twilight hours were upon them, they arrived at Tristol. It was nothing more that a collection of various non descript small aged buildings and stores. They slowly made their way through to the pier. They saw multiple boats of all sizes, and a large ship was berthed in pride of place at the end of the dock. They could just make out that the boat was carrying the royal crest at its stern.

"This is the Endeavour, the royal warship of the elves," Aetherhard told them. "Come, they are expecting us," and he dismounted and tied his horse to a railing at the beginning of the pier.

"Get the supplies off and onto the ship and get the horses housed," said Aetherhard to one of the royal guards who were dismounting as he spoke. The rest of the party followed Aetherhard's lead, gathered their belongings, and made their way to the ship. Two guards were discussing something with Aetherhard at the gangway. They stopped and bowed when they saw Princess Elisha.

"Princess, I was just telling Captain Aetherhard that all the rooms are ready. I will inform the captain of your arrival whilst Arlo takes you to your quarters at the stern under the bridge." Then, looking around the companions, he continued, "My name is Freolo, and I will be the person to shout if you need anything."

Freolo started climbing the gangway.

"Come this way, please," Freolo called.

Freolo led them to their cabins. Talis, following Arlo and the others, watched Elisha go into what was apparently her own cabin by the royal crest outside. It must be because she was a princess. Maybe, it was the king's quarters, thought Talis. Luckily, he shared with the dwarf Helm as Arlo pointed them into a side cabin, and it wasn't Luther. Talis guessed that might have been awkward if it had been Luther. Berolarn and Luther were together instead, in the opposite cabin. The three girls. Lilla, Lauren and Jenna were in another. Aetherhand bid them farewell as he was staying with his command in the quarters below deck.

Talis and Helm dropped all their gear next to each bunk. They chatted about how neither had ever been on a ship before. Talis confessed to Helm that he wasn't a good swimmer because he was scared to death. Generally, he had paddled in rivers. Helm found this quite amusing. He couldn't swim at all. But Helm was a dwarf, and dwarves feared nothing. He said if there was a need, he would learn a way. Talis thought you really have no idea Helm on the perils that water brings. But nodded in agreement.

There was a knock at the door. Freolo entered and told them they were invited to eat with the captain in an hour. Talis and Helm readily agreed, both realising how hungry they were. The hour dragged for both of them as they made idle conversation.

Finally, the hour passed, and they all came together in the large quarters of the captain. Sitting around a large table made for banquets, they talked and ate. There was no discussion of the trip ahead, and Talis was thankful for this. He was tired and hoped he could spend some time with Lilla up on deck as soon as they had eaten. Finally, when all their bellies were full, the captain bid them farewell, telling them all they might have set sail before being awake, depending on the tide and weather. Talis made a play for Lilla to come with him.

"Lilla, would you like to take a stroll with me up on deck? Maybe along the pier." Talis finished quickly, "I would like a bit of fresh air before we sleep," as he saw Luther looking at him with piercing eyes.

"That's a great idea," replied Lilla. "You coming, Lauren?"

Lauren catching the look on Talis's face, smiled at Lilla.

"No thanks, I've had enough walking, riding and outdoor activity to last me for a few days," Lauren replied. "You two go and have fun."

"Ok, I'm sure we will not be long, will see you in a bit," Lilla said, smiling back.

Lilla and Talis exited the stern and walked down the gangway.

"Can you smell the air and hear how the waves crash against the ship's hull, Talis," asked Lilla.

"I can smell the air, and yes, the waves. I realise again how cold it is," said Talis pulling a giggling Lilla close to him.

"I've missed you," whispered Lilla.

"I know, me too," Talis whispered back. "You realise we are now not going to be alone for weeks, months, now," he continued sighing.

Whispering again to Talis with a giggle, "come, let's go quickly and find somewhere. I know there will be plenty of warm hay in the stables," said Lilla, now laughing. Holding her hand, Talis quickened their pace to even more laughter from Lilla.

"Ssssh Lilla, someone will hear," Talis moaned.

"They might if it's as good as last time," Lilla cried with laughter as Talis pulled her into the stable.

Over an hour later, they both still lay in a state of undress, deep in a pile of hay.

"I think we better go," said Lilla kissing Talis. "We have been gone some time now."

She jumped up and realised how cold it was as the goosebumps hit her skin. Lilla did her best to quickly brush the hay out of her hair and off her body. She then started to put her clothes back on. Talis was feeling quite content and didn't want to leave yet. But watching Lilla admiringly, he knew she was right. So he jumped up and was hit by the same freezing sensation as Lilla and rushed to get dressed.

Luther was pacing the deck. He was annoyed. He never got annoyed, yet Lilla always managed to bring out any hidden anger. Damn that girl, he thought. Luther loved her like a real daughter, whatever that meant, and it was now his weakness where Luther never had any. He constantly struggled with the demons around him doing the right thing for Lilla, and in the end, he left her to Biggy to look after. But Biggy wasn't here, and he now had all the responsibility.

Then there was the boy. That damned boy who was vital to the war effort. He could see how she looked at him and him, her. There was such a danger in such a friendship. He could see it as plain as day, and so could Berolarn. Berolarn had said it mustn't happen. But what was he supposed to do? Bind her to him and put a gag on her, he thought as he saw them walking back up the pier. Luther walked down the gangway to meet them. As they got closer, he saw her state, bits of hay in her hair, and dishevelled clothes.

Losing his head, Luther punched Talis, knocking him down.

"What are you doing," fumed Luther as he grabbed Lilla. "Are you a slut?"

Lilla was incensed and went for Luther, fists flying everywhere. Luther pushed her hard, and she fell.

Luther was suddenly hit by an unnatural force that carried him several metres through the air. He landed, and in a fluid movement, he was on one knee, knife drawn in a predatory position. It was just in time as Talis exploded on him with red flame all around him. Tearing at Luther in an attempt to kill him. Luther realised immediately that Talis was in the grasp of the hunger, and now it was life or death.

They circled each other looking for a moment's weakness, Luther saw Lilla rising, and that momentary lapse allowed Talis the opportunity. Suddenly he was upon him. First, Talis knocked the knife out of Luther's hand. Then, grabbing him, he smashed Luther into the ship's side. Luther started to rise, trying to work out how to stop Talis without resorting to killing him, when he saw Lilla grab Talis's arm.

"Stop, Talis," Lilla screamed.

Talis grabbed her by the throat, lifting her off the ground and pinning her against the ship's side. He was to drink, feast upon her blood. He then heard a faint plea.

"Please, Talis," whimpered Lilla.

Talis looked at Lilla's tear-filled face ….. It's Lilla ….. He was suddenly confused as recognition started to take hold. Why was he holding Lilla by the throat? He began to lower her as he was filled with overwhelming grief. Then the world went dark.

Talis awoke with a start and looked around in panic. His head was pounding. Then he focused on Lilla, leaning over him. She looked as if she had been crying. Her face was a mess. She was wiping his face with a damp cloth. Talis saw Lauren was there. He then saw all the bruising on Lilla's neck. Talis started crying.

"I am sorry, Lilla," Talis whispered as the memories flooded back. "I don't know what happened. First, I saw Luther strike you and the anger, hate, and darkness …… then I saw your face crying as I was hurting you."

"It's ok, Berolarn has explained to Lauren and me. I love you," whispered Lilla.

"Yep, stupid, looks like I am to share another thing with you," laughed Lauren as she looked at him with sisterly love.

"I told Luther as well, said I loved you, and we will marry," Lilla said, grinned and then winced in pain. "I told him to keep his big fat nose out of it. It was him that hit you over the head and knocked you out. Luther sarcastically said he would have definitely killed you if he had known I loved you!"

"Berolarn said he would talk to him. It will be ok. He told me Luther doesn't understand how much he cares for Lilla. Adjusting will take him time. But, once he gets used to the idea, it will be a relief that Lilla has someone as unique as Talis as her protector. It will ease some of his responsibility and, in some ways, free Luther from becoming Lilla's protector on this journey," said Lauren.

"Well, that's what Berolarn said to me, ….. Lilla," Lauren exclaimed as she noted the scorn on Lilla's face.

Lauren continued.

"Anyway, Berolarn thinks I should stay with you two love birds and ensure you are ok. The good news is that Helm has agreed to move in with Jenna. Jenna is fine with it. She said it would be good to return to being Garrett, and we are way too girly for her anyway. She would take a dwarf as a roommate anytime. Also, I can stop the pair of you from getting up to no good. You obviously cannot manage it yourselves," laughed Lauren.

"Right, I will give you thirty minutes. I will tell them that you are awake. But everyone is banned from entering until I say. In fact, I will say you have asked to be left to sleep until tomorrow. So I will give you an hour alone before I return," said Lauren as she left the room.

Lilla laid down next to Talis. Talis couldn't stop looking at the bruising and scratching on her neck. He was still mortified about the pain he must have caused her.

"Does it hurt? I am so sorry, Lilla. I feel broken that I have done that." Talis whispered, looking deep into the once again tearful eyes of Lilla.

"I have never ever become that creature before until Berolarn brought it out. I thought it had gone. Does it hurt? I can't tell you how sorry I am."

Smiling through her tear-strewn face. "Will you shut up saying sorry! I knew you were different before this. Berolarn has since explained it to me, or I think he has. I didn't understand everything, but I got most of it. He said it showed that you were already its master. You came back when I called. Berolarn thinks soon you will be able to control it, but you will also be able to bring forth the power without the thirst to kill or something along those lines," replied Lilla.

Luther and Berolarn were in deep discussion whilst Talis and Lilla was with Lauren. Luther was furious with Berolarn.

"I told you this would happen, Berolarn, if we didn't split

them up. I saw it as soon as they met. They had an instant attraction, chemistry. You know better than anyone how dangerous this is for everyone. You are lucky I remembered your master plan down on the dock. He was this close to death," said Luther snapping his fingers.

"Luther, it is imperative that Talis remains safe. He is essential to the war effort alongside Lauren and the defeat of the dark lord. You know that," sighed Berolarn. Then shaking his head, continuing with a real emphasis in his words, "you need to keep a close watch on the pair of them. Making it difficult for their relationship to blossom any further. Concerning Lilla, we still do not know what part she has to play in this, and she must be kept under control."

"You know she is headstrong ever since she came to me, and the heat in her blood runs like fire," growled Luther.

"I have spent many years trying to temper her spirit. I have failed. I am not sure that she was ever destined to fulfil her destiny. She can become more dangerous than another one of your saviours, Berolarn. I fear for her; she is my number one priority and should be yours, Berolarn. If Talis hurts her again. I will kill him," replied Luther coldly as he started to rise.

Garrett moved away from the cabin door and hastily made her way down the corridor to the deck as it sounded like Luther would exit the room. Well, this is interesting, she pondered. I thought it was the twins who were vital to their plans. Maybe the girl Lilla is important too. Magma knew they were coming. She had sent messages to him. When we arrive, should I try and send some further news about this girl, Garrett considered as she walked? I suspect he is waiting and might need to know about this girl. Magma will be pleased with me regardless, and the rewards would be great if she pulled this off. But did the girl really matter? She argued with herself. Was it worth risking being caught as a spy?

Garrett had decided long ago she would always be on the winning side. It was a real shame that things were turning out this way, and she hadn't foretold this was what would happen. Garrett liked Luther a lot, and admittedly she enjoyed the company of the children. But she must do what she agreed to do. So when Garrett decided to join Magma and his alliance with the dark lord, Garrett feared his power but could see they would rule the lands. She had no idea that Luther would be involved, but he was always involved somewhere.

Garrett should have considered this. It would be more difficult as well. These were not ordinary people, and then there was ….. Luther, the indomitable one. Then again, Magma was far from normal, even as a human or whatever he was.

She had made the right choices. If fate decided, Luther and the children would die, and probably the warlock. Then so be it. The princess would be taken and used as a bargaining tool to force the elves to surrender. Or maybe the initial choice would be to keep out of the wars with the dwarves and men. That would be the logical choice, Garrett thought.

The ship sailed early in the morning as planned. The waters were calm, and the weather had remained reasonable for the time of the year. Over the first few days, Talis and Lilla suffered severely from seasickness. They had often wished death to come quickly as they felt so ill and stayed in their room. Lauren was fine and, therefore, very bored, stuck in the room with them. Lauren became very annoying at the expense of the Talis and Lilla as she tried to get them out of bed and do something other than moaning. Besides Lauren, they were generally left by the others to suffer alone.

After a few days, they both started to get accustomed to the constant rocking and the ship's motion as it ploughed on through the sea. They began to move about the craft and mingle with the rest of their companions. Luther had managed to get Lilla alone, Lilla told Talis. Lilla explained to Talis that Luther had been full of apologies, how much he cared for her safety and all he ever did was for her best interests. When she was telling Talis about her discussion with Luther. Talis agreed with Lilla. It was great news that Luther was apologising. But, he decided that he was right not to tell her about how Luther had cornered him and had told him in no uncertain terms that his death would come quickly if he ever hurt Lilla again. That Talis was highly fortunate that Luther had considered his worth on their first encounter, next time, Luther had no doubt, he would not make the same mistake again.

The weather was generally kind to them as they sailed to Caledonia. The two of them, Talis and Lilla, continued to spend much of their time together in their room or just meandering around the deck. Over the next week, Lilla recovered from her injuries, and everything was back to normal. However, the same could not be said for Lauren. She was highly inquisitive, one who had a tendency to become bored exceptionally quickly. She spent her time pestering everyone for conversations. Most of the time, she could be found in the company of Elisha or Jenna.

Lauren was considering what to do one day and thought about who to go and see. She liked Jenna as she was hilarious, crude and had no actual boundaries. Jenna had constantly been playing jokes on Helm, who had become notorious for being grumpy most of the time and not having much tolerance for anything. This just stoked her playful nature. She had managed to set his beard on fire and then proceeded to chuck a bucket of water over him. He had chased Jenna around the ship after that one. Luckily Jenna was highly agile in comparison to the stout dwarf.

In the end, after multiple encounters between Jenna and the dwarf. Luther had to broker peace between the warring factions by grabbing hold of Jenna in one such melee and telling her in no uncertain terms that he would be throwing her overboard if she didn't stop teasing Helm. Although to be fair, Lauren did actually really like the dwarf. She had spoken to him a few times now on his own, and she found once you got his grumpiness out of the way, he was full of more stories about the wonders of the dwarven halls under the mountain.

Her time with Elisha was different. Lauren couldn't really explain it. It was always very calm and spiritual, if that was the word. When she was with Elisha, she felt the weight of what was happening disappear. She would even just sit with Elisha in the room reading. Lauren never read, really, but it was something Elisha liked to do. So Lauren would sit there for hours reading with her. She just loved being with her.

She thought about going to Elisha, but she was busy today with Berolarn and Aetherhard. She guessed it was the cost of being a princess and the next heir to the throne. Elisha had confided to Lauren that her father was among the mightiest kings in elven history. The elves had significantly prospered since he took the throne, and now that Elisha was the heir to the throne. There was a lot of pressure on her. She was living under the shadow of what her father had done, and at times she wished that it was not so, that she maybe had a brother to take the throne would be best. However, she was expected to marry and continue the bloodline. The king was always trying to force her by suggestion to marry an Elven lord. Yet, she wanted to marry out of love, not need.

There was an alternative, though. Lauren could go to find Luther. See if he had anything interesting to say. Lauren had never really spoken to him, she knew quite a bit about him, but she had probably talked to him once or twice in the briefest of passing. So Lauren knocked on the cabin of Luther and Berolarn. She heard Luther ask who was there.

"Hello Luther, it's Lauren. Can we talk?" she shouted at the door. She heard movement, and then the door opened with the stern face of semi-naked Luther staring at her.

"What do you want, Lauren?" he asked, looking at her, then along either side of the corridor.

"Errr.....I've got a few questions about Berolarn," she answered.

"Like what," snapped Luther.

"I know nothing about him, and we are supposed to trust everything he says. Talis and Lilla have bought into everything he has told us. But I feel he is hiding something. Well, Lilla says you know him better than anyone, so I thought you might be able to give me a few answers," stammered Lauren as she suddenly thought, why does this man make her nervous?

Luther paused before answering, looking deep into Lauren's eyes for a few seconds.

"Come in," Luther sighed and turned. "Sit where you

please." He threw himself onto his bunk. Then, lying slightly upright, he turned to face Lauren with his hands behind his head.

"Well? What do you want to know, Lauren?" asked Luther

Lauren looked at Luther properly for the first time. He looked in his thirties, maybe forty, but she suspected he was older. Luther had piercing blue eyes that didn't go with the ponytailed long dark hair flecked with grey. Then with him just having undergarments on, she could see his legs were like tree trunks. His waist was ripped with muscle, as was his chest. Then his arms looked as if he could crush a bear with each hand. She had to admit he was an imposing sight. She could see what Jenna meant about him being lethal as she noted all the scars he carried as medals of his previous encounters. Luther was covered in them, and his back was worse. It looked like he also carried the scars of a flogging.

"To be honest, Luther, I am unsure what I want to know. I have no idea who Berolarn really is, except everyone trusts him implicitly. But I don't really know him," answered Lauren.

Luther smiled. It looked like the first genuine smile she had ever seen from Luther.

"No one really knows Berolarn, Lauren. He is a mystery to me as he is to you. I know little of his history, and my time in that history has been short," replied Luther.

"C'mon, Luther, you seem to be his closest confidant and advisor. May I even venture his friend?" Posed Lauren.

Luther laughed.

"I will tell what I know in terms of trying to help you

understand Berolarn. I wouldn't say we were friends as such; more, I work with him to ensure the safety of the weak and vulnerable," said Luther.

He stopped, thinking for a second and then continued.

"This is what I have pieced together over the years. I think actually it is appropriate that you know. Berolarn is a Solarian, as you have recently found out. He has lived amongst the races for a long time. He was not young when the blood prince, or should I say the dark lord, first rose. He was there at the final battle of the race wars. He was strong amongst the Solarians back then. A chief warlock, great in magical forces and of skill."

"After the wars ended, I recently discovered he married the vampiress Selene as he was overcome with love, though he was much older than her. He helped her battle her thirst and anger, and they lived happily together for hundreds of years. They had a child, and throughout he had a new purpose away from the doctrines of the Solarian Knights. He forgot about the races and left that to others."

"Then Selene and the child was gone. She had heard the call of her father. What choice Selene had, I do not know. But she left. For several years, he mourned them as dead and in the darkness when no light was left within him. Then, finally, Sol came to him in a dream and helped him renew his purpose. His search ended abruptly. He now had a new purpose. He travelled the lands again, once more helping the races and fighting the works of the dark lord."

"I had heard some of this story. To be honest, Luther, Talis and Lilla had told me bits. But why you? How did your paths cross?" she pressed him.

"I can see you will be a nuisance unless you feel you have what you think is the full story." Luther laughed. "Our story is quite simple. I was a hired hand as I was fighting the tyrant, King Jed, in the lands of Breear. Berolarn was advising the King in waiting, who was leading the uprising. Our paths crossed, we talked a few times, and I helped save his life when he was ambushed by King Jed's hags, evil witches of his cursed occult. Since then, he has asked me to do specific tasks and look after what is most important."

"Do you trust him?" asked Lauren speculatively.

"Trust, what is trust Lauren to you? Everyone has their own reasoning and purpose that never fits precisely with the next person. Therefore, you will never entirely trust what a person does or wants. But you say you trust them? Yes, I trust Berolarn. Does he tell all his plans and what his desires are? No, he doesn't. Does he keep things from us? Yes, I am sure he does. Why? He has many different forces he has to negotiate and appease. He also thinks, as do I, that sometimes you have to follow a path, making multiple pivots before you reach the end. If you start at the end, you are actually at the wrong destination," signalled Luther.

Lauren hated when older people talked in riddles.

"Do you think we are following the right path?" asked Lauren.

"That is the question, Lauren, and unfortunately, I do not have the answer. Berolarn thinks so. We must therefore trust his judgement," advised Luther.

As she spent the next few hours in Luther's company, Lauren learned she didn't mind Luther. He wasn't the total yardstick she had surmised he was from her discussions with Lilla and what she had seen. His problem was that he was like Berolarn. Their purpose had taken over their personalities. After leaving Luther, she returned to her room with Talis and Lilla. She considered telling them about her conversation with Luther. Then thought better of it, pointless antagonising Lilla. She might say something wrong if she tried to tell them. It was apparent Lilla had a problem with Luther, as did Talis. Perhaps over time, she could broker some form of peace. Now, she had Luther's ear.

The day passed relatively quietly after she met with Luther, as did the next few days. Then the weather started to slowly turn, and soon they were being battered by storms, snow and rain. Talis and Lilla suffered from seasickness again, and even Lauren sometimes felt queasy. A lot of the time, there were confined to their rooms as the deck was made out of bounds. The captain was worried that his passengers could be thrown overboard, not being used to such travel. When the companions began to think that they could stand it no more. Finally, the captain told them they would be at Caledonia within a few days.

Chapter 21 – Land of Ice and Snow

They arrived late morning on the nineteenth day since they set out from the Port of Tristol. The captain told them that the place they landed was once the harbour of a massive city, but it had been consumed by the changing world and was now buried under stone and ice. The elves had landed here a few times and had built this rudimentary docking place. They had found no life in this area and felt they should be safe in the initial part of their journey.

The stone pier's walkway where they had disembarked was slippy even though it had a covering of snow. It was thick ice underneath, which could have been a foot deep from what he had seen from the ship. Talis couldn't believe how cold it was. Everywhere as far as the eye could see, was covered with snow. The mild breeze was already biting at all the companions, eating through their clothing and chilling the bone. This was going to be a long journey, Talis thought miserably as he surveyed the vast mountainous wilderness. He and the others stood around as the elves unloaded various items and prepared for the companion's journey.

Captain Aetherhard told them not far from here, there was an old ruined castle that sat just above the ice cap. Over the years, when the elves visited the lands, they used the castle as a base to explore from. It was only several miles away. They were initially going to be making for the castle. They needed to be there before nightfall and before the temperature dropped. It would afford them initial shelter and warmth on their first night. Talis, Lauren and Lilla, being less travelled than their companions, could not imagine it getting any colder. As they breathed, their breath turned to iced smog.

"If it gets any colder, I am sure all our eyes will freeze solid," moaned Lilla to the twins. "It is so cold!"

Overhearing Lilla's comments to Talis and Lauran. One of the elves who was unpacking came over and said. "Come, you are not dressed for this weather."

The three of them had not noticed that everyone else had been routing through the items the elves had been unpacking. They were all in different states of putting on large fur coats, hats, boots, and mittens.

"Come, come over here. Your items are here too," beckoned the elf.

"I am surprised no one had the common sense to give us these before we left the boat," muttered Lauren as she changed her small boots for the heavily furred knee-length leather boots.

"I thought we were going to die a death as sure as Talis is better suited to being a cow herder," she said, smiling at Talis. Lauren then elegantly scooped up a ball of snow and threw it at Talis, who, in mid-battle of getting the new boots on, was hit square in the face with the ball of freezing snow.

"Lauren, for god sake," Talis shouted. Lilla and a few others laughed at the now red-faced and wet Talis. "Honestly, I will kill you one of these days!"

"Now, Talis, I am just trying to warm up your cold spirit," she laughed as she put on the luxurious fur coat. "Crikey, have you felt how warm you feel in these coats and boots." She exclaimed as she laughed at Talis, who struggled to get on his boots. "What on earth are you doing, Talis Quicksilver?"

"I cannot get these damn boots on. They're too small," snapped Talis.

Lilla couldn't help herself but giggle at the struggling Talis. But, unfortunately, he was putting the boot he was struggling with on the wrong foot.

"Try the other way round, Talis," said Lilla, trying desperately not to join Lauren in laughing at him.

"Oh," muttered a red-faced Talis.

Then as quickly as he could, hoping no one else was watching, he swiftly swapped the boots around.

"I was so damn cold, I wasn't thinking what I was doing. I was desperate to get the boots on," said Talis with a sheepish grin.

Talis looked around to see if anyone else had noticed. Even though Lauren was in hysterics and actually crying with laughter. Luckily it appeared everyone else was too preoccupied with getting dressed to be concerned about what they were doing. Talis was highly thankful, especially as Luther currently held him in little regard. Lilla and the twins joined the rest of the company in being fully clothed in boots and furs for such climate extremes.

Aetherhard looked around and saw that everyone had assembled all their equipment. Finally, the companions appeared ready for the trek to the castle.

"Princess Elisha, are you ready to go?" enquired Aetherhard. She nodded in reply. Turning round to everyone, he commented,

"It should be good walking conditions as it is so cold, the snow will be hard underfoot, and we should make light work of the walk."

The companions followed Aetherhard with the Elven royal guard split between the front and rear of their ranks. They found that it was true, the feet hardly sunk into the untrodden snow, and they started out at a good pace. They travelled for around thirty minutes when the landscape started to change. What had been a gradual incline after leaving the ship had reached a plateau. Before them, they now saw a vast range of hills, mountains and forests entirely covered in deep snow. The predominant trees struggled to breathe in the deep white covering. Most of the trees seemed to be a kind of blue-green pine, interlaced with birch, willow and red-berried trees.

"The red-berried tree is a rowan tree and was now only found here. But be careful of the berries, as they are succulent to look at, but they bring illness if you eat them," advised Berolarn as he pointed at a collection of trees.

"Is it too cold for animals? I haven't seen a sign of any life since we left the ship," asked Lilla.

"Me neither," piped up Lauren.

"There are plenty of wild animals in the forest," answered Aetherhard. "Some are more dangerous than others. But, as we move further south, we will also find that the lands occasionally have more warmth as the sun stays longer in the skies. It will fill with birds, and I think more beasts will cross our paths."

"Is it still this cold, and the lands covered in snow most of the time then?" asked Talis.

"Unfortunately, Talis, Yes, the lands are still full of snow and yes, it will still be cold," laughed Princess Elisha joining the conversation. "However, you should stay warm now you have your boots on the right feet."

All the elves, Lilla and Lauren, laughed. Talis going red, realising they all must have seen him, grinned in acknowledgement of his stupidity.

"Can anyone tell us more of the history of these lands whilst we walk?" Asked Talis as he tried to deflect the attention away from himself.

"I will tell you what I know, Talis," said Berolarn. "I spent many years reading the histories of the third age and the doom that men brought upon themselves. These lands were once a central hub of civilisation. It was made up of two large islands and many small islands, and its name was Britannia. It consisted of many warring tribes who, as they evolved, became three of four distinct tribes."

"Mighty in the world's affairs did the Britannia people become, controlling many lands around the planet for a time. As a result, they had perhaps one of the most significant histories of all the lands. They invented the first machines as part of what was known as the Industrial Revolution. Some machines could carry people across the lands and seas at speed. Devices that created steel, clothing, and food. Machines did everything for man. But Britannia also made some of the first weapons of mass destruction." Berolarn shrugged, "With hindsight, they should have seen that man's greed would ultimately nearly destroy them."

"But, they have all gone now?" asked Lauren.

"Oh yes, indeed. As the lands shifted at the height of the cataclysm that man brought upon itself, the world shifted significantly over a few years, and these lands re-joined and became one with the giant continent that we now stand on. But, as I discussed in the council, many of the world's people perished or maybe in the case of Britannia, they migrated out of these now harsh lands and moved further south. Left behind were the tribes of the strongest Celtic ancestry who roamed the most northern parts of Britannia. Instead, they did not go and made their homes in these newly formed lands, even though the environment had become harsher. They are now warrior tribal people as they were of old. Flowing long red hair and the men full-bearded, they are quick to anger and quick to kill. We will hopefully avoid them as we make our way south."

"But these lands for two thousand years were full of many wonders and riches as were many lands. Many kings and queens ruled during this time. Many mighty castles were built, and wars were fought as the power constantly shifted across the lands. Yes, a land full of history is the history we seek now," revealed Berolarn.

"History we now seek?" asked Lauren.

"Yes, Lauren. Do you remember we are here for the Dragonheart Stone? Do you remember what I mentioned in the council meeting? That the stone is mounted in a golden sceptre?" replied Berolarn.

"Yes, I remember," replied Lauren.

"I remember, too, lies in the sceptre's golden cross," Lilla said.

"Good," stated Berolarn. "Well, the sceptre belonged to the

Britannia kings and queens of old. They had no idea, what they had in their hands, but saw it as a thing of great beauty and signifying the power of the monarchs of the land. So they mounted the Dragonheart Stone in a golden sceptre and kept it with other items of value that signified their rulership of the lands."

"Do the other items have powers then Berolarn," asked Talis.

"Only the power over those with greed, ones who covet gold and precious stones," replied Berolarn. "I expect that all are still intact, within what remains of the tower that protected them. As they were well protected from theft.

"It will be finding the tower that might be the tricky part. The lands have changed considerably since that time. For instance, there are now mountains that you see in the distance. Well, they did not exist at that time. The land has disappeared and changed much at the end of the third age. Still, from what I have seen in the histories and ancient maps. These are still the right lands we are travelling, and as we close towards the death lands, I expect to find what we seek," finished Berolarn.

"What is the place we are currently travelling to? You said the remnants of a castle?" asked Lauren.

"There is not much left of what was," replied Aetherheld. "I have been here a few times, and the elves who visit have made repairs to make it usable."

"It used to be a castle of the Celtic kings, standing on what was known as Castle Rock. It stood high above the lands, looking down on a great city. All have now gone, and the rock has submerged back into the underbelly of the land. You will see only a small part of what was," commented Berolarn.

"How long before we arrive?" asked Helm.

"Not long now, my good dwarf," said Aetherhard as he stopped and surveyed the lands. "You see over there." Aetherhard then pointed slightly towards a small pass cut between the hills and trees.

Everyone turned and looked in that direction.

"We cut through there, and when we come out the other side, we will see the castle in front of us on the right. "Maybe another hour or so, and we should arrive. Even though night settles early in these lands, we should arrive before sundown," indicated Aetherhard.

"Ah, I am glad, master elf. I am more tired than expected, even after such a short journey. I think lazing on the ship took away some of my metal," commented Helm.

Talis hadn't thought about it, but he agreed with the dwarf. He was fatigued, too, though they had only been walking for a few hours.

The companions continued walking towards their destination, making their way down the valley and out the other side. As Aetherhard had predicted, once they came out the other side, they could see a sizeable low-lying hill in the distance coming out of the snow and ice. Sat upon the hill were the remains of ancient crumbling walls and a few buildings with a half-round stone building behind a gated rectangular front.

"What you see now is only a small part of what was," said Berolarn as they got closer to the building. "That building was designed for war, not people, and was known as the half-moon battery. I came here once with your father, Elisha, many years ago."

"I also came with my father, too," replied Elisha. "He used to like to come to these lands from time to time. He said the harsh environment cleared his mind and helped him see things clearer."

Soon they were climbing up the hill toward the gate of the building. With some effort, two of the royal guard opened the large gate and went inside. All clear, the companions heard one of the elves inside shout. The rest of the party made their way in. The place was absolutely antique. Lauren looked around, amazed that it did not fall down around their heads. She looked at Talis and Lilla, seeing they were having similar thoughts.

"This way," called Aetherhard. "We will make camp in the great hall."

The companions entered a courtyard on the other side of the battery building and made their way into a heavily repaired long building. Once inside, they saw just one massive plain long interior with an enormous stone fireplace at one end. The elves quickly lit a large fire and had food cooking as everyone else made themselves comfortable. Berolarn told them that he had seen pictures of what the building once was. This was indeed called the great hall. When it was a centre of the hustle and bustle of many people, it had not the plain roof they saw now but an iconic ornate ceiling and wood-panelled walls. It was once a thing of great beauty.

Not before long, the companions had eaten a warming stew and passed the evening with more stories from Berolarn of what once was the country of Caledonia. After a few hours, the elven royal guard had arranged the watch for the evening, and slowly everyone started to sleep. Talis and Lilla were slightly apart, parted by Lauren. Both were fully aware that they were still under the scrutiny of Luther and didn't want to antagonise him any further. However, Talis wanted to mend some of the bridges between them, and they had discussed that some separation at times might be helpful.

They were awoken the next day by the elves as they prepared breakfast for the party. Lauren and Lilla went to the door as they thought they would look around.

"It's still dark. Why are we up at this god-earthly time" cried Lauren humorously.

Elisha smiled. "It is not that early, Lauren. But unfortunately, we do not see much daylight in these lands. The night rules and the hours for walking in the sun are five or six hours. So we will not see the sun until mid-morning."

"How depressing," muttered Lauren. As she dragged Lilla back inside and glumly plonked herself back down near Elisha. "Someone might have mentioned this in the council. I could still be in a wonderfully comfortable bed back at the palace of elves." She said accusingly whilst looking and grinning at Elisha.

Elisha loved being around Lauren, she made light of everything, and her dazzling smile lit up every day she was in her company. Elisha had not encountered many humans, and she believed that man was selfish and careless. Likening everything they were to the destruction of the lands. Now she saw this was not true. Lauren and Talis were not human, but they had grown up as such, as had Lilla. She could now see that there were those of the human race generally of good character, and in Lauren, she felt an overwhelming love for the child. She hoped that this journey doesn't taint the goodness in Lauren's heart.

"Lauren, if I said we were going without you, I am sure you wouldn't have been happy with that? I didn't think so." Elisha smiled as she looked at Lauren. "You know you are here to look after Talis and Lilla."

"Yes, absolutely. They wouldn't be able to manage without me!" Lauren laughed. "You wouldn't be without me anyway, Elisha. Who else would take no notice of you being a princess and not subject you to all this royal highness stuff? Me!.....Which, by the way, must drive you insane. If I was in your position, I would ban it ...." As she was speaking and picking up pace, Elisha saw the signs. She knew Lauren was going to go off alarmingly. Which she did when she got excited.

"We must start packing our gear away. Lauren. You need to be getting ready. I think we will be off shortly," said Elisha, cutting Lauren off mid-sentence.

"Oh yes, you're right," said Lauren as she surveyed the room in a state of busyness. Elisha smiled as Lauren jumped up, pulled her stuff together, and started talking to Lilla and her brother Talis about today's trip.

"I wonder how far we will travel today, Talis. Did Lilla tell you it is still dark outside, even though it is morning?" said Lauren to the back of Talis's head, who was busy sorting his backpack out.

"I asked Aetherhard, and he said we were making for the large river that still flows. It is about eight hour's walk due south. There is the benefit of shelter as the lands are generally forests for many miles. However, he said that the further south we went, the more cautious we would have to be. We would start to risk encountering the Celts, wild beasts and maybe even goblins. He said the clouds look full, and we should expect the weather to turn against us. He wasn't a barrel of laughs about how the day will turn out to be fair." Talis said, looking over his shoulder at Lauren.

"Well, I cannot wait to get to where we are going and get back to the palace," said Lauren earnestly. "I think I am not very good for this adventuring stuff," she grinned.

"Me and you both," laughed Lilla. "When they talked about finding this stone and travelling inland for twenty to thirty-odd days to where it is hidden. Didn't seem such a big deal, if I am honest. Now, we have walked in bitter winds and snow for just a few hours." She shrugged, raising her eyebrows and pulling a face of surprise. "I am not enjoying this as much as I expected," she laughed again. "Or the thought of doing it day after day with probably nowhere to stay on the journey, and now your throwing mad red-haired natives and wild beasts at me.

Talis and Lauren laughed with Lilla, and Elisha smiled while hearing their conversation. It was refreshing that they were young at heart, and she hoped they kept this part of their childhood with them. Even though she did worry that the journey each of them would have to take might change them irrevocably.

"Is everyone ready?" Said Aetherhard looking round at the companions. "Good, let's make a start then. If we try and make a good pace before the weather hits us, we will not lose time for the day. With the wind picking up speed and the darkness in the clouds, it looks like a storm will be coming down from the north. We should spend as little time as possible in it."

Chapter 22 – The Journey South Begins

Aetherhard had been right. They had walked for several hours, and little by little, the wind grew in intensity, and they were now being hit by a constant barrage of violent gusts. They all had their furs wrapped tight around their necks. Heads bent downwards. Their hoods took the full force of the wind that swirled around them.

As predicted, the wind brought with it the denser clouds and soon the snow came, heavy and driven into a ferocious blizzard by the unrelenting wind. They huddled together as they walked, hoping in their subconscious that their fellow companions would help remove the harsh coldness creeping down their limbs and into their very being. But unfortunately, this was not to be the case. And the companions were virtually bereft of light, and the clouds continued to darken in the howling winds.

Even Aetherhard was beginning to lose his way; eventually, it was no good. Finally, he admitted he had lost all sense of direction and wasn't sure how they could continue. In the end, they had to rely on Luther, who took the lead as their guide and whose years of experience as a ranger ensured that they stayed on a true southern path.

Finally, just as Lauren thought, her legs would carry her no further, and she would fall asleep standing as she was so tired. Luther called the company to a halt to much relief to all the party.

"We are nearly at the river by the sound of the wind. Let's make for cover in the trees here. It is dense and will afford the tents some relief from the wind," said Luther as he was surveying the land.

As they moved through the trees, Luther stopped the party where the forest started to climb. "Good, this will do. The incline will offer us more protection from the weather." He muttered as he continued to walk back and forth around the area as the rest of the company watched and waited. "Yes, this is fine. Make camp."

Soon everyone was busy collecting whatever long branches, brush and vegetation they could find or cut from a tree in the nearby area as guided by the elves. The elves quickly assembled broad, stocky structures lashed with elven rope to form three-domed round shelters covered in the brush and vegetation they had collected.

"Are you sure these will stay up?" asked Lilla apprehensively. She had a vision of them collapsing under the burden of the snow and wind. Even with the cover the trees were affording, she had never seen such a structure, and it didn't look solid or that strong.

Some of the elves laughed lightly.

"There is magic in elven ropes. Once tied, they do not come undone, and the wood is strong and flexible, Lilla. They will not fall, no matter how much the wind from the north growls," smiled Aetherhard.

Lilla was still unsure, and Lauren thought she agreed with Lilla's pessimism about their safety. As the conversation about the strength of the shelters was ensuing, Luther appeared in front of Talis

"Talis, you can come with me whilst the others make the fires. Let's go down to the river and scout the lands around," said Luther.

Talis nodded, following the giant ranger back to the path they had been walking and continued to where Talis presumed they would find the river. Unfortunately, the blizzard had not let up in the hour they had been in the deepness of the forest, and now it felt pretty surreal to Talis as they crept along the path in the darkness. Their only light came sporadically as it fought to break through the fast-moving clouds. As they approached the river, Talis could hear the river grumbling as it flowed.

"Stay down. Someone is here," whispered Luther urgently.

Luther dragged Talis sidewards into the trees and bush, not ten yards from the riverbank. Then, urging Talis to follow him quietly. Luther edged forward slowly in a semi-crouched walk towards the riverbank. As they moved closer, Talis could make out voices talking.

"They are around here……. somewhere, Angus," said one heavily accented voice.

"Aye, Bear and Bronte can smell their hides, Murray. I have no doubt about it," said another voice with a similar tone.

Luther continued edging forward, and Talis attempted to follow, mimicking Luther's stealth. Talis gazed in wonder as his eyes broke through the clearing and focussed on flames flickering from torches held by two wild-looking men. Though clothed heavily in furs, Talis could make out their long red hair and beards as the light of the flame danced back and forth in the wind.

However, what really took Talis's breath away was their steads. These giant men were mounted on the biggest bears Talis had ever seen. They were five or even six metres in length and maybe two and a half metres in height. Covered in thick pure white fur that covered massive broad torsos. The Paws were as wide as tree trunks, and Talis hated to think how big their teeth were. Each had a large saddle fastened around their girth and an armoured steel plate around their chest. Each man stood up in their stirrups, looking back and forth, and both bears sniffed the ground.

"Come, we must go before they catch our scent," whispered Luther urgently.

Luther rose and started to deftly move back down the path they had followed. Talis gave the bears one more glance and followed Luther. As they stealthily walked back towards camp, Talis tried to talk to Luther. Luther swiftly brought his finger to his lips, ensuring Talis understood that he should be quiet.

"We are being hunted, I think," said Luther to Berolarn and Aetherhard as they came through into the slight clearing where the camp was.

"What have you seen?" said Aetherhard.

"Two Celtic warriors, not sure which clan, could not distinguish their insignia in the dark. They were mounted on snow bears, plated for war," answered Luther.

"A hunting party in the dark, in this weather? Well, well, well, that is strange even for the Celts who live in this land. You do not think it was a coincidence, and you passed each other by chance," asked Berolarn.

"No, I do not think so," answered Luther.

"I heard them.........said they are around here somewhere," chipped in Talis.

"You are sure, Talis?" asked Aetherhard.

"Yes, definitely, I got the impression that these ….. snow bears could smell our scent or the scent of what they search," answered Talis.

"Hopefully, we will be lucky. But fortunately, it is unlikely that the snow bears would come deep into the forest unless they had the whiff of the hunt. I should imagine their confusion because they keep catching a scent, but it is lost to them in the storm," replied Luther looking thoughtful. "Whichever the case, we have trouble if we run across snow bears again, never mind their riders. We must keep vigilant tonight and keep swords to hand."

"Agreed, we will triple the watch," said Aetherhard.

"I would like to take my turn in the watch," said Helm loosening his axe from his back.

"Thank you, Helm," said Aetherhard. "You can take first watch with me and ….. Davel," he called to an elf as he looked around his troops. "First watch after we have eaten," he called to the elf, who nodded.

"Luther, it is unusual for the Celts to be this far north, is not?" asked Berolarn.

"Yes, they are usually at least fifty leagues further south. This is quite far north. But, even for them, it is too cold, and food is more scarce," answered Luther.

"I wonder why they are here?" mumbled Berolarn. "They must have had wind of us arriving in their lands. Why else would they arrive in the same area we travel."

"Are they hostile?" asked Lauren while listening to their conversation.

"I would say neither friendly nor hostile as long as you do not travel near their communities. They class this land as their own and do not like outsiders. Yet they tolerate people travelling their lands in the rare instances it occurs," said Aetherhard, who shrugged. "But, if you do not bother them, they do not bother you."

"We forget, Aetherhard, that we are an armed party of nineteen. They would see us as invaders, perhaps or worse. Therefore, it is dangerous for us to parley with them, "Luther responded. "Why or who are they searching for? No, I do not like it."

"Yes, I agree, entirely Luther. Let us hope their mission is not us," replied Aetherhard. He then warned them they would enter areas where he knew the Celts had communities. This would mean that it was a possibility they would come across them. Therefore, they should under no circumstances engage in any form of hostilities with them unless they were attacked.

"Can I ask a question? What are snow bears?" asked Lilla

"They are what the name implies, Lilla," replied Berolarn. "They are great white bears that live in these lands. But they have mutated into a much larger, extremely intelligent group of animals over the last thousand years. You could say they have become comparable to wolves and dogs in some ways, if not even more intelligent and are loyal companions to the Celts.

They are extremely dangerous and challenging to stop in battle. They are brutal in the fight and can take many blows before they fall."

"I take it we need to stay clear of them then," said Lauren with a grin at Lilla.

After discussing Celtic warriors and snow bears, the companions settled down to eat. It could be said that everyone was slightly more nervous about the environment outside of the wind and snow. Yet the hour passed with the weather unrelenting but with no signs of the Celts. After eating, the first watch began, and the others prepared for bed and sleep.

The evening passed uneventfully through the night to morning. It was still dark when Lilla nudged Talis awake.

"You awake," she whispered as she prodded him.

"I am now. What's up?" asked Talis through squinted eyes as he pulled his blanket tighter to keep the shiver from running up his back.

"I've been watching you for over an hour. It is still snowing, but the wind has died somewhat. I think it will be hard going once we set off. It's going to be really deep in places," smiled Lilla.

Opening his eyes further and seeing Lilla's beautiful smiling face warmed his heart.

"Morning, you," he said hesitantly as she moved closer and kissed him.

"Morning, Luther is out and about from what I can see," she answered as if reading his mind. "Most are already up and about, sleepyhead. Lauren is over there with Elisha." She said as he looked at the missing body under Lauren's blanket. "I think we should get up and eat, or they will be setting off before we know it."

Talis stretched and jumped up in an attempt to show the cold he was ready for anything that it would throw at him. He helped pull Lilla up, too, and they moved towards the fire's dying embers from the night before. They stood there for no more than a minute, trying to gain any heat it had left. Before they grabbed all their furs and put them on as quick as possible. Then set about eating the cold rations with freezing cold hands. Unfortunately, they found it was a joyless experience and the food offered little to them.

"When are we leaving?" asked Talis to anyone who was listening.

"Luther and Aetherhard are out scouting at the moment. We will leave as soon as they return," replied Elisha breaking her conversation with Lauren. "A wooden bridge nearby will take us over the river."

The group waited for some time as morning light started to break through the forest canopy. Then, finally, Luther and Atherhard returned. The scouting trip had been good. They found no more evidence of the Celts or their beasts, and their tracks had been covered by the snow. Luther could see no new ones had come in their place anywhere in the surrounding area.

"Hopefully, it was just a scouting party, just travelling the lands," said Luther. "We ventured a little over the bridge, and again no sign."

"Good, let us be off then," replied Berolarn. "We have a long road ahead, and the quicker we get further south, the less harsh I hope the storms will become, even in this land of ice."

The companions finished packing their belongings and started back on the trail towards the river. Lilla had been right. The overnight storm had cleared but had left the track now nearly knee-deep in snow, and it was going to be hard going and would inadvertently slow them down. They noticed that none of the elves actually sunk into the snow as they walked. They were all walking on the snow as if it was solid land. Elisha was the same as the soldiers. Lauren marvelled at this and whispered to Lilla and Talis.

"How are you doing that, …… Elisha," Lauren called out to the Princess.

"What is it, Lauren?" replied Elisha.

"You elves can walk on the snow without sinking," answered Lilla as she could hold her surprise no longer. Elisha and some of the elves close by smiled as if Lilla had said something amusing.

"We are gifted with magic, Lilla. I ….. we….." she said, looking around at the other elves with her arms motioning. "….. have decided we will use a little magic to stop us sinking."

"Can you do that for us," said Lauren in awe and excitement.

Elisha giggled and found this very funny.

"I am sorry, Lauren, I jest it is no magic as you know it. It is ….. how can I put it ….. we inherited a skill from our ancestors, we do not even realise we are capable of doing it. It happens naturally with every step we take. You would struggle to find many blades of grass that have buckled from the weight of an elf. Only someone such as Luther would note our passing," answered Elisha.

"Wish I was an elf," she muttered slightly too loudly.

The comment caused everyone to laugh. Which made Lauren grin.

It is good that they are all smiling, thought Berolarn. This weather is depressing enough. As Berolarn followed those in front of him. He looked at Lilla and Talis intently as they talked, trying to ascertain if they spoke to each other with the exuberance of youth or if it was more than that, was it, young love. Berolarn was sure it was the latter and wished it could have been different. What concerned him now was how this was all going to play out.

There were many moving parts to this war, which could jeopardise things if they didn't all fall into place. He had already forfeited much in his attempts to stop Olgrich, and was he prepared to lose more, he asked himself? He wasn't sure he was. The intertwining of fate and destiny could not have their paths altered. Berolarn knew this, though he often tried to change this final destination. It was the primary order of nature and the gods. Only the strongest of magic could cause a ripple in the fabric of time. He sighed to himself. For some reason, he was feeling his age today, and the aches of a thousand years had come to strike him. His mind was full of riddles he couldn't hope to solve as he trudged through the thick snow.

"Lilla, come talk to me….. only for a little while," he requested as he saw she was torn already from leaving Talis's side. Perhaps the bonding of these two is by the design of Sol. Thinking back to the pendant and the ring.

"I would enjoy your company for a while as I am weary, and

I need something to kick the cobwebs from my mind this morning." He added as she waited for him to catch up with her.

"Thank you, Lilla. We haven't talked much since I arrived at the inn," he said in a jovial manner as he tried to lighten his usual tone. "Funny to say how much we have recently travelled in each other's company."

"I must admit I thought you were avoiding me a lot of the time or perhaps thought I added little value to the company," Lilla said apprehensively.

"No, that was never my intention, and to be honest, you never should underestimate or overestimate the value someone has or can bring to any situation. This is something you should never forget. No one knows what is on the other side of a person's destiny. So many people live a life half in the shadow and half in the light as they battle whatever life throws their way. People's choices tip the scales one way or the other, like throwing dice. They are usually quite random," soothed Berolarn.

Lilla nodded as she tried to work out what Berolarn was mumbling about. She always knew what she was doing. She was sure of that.

Lilla and Berolarn continued to talk for several hours as they travelled, and to be fair to Berolarn, Lilla found the conversation not as bad as expected. He was always lovely when you started to strip away all his words of unfathomable wisdom. Berolarn told her little snippets of his life and travels. He talked of the wonders he had seen worldwide, ancient buildings, exotic plants and wildlife, great mountains, rivers and deserts.

As Lilla continued to show signs of feeling safe in Berolarn's company. Berolarn started asking her many questions, and he showed a great interest in Lilla's life. He wanted to know everything about her time growing up at the inn, how it was in the care of Luther and Biggy, her friends, what she did when she had not been working, and her whole Lowedom life. Berolarn was interested in all the small details. Lilla occasionally thought to herself, why is he interested in what I have been doing all my life? Her life at Lowedom seemed now to be a different world and a million miles away from who she was now, even though that life she had left behind could be measured in years, not months.

Berolarn was keen to see if she remembered anything from her childhood, which she didn't. She had banged her head when she was a young teenager, and Lilla remembered waking up having no recollection of who she was and her childhood. Luther had filled in the gaps and told her everything about her rescue as a baby. He has explained how he looked after her, though that last statement was incorrect. It was Biggy who looked after her. She told him this story again, and he talked about destiny and mumbled that it was a shame things couldn't have been different. This is where he started to lose her again.

"And what about Talis?" Berolarn finished.

"Sorry, what?" Lilla asked, making sure she heard him correctly.

"Talis ….. you pair seem to become extremely close. I wondered if you would share with me your thoughts on Talis," challenged Berolarn.

Lilla was taken aback by the question. Though she had played out many scenarios in her head of a life with Talis. Lilla had not discussed it with Talis, and though Lilla felt he cared for her, maybe even loved her. Lilla was scared if she mentioned any future plans to him, he might push her away. Especially when they were in the middle of all this confusion. He was a man, after all. Her friends from her former life had told her all about men and how weird they could be around the subject of settling down. She was sure Talis was the one. She thought to herself. Talis made her stomach flutter and her brain all mushy. Yes, she loved him fiercely.

"What would you like to know?" Lauren queried Berolarn.

"Anything you would like to tell me," probed Berolarn.

The pair continued their war of words on Talis, where Berolarn continued to ask Lilla teasing questions that brought out a continuous stream of answers from Lilla. Little by little, she started to pour her heart out about her hopes and dreams for the future. Finally, Lilla realised, after the long discussion, that Berolarn had somehow stripped her soul bare, and she had told him everything about her relationship with Talis. Berolarn noticed the look of realisation cross over Lilla's face.

"Do not worry, Lilla. Your secrets are safe with me, I promise." Berolarn acknowledged smiling and patted her hand. "It is good to love and hold what is dear to you close to your heart."

"Well, I better go back to Talis. Look at his face. He looks as if he is miserable without me," chuckled Lilla smiling.

Lilla was wondering how Berolarn had managed to extract all that from her and how he knew she had realised. She jogged forward to catch up with Talis and started talking to him, looking over her shoulder at Berolarn.

Berolarn was happy for the child in some ways. Love was the most potent force in the universe. If perhaps the most dangerous. It was well known to him that love clouds the mind and good judgement. He had suffered the perils of love himself and had made poor judgments and irreversible decisions on the back of it. He thought about how he had told Luther they must stop this relationship from continuing. Was this the right decision? Berolarn was beginning to think that perhaps it wasn't. It was an attempt to interfere in their destiny for the greater good. But maybe this love would be what is needed. Yes, he would speak to Luther and advise him to let things lie.

After Berolarn and Lilla had finished their conversation, the companions stopped for the evening and made camp. They had encountered no living soul on their second day of travelling south, and the weather had been a lot kinder on them.

Throughout the evening, Talis periodically enquired of Lilla why she had spent so much time with Berolarn. She made light of the conversations they had, had. She concentrated much on what Berolarn had told her about the lands he travelled and Lilla's life at Lowedom, much of which Talis knew. Talis got bored with the questioning, and much to Lilla's relief, he had engaged the two in conversations with Lauren and Jenna. Jenna was telling Lauren tales of high adventure, and Talis was keen to listen.

The companions continued travelling for two weeks southwards, and Caledonia's lands had not changed much. It was still all mountainous regions and woodlands. The weather had been unrelenting for much of this time. It was with great relief that the wind didn't howl or the snow relented for a little while. However, everyone had generally remained in good spirits. Even the dwarf, Helm. Who was noted for grumbling about many things! He had trudged on with little remark on the weather, their main problem.

Chapter 23 – Fergus and Heather

The next day they had set off early and had been travelling for a few hours when suddenly, in the distance, they could see a host of beasts baring down on them.

"Quickly, make for the trees, Celts," shouted Aetherhard as he turned and started running towards the nearby wooded area.

As the companions ran for the cover of nearby trees, it was evident that the Celtic warriors had seen them and were giving chase. There were several warriors mounted on snow bears bearing down on them.

"You there, stop," shouted a booming voice. "I said stop, or the penalty is death."

"Everyone, stop where you are and let me talk," urged Aetherhard. They all turned and waited as the great snow bears bore down on them and started to circle the company.

"Greeting friends, we are travelling through your lands, bringing no harm to them. We ran, unaware that a noble Celtic clansman was bearing down on us," said Aetherhard.

"Aye, hear this, men. We have an elf, in fact, many elves amongst us," said one of the warriors, who was obviously the leader, as he pulled up in front of Aetherhard. "What are you doing in our lands, elf," he said with humour in his words.

"Whoa, hold on a minute. I recognise a few here. Well, well, well......look who we have here.......Princess Elisha, no less, unleashed from her father's side, I see. No daddy here with you?" he laughed and then turned towards Luther.

"And then the dog's turd himself," jested the man, spitting towards Luther. "Luther, how are you? Still look like shit to me, if I am honest," he laughed as he continued to peruse the companions.

"Ah, your Master Berolarn," he marvelled, pointing at Berolarn accusingly. "Long time since we have seen you grace our lands. I think I was just a young man when they last talked about the false prophet, the shaman, the infidel."

"Oh my, look at these two beauties you have brought me ..... mmm, you look good enough to eat." he drooled towards Lauren and Lilla.

"Come near me, pig, and I will slit your throat before you draw your next breath," hissed Lauren as she drew her long knife without thinking. In doing so, all the Celtic warriors around them burst out laughing.

"Oh my," said the man, rubbing his crotch. "Come here, girl. Let's see if my weapon is longer than yours," the man roared with laughter.

With this, he fell off the snow bear in his hysterics. Then, jumping to his feet, feigning movement toward Lauren and continuing to laugh really hard, he abruptly turned direction and gripped Luther's arms.

"My dear friend, it has been a long time," he said. "Sorry, Princess Elisha. We have to have some fun and, again, a very long time." He said with a mocking bow. "Berolarn, what I said still stands," he grinned as he turned to Lilla and Lauren. "Many apologies to both of you. But you are stunning, young and full," he jested. "I sure we have many who need a wife."

"How much?" he asked as if he was looking for takers.

"No?" He laughed again.

"Come Luther, why are you in my lands, you old dog." He smiled as Lauren and Lilla looked around at the circling men apprehensively.

"Do not worry. You are all safe," noting the worry on Lilla and Lauren's faces. "Now come, Luther, speak before I run you through."

"Hello, Fergus, I see you have lost none of your wit and charm," remarked Luther with a wry smile. "It has been a long time, my pig-snouted, vomit-eating friend. I wondered if we would have the misfortunate to cross paths on our journey. But, unfortunately, it appears fate has again not been kind to me."

"Ah well, you know what I say about fate, it is a treacherous old dog, and only the village idiot would believe in such things," Fergus replied, laughing. "Tell me why you are here ….. no, in fact, why not come back to the village as my special guests," he said, grinning at Elisha. Who nodded in return. "The night will be on us, and it would be good for you to come and make merriment. You will be fed well and given a warm bed. I am sure Heather would love to see you again."

"How far is it?" Blurted out Lauren as she dreamed of warm food and a bed.

Fergus turned to Lauren, trying to give her an over-comical smile.

"Not far, beautiful. We can carry you all on our steads. No problem carrying three or four each. I would have you three ladies ride with me," pointing at Lauren, Lilla, and the Princess.

"Don't worry, Luther or you, my good captain. That's what you are, is it not? Elf," he said, looking at Aetherhard. "They will come to no harm. I only jest," Fergus stated thoughtfully. "It would be my honour to take the royal highness and the two ladies on my ride. His name is Bobster, and he will carry you truly and safely."

Luther nodded to Lilla to confirm it was ok.

"That sounds a great idea, Fergus. Thank you for your offer," said Elisha.

"Is that ok then, Luther? We can talk as we eat?" asked Fergus, grinning at them like a lunatic.

"Yes, sounds good, my old friend," replied Luther.

"Good, Ladies, this way," he said as he escorted the three women to the side of Bobster. Then, he scooped up Lilla with one momentum and threw her upwards onto Bobster.

"You are not….." Lauren started to say as he grabbed hold of her and did the same as he did to Lilla. "Doing that to me," she finished as she started to sail through the air.

Elisha seeing what was happening to the joy and amazement of Fergus, ran at him at speed, jumping and pushing herself off his giant shoulders and flew upwards through the air. She somersaulted as she passed and landed perfectly in front of Lauren, Lilla, and behind Fergus's massive saddle.

"That was amazing," crowed Fergus, laughing with an open mouth. "you must do that again before leaving. So come every one, pick a mount and let's be off."

Everyone else proceeded to get on top of a snow bear, taking help from a rider where needed. Soon they were off, Fergus gave his snow bear his head, and he and the other snow bears ran at pace. Yet, though they ran as fast as any horse, the companions found the ride was smooth, and they did not have to cling on for their lives. Instead, it was like sitting on top of a slow-moving horse. The only thing that showed they were running was the quickly changing landscape and the wind in their hair.

They rode for nearly an hour, and the night was indeed drawing in when they started to make out the lights of fires in an area cleared of any trees. The closer they got, Talis and the others saw it was a large village that backed onto the side of a mountain. It was enshrined in a surrounding wall of tree trunks, some thirty feet high.

As they rode towards the massive gates, they heard the bellow of what must have been a large horn which seemed to emanate from one of the three watchtowers that soared upwards out of the fortress walls. Then, with the horn blast, the gates opened, and the snow bears all galloped in.

They worked their way through the village. Which was a collection of various wooded buildings laid out across the area in no particular fashion. Finally, they advanced towards the mountain where a large wooded two-story building had been erected against it. As they got closer, the Celtic warriors started jumping off the snow bears mid-flight as the snow bears continued towards another massive building.

"Bobster," shouted Fergus. His snow bear stopped, which led all the others to stop. "Sorry about that, I forget. Please dismount and come this way."

The other warriors left Fergus waiting for his guests to

dismount and join him. When the last of the companions had worked a way out of the throng of the snow bears. Fergus shouted again, and the snow bears trotted off into the other massive building.

"Sorry, sorry. The bears are used to just going straight to bed. They do not usually take any further heed of people still being on their backs. They just expect all who ride to have jumped off. Come, come..... this way," he said as he guided the company into his home.

As they walked through the significant doorway, they heard a lot of commotion as many people were laughing and joking in the great hall they had just entered. Circular in size, it could probably have held two hundred people comfortably. Rows of large tables were at one side, obviously used for banquets. A sizeable area was roughly marked out next to the clear banquet area. Perhaps this was used for dancing and merriment, thought Lauren thinking back to their inn. Then opposite the doors was a large raised stage area with steps leading up to it. There was a smaller table at the side of the stage and some oversized chairs looking out into the room. They look like thrones, thought Talis.

"Heather, where are you, woman" shouted Fergus as he walked towards the stage, turning around to the companions, "over here," and then crying again, "Heather."

"What are you shouting for, you flee bitten bastard son of a ....." said a red-haired woman as she entered the hall.

"We have guests, my love," hooted Fergus as he waddled over to her and attempted to start waltzing by grabbing her roughly by the waist. Which resulted in her knee rising upwards and her hand striking him hard across the face.

"You drive me insane," she said as she pushed the now prone Fergus over.

"Please forgive that doggard for everything he has done and, unfortunately, anything he is bound to do whilst you are in our company," she grinned as she came up to them and started greeting them all. Then, stopping at Lauren, she stepped forward and ran her hand through Lauren's hair and down her face.

"So pretty, you are beautiful and what lovely hair. I have never seen anything like it before …… so pretty," Heather smiled. Much to the annoyance of a now red-faced embarrassed Lauren. Then she came upon Luther.

"Ah, I see why he is giddy now …. Luther, you have him dreaming of war. I bet. Well, that old fool is no warrior anymore. He eats and sleeps more than he wields a sword nowadays. He is good for nothing, Luther….. Nothing."

"Hello, Heather. I see Fergus is still the most loved husband one would ever wish to meet," joked Luther.

"He's nothing but filth, you know it, I know it. But he is my filth," beamed Heather, looking back at Fergus.

"I am still here, you know." winced a red-faced Fergus.

"Well, get up then and make our guests welcome, fool," shouted Heather.

Lauren, Talis and Lilla were all thinking the same thing. They had never ever seen anything like this encounter between what was obviously man and wife. Fergus got to his feet unsteadily and started barking orders as he walked across to the stage.

He gingerly made his way up the steps and sat in the main chair, his throne, as Heather gracefully sat in the one next to him.

Fergus shouted down. "Elven warriors, please sit on the side down there, and food and drink will be brought."

"Princess Elisha, Luther, get the rest of your party up here and sit at my table…… I will come and join you in a second once the pain has gone," he hissed at Heather.

Fergus and Heather joined the party at the table as young teenage boys and girls started bringing food to the tables. Talis noted that the downstairs tables had also begun to fill, and the room was a hive of noise and activity. As they all started to eat, they participated in various conversations. Then, suddenly, Fergus banged down his tankard after they had eaten what the bulk of the meal was.

"I will ask again," he thundered, looking from Luther to Berolarn and Elisha. "Why are you travelling these lands? It appears strange that there is unrest in the clans, years of peace between brothers are almost gone, and brother now fights with brother. Goblins, creochs and ogres now dare to walk these lands."

He looked down into his tankard, drank out of it as he threw his head backwards and again, he brought the tankard back down with a thump and stared deep into Luther's eyes.

"Now you return, Luther. Friend or foe, I ask. Walking alongside elves dressed for war and the warlock himself. Tell me now, what are you doing here," he asked with his loud booming voice.

Fergus's tone irked Heather enough for her to yank down on his beard and hiss at him to watch his tongue.

"I am sorry for the way Fergus was talking to you. He is a scoundrel who knows no better," she hummed sweetly.

"Damn it, woman, will you stop doing that. We do not know that they come in peace," Fergus cried.

These people are absolutely raving, Talis thought.

Luther smiled and then spoke to Heather,

"It is ok, Heather, honestly. You have known me a long time now, and I am used to Fergus." Then, turning to Fergus, "The dark lord has risen again, Fergus."

With that, Fergus jumped up excitedly and started pacing back and forth at the head of the table.

"I knew it, I knew it. Didn't I tell you, Heather, that something was going off? Oh yes, I told you. But you mocked me, eh….you see, I was right. The dark lord, you say, the rumours of the bloodsuckers are true. Very interesting, is a war coming? Do you need help? I am there for you, Luther, my men and me. All you need to do is ask," vowed Fergus.

"Shut up, you old fool," hissed Heather. "Let Luther speak and hold your tongue before I rip it out."

Fergus turned to his wife about to retort, and Lauren, who was closest, could see by the look in Heather's eye that there was a good enough reason why Fergus slumped back down into his chair. Lauren was thinking along similar lines to what Talis had been thinking, though amusing. These people are mental, and therefore they are dangerous.

"Luther, I must apologise again for Fergus, he has sat on his backside for far too long, and he craves his youth again. But, please do continue ….. and Fergus, calm down, or you are asking for it," continued Heather smoothly.

"Heather," nodded Luther before he continued. "Fergus, yes, the dark lord again arose out of the ashes, and the black cloud you see on your lands is the same cloud that all the lands are seeing. He has brought all the clans of goblins and ogres together under his banner and now seeks to wipe out all we know and create his new world order."

"The goblins you see in your lands are part of him flexing his arm, and his arm has grown very long. He is pushing down on the wills of men, dwarves and elves. I think he is looking at who will fall first. This party, assembled in the land of elves, is following the advice of Berolarn. We are searching for an ancient relic that will help us equal the might of the dark lord and give us a chance. Ancient scriptures reference where this relic once resided, and Berolarn has ascertained that it is highly likely to live in an area once called London. So that is where we strive to reach."

"Bah, London is smashed to pieces, now a legend of forgotten times and definitely a forgotten people," scoffed Fergus. "As for this relic, I say how sure you are it exists." Luther looked over to Berolarn.

"Fergus, you know who I am," asked Berolarn.

"I do. I hear you are a fake wizard and a bringer of ill omens," laughed Fergus. Then looking at Heather, quickly wiping the smile off his face.

"Look, Berolarn, you, Luther, ask me to believe in fairy tales.

The only magic I have seen, and all the magic we need, lies in steel and the hearts of men. I think you are chasing a dream," indicated Fergus as he took a massive gulp of mead and belched.

Berolarn opened his hand, spoke a few words under his breath, and suddenly, a blue and white flame danced in his hands.

"Look closely into the flame Fergus, you too, Heather. You will see what we seek and where it resides. Look closely. It will not harm you," explained Berolarn as the images flowed quickly into their minds. "Now see it in hand being presented against the dark lord and hosts. See the roar of the flame as it rises and falls in its path." Then Berolarn closed his hand, and the flame was gone.

"What witchcraft is this," shouted Fergus as he jumped up and was swiftly pulled back down by his beard courtesy of Heather. "You dare use witchcraft on me, Berolarn, the chieftain to my people."

"Will you shut up for one minute," hollered Heather. "Berolarn, unlike my foolish husband, who should know better if you travel with Luther and what we know of your work across the lands. If we say we believe you, what would you have us help you with?"

"I was going to say that," grumbled Fergus. "you always interrupt me and spoil everything."

Heather just gave Fergus a withering look and returned back to Berolarn.

"As already offered, you are more than welcome to stay the night. Rooms have been prepared for all of you, including your men. You are safe here, on my honour and have no doubt about this. You can decide in the morning if you require our help. We would be able to send men with you or offer anything else you want." Heather stated. "As for you," turning on Fergus. "One sniff, one little sniff of anything underhand from your direction, and you will wish you had never met me, do you understand"

"Oh yes, I wish I had never met you," Fergus muttered.

Lauren nearly gagged on her drink as she tried to stop herself from laughing at Fergus's comment.

"I said, "do you understand." Heather literally screamed at him.

"Yes, damn it, I understand," Fergus shouted back.

"Good," replied Heather with a smile. Then she looked at Lilla and Lauren. "Make sure if you ever marry that you get a good vision of what might be, keep him under control and don't marry something like that," she sighed as she nodded towards Fergus.

"More drink," Fergus bellowed. "Let the merriment begin!" he shouted over the balcony.

Berolarn and Luther continued to talk to Heather, mentioning the two Celts they had seen by the river searching for something. On naming Angus and Murray from the conversations, Luther had heard. She knew them. They were their kin. They had been out roaming the lands searching for goblins. They had returned this very day. Though she was surprised, they were so far north. Indeed it was worrying if the goblins were being tracked so far north. Heather told them that she would find out the truth in the morning, as they would be too drunk by now. After that, the chances of making sense of anything coming out of their mouths would be slim.

The companions spent the next three hours drinking, talking, laughing and enjoying Fergus's merriment. All the past tenseness at the table was forgotten. Instead, music, dancing and games were the order of the night.

Lauren discovered she was an expert at hand axe throwing and had come an honourable second in the game, outdoing much competition. She had a brilliant night. It was only later, when, much to his amusement, Talis told her that Fergus and others were trying to buy her off him as her brother, an apparent guardian, that the night slightly soured. Luther had overheard Talis telling her this. Luther interrupted the conversation and told her it was the way of the Celts. Whether it was right or wrong, they traded daughters and sons for marriage to keep the peace between different chieftains and their respective families.

It was called '*the way*'. It was meant to mean no harm, and in their culture, it was believed to be a good thing, and she should view it as a great honour that they considered her, an outsider, good enough to join the family. Lauren was not sure this was a compliment but kind of begrudgingly understood it was their culture as abhorrent as it seemed.

However, as much as she hated admitting it, she actually trusted Luther, and when Lauren told Elisha, Elisha smiled and agreed it was their way and to pay no heed to it.

Finally, after much of the night's festivities started to draw to an end. All the companions made their way to the several large rooms that had been prepared and went to sleep with a warmth that only alcohol could bring. Sleeping heavily, the night went unhindered for all as they lay restfully in the wonderfully comfortable beds.

Lauren was one of the first to wake, stretching and emerging bleary-eyed from under her blankets. She saw Talis and Lilla lying together. Lauren smiled as she gazed at them. Then, quietly rising out of bed, Lauren quickly put her trousers and tunic on. She ran across the room and jumped on the pair of them, causing a startled reaction, especially from Lilla, who still wasn't used to a Lauren wake-up call.

"C'mon, lazy heads, it is morning already. Let go and see whose up and if anything is going on." Lauren whispered rather too loudly. Looking around at Jenna and Elisha to see if either of them stirred. No sign there.

"Please, Lilla, get up. Talis, come on, get up. I don't want to go out there on my own," moaned Lauren.

"Lauren, you are such a pain. I would sell you to the lowest bidder if I could," grumbled Talis. Then, feeling that familiar punching sensation in both arms. He realised that not only had Lauren punched him, but Lilla had given him a playful dig. Just for good measure, he thought.

"Ok, I am getting up!" Talis said as he swung his legs out of bed and sat there, feeling harassed.

"You too," nagged Lauren as she grabbed Lilla by her arms and pulled her into an upright position.

Soon the three of them were walking into the main hall. It was a real mess. It looked like the villagers really did have fun last night. Then to their amusement, as they walked towards the stage, they saw Luther talking to Heather again, with a comatose

Fergus slumped over the table.

"Drinks himself to sleep, most nights does, my love," chuckled Heather as she saw the three of them walking toward them. "Come have a seat. I will have breakfast brought out, and do not worry about Fergus." Then, walking off, Heather continued, "We will not see his eyes open until after midday. That's one you cannot wake, I can assure you."

"Morning Lilla …. Talis ….. Lauren. Did you have a restful night?" asked Luther.

"Yes, what are you talking to Heather about?" inquired Lilla.

"Morning Luther," Talis replied for good measure.

I asked Heather many things, Lilla. Specifically for our purpose, I wondered what she knew of the goblins in the land, and if she had any news from the two Celts, we saw at the river chasing goblins. Finally, I asked if we had to be wary of other Celtic tribes," said Luther.

"And," challenged Lilla, slightly shaking her head and opening her hands for more information. Luther sighed to himself. Still the same inquisitive impulsive child. Lauren and Lilla are alike in spirit.

"Goblins are now everywhere but in smaller splinter groups rather than in a full invasion. Heather is very aware that it is now a difficult time for the clans. The two we saw at the river two weeks ago were indeed chasing goblins, and now they know we were there. They think they were tracking the trackers. They believe the goblins had wind of us and were searching for us. So they killed the goblin hunting party when they finally found them. Probably twenty or more were looking for us. As for the

315

other clans, she didn't believe any would harm us. But she couldn't guarantee this. Strange times mean strange things happen. Heather says she has an idea to help speed up our journey and needs us to wait until tomorrow as she must convince Fergus it is the right thing to do." He replied, "Is that enough for you, Lilla?" Luther asked sarcastically.

"No, what is this plan of Heather's," Lilla replied.

"I am not sure anyone will like this," Luther smiled wryly.

"Well?" asked Lilla

"Heather is proposing that she give us, or should I say, loans us a few snow bears to take us to our destination and protect us," stated Luther, who laughed at their faces after this news.

He could tell they were not overjoyed by the idea of managing these fantastic beasts.

"It will be fine if she can convince Fergus. It is an excellent idea. They are fast, brave and sagacious animals. It can only be seen as a positive for our quest," grinned Luther.

"Did I hear that correctly," said Berolarn as he appeared from behind Lauren.

"Yes, if you heard him mention the snow bears and heather's plan," Lilla answered.

"That is a wonderful idea," exclaimed Berolarn, looking doubtfully at Fergus. Knowing the love the clansman has for these animals. To part with even one was like mourning the dead.

"Heather will convince him. We spoke at length this morning, Berolarn." Luther said, nodding. "Ah, I was just talking about our host, Heather."

"Nothing bad, I hope. I have told all your companions that breakfast will be ready soon," said Heather as she walked up the steps and sat back down.

Not before long, all were assembled and were eating breakfast. Luther explained to Elisha, Aetherhard, Helm, and Jenna about forming the new plan. Lauren, Lilla and Talis went for a walk around the village after breakfast to get fresh air as the snow was light and it would pass the time.

When they arrived back and entered the halls, they could hear shouting that was obviously Fergus. It was clear to all of them that he must have woken, and Heather had broached the subject of the snow bears.

"No, No, No. What is hard for you to understand, Heather? They are not having one of them, never mind.....what did you say .....FIVE! Five are you mental," screamed Fergus.

"You listen here, Fergus. You do as I say. The outlanders need them. It serves us as it serves them," Heather shouted at Fergus. "You will do as I say, or help me, god. I swear I will make your life miserable."

"What will change there," Fergus shouted back.

"Damn your worthless hide. You give them the snow bears. I will not have us all perish because of your high and mighty stubbornness," threatened Heather menacingly as she stepped forward. "I am warning you, last chance."

"I said no, I am chieftain, like everyone else, you do what I command," Fergus screamed back.

With that last word leaving his lips, Heather was flying

through the air at Fergus and was grappling him to the ground. My god, she can fight, thought Talis, as the woman half the size of her husband had successfully gotten him to the floor and was grinding his head into the ground from her vicious headlock.

"No," came to a muffled comment from the red-faced Fergus. Talis looked around as he started to hear laughing. He noted that the hall had some of Fergus's warriors hanging around, and they seemed amused by their chieftain's predicament.

Fergus was now turning to the colour of a blueberry. Heather was still pushing on, shouting at him to yield and hand over the snow bears.

Finally, Fergus whimpered, "ok, fine."

"I knew you would see it my way, my love," soothed Heather as she winked in their direction and let go of Fergus, who rolled onto his back with his eyes closed, drawing deep breaths.

"I will let the beastmaster know that they are to be prepared for the morning," said Heather as she rose. She then exited the hall.

Finally, Fergus rose. Talis, Lauren and Lilla had not moved, held by shock and wonderment at what they had just seen. Fergus called them over and chided the warriors who had dared to laugh.

"I suppose this is your fault. You fell in love with my animals," said Fergus accusingly.

Lauren quickly answered, "Sorry, but I think it was Heather's idea. It was definitely not ours. They are beautiful animals, and I will do everything to keep them out of harm's way. I promise."

Fergus smiled, probably his first genuine smile.

"Thank you, girl. Those simple words are important to me, I love these animals like children, and they are dear to me. My wife is very clever, is she not? She always knows what is best. It takes me a bit sometimes for what she says to sink in." Rubbing his neck, Fergus continued, "usually it sinks in with pain, but I love her dearly," he laughed.

"The snow bears will be prepared, as Heather requested. I will speak to Heather and the beastmaster and ensure you get the strongest, fastest and wisest of them. No one will ever say, I did not do everything possible to aid the war."

Fergus then proceeded to call for drinks.

The companions had another day of drinking, eating and an all-around entertaining day. They found that Fergus and Heather continued their ongoing matrimonial arguments throughout the day, and they continued to amuse Lauren greatly. She did concede that this was definitely a place she could live. But finally, the day was ending, and the companions made their way to bed one by one. Lauren, Talis and Lilla discussed their apprehension about the next journey stage as they lay in bed. The wind had been ferocious all evening, and even in the great halls of Fergus, they could hear it howl.

Chapter 24 – Snow Bears

"Over here, this way," shouted Fergus as he walked across the yard.

He was dressed in his nightshirt and great fur boots. He looked hilarious to Lauren as she struggled to suppress her giggles as they followed him through the snow. How he wasn't freezing to death was beyond her, it must be all that alcohol still in his gut, she thought as she continued to smirk behind his back.

"What are you smiling at, Lauren?" asked Elisha as they walked together.

"Oh, nothing. I am just really excited to see the snow bears again," Lauren answered with a permanently fixed smile.

"Will you ride with me, Lauren? It had been a long time since we had spent quality time together. It would lighten my heart to have you alongside me," asked Elisha, returning Lauren's smile.

"Would love to. If I am honest, it would be good to give Talis and Lilla more quality time together without me being there. You know what young love is like," laughed Lauren, grimacing in mock at the thought. Elisha laughed.

Lauren has this unique way to my heart, thought Elisha.

As they entered the ginormous stables with the others, Lauren thought it was an unbelievable sight. Huge pens, lined in rows along either side, must be thirty of them. Elisha could see running all along the pens that whatever lay behind them was exhaling steam from their frosty breaths. If Lauren hadn't known better, she would have thought the stables were on fire. The smell was horrendous. Lauren thought it smelled like a thousand head of cattle must have deposited all their waste in the building.

"Welcome to my favourite place," said Fergus as he brought back the attention of both Elisha and Lauren. Lauren looked around excitedly for Talis and Lilla. Seeing them, she grinned.

"I have decided that you will take my snow bear, Bobster," he choked as the words left Fergus's mouth and pointed to the first pen. "He is the most intelligent, strongest, and bravest of all my bears, he will serve you well, and the others will do as he says," he said, rubbing one of his eyes with his giant ham hock of a fist.

Is he crying? Lauren thought as they followed Fergus along the pens. Finally, he stopped at two opposing pens and pointed to each.

"With him will go two you have met before out at the river, Bear and Bronte. Bronte is our most ferocious snow bear. Whereas Bear is just Bear," grinned Fergus.

"He is unusual, he is, hmm, how can I put it, clever but a bit soppy, his first thought is always friend rather than foe. However, where Bear goes, Bronte follows. They go together as one. Bear will serve you well. You just have to get accustomed to his character." He finished as the giant snow bear, Bear, popped his head through the colossal steel bars set above the half-door. He is beautiful, thought Lauren as he cried and started banging his huge paw against the bars.

"Bear, give over, get down, I say," shouted Fergus, much to the annoyance of Bear, who roared at him.

"Quiet, goddamn you," snapped Fergus, and he continued down to the following pens.

"Here is Bronwyn. She is ferocious like Bronte. It is a female thing, if I am honest. They are like Heather," cackled Fergus. "And finally, here is Baldrick. He is young and has the making of being the dominant male when Bobster retires."

"We cannot thank you enough," said Berolarn.

"Indeed, to allow us to loan such magnificent beasts must be a hard endeavour," commented Aetherhard.

"Think nothing of it, and to be honest," said Fergus pulling down on his beard, "I would have come, but Heather will not let me ….. anyway, come, let's go back and have breakfast and by the time you have finished the snow bears will be ready for the journey."

"What do they eat?" asked Lauren.

"You, if you are not careful," said Fergus playfully as he laughed. "Do not worry about that. Just let them go when you make camp. They will return when they have found their fill. You will find they will be gone no more than a few hours each evening."

After they had eaten and said farewell to all their hosts. They returned to the pens with a now-dressed Fergus and his wife, Heather. The five snow bears were all outside the stables. Each snow bear now carried a war plate on its chest. In addition, they now had a steel helmet with a prominent horn of steel protruding out of it like a spear. Each one was saddled for a lead rider, with giant reins tied to the front of the saddle. It was apparent to the companions that they would ride bareback as they did before when they first came to the village.

After much discussion, they had decided who would go together on which animal. Luther, Lilla, Talis and Jenna would go on Bobster. Helm, Berolarn, and two of the elven soldiers on Bronte. Princess Elisha, Aetherhard and Lauren would go on Bear at her demand. The rest of the elven soldiers then split evenly between Bronwyn and Baldrick. Finally, they all mounted the great snow bears and bid their farewells. Fergus paid particular attention to Bobster as tears flowed freely down his face.

"Goodbye, my friend. You keep yourself and your charges safe. Do you hear me, goddamn you? You better return, you big soppy idiot," he cried as he threw his arms around Bobster's lowered head as the colossal bear licked him. Fergus buried his head into Bobster's head and started crying uncontrollably.

"Come, Fergus ….. Fergus, he will be fine, my love," said Heather gently as she pulled the sobbing chieftain away from Bobster and pulled his head into her chest.

Lauren had never seen such a grown man cry so hard and was amazed at the love Heather was showing him as she tried to console him. Then, looking over Fergus's shoulder as she held him tight, she smiled at the companions.

"It is time for you to go, my friends. Go on, go. I will look after him," whispered Heather. "Go, Bobster, go, we will see you soon, I am sure," she finished with a stronger voice. Bobster, hearing the command, roared and started moving towards the large gate that exited the village. The other snow bears instinctively followed when the lead snow bear started moving out.

Luther quickly got a handle on controlling the mighty snow bears, shouting instructions backwards to Aetherhard and the three elven royal guards managing their respective snow bears. They followed his lead and gave the snow bears their heads. Then, within seconds of great roars coming from all the snow bears, they crossed through the wilderness at breathtaking speed. Unhindered by the deep thick blanket of snow, it was apparent how much time this would save the companions. Berolarn estimated that this would save them several weeks and that, all going well, they would reach the outskirts of London within three or four days.

Though the snow bears slowed down as the morning long disappeared and the afternoon was well underway. The pace was still faster than they had expected. The snow bears were faster than what horses would be on summer fields.

"I think we will make camp here," said Luther as he started to bring Bobster to a halt. "Night will soon be with us, and I think this place would be ideal for the snow bears and us," he continued as he surveyed a pocket in the woodlands. The companions were just about to pass the area when Luther noted that it would not only house the companions but would afford enough room for the animals to rest comfortably.

"Agreed," shouted Aetherhard towards Luther.

"Let's make camp then, and we can let the snow bears go on their way to feed," returned Luther as he started to guide Bobster into the woodland area.

Once they all were there, they dismounted and made busy making camp as Lauren helped two of the soldiers go around the snow bears, taking off their saddles. Lauren kissed Bear as she went past his curious face. She couldn't help herself. In response, he gave her a massive lick with his huge wet rough tongue. Then, giggling and looking back at Bear, she ran on to Bobster and whispered in his ear.

"Time for you to go and eat, my friend, be safe and return well-fed," she whispered. Bobster let out a deafening roar, and all the snow bears started to move out. Soon they were running into the distance and out of sight.

A few hours passed peacefully when suddenly Luther jumped up.

"Sssssh," Luther hissed.

Luther then moved in a circular movement around the camp.

"Goblins, and…. creochs," whispered Aetherhard as he got to his feet and sniffed. "I can smell them in the air," he whispered as he motioned the royal guard to their feet.

"Yes, I can smell their dirty hides, too," whispered Luther. "Everyone get ready for ….."

When there was an almighty crash, masses of goblins and creochs came at the camp from all directions.

"We are trapped. Fight," shouted Luther as a colossal goblin chieftain clad in black with the red insignia of the dark lord on his shield bore Luther down to the ground.

Within seconds chaos ensued as swords met with a deafening clash of steel, and shouts and screams echoed around the camp. Lauren jumped up at the beginning of the melee and, grabbing Lilla dragged her to a nearby boulder where they would have an advantage. Swinging her sling, she let fly with what round stones she had collected. Lilla desperately tried to keep the goblins at bay with her short sword. Preventing them from climbing the rock to get to Lauren.

At the same time, the elven royal guard stood in two ranks of five in front of Elisha. Working in unison, the two lines cut down many goblins and even two creochs. But they struggled to hold the weight of the goblin and creochs coming at them from all angles. Berolarn, conjuring magical flames from his hands, had a snapping creoch by the throat, and the smell of burning flesh was filling the air.

Looking around as she spent her last stone, Lauren could not see Talis, Helm or Jenna. Luther and Aetherhard were hard-pressed in battle with several goblins, and more were running in. The elves were falling, and Elisha would be alone. Making her mind up, she saw now that several creochs were circling the remaining two elven royal guards and the Princess. She grabbed hold of Lilla.

"Come, we must help Elisha," shouted Lauren.

Lauren jumped, pulling Lilla with her, and they attacked the flank of the creochs. It was all in vain. Three creochs had forced them back against the rock, and now Lauren couldn't see what was happening. All she could see was the colossal snapping jaws closing in on her as they fought for their lives. Suddenly as one jumped at Lilla and Lauren. A huge roar echoed around them as the creoch was caught mid-air and thrown like a toy. She saw it was Bear, and as she looked around in the slow-motion of flying snow, bodies and blood, to her sobbing relief, the snow bears had arrived. She had never seen such brutality and savagery as they cut down the goblins and creochs. Then, within a minute of the snow bear's arrival, there was a deadly silence as the last foe met their deaths. She looked around and threw her arms around the princess's neck.

"I thought you would die," Lauren sobbed as she clung to Elisha.

"Not today," Elisha said soothingly, stroking Lauren's hair. "Come, there are wounded. We must help."

Lauren's thoughts immediately went to Talis as she looked around with fear in her eyes.

"Talis" Lauren shouted as Lilla did the same.

"I am here," called Talis as he came out from the trees. He was like the snow bear's, covered in blood around his face and body.

Lauren and Lilla ran at him, grabbed hold of Talis, and dragged him close, unconcerned about the blood dripping from him. At that moment, they were joined in fear and relief as one.

"Lauren, Lilla. Come, we must help the others," shouted Elisha as she was helping up Aetherhard. He held a limp blood-stained arm with his other.

"I will be fine, princess. Please check our men." Aetherhard said respectively, even though he was in much pain.

Luther was helping Berolarn to his feet. Talis was trying to revive the dwarf, Helm, who had been knocked unconscious. Lauren and Lilla ran over to the elven guard who had been protecting the princess. Tens of goblins and creochs lie dead amongst the fallen elves. As they ran around searching for each elf. Tears were streaming down Lauren's face.

"They are all dead, all of them," she cried in shock and ran back to Elisha. "They're dead, Elisha, all of them." She could see the tears in Elisha's eyes, who shook her head.

"We mourn greatly the loss of such full lives that had much more to give, Lauren. But we also celebrate what they were and know they are now on the next stage of their journey to the kingdom of Sol. In that thought, we should take comfort and not let the grief overwhelm us. Do you understand that Sol has deemed this is their fate?"

"No," Lauren cried. "I don't understand all this death. It is pointless."

"I know, Lauren," Elisha said, kissing Lauren's forehead and wiping away her tears.

Berolarn looked on as he brushed himself down. Lauren will be powerful as her love of life runs very strongly within her.

"Where is Garrett?" snapped Luther as he looked around the fallen.

"She is gone," answered Talis, who was sitting down cross-legged, rocking back and forth as Lilla tried to talk to him. This was made an even stranger sight as Bronte, the snow bear, came behind him, and the great bear started licking the blood off the back of his head.

"What do you mean she is gone," growled Luther.

"Is it that hard to understand, Luther? I said she has gone." Talis shouted at him.

"You better start making sense, boy. I have no time for your games," said Luther menacingly.

"When we were attacked, she attacked me!" shouted Talis.

"What do you mean she attacked you? Speak Talis, I need to know," said Luther, now sounding shocked.

"She tried to hit me over the head," Talis answered. "I just saw the blow coming and managed to parry it. After that, we circled each other, and I was wary of her skill in combat. Bodies were flying through the air all around us. But my eyes never left hers. She grinned at me, and then she somehow had taken my legs from below me in an instant. Down I tumbled onto my front, and my head was being yanked back. A knife was about to run across my throat, and I saw Lauren and Lilla fighting for their lives. Then, in an instance, I had thrown Jenna from my back."

"I changed, ok! Jenna was gone ….. and I was flying through the air, biting, tearing, killing, and I loved it. I craved it, blood everywhere. I had changed, and this curse had taken hold of me. But for the first time, I could control it. It was now mine. I killed many, many with ease. Then the snow bears came." Talis shrugged, "I just let the hate slip away, and I was back."

"This is good news, Talis," said Berolarn excitedly. "No, it is," seeing Talis shaking his head in disbelief. "You are getting closer and closer to being its master. With mastery, great power and responsibility will be yours."

"This is all very well, Berolarn. However, I am more than concerned about Garrett," Luther shouted at Berolarn.

"I know, my friend, you are right. But, unfortunately, it seems that a long-time friend has turned spy for the enemy," said Berolarn.

"I just cannot believe it. Are you sure, Talis?" asked Luther.

"I am sure," replied Talis.

"It is an evil day. I have known her since she was a girl. I thought the gutter she was pulled from had been washed from her. But unfortunately, she still carries that burden of looking at the world from a self-first ideology," muttered Luther walking about, shaking his head.

"Well, it is what it is. This was no scouting party. I am not sure how Garrett communicated our position. But now I am sure she did. There must be over one hundred goblins here and what.... A score of creoch. This was no ordinary encounter," concluded Luther.

"Sorry, Luther, look, one of the snow bears is hurt," said Lauren as she lost interest in what Luther was saying.

Lauren had moved towards the snow bear, who was lying down. One snow bear was licking its leg, and Bobster was sniffing her. It was Bronwyn. Lauren could see she had a nasty sword wound in her rear by looking at her leg. Running to what remained of their camp beds, she grabbed a blanket, ran back to the snow bear, and started cleaning the wound as the other snow bears looked on. As she did this, the others discussed how to bury the dead. Lilla was helping Helm, who was just coming around from the blow that had rendered him cold. Helm ensured Lilla understood as she helped him to his feet that it was only a slight knock. He hadn't been knocked out. He was just taking a breather, and the girl should remember that he had killed several goblins in the battle.

Lauren stroked Bronwyn's giant head soothingly and whispered that was all she could do for her in Bronwyn's giant ear. The colossal bear nuzzled into her and rose gingerly, testing her leg. It was apparent that she would be limping for the rest of the journey. Bobster again came up to Bronwyn, and this time he growled at her and then looked at Baldrick with a growl. It seemed he had told them to go as they rubbed past him and started to leave the camp. Lauren ran in front of Bronwyn and tried to stop her, pushing with both hands on her chest. But the snow bear just looked at her and kept moving gingerly forward.

"Leave her, Lauren. Bobster has seen she is injured and sent her home with Baldrick as a guard," called Berolarn after her.

Though Lauren had her doubts and was fearful for the giant bear. She did as requested and returned to the camp.

"Let's build a pyre for our fallen," said Aetherhard, "and leave this disgusting garbage to any carrion who walks these lands with the stomach for such food."

"We must be quick," said Luther. "We have no idea if there is more already out there or if Garrett will bring more hunters. I say the bears have had their fill. They should be able to gather pace for a few more hours. That will significantly change our location to return us into the searched for, rather than the found."

"I agree. Everyone finds enough firewood to build the pyre over there," said Aetherhard. "And we can say goodbye to our friends and be off."

Within the hour, they were galloping hard, leaving the large smoking fire and a parting prayer behind them.

Chapter 25 – The Enemy Marches

They rested less and less over the last few days and pushed the snow bears hard to avoid the enemy. Luther was convinced there was now death all around them. He had told them he could smell war, the enemy's scent was in the air, and the chase was on. Maybe the southernmost clans were fighting the enemy. Perhaps the enemy had unleashed his hordes on Caledonia. Though one of the most challenging terrains, the Celts had no one to come to their aid. It was the Celts versus whatever the enemy threw their way. He thought that there was a potential that their coming to these lands and Garrett's treachery could have set the wheels in motion. To which Berolarn agreed it was a highly likely outcome. The dark lord would be highly concerned that such a group was banded together searching for the Dragonheart Stone. He would know exactly what it was and more than likely know what it does to his plans.

"How many leagues do you think they are, Luther" questioned Aetherhard.

Luther put his head to the ground. "No more than several leagues as the crows fly. They are close. I can hear they're running deep in the stone of the earth. We must flee." Luther urged.

"How do they keep tracking us, we have been running now for two days, and still, there is no let-up to the hunt," boomed Helm from the top of Bronte.

"Who knows what madness is driving them or what is chasing us? But we must go," hollered Luther as he mounted

Bobster again and shouted ride.

The snow bears, hearing the call, set off again at a thunderous pace. The scenery of the land was now flashing past the companions at such a speed. Lauren could only frame a hazy picture of lands, white with a splattering of grey stone and greenery trying to break out from the woodlands as they battled the blanket of snow. They seemed to be riding for hours, and it had been dark for a long time. The wind was starting to bite the companions, and most were now extremely fatigued, cold and hungry. But, as Lauren thought, they would never stop. Finally, Luther brought the company to a halt.

"We need to get off this road now." Luther hissed. "Look up there….. at the mountain, you can just see an alcove. There behind the tops of the trees on the rock face. It should be reachable for the bears as they can climb as well as men. It definitely looks big enough to house us all." Luther spoke with haste as he pushed Bobster towards the mountain and beckoned the others to follow.

Luther was right. The snow bears made easy work of scaling the side of the mountain. The party entered the alcove and dismounted. Berolarn went straight over to Luther.

"What is it, Luther," asked Berolarn as he grabbed Luther's arm.

"They come. The dark lord has unleashed his army. I can feel the thunder of iron-clad marching feet," replied Luther.

"Are you sure?" Berolarn asked, gripping tighter on Luther's arm.

"Yes, I am as sure as I am sure day is full of light, and the night is full of darkness," muttered Luther, pulling his arm away. "Now be quiet, all of you and no fires." He whispered over his shoulder as he went back towards to alcove entrance and the cliff overhang.

He knelt and looked out over the lands.

Maybe twenty or thirty minutes had passed when the companions started to hear a noise. A noise that was getting louder and louder as the minutes passed. The companions all moved to join Luther.

"Down, down, do not be seen," he whispered as he motioned for all of them to crouch lower.

The noise was deafening as the throng of many marching feet was now upon them. They could see many torches mingled within massive formations of marching goblins and men intermingled with lines of giant ogres pulling machines of war and goblin riders on the backs of creochs.

"There must be several thousand," whispered Talis as the backs of the army were now moving into the distance.

"The war machine is now moving. The chain of events we foretold has begun. The dark lord has now unleashed forces on two fronts. The time for guessing is over. I fear we may have finally tipped the scales, and the dark lord will now march openly on the lands. We must make for London as fast as the wind will take us. The time for any stealth is over," returned Berolarn, whispering.

"I agree, Berolarn," said Elisha, nodding. "I now fear for my people and wish to be done with this quest. The time to march to war is upon us."

"I agree also. But, I have pushed us, including the bears, hard. I will still advise that we take this opportunity to rest. I feel no more feet around us. The chase is done. I surmise the chaser has now joined the rest of the dark lord's legions as they march on the Celts," muttered Luther as he continued to survey the landscape

"We must leave early in the morning," stated Berolarn.

"What about Fergus, Heather, and the Celts," asked Lauren with concern in her voice. "They will all be slaughtered!"

"Do not be so sure, Lauren. I am not as worried as you might think. There are many clans. Fergus's clan is one of many. They know these lands better than any. They will all know of the march of the goblins already. News travels faster than goblins. The clans will come as one and will be a force to match what you have seen. As the war spreads and grows, they might fail as we all might fail. But that future is currently undecided," smiled Berolarn as he answered.

"Are you sure that they will join together?" asked Lauren

"Oh yes, of that much, I am sure, regardless of how they appear to the outside. The clans do have a form of government. Or perhaps I should say a loose form of allegiance to each other. They will sit in council, all the chieftains, and come out fighting. I discussed this with Heather, and she will already be putting the wheels in motion. Heather understands more than Fergus, and she will guide him accordingly," said Berolarn.

"Do not be put off by Fergus. He is not what he seems. His brain is sharp once the drink has cleared, and Heather could rule all these lands on her own. Have no doubt about that," added Luther with an uncustomary grin.

"Come now, the enemy has passed. We should build what fire we can, eat and get some rest. I fear more storms are in the air, and tomorrow will be another hard day."

"How much further now to London?" Asked Helm.

"By foot, it would still be several days, I expect with the snow bears......no more than one more day," answered Luther as he turned and indicated to all to find wood for a fire."

Whilst Helm was striking up the fire with his tinder box, the others made small conversations. Lauren went over to the now resting snow bears.

"Hello, Bobster," she said to the lead bear as she rubbed her face against the giant muzzle.

Then, walking over to Bronte, who lifted her head in waiting, she rubbed the great bear's ears as her hands caressed the snow bear's head.

"Hello, Bronte," she repeated.

Lauren suddenly found herself airborne as Bear lifted he up and pulled her over to where he had been lying. Before laying back down, Bear proceeded to drench Lauren's face with multitudes of licks, much to her amusement.

"Bear, stop, Bear will you stop it," she giggled, trying to push the giant bear's head backwards.

Bear finally gave Lauren a nuzzle with his enormous nose and dropped back down. Lauren sat down and slouched back into the snow bear's chest. Letting Bear's fur envelope around her. The warmth of his body and the rumble of the constant beat of Bear's heart and breath was very soothing, and Lauren dreamily thought of a new life in a small house with beautiful gardens, children and snow bears.

"I am not sure I will ever have a normal everyday life again, Bear. Already it seems a long time since I was home, not that home exists anymore," Lauren sighed. "I wish everything could be undone, my friend and none of this had happened."

The bear seemed to understand precisely what she was saying and growled gently in response.

"I think I will let the evening quieten down, eat with the others, and then I must speak to Berolarn." She continued and then was silent for several minutes as she sank deeper into the warmth of Bear's fur.

"You know, Bear, everything happening to Talis and this Solarian and Vampiri stuff. You see ….. the killing, …. the wanting for warm blood. Which I must say is extremely weird! ….. why is it not happening to me if I am a Solarian? I just don't get it. You know ….. when will I become this lunatic who kills everything in its path?" Lauren whispered and went quiet again for some time as she watched the fire roaring in the centre of the sitting companions, who were now eating some of their iron rations.

"Yes, no one has really told me, and I need to find out," Lauren finally said to Bear, and she pushed herself up out of the folds of his fur, kissed him farewell, walked over to her gear, and pulled out some food. She then went and sat close to Berolarn and started to nibble on the mundane crackers.

After a few minutes, no one was really paying much attention to each other. Lilla and Talis were talking to each other. Helm was already asleep. Aetherhard was with Elisha, who was busy changing the dressing on Aetherhards arm. Luther was outside looking into the wilderness. She decided to brooch the question with Berolarn, who was looking at something he was holding in the palm of his hand.

"What you looking at, Berolarn?" asked Lauren.

"Nothing, just a small child's trinket, an old family heirloom," Berolarn said as he put whatever he held into his pocket. "How are you doing, Lauren? It has been a strange few days," he smiled.

"I'm ok, I guess, though for weeks since we were at the palace, something keeps playing on my mind now and then. I wondered if you could help me understand, ... maybe help me make some reason of it all. I have tried to rationalise everything I have been told and logically thought about all the events since our village was attacked. But, I still come back to the same question," sighed Lauren with some apprehension as she felt she needed to say the right things to Berolarn to get the correct answers.

"What do you want to know? Lauren. Please tell me what is playing on your mind," questioned Berolarn.

"Who am I," she whispered and looked at Berolarn pleadingly. Berolarn expected that this time would come. In fact, he was surprised that it had taken Lauren this much time to inquire more, he thought.

"What exactly are you looking for, Lauren? Please expand a bit more, then I will try and answer as best as possible," probed Berolarn.

"It's all this Solarian and Vampiri ancestry stuff, the dark lord, magic, living for thousands of years .... it frazzles my brain. Then my twin is suddenly a potential lunatic," Lauren said, looking over to Talis and clearing her throat. "Virtually flying through the air, with some new unholy strength, ripping out throats, killing, murdering.......wanting to drink blood! .... And I am the same? Are you the same? I do not ..... understand ..... why am I not changing?"

"This is a good question, and I wondered when you would want to discuss it. But, I decided I would wait and let you find your own time to ask, and when you were ready, I would tell you," said Berolarn.

Berolarn started playing nervously with his hands as if searching for his following words.

"You remember when we were back in the council meeting discussing the histories of the world and the birth of the dark lord Olgrich Validoral? Birth of a terrible being through the use of the black book of Hel? Then we discussed the deliverance of the Solarians through their understanding of the works of Sol as laid out in the white book. The Solarians, I guess, is a term the breakaway group of Vampiri gave to ourselves. An appropriate term in reverence to the god Sol. But, Vampiri, we are, and Vampiri will always be at the core of our being. Did you understand this?" Asked Berolarn.

"Yes, I think so," Lauren replied.

"Good, as part of all Vampiri lives is the awakening," continued Berolarn. "The awakening takes you from what I guess you would say is a realm of what is considered normality for man to what you see in Talis. The thirst or the hunger, it is called. This occurs very early for Vampiri and is always on the date of their thirteenth year. The transformation is what you would call a managed transition. The Vampiri children are taught how to manage their thirst and control it though they do not stop it. Instead, they call on it and use the incredible power it brings. This power is not only extraordinary physical strength, agility, and the ability to self-heal and fly. It also brings an inherent magic capability and an ability to transform one's physical being. All this power varies from Vampiri to Vampiri. The males are usually physically stronger as with all kinds and call more to this side. Where the females are generally the wiser of our kind and master the magic more easily," pondered Berolarn.

"At first, I thought your father had somehow stopped this transformation, and I had to call it from Talis using my own magic to break through the walls created within Talis. I deemed wrongly or rightly that he needed to be able to defend himself. But, remembering, I had no idea who could be chasing him or how many of the dark lord's forces were on the hunt. As for you, you were lost to me until we met at Solanstar. Now, this is important to understand. When I broke down the walls in Talis, I was convinced it was magic from your father that controlled the rage from within, stopping it break free. I thought the same would be of you. Do you understand so far?" asked Berolarn.

"Yes, I have this magical wall also, and you think it was my father's creation using magic, and now you are not convinced. Which is fine. But, you are not telling me why you haven't helped me master it?" Lauren asked questionably with an evident frustration at Berolarn. Why does he never get to the point? She thought.

Berolarn smiled as he spoke.

"Patience, Lauren. You will soon have some answers. Firstly, it is something that is managed. We are out in the wilds with whatever hell the dark lord throws at us. It is difficult enough to be concerned with one going through the transformation in this chaos. Never mind both of you. Secondly, you are a female. Females are different. Powerful, terrible, and violent is the change. You are not only changing to become a predator, but you are also becoming a woman at the same time."

"We do not evolve like humans. Our timeline is definitive. The age of puberty at thirteen years is a traumatic time for Vampiri girls. You are emotionally vulnerable, and you don't understand why. Like males, there is rage and hunger. But, it is more. There is indestructible, overbearing wrath and terrible hate for a world that is impossible for the brain to untangle. Yet, in another moment, there is violent distress. You are full of anguish and flooded with tormented tears. A young sapling being violently bent back and forth in a storm. The change is much worse for the females of our kind, and it takes much longer."

"This is the premise of the change. The training is a few years for males and several years for females. The environment for Vampiri, as well as Solarians, is controlled. You are taught to manage your thirst. The management is obviously different. Vampiri still kills and feasts on the blood of others. Solarians have eradicated this overwhelming need for blood and ensuing carnage."

"We are now clear on this element?" asked Berolarn, looking at Lauren. "It takes time to become accustomed to your body and manage your hunger. There is also this added complication with Solarians; you are taught not to crave blood and the death of those weaker than you. You do not want those around you to bow down in reverence as if you were a god. We are here to serve the god, Sol".

"Ok, also with this comes the magic, as I have mentioned. So part of the training is to learn to harness the four elements of air, fire, water and earth and make them your own. These elements are the lifeblood of who we are. The extent of the power is dependent on the individual. The harnessing of the body, mind and soul in every one of us is different. The greater the bond, the greater the power. But we are born with magic. Yet, there is no control or order without the training, just chaos. Talis hasn't been able to use any magic even though the transformation is well underway. But, he could unleash it at any time with unknown consequences. If we had more time, I would also take you on that journey and help you become what you are meant to be. But time is currently against us," admitted Berolarn.

"Could I change then at any time?" Lauren asked after a few seconds of thought.

"I do not know, Lauren. I have held the change from another for my own reasons only once, and it takes great magic to do so and comes with unexpected costs. But, unfortunately, these costs are my own, and your father was never one to go deep into the magic. I have considered this often on our trip. I had thought it was your father. Then a dawning came onto me. It could be your maternal side that is controlling the change," divulged Berolarn. He paused himself whilst deep in thought. "Yes, it would make sense," he said to himself rather than to Lauren.

"What, my mother? What about our mother? We didn't know our mother. All we have is vague memories of someone who might have existed. What has she got to do with this." Lauren demanded.

Berolarn realised his tongue had once again gone too far. It was happening a lot to him recently as age was taken hold, bearing down on him.

"I only saw your mother once, before you were born. Who she was, I do not know. She was not a Solarian. Perhaps, an elf ….. or maybe a human. It could be that side of you both holding the Solarian half at bay. I would have thought the Solarian inside you would be more assertive. But maybe not. I am mumbling now of things I do not know," hinted Berolarn as he assessed the different possibilities.

He hoped this was enough to quench Lauren's need for knowledge as she tried to understand her being. He had an excellent idea of who Gabrielle was. The prophecy he had read told of it, though he had struggled to believe it. How had Loran met her? ….. and their love formed, he had no idea, though the Palantari stone could be part of it. Because then again, no one walked the paths that Loren had walked.

Berolarn had also dreamed, dreams that spoke of what their fate could be. He was sure they were muddled, confusing dreams directly from Sol and their destiny which was not closed, came with many options. The choices they made would tip the scales one way or the other.

"They say my hair is my mother's. My love of the people and the lands also come from her. My father said he would spend much of his time walking the lands, being taught the many wonders of nature with my mother. Many in the village said Gabrielle was a druid who brought healing to the surrounding lands, and food was plentiful through her work with nature. Do you know of this?" Lauren asked before continuing ….. "Anyway, one day, our father said she started to grow ill, that she was tired of this world and peacefully became a shadow and moved on to be with Sol".

"I am the hurricane in the mountains

I am the earthquake that moves the lands

I am the fire of the sun

I am the crashing wave of the sea

I am wrath

I am the one that gently blows your hair

I am the one who holds your steps

I am the one who warms your heart

I am the one who cleans your soul

I am love

I am the protector of the land

I am the lion in battle

I am the eagle in the air

I am the lamb who heals

I am the messenger

I am nature

I am knowledge and wisdom

I bring the word

I am might

I am all

I am peace

I am the weapon

Who I am and what I am

I am your servant

For you are the all-powerful glory"

"Sometimes, my father would say this canticle when talking about my mother. I asked him what it meant. He said it was an ancient hymn about those who are the greatest servants of Sol. I always took it that my mother was devout and a deeply pious woman, as was my father, I believe, at one time. But, like many recent generations, I did not really believe in the gods," admitted Lauren.

"I have not heard that rhyme before, if I am honest, Lauren. But, it definitely seems to be a tale of Sol and those who serve him at his very heart," concluded Berolarn.

"I think there will be a time when Sol's path that has been laid out for each of us will become clearer as we travel on our quest. Also, what is buried deep inside you will emerge if that is the will of Sol. If and when that time comes, I think, like Talis, you will become its master. You are strong of mind, yes? And of body and soul? You have all the keys to the door, Lauren. You will unlock the door and push it open when the time is right. I am sure of it," stated Berolarn.

"I am still confused, Berolarn, and scared. What if I cannot control this darkness inside?" asked Lauren.

"You must and you will," insisted Berolarn. "Now, I think we have discussed this enough for this evening. Also, I would advise not telling Talis of our conversation. Not for a little while, at least. He carries enough of a burden at the moment as he bonds his body, mind and soul together. Is that ok?"

"I guess," momentarily confused. "I will think of more things to ask you, maybe at another time," Lauren finished with a smile.

"Good, I am tired and think we should join the others and rest," Berolarn proposed as he surveyed the alcove, noting everyone else was now settled and attempting to sleep.

"Thank you," Lauren said as she rose and walked back towards Bear. Then, grabbing her blanket, she laid down alongside Bear. She let the mammoth snow bear's fur envelop her in warmth, and soon she was asleep.

Berolarn pulled the child's trinket back out and gently fondled it again as his gaze went from Lauren to Talis and then onto Lilla. He hoped all his decisions were the right ones. If only Loran was still here, he thought absentmindedly. Finally, after several minutes of deep thought, Berolarn put the trinket away and let the tiredness take hold; soon, he was also sleeping.

Chapter 26 – London and Significant Loss

They awoke early, it was still dark, and the morning was still asleep. A storm outside was howling, and the driving snow had started to enter the alcove. Nevertheless, Helm had been feeding the fire and kept it alight, and at least they were being afforded some warmth as they began eating some of the meagre iron rations.

"What is our plan for today, Luther?" asked Berolarn. "You said we are about a day away. Do we ride to the outskirts and make for the centre the following day?"

"I would think so. If the location of the white tower is still correct, it was near the centre of the city in the old world," replied Luther. "All of you should be aware, this place London was once one of the jewels of the world, massive in size, it had millions, not thousands of inhabitants. Much of what was, has gone, sunk under the ice that now covers these lands. Yet, even after thousands of years, much still exists, held together by the elements. No one goes there now, not even the Celts or goblins. They say do they not Berolarn that spectres now walk there in man's place."

"This is true in terms of the legends that haunt the minds of the Celts. I have been here once before, as have you, Luther, and we saw nothing to indicate any truth to this. Yet, there is no doubt that they exist in other realms."

"What are spectres, might I ask," said Helm.

"Spectres are apparitions, similar to what people call ghosts. But, they are not bound by any location. They were vile humans who committed heinous, murderous acts in a past life. It is said that they are cursed undead who must now walk the lands for all eternity. Their touch freezes the skin and steals its victim's life force by draining the soul of its essence," replied Berolarn indifferently. "They are the pets of the dark lord. Of that, I have no doubt. Some of the undead will be his attempts to create life."

"Are they similar to the deathwalker's?" asked Talis.

"They are both undead, yes. But the deathwalker's are more powerful, and they are the soldiers of Hel. The dark lord might use their being for his designs, but he did not create such monsters," answered Berolarn.

"More doom and gloom," whispered Lauren to Lilla, who giggled at the deep, ominous voice, Lauren portrayed.

"You would do well, Lilla, to keep your wits about you and listen to what you are being told," growled Luther.

"Luther, will you get off my case? I get we are in constant danger, and death is just one step away. I get it," she snapped back at him.

"Ok......., what happens? Say we meet one of these spectres things, what do we do," chipped in Talis.

"In general, I would say hide. They should pass you unharmed, and it's a big if we come across them. Then we will have to stand there and fight," answered Berolarn.

"They don't sound any worse than a goblin to me," said Helm. "I am sure my hammer will deal with as many as needed. What I want to know is where this stone is."

"It is at an ancient fortress, Helm. It was known as the

Tower of London in ancient times," replied Berolarn. "It is a castle of stone. Once a grand palace for a royal residence, it became a prison and the home of Britannia's crown jewels, as they were called. This included the sceptre we now seek. So when do we leave Luther?"

"I do not think this storm will pass. We must travel within its wrath. But, say, thirty minutes, the day should start to break. Seems the opportune time to start our travel," replied Luther.

The time came for them to leave, and they worked their way back down the hillside with the snow bears dutifully following. Finally, they mounted the snow bears on reaching the bottom and set off for their destination. The winds were blowing a gale, but luckily it had stopped snowing and at least they could see where they were going and the landscape around them. They all noticed that the land was starting to flatten, and they were leaving the mountain ranges and hills behind them. The woodlands, however, were still as dense as they had been throughout Caledonia.

Several hours later, after leaving, the afternoon was coming to an end and with it came the snow. A blizzard was now taking hold, and the companions were fighting against the wind.

Around this time, they started to see various structures frozen in a timeless state rising out of the frozen ground. It was challenging to work out what they were. None of what remained of the buildings resembled anything they had seen before. Some stood straight, others nearly fully submerged under the ice and some were dangerously tilted on their side, looking like they would fall over any minute. They were all in various states of decay. Some were damaged beyond any recognition of what they were. Ripped asunder by whatever struck the lands in the cataclysm, they were frozen in statue from another time. Corroded mangled steel was everywhere, as were the unusual materials the buildings had obviously been built with.

"What is this place? What happened?" shouted Lilla over the howl of the wind.

"Welcome to the outskirts of London. We are not far away now," answered Berolarn. "You see the beginning of what was the end. Mighty structures of old you are now looking at. Ripped apart by the actions of man, the effects of the cataclysm."

"Come on, let's go on until we can find some shelter in one of these buildings. We will not reach our destination tonight. It seems the perfect time to rest. Also, I am not overly keen on travelling through this place at night," shouted Luther.

"Agreed, lead on Luther," shouted Berolarn in return.

They actually travelled for a few more hours, and nighttime was upon them when Luther indicated a perfect spot. A colossal structure was in front of them. It appeared to have once been oval in shape. But half its structure was a mangle of frozen twisted steel that looked like it was about to drop down the giant slope it hung onto. But the rest of the structure, including the steps, seemed pretty sound.

They dismounted the snow bears and slowly walked up the steps with their weapons drawn.

"What is that," said Talis, pointing at a significant symbol of a cockerel that stood upon a circle.

"Interesting, I have never seen such a symbol before," said Berolarn. "Have you, Luther?"

"No, perhaps it is a symbol of a clan of old? Maybe one that was mocked? It seems to be a weak symbol whichever way you look at it," replied Luther as he looked up at the unusual motif that hung on the side of the building.

The party came upon some doors hanging loosely on the side of the building. Luther went in first, followed by Helm and Aetherhard.

"Looks all clear," shouted Helm to the others. "It's a large entrance area of some kind."

The rest of the party entered. It was one of the most oversized rooms any of them had seen. Several stories in height with corridors, rooms and stairs leading off it. Another cockerel symbol was on the wall with grandiose Letters To ten m otsp r underneath it. As they worked their way around the building, Lauren indicated a massive exposed area in the wall where they could lead the snow bears into the building.

Luther agreed, and Lauren and Lilla went down to fetch them up. The others continued to look for somewhere suitable to set up camp. Finally, Talis shouted he found somewhere not only big enough for the snow bears but also ideal for protection from attack. He led Luther to a room with two massive double doors that opened to a single-storey room, again large but long and thin, with an open plan side room, making it t-shaped. Large intact sheet glass windows along its outer wall gave a hazy view of the outside world. It had a smaller side door leading down a corridor with multiple exit points.

"I think it's ideal, Luther. I guess we can get the snow bears just through the double doors. There is an exit for them and maybe us through the windows, giving us an ideal opportunity to see any enemies coming. Look, you can see for a fair distance any approach. Then there is this door which leads to multiple exits down its corridor. Which we can bar, yet open in need," said Talis.

Luther looked around. Not totally ideal. Talis had missed the point that they could see any approach, but any enemy could probably see them if they made a small fire or lit some torches. But, It would do. In the city's wreckage, it was perhaps as good as anywhere. It looked like they could use the side room to rest, surmising they could build a small fire and with the bears on the outside of this room. They would probably block most of the light of the fire.

"Yes, I agree, Talis. This is as good as anywhere. A good spot. Let's get the others." Luther said to Talis as he looked around further.

Soon, all the companions were in the side room. Talis had jammed the small door in the main room from being opened outside. He had also managed to pull the double doors together and put a thin steel bar across their handle. He knew the doors were weak, and perhaps it would only afford them an extra second, but Luther thought it was a good idea. Soon a tiny fire was alight, and the companions were huddled around it, chatting.

"Luther, how long ….. will it take to ….. reach this tower? Any idea?" Asked Helm as he munched his way through a cracker and some dried fruit.

"Several hours at best. We could be there by midday if the weather is with us and the path is clear for the bears," answered Luther.

"Berolarn, can you look at Aetherhard's arm? It gets no

better. I think he is coming down with a fever," said a concerned Elisha, who had been dressing her Captain's arm daily. Berolarn got up and looked at it.

"I am not a healer," said Berolarn, "I do not have the skill for his arm," he continued looking concerned.

"Lauren, why don't you look at it," said Talis.

"Talis, I don't think …." Lauren started to reply.

"You have the skill. You used to look after the ill in the village," interrupted Talis.

"They were just aches and pains, Talis. The wounds of old age," Lauren snapped angrily. But Lauren was thinking, why on earth would he offer hope when she didn't have the skill?

"Well, you are the only one amongst us who has any of the healing art. So please, Lauren, come look," asked Elisha.

"I will be fine, Princess," said Aetherhard. Lauren hadn't noted until now how pale he was looking.

"No, Aetherhard, you are not alright, Lauren, please," asked Elisha again.

"Go on, Lauren," said Talis.

"Yes, please try, Lauren. You might be able to help," requested Berolarn.

Lauren was really annoyed by this. She really wanted to help Aetherhard, but what did she know about war wounds? Yes, she had treated people with fevers, using herbs that her father had said her mother had used. But Lauren didn't have any of them with her. So what was she supposed to do? Pat his arm and say there you go.

"Ok, I am sure I will not have the skill or art to do anything," Lauren said impatiently.

Elisha slowly unwrapped the dressing she had placed on his arm and showed Lauren. It looked terrible, inflamed around the wound, and it looked like a pocket of yellow fluid under the skin. She had seen this type of infection before, and it could kill.

"We must lance it and try to get the pus out of it. It is infected. Talis, heat the end of your knife on the fire." Then, looking at Elisha, "we need something for him to bite onto. This will be really painful, Aetherhard," warned Lauren.

Elisha thought a moment, then reaching into her backpack, she pulled out a thin leather belt. "Will this do?" asked Elisha.

"Yes, that will be brilliant," Lauren replied. "Talis, is the knife ready? Aetherhard, I must burst the infection and squeeze out all the badness. This will hurt. Put the belt in your mouth and bite down when I tell you,"

Talis passed her the knife, its tip glowing red. She tenderly reached out to Aetherhard's arm. As her hand wrapped around his forearm, she started to say,

"bite down….."

Lauren suddenly stopped, dropping the knife onto the floor. Her chest exploded with warmth, and in that moment of shock, a faint blue light encased her body and travelled along Aetherhard's arm. She watched, as did others, in amazement as Aetherhard's wound started to shrink before their eyes. Then, finally, Lauren heard Berolarn whisper Sol as the blue light began to fade and the heat from her chest dissipated.

"What the hell, Lauren," said Talis as he dropped down to

his knees next to her and looked at Aetherhard's near perfectly healed arm and then into Lauren's eyes.

"I …… don't ….. understand," was all Lauren could say as she let Aetherhard's arm slip from her hand.

"What happened, Lauren," demanded Berolarn.

"I was …… just about to stick the knife…..into the wound, Berolarn. I reached out ….. reached out ….. to his arm, and, and…..my chest went really warm, then my whole body ….. a feeling of peace and a reverence hit me, and like you, I ….. err ….. watched his arm heal," gasped Lauren, sounding really confused. "I didn't do anything," she finished defensively.

"Magic …… you have the power of true healing!" said Aetherhard in awe as he turned his arm back and forth, looking at it. "It feels nearly as good as before."

Berolarn kneeled beside her, looked into Lauren's eyes, and slowly pulled the chain around Lauren from under her blouse. Then holding the sapphire pendant in his hand, he looked down at it and then back at Lauren. It was still lightly glowing.

"You have the Palantari Stone, the sapphire stone. I now know what you hold. I have heard much of its legend; it is the Airmedial Stone, perhaps the most powerful of the palantari stones. It is a gift from Sol indeed. It is said that Sol blessed it for his chosen cleric so that whoever wields it can bring true healing to the world." Berolarn said with a certain awe. "It is a special gift you have, Lauren. Sol, for some reason, has brought this stone to you. You have been chosen. You can bring real healing back to the lands," illuminated Berolarn in wonder.

"I don't understand what you mean?" Lauren said with real

uncertainty about what Berolarn was talking about.

But, like, most, she had never really believed in gods. Lauren had only seen any supernatural signs and a belief in magic in the last few months. It was all very confusing, she thought as she tried to recall what her father had said of Sol. She and Talis had listened dutifully without taking much of Loran's lessons to heart.

"It is a sign, as the stones do not work for just anyone. To others, they just appear to be precious stones. But, the chosen of Sol, the stones imbue the holder with different and very distinct unique abilities. They are gifts from Sol to the lands. It appears that Sol, in his wisdom, had decided you are the one to bring the word back to the lands," heralded Berolarn.

"What do the others do," asked Talis.

"Well, after you managed to acquire them, I looked in the old Atlantean archives that the elves still hold. They are mentioned but not in great detail. However, the stones all afford the wearer a gateway to communicate with Sol," replied Berolarn. "How I do not know," Berolarn added as Talis pulled out his pendant and looked at it questionably.

"We now know Lauren has the Armedial stone due to its healing powers. The others are called, Astrayus, the astral stone. Creatil, the nature stone and Elemar, the elemental stone. From what I have read, Astrayus, it seems, give you the ability to travel space and time to other planes and worlds, perhaps even the homes of the gods. Creatil, on the other hand, gives you the ability to communicate and control the living world in some part. Finally, there is Elemar, the energy stone. You can manipulate the elements around you, earth, water, air and fire, to a great effect," revealed Berolarn.

"What do I have," said Talis looking at the Emerald stone in his father's pendant.

"I do not know Talis, as I didn't know until now in all surety that they were indeed palantari stones until Lauren healed Aetherhard. The histories are unclear which stone conveys which power. How you call on the power also is unknown to me. However, it is also apparent." Berolarn said, looking at Lauren, " Lauren didn't directly call on it as she had no idea what hung around her neck."

"And the ring," asked Lilla.

"It is a ring of protection, I believe. It affords the wearer some resistance to magical attacks from the forces of Hel," replied Berolarn. "I believe it will afford total protection from lesser forms of magic. But fortunately, it will also weaken a more powerful spell."

Turning back to Lauren and Talis.

"What is true about all the stones is that they also rely on the bond I mentioned, the bond between the body, mind and soul. The stronger each one is and the stronger the bond, the more potent the powers of the stones become. Hopefully, Sol will deem you worthy, Talis, and at some point, will reveal the nature of your father's stone."

"Where are the other stones, Berolarn?" asked Helm.

"To be truthful, Helm. I have never given the stones any consequence. I have never had any reason to believe they still existed. I thought they had passed with the age of dreams," answered Berolarn.

"I hate to say this, but I think my Father has one, Berolarn. He carries one identical to these. It has an opal, jet black, yet imbued with flecks of silver in perfect symmetry. It is handed down to each heir to the throne on the passing of the ruling king or queen," said Elisha with excitement.

"It seems to me that it is no coincidence that three of the four stones are now with us if what you say is true, Princess. I would say that Sol, ..."

Berolarn was cut short as suddenly there was a massive explosion, and the wall of glass was smashed apart by an invisible force.

There was a certain calm for a split second as the companions watched several figures slowly fly into the room and gracefully land on their feet. But, then, the snow bears, with great roars, were running at the intruders. As they darted across the floor, one of the black-clad individuals raised their hands, and red magic spewed forth, encasing the racing snow bears. Then, using the momentum of the snow bears, the warlock holding the bears in a magical entrapment swung around and sent the three bears hurtling past the enemy and out through the hole in the wall. The enemy continued to point his magic outside.

With a cry, Lauren jumped to her feet. She had to protect the bears. She had taken two steps forwards when she felt herself being yanked back.

"Don't move, Lauren," whispered Luther in her ear and gently let go.

One of the intruders stepped forward, he was clad in the same black and red attire that the Vampiri Selene had been wearing, thought Talis.

"No, come to me, child. It is for you that we have come," called out the tall man grinning.

"Me, my brothers and sisters, have been searching for you. But, much to the blood prince's frustration, we have struggled to find any of you again. His daughter, Selene failed him badly, didn't she Berolarn, and he has to keep punishing her, but she never learns. So anyway, here we are, and here you are. Together at last." He laughed.

"Darius, go back to whatever hell pit you came from. You are better served to be with the sewer rats than bothering us," spat Berolarn.

"Now, now Berolarn, my good fellow. No need to be hasty with your words, especially for one who has not enjoyed your company in centuries. We will leave your party unharmed. We want the three children only," replied the man Berolarn had called Darius.

"Darius, I repeat, you and your kind are not welcome. Go back to your master with your tail between your legs and live another day. Now go, I say, before you regret it," commanded Berolarn as his voice echoed around the room.

"Berolarn, don't be a fool," mocked Darius. "You cannot hope to prevail against the might of the Vampiri. You know this, Solarian. There is no point in your deaths being now, that will come in due course, but it doesn't have to be now. Lauren, Talis and is it Lilla. Come to me," beckoned Darius. "The great snake wishes an audience with you before we take you to the blood prince, and grateful will he be, and many rewards will be bestowed on you."

Lauren, Talis and Lilla all felt the pull to move towards the man speaking as he beckoned them forward.

"Unfortunately, your powers of suggestion have no hold on them," said Berolarn as he moved in front of them and was joined by Luther, Helm and Aetherhard.

"So be it," said the vampire Darius with a mock yawn. "Hold the bears at bay, Luca."

Glancing at the vampire whose magic was now raining through the hole down on the bears, stopping them from returning. He then turned his attention back to the companions.

"Here we come," Darius laughed, and the five vampires flew straight at them.

Suddenly Talis found himself flying backwards as a vampire propelled him back, holding him by his throat. He smashed through the wall behind him. Lauren didn't know what to do. Everything was happening fast. Berolarn and this Darius were in the heat of battle. Locked together in white and red flames as the magic coursed through them. Each was grappling with the other for a sign of weakness to gain the upper hand and mastery. Lilla was running towards the direction Talis had gone.

Luther was deftly parrying and circling another.

Helm's lifeless body was on the floor nearby, with a Vampiri tearing at his throat. She would never forget the sight of the female Vampiri ripping upwards and pulling the poor dwarf's throat away in her mouth and blood spurting everywhere. She screamed with gurgling joy as she threw her head back. Slowly the female vampire lowered her head, blood slowly dripping down her face from her large protruding canines.

"Hello, pretty," she said viciously, and grinning at Lauren, she flew at her.

Lauren instinctively brought her hand up to protect herself. The knife she held plunged deep into the vampire's chest. The vampire's eyes and hers met. Lauren could see hate, lust, fear and shock in the female's eyes as the vampire's blood started to wash over Lauren's hand. The vampire then began to violently struggle to get away from the pain. How had this happened, the vampire thought as she felt her life force starting to ebb away. Then she slumped forward onto Lauren, her head lifeless against Lauren's chest. Lauren pushed the vampire away, and the girl slipped off Lauren's knife and fell to the floor.

She quickly scanned the room. Talis and Lilla were nowhere to be seen. Aetherhard was also lifeless on the floor, and another vampire was feasting on his corpse. She saw Elisha lying on the floor, also dead? Luther was running towards the vampire, feasting on Aetherhard. Berolarn was now nearly on one knee as the vampire Darius was overpowering him. They needed the snow bears. She knew what to do. She ran at the vampire holding the bears in his magic. She sprinted towards him, and he turned too late as Lauren's knife protruded from his back. The magic died from his hands. Lauren heard the tremendous roar of the snow bears. She turned to see Talis emerging from the wall, carrying an unconscious Lilla in his arms. Lauren whipped round to see Luther's sword parting the head from the neck of the one feasting on Aetherhard.

Darius saw all that was transpiring around him as he nearly had the old Solarian on his knees. He was close to ridding the world of this meddler. But Darius saw the one he knew to be called Luther, the infamous master of combat, starting to come towards him. The tides had changed very quickly, and he was now at a disadvantage.

Then the children were imbued with powers that no one but he, the blood prince, understood. The snow bears were coming ….. It was time to go, but he couldn't fail and suffer the fate of disappointing the blood prince or the giant snake. Damn their hides.

A massive bolt of red flaming energy erupted from Darius's body with one great effort, throwing everyone to the ground and sending Berolarn flying across the room. Before Lauren's eyes, as she was picking herself up, she saw Darius transform. It was not a man before her. It was a demon. Its horned head now touching the roof of the room, huge red spiked wings appearing on either side of blood-red muscular form. Even his eyes looked on fire.

It was flying now at her, too quick. It was upon her. She felt herself being hit in the stomach as if a horse had smashed into her, and she was now held tight in the monster's arms as the cold air hit her face as she desperately struggled in its arms.

Lauren was gone.

Talis ran towards the hole in the wall, screaming for her.

But all he saw was the snow bears making their way back and snow falling from the sky. So he ran back towards Berolarn.

"Quickly, we must go. We must give chase. He has Lauren," screamed Talis in frustration.

"Slow down, Talis," said Berolarn, pushing Talis out of the way as he surveyed the room.

"Talis, where is Lilla?" he demanded. "Are all the Vampiri

slain? Or gone?"

"I'm fine, just a bit groggy," called Lilla from the opposite side of the room, who Berolarn saw was being licked by Bronte.

"Yes, all dead. Over here, Berolarn. It's the princess," shouted Luther. "She is losing blood from a neck wound, but she is alive. Aetherhard and Helm have left us."

Berolarn pushed past Talis again and rushed to Elisha. He saw blood slowly dripping out of two puncture marks at the side of her neck.

"She has suffered the bite of the Vampiri. Unfortunately, I am no healer but can help this wound," panted Berolarn.

Berolarn ran to his backpack and fumbled inside. Running back, he unscrewed a small bottle he was holding. He dripped a drop of liquid on each skin puncture. The skin around each wound on Elisha's neck sizzled with a bubbling effect as the skin smoked and gave off an acrid smell. Talis watched in wonder as the injury seemed to melt together until it was totally closed.

"She will have the scars of the bite for life and perhaps will feel pain there forever. But she will now live," assessed Berolarn.

Now he turned his attention to the highly frustrated Talis, who was pacing up and down.

"Talis, we now have two concerns. We have to look after Elisha until she comes around and shows us she is fit to travel, and we have to find Lauren. But, Elisha, we cannot give up on and leave alone. Even with the snow bears you have seen, they can be restrained by magic. As for Lauren, it has always been clear to me that she is only part of the prize the dark lord seeks. He seeks……" Berolarn said, pausing to Talis and glancing at Luther before continuing. "You both. He will know what we seek, I am sure. Darius will lay in wait at the Tower, knowing that we come for the stone, but also Lauren. He will have deduced we will have worked this out. He will attempt to thwart us from getting the stone and use Lauren as an incentive to guarantee you are there. She will be safe for now. Trust me."

Talis had a solid urge to disobey Berolarn and leave immediately. But he didn't know where he was going, and he guessed Lilla would be safer with Berolarn and Luther than him alone, and she would not let him leave without her.

"Ok, you better be right, Berolarn. If anything happens to her because we waited. I will blame you. I want you to understand this," snarled Talis as he went over to Lilla.

"Luther, help me get Elisha up. Let's sit her up against this wall. She should come around soon as the balm I used works through her system," muttered Berolarn.

Luther and Berolarn lifted the princess gently and moved her against the wall.

"Luther, close Aetherhard's and Helm's eyes, please," requested Berolarn.

He crouched next to Elisha and started looking for other signs of injury.

Luther walked over to Helm and then Aetherhard, muttering a quick verse of the Fallen Warrior as he closed their eyes.

"Though you now walk through the black night

The edge of your swords and axe now blunt

Your name and deeds ring in the halls of Sol

You now go on to meet Sol

In full glory, you stride to his gate.

There he will greet you

Your path is his path as you walk towards his heavenly home

Farewell until we meet again, the fallen warrior"

"It is done," Talis heard Luther say to Berolarn.

"You ok," Talis asked Lilla as he pushed Bronte away.

"Yes, thanks to you," she smiled weakly. "Just another one of those bangs on the head. I am getting quite good at getting them." Then, pushing herself towards him and hugging him, she continued," I see you can now control changing into whatever you become.

"It was strange, but you are right in a way. I didn't call it. The attack triggered it, I guess, as a kind of self-defence mechanism. The anger and the hate were buried deep inside. It was there, but I didn't have a burning need to drink …..blood," Talis said as he smiled sadly. "Then the power dissipated as quickly as it came. ….. I wish I knew where Lauren was," he muttered at the end.

"She will be fine, Talis. I honestly believe that. She is strong and resilient. I actually agreed with Berolarn's logic for once as well," replied Lilla.

"I guess you are right. Anyway, I was going to say I was sure you helped me beat that Vampiri when he gave you a clout. You had stuck him in the back with your knife, hadn't you?" Asked Talis.

"Ah, you saw," Lilla grinned. "I didn't want to take away from your kill, warrior." She kissed him lightly and cupped his face. Lilla then looked deep into his eyes as she spoke. "Lauren will be fine. We will get her back. I know it. You must believe it."

"I do, Lilla. Honestly, I do. As annoying as Berolarn and Luther are, I know they are strong and wise. They say she is the key. They wouldn't let her come to harm if they believed anything other than they could get her back. Let's go and see how Elisha is," Talis said as he got up and helped Lilla get to her feet.

"You ok?" Luther asked Lilla as they came over to where he stood.

"Just a knock on the head. How's Elisha?" replied Lilla.

"Feeling drained," answered Elisha weakly with attempted humour as Luther moved sidewards to show Elisha lying against the wall with Berolarn at her side.

"Oh, Elisha, you look pale," said Lilla shocked at Elisha's appearance.

"I will be fine. I just need to rest for a while," replied Elisha closing her eyes.

"She needs to sleep for a while. I think you three should also rest for a few hours. Then we will set off. The liquid I have applied to Elisha needs to work its way through her system and remove the Vampiri parasites, and she will be nearly as good as new. I will guard your rest with the bears," said Berolarn.

"No Luther," seeing Luther about to protest. "You too, I am fine, and I need to think a while. It will be no good if you do not rest. We will have a challenging day ahead of us, and I need you sharp. Go to sleep."

"What about you being sharp and ready, old man," asked Luther, labouring on the old man's part.

"I know what you are doing, Luther. You think a little insult will convince me otherwise," Berolarn smiled and chuckled. "Luther, I am a Solarian. I can draw my energy in other ways, as you know. Go sleep, I insist!"

"Berolarn, I seemed to be able to control what I am now, though not knowing when it will come or how to even call it. I need to know now what we saw, that Vampiri you called Darius. He turned into what the stories of old would call a demon. What was that? Will I become that? Please tell me before we rest," asked Talis.

"I agree, Berolarn. I would sooner go into battle with eyes wide open than flounder because my eyes were half shut. I have seen Vampiri before, as you know, but have never seen them transform into that," said Luther.

Berolarn nodded and then replied.

"What you see there is perhaps the true form of a Vampiri from ancient times before they took on the appearance of the Atlanteans, I think. I do not know the entire history and only have this as a theory. Anyway, only the chosen of their kind can transform into what you saw. I understand it takes the power of will and learnings from the dark book to take that form now. They are stronger, faster, more powerful in magic, and much harder to kill in this form.

Darius is of high standing and has the ear of the dark lord. Not so much a surprise that when the going was not in his favour, he transformed into the Vampiri demon that evened the odds," explained Berolarn. Then looking directly at Talis.

"This is good, Talis. Now you control it instinctively, and it comes unhindered when danger is in front of you. Soon you will be able to call it without thinking. The powers you see that I have. I do not have to call it anymore. It is now a part of me as much as I live and breathe. You will progress to this soon. You have come far really quickly. Well done. Now I really do insist," said Berolarn looking around the companions. "You must rest. Go on sleep."

Talis and Lilla helped Elisha to her feet and moved back to the side room. Talis searched through Helm's backpack and relit the fire on finding the tinderbox. Slowly bringing warmth back to the room. Luther entered after several minutes as the others huddled together. Lilla had her arm around Elisha, helping her get warm.

"I have discussed further with Berolarn. We will rest here now until tomorrow. We do not expect any further attacks. It would be best that we rest until we recover our full strength. He is currently creating an invisible magical wall around the room. He says it is devilishly difficult to break down even by the strength of numbers or magical attack. But, he says, if and we both think, if they decide to come back, we should not only have time to make an exit. Then, they will not be able to get to us due to his wall," clarified Luther.

"You agree with Berolarn. You think Lauren is safe?" asked Talis.

"I do not know, Talis. I cannot lie, but I believe in Berolarn's judgement, and his logic seemed sound, and I again queried him on this whilst we decided how long to rest, and he did not shift his thinking in any way." Luther answered as he lay down.

Soon the companions were asleep. Berolarn was considering the night's events. He mourned the loss of the dwarf and the elven captain. However, he felt relief that Talis, Lauren and Lilla were still alive, though he had managed to lose Lauren. It was very concerning that Elisha had come close to death.

He had argued with Ethera about her coming. But she had insisted that the elves needed to play their part and that anyone else was a token gesture. Likewise, his father had argued with his daughter. But, as he told Berolarn, she was the heir apparent, old enough and wise enough to make her own decisions. Moreover, she was highly skilled as a warrior and had elements of magic still within her. Nevertheless, he did worry that losing any of them could have significant consequences for the world's fate.

What if he lost Elisha and something happened to the King? The elves didn't have a natural successor. Unless Eleran took over. She was wise, but she had lived the life of a soldier and didn't understand the world's politics. The retrieval of the Dragonheart stone and the journey of Talis, Lauren and Lilla were just part of the puzzle. The full might of the elves and their armies would be critical to their success in defeating the massive goblin and ogre armies.

With the potential of Garrett being a spy in the camp and selling out to Olgrich or probably one of his subordinates, they would know who was coming. They knew everything that he had told the council and all their plans. They would know the companions were coming for the stone, which was in the icelands of Caledonia. But luckily, he hadn't mentioned the tower or the sceptre.

But, Olgrich would know many world histories and probably worked it out as Berolarn had done. However, he didn't have all the Solarians' records, as their quest for knowledge was not of interest to him. He only quested for power. He hoped that he would not understand the power of the stone. He had only come upon the truth by chance and tied it with the prophecy he had found, indicating Loran and the children.

A few hours later, Luther came over to Berolarn, sat beside him, and looked out of the gaping hole to the desolate remnants of a city that had once been here.

"You realise we have little chance of survival, Berolarn, if we continue on this path?" stated Luther.

"There is always a chance, my friend, no matter how small," replied Berolarn.

"We risk much for a prophecy and the children. We could walk away, regroup and begin again. This war will go on for years, I am sure. We will have many more opportunities to work out how to defeat the dark lord, Berolarn. You know this?" Luther asked questionably.

"Luther, the possibilities are endless, and we might indeed delay and thwart the dark lord many times. But we will not defeat him, he will always return, and we will not put his soul where it belongs with his master Hel. If he manages to get his hands on the children, who knows what foul malignant plans he has for their use? But nevertheless, they are the ones foretold who can end this war and bring peace to the lands. We have discussed this," responded Berolarn.

"I know we have discussed this many times. But if you play a dangerous game, be warned. You are in motion with forces you potentially cannot control. I must reiterate that our chances of survival will be limited tomorrow. They know we will come. They know we defeated a selection of their elite forces. This would have been unexpected, but they will ensure it doesn't happen again. You know all of this." Retorted Luther slowly and meaningfully, ensuring his words would not be lost on Berolarn.

"I know, my friend, everything you say has truth to it. But I will not change my path and will not forfeit Lauren. I will not let him have the child. I will not risk not following my gut on what the prophecy has foretold. I have often meddled wrongly with fate and destiny and have lost much as a direct result. I will not offend Sol this time. If you wish to follow other paths, I will not blame you, Luther," smiled Berolarn.

"There it is," grinned Luther. "You are a wily old dog, Berolarn. You finished with a smile and a lack of blame, knowing I would not turn my back on you. How many times have you said you wished you had followed my wisdom? Yes, all the damn time." Shaking his head, Luther continued. "Maybe we can create a finish that will be worthy of a song in years to come. Perhaps this is our time, maybe my time. I have often wondered if I would meet a foe who could better me in combat," Luther grinned. "Tomorrow, maybe we will see. But, come, you must go rest. I will take watch if your magic wall will hold."

"Thank you, Luther, and yes, the wall will hold," he answered as he got up, walked over to his bedding, and laid down. As Luther kept watch, Berolarn's mind was still restless as he reconsidered all their options. After several minutes of considering things. With much effort, Berolarn tried to clear his mind so he could sleep for a little while.

Luther sighed to himself as he yawned. He was sure this was a terrible idea. It was near-certain death if they made one false move. They had little time left before she would need to know. He wished he had more time to explain to Lilla who she was and how much he cared. Luther hoped that Berolarn would allow the secret out. He felt it was wrong in the current situation to withhold so much. But, Berolarn thought it was best for each of the children to discover their own paths little by little. It might tip them over the edge too soon and cause destruction if they found everything all at once.

The ways of the Solarians were as much a problem as they were a solution. He always thought as much. Too much secrecy and manipulation. He could actually see as good as the Solarians were. As much as they cared for the lands, there was a synergy to the doctrines of the dark lord. They wanted to control as much as possible all outcomes. As much as he battled this in his head and heart. He followed Berolarn like no other. Why was that?

Perhaps where others talked of honourable and good deeds for the races, theirs were nothing more than talk. Berolarn lived it, if maybe in a peculiar chaotic fashion. Luther had decided his skill would either benefit himself greatly or others. He had decided long ago that others needed him more. So it was a natural joining with Berolarn. They both followed the same ideology, even with slightly different approaches.

He gazed outwards and waited for the morning to come.

Chapter 27 – The Wasted City

Talis awoke to see that all his companions were busy packing up. He glanced towards the hole in the far wall and noticed that morning had already broken. Talis had a terrible night's sleep. He felt like he had been tossing and turning most of the night. He had intertwined this with fitful sleep full of dreams. A dark world filled with images of Lauren, torture, fire, unseen death and a deep horrendous laugh that even now he was awake filled him with apprehension and unwarranted fear.

"Morning, sleepyhead," said Lilla softly as she walked across the room to his side.

"You better eat quickly. I think Luther wants to be off soon. He wants to ensure we make the tower as early as possible. So he can scout the surrounding area before it's dark. He thinks this might give us an advantage rather than rushing in."

"As long as he and Berolarn understand, my priority is Lauren, not this damn stone. Sorry, Lilla, I'm already ranting at you." Talis smiled sadly as he saw Lilla's concerned face.

"I am just scared for her. This feels worse than when she went missing in the village. I thought she was dead, and then I knew she was safe with the elves. This time I know she is with a crazed blood-sucking demon who wants to conquer the world," brooded Talis as he searched for more words.

"I know, Talis, it's ok. I love you so much. We will get through this together," smiled Lilla, though she went slightly red as she spoke. She couldn't believe it embarrassed her so much. It was daft admitting your love when death was around the corner. She then laughed and kissed him.

"I love you too," he smiled back as she broke away. "Know this, Lilla. Whatever happens, I will always be there for you. Always will be with you. You are definitely my one too." Talis said lovingly as he hugged her and held her for a long time, but his mind drifted towards Lauren. But it gave him some measure of comfort holding Lilla.

"Right, Talis, eat now. Quickly before we set off. You will need your strength," said Lilla.

Lilla pulled away, rummaged in Talis's backpack, pulled out some rations, and passed them to him.

"How is Elisha?" asked Talis as he started to eat.

"She is okay, though she is really upset about Lauren and the loss of Aetherhard and Helm," answered Lilla.

"Now she is fully aware of what happened. But, if I am honest, Elisha has taken it badly, no doubt about it. She had tears in her eyes. They are perhaps a lot closer than we realised. This morning, she talked about her to me as if she were her sister or best friend," revealed Lilla.

"Well, she is infectious, I have no doubt. Lauren occasionally disappeared when we were in the palace to spend time with the Princess. Not sure if you noted that if she didn't spend time with us, she spent time in her company," conceded Talis as he considered the relationship between Elisha and Lauren.

Talis then shrugged and continued. "We will find her. We will get her back. I know it," enthused Talis with finality as he bit into a cracker.

They walked out the door ten minutes later, mounted the

snow bears, and set off.

Though Lilla hadn't told Talis, she was genuinely scared that today was the day they would all die if anything of yesterday was to go by. However, Lilla was glad to leave that building and get the journey back underway. It was terrible being in the same room as Aetherhard and Helm, lying in a corner, just covered over.

The companions found that the day was as cold as ever. Usually, there seemed to be no let-up to the howling wind or snowfalls that created the horrendous blizzards. The only occurring difference was usually the size of the snowflakes. Talis usually found it hard to concentrate as his face burned with the coldness of the environment that managed to creep through his face coverings. He had to admit that the harsh climate was very fitting for the lands they travelled in. But today though freezing cold, the wind was virtually non-existent, and the sun was high in the sky, and it was pretty weird to have the freezing air competing with the sun's rays on his face.

As Talis surveyed the area they were travelling through, he had to admit he had never seen something so grey, miserable, and deathly in appearance. Whatever had happened here must have been horrific. Evidently, the whole area had been bursting to the seams with buildings and life. Yet, the buildings were nothing but frozen rubble on the ground showing no signs of what they had been. If they did exist, they were either half-submerged in the snow & ice or were just a shell of what they once were. They looked like carcasses stripped of their skin and had all the meat torn off their bones. Yes, the remnants of the buildings looked like they had been scavenged by a massive predator that went from building to building, never able to quench its hunger.

"Berolarn, what actually happened here," Talis asked. "I have never seen such destruction, and when you said city, I imagined something like Solanstar. This place goes on for as far as the eye can see. What evil could have caused this."

"You remember, Talis, that I talked to you about the third age?" replied Berolarn.

"What you see is the end of the third age, the cataclysmic effects that emptied seas, created volcanoes, raised mountains and tore the lands asunder."

"Yes, I remembered that, to be honest, Berolarn. I wondered what exactly led to this happening and how. I guess," said Talis.

"Well, it is a long story," Berolarn sighed. "….. and it shows what happens if power is not kept in check." He went quiet for a few seconds and then continued.

"In the third age, what man is today, was the same during the third age. They had the same innate intelligence and, unfortunately, similar greed as you see across all the races of man. They had not started this way when the third age began. They had been simple primates like apes and gorillas, though more advanced. But they began to evolve as a new species from these simple primates. For thousands of years, they grew and changed as they roamed the lands and developed to become a highly evolved race."

"In fact, man has significantly gone backwards since the cataclysm. Throughout that age, they started to create social systems with small groups and competed with other species for food and the right to live. These social systems or groups of people afforded them greater protection and more significant numbers to hunt."

"As they spread out across the lands, they had a high rate of births and constantly increased in number. As they grew in numbers, small groups became larger, large groups became communities, villages, towns and cities, and these became countries. Do you see similarities with the current world, how men and women of power now have control of the many as these communities formed into countries? How the people on mass need to follow and be told how to live?"

"Yes, to be honest, it sounds similar when you think about it. I have not really thought about it before. But everyone bonds together for safety, I guess," answered Talis.

"Exactly, the system should work well in theory. When countries are run well for the benefit of all, such as what we see with the elves. Then this model works. But, then, some fall out of this intellect, such as the dark lord, those who want more. There are always those who want to own what is not theirs. They want more food, money, jewels, land, husbands, wives, and people to pay homage to them. The list is endless. You see this from the beggar to thief, brother to sister, friend to friend, king to king, country to country. It becomes all-consuming. It leads to robbery, murder, destruction and many other heinous crimes against life. It is inherent in most forms of life, especially man, and you can argue at its pinnacle, funnily enough, is the Vampiri," replied Berolarn.

"Do you start to see a picture, Talis? ….. Lilla?" Asked Berolarn. Noticing that Lilla was enthralled by his words.

"I guess nearly every day, you see some form of this greed," agreed Talis.

"Everyone is out for themselves to some degree. But, when I think back even to the inn, I bet you saw the same Talis? All the fights, arguments and the like were caused by greed, power and things of that ilk. It can be minimal, can't it, Berolarn? But it's always there bubbling away," added Lilla.

"Yes, when you look deep down into it, all these different elements competing together, you will start getting problems. So man tried to control these factors with laws, religion, agreements of peace, and many other things to hold this social system together," volunteered Berolarn.

"At times, it was successful. The world had peace. Yes, it still had greed, and crimes occurred. But for short periods in history, the world was calm. However, this was not the norm. The underlying problem of man's nature was still there, bubbling away."

"Neighbour warred on neighbour, country warred on country. Usually, at its centre was a regent or a group of power-hungry individuals who wanted more than what was theirs. It is always the way," conceded Berolarn as he shook his head.

"You are correct, Berolarn. It is still the same, even now. Though we fight the dark lord throughout the history of the lands since the cataclysm. Wars are fought on small differences or a want for something that is not theirs," said Elisha sadly.

"Yes, it is true. But, unfortunately, history repeats itself constantly, Elisha. But, we must live in the hope that we will finally learn from the lessons of the past and that history doesn't repeat itself in the end," said Berolarn.

"The elves had hoped to do their part as they understood the frailties of this system and the near end of the world. We had planned to leave our lands and bring our love to people. But as you know, we were back to the same old problems as the Vampiri returned," said Elisha.

"Indeed, and this is still a problem for the future, Elisha," replied Berolarn.

"I hope one day that the guiding light will stop the manipulations of Hel on this world and bring to the world a new order of peace."

"We have man, a highly evolved race, who suffer from the needs associated with greed and a hunger for power. We also understand that a few men and women stand apart from the many. These people want to have as much as they can at any cost. When these ascend to power and lead countries, the problems for the world are significant," stated Berolarn.

"Caledonia was one of these such places?" asked Lilla

"Yes, as I told you before, Caledonia was a powerful country called Britannia and played a significant part in the world during the last thousand years of man before the cataclysm. During this time, many countries of large size and massive populations began to form. Instead of thousands, we are talking about millions of people. In fact, in London, which was just a city in Britannia. There were several million people," revealed Berolarn.

Berolarn noticed the open mouth of Lilla and her astounded look.

"It is true, Lilla. So many people lived here," said Berolarn.

"So many people, I can't believe it," gasped Lilla.

"It is true though hard to believe," Berolarn replied, "and in the last one hundred to two hundred years, the evolution of man hit rates that have not been seen over the previous ten thousand years. They had learned how to create big, powerful machines to make their lives easier. They knew of science, new ways of manipulating nature resources, and ways to generate energy and heat. They even used science to control an individual's life force."

"They used these machines for war. Significant wars were fought using air, sea, and land machines. They used these sciences to create weapons that easily killed soldiers and people. And their knowledge continued to grow and grow, and soon as I said to you before, they made medicines to cure all illnesses, creating machines and weapons that could kill millions in one blow. There was actually a period of relative calm for a time. The weapons became a deterrent."

"There was a wave of peace for some time? What happened to break this peace? Asked Talis.

"From what I can ascertain from the histories. Life became unsustainable, and the world population was out of control. Millions became hundreds of millions which became thousands of millions. They began to suck the very life out of the planet. Not enough food, not enough natural resources such as steel. All the items they had become accustomed to for maintaining the level of evolution they had reached," answered Berolarn.

"That is what caused the cataclysm?" asked Talis.

"In part, yes. But more so, the world began to run out of energy. They had found materials in the ground that their machines used to create heat and power. These were a type of oil we use today in our lamps, and like the air we breathe, they called gas, which they burned. They used their science to understand the heat of the sun. They had already used this science to create weapons of mass destruction. But, so deep, they delved into this science and tried to capture Sol's essence, the sun's power. They were close, I believe. They were so advanced in their understanding. But they rushed the science as their need was great," said Berolarn as he narrated the histories of the third age.

"What happened?" asked Lilla excitedly.

"This part of the history is more unclear, to be honest, Lilla. However, the narratives are reasonably detailed up to the point when the cataclysm struck. After that, it is a bit of a jumble of broken histories from what scholars survived. I understand that they created a big machine that simulated the very essence of creation. When the gods stood as one and made the planets and the stars. In excitement, they rushed ahead and created a new machine to simulate the sun's power. It would mean infinite energy for all. So quick they rushed on, so many shortcuts they took, and errors of judgment they made," said Berolarn.

Berolarn shrugged and then sighed.

"They turned on their machine. It became self-sustaining and out of control. The scientists could not turn off their device. It was out of control and growing. They were actually giving birth to a small sun on the planet. The planet was being consumed, and the world started to collapse. In an attempt to stop it, the scientists attempted to destroy it using one of these weapons of mass destruction, something they called a nuclear weapon, which they aimed at the heart of their machine. I am not sure why but it set off a further chain of events, and soon different countries unleashed all their weapons of mass destruction, and soon the air was full of these nuclear devices as countries led by power-hungry fools sent thousands flying around the world."

"What you see in London is what is left of a colossal city. It had become a victim of these events. Hit by the power of the scientist's machine and weapons of mass destruction. These events unleashed the most horrific of destructive forces, flattening the city. Millions of innocents died. You cannot imagine the power unleashed," reflected Berolarn as he went deep into thought.

"Where the lands are now ice, they were not in those times. The lands of Britannia were changed dramatically as the world was ripped apart and shifted. The lands were three times as large and vastly different in shape and location. It is terrible to think of the loss that occurred on that day and the short scream of the world." Berolarn finished with a sigh.

"How did anyone survive? I know you explained it was more due to the volume of people, but I do not see how anything could have lived," asked Talis.

"Your people Elisha, were descendent from another time? How did elves live on?" Lilla asked.

"For our part, as you say, elves were the direct descendants of Atlanteans. We were chosen by Sol," said Elisha, and she stopped as she looked for her following words.

"He gave us great magic, and we had used this magic to withdraw from this world of men. When the cataclysm hit the world, the magic held on and saved us. But after it was finished, the magic had done its part, and it crumbled away and was no more. It was a sign for the elves to return to the world. The world was suffering. Everything was struggling to grow as an everlasting winter took hold. For those who had managed to survive, there was no food, crops they tried to grow failed, and famine. Perhaps if the elves had not intervened, the races of man would have completely died out," said Elisha, then looking at Berolarn, who nodded, she continued. "The elves spent a century using what little magic they had left to stabilise the world and breathe life back into the earth, and from then to now, we continue to spend much of our time nurturing the lands."

They had been discussing this for over an hour when Luther brought his snow bear to a halt.

"We are being followed," he said to the others as they approached him.

"Are you sure?" asked Berolarn.

"I am not sure by who or what," Luther nodded. "Whoever it is, they keep some distance and move very fast. All of you, be on guard with your eyes wide open. You need to be ready with your swords to be in your hand."

Chapter 28 – The Abduction

The force that hit Lauren momentarily took her breath away as the demon flew out of the building with her in his arms. His veins visibly moving under the skin of the red arms of pure muscle and sinew that held her tight as she struggled. She could feel his long bony fingers which ended in sharp claws, painfully and teasingly penetrating her skin. The smell of him nearly made her sick. He smelt of carrion, decaying rotting flesh. His skin was slimy and amphibian to the feel as she looked up at his face. He was gruesome to behold, deformed by large horns and canines that protruded from his mouth on either side. They were at least an inch long. His head was red-skinned like his body, with long black hair. But it was his eyes, slit like a cat's black pupil set in blood-red where white had once been when he was in human form. His eyes showed nothing but evil inside.

"Stop struggling, woman or I will drop you and then he will not get his prize for the blood prince," he shouted as they flew.

Lauren did continue to struggle for some time, but she didn't have her furs on, and the coldness and pain stilled her movement finally, and she started to lose any sense of what was happening. She ultimately lost consciousness, and the world turned black.

When Lauren awoke, she was on the floor of an ornately decorated circular room in front of a large stone hearth fireplace, where a fire roared and licked its way up the chimney. The room, panelled in exotic wood with various tapestries depicting war, torture and death, had a sinister feel. As Lauren rose to her feet and let her mind clear, she saw the room had a variety of furnishings, including a desk with lots of books and papers on it and two luxurious plump sofas set opposing each other. There was a large door at one point in the walls. She crept towards the door and gently tried the handle. The door was locked. She was stuck here until her captors came.

As she paced around the room, Lauren realised she was really thirsty. She noticed there were bottles and glasses on a side table. Lauren started sniffing the bottles until she was convinced she had found one that was water. She put the bottle to her mouth and started to sip and drink heartedly on what was indeed water. Then, the door began to open.

"Ah, you are awake," came a voice. As Lauren turned to the doorway, she saw Darius, now in human form, in the company of a female entering the room.

"He comes to see you soon. Get changed," said Darius as he grabbed a dress out of the female's arms and chucked it at Lauren's feet.

"He will be angry if he sees you wearing that elven gear covered in filth. Take off your clothes and change now," snarled Darius.

Then turning to the woman,

"See that she is changed and looks presentable…..In fact, I've had second thoughts take her to the wash house and have her scrubbed. Then bring her back here when she is ready."

Darius turned and walked out. Lauren's eyes darted to the open doorway, and she was just about to attempt an escape when as fast as her eye could see, the woman had flown across the room and was standing in front of Lauren.

"Ah, now, you do not want to be doing anything silly," the woman said as she grabbed hold of Lauren's hair and yanked her head back with painful force. "We do not want to make Tarani hurt you, do you?" the woman said.

Lauren felt the woman's long fingernails run up and down her neck.

"You are pretty, a great prize you are, oh yes, special you are," whispered Tarani as she pulled harder on Lauren's hair until she heard Lauren wince in pain.

"Time to go and get rid of all those nasty smells and dirt," Tarani laughed as she dragged Lauren by her hair out of the room into a corridor.

They walked for a minute down the corridor, then another. Lauren was in a lot of pain when the woman opened another door and threw Lauren across the room with tremendous force. This caused Lauren to wince further in pain as she landed on the wet floor. In the small stone room. Two girls in rags were in there and immediately started filling up a tub with hot water from a cauldron of a fire nearby.

"Get her undressed", commanded Tarani to one of the girls.

One of the girls walked over to Lauren as she got to her feet and attempted to start undressing Lauren. Lauren instinctively pushed the girl away. Again Tarani came over, grabbed her hair and pulled her head back even harder than last time.

"You might be the prize to some girl, but not me. Now, if I have to tell you to get undressed again. I will gladly rip out your throat," laughed Tarani with malice.

"Now, let's try this again ….. you get her undressed now,"

shouted Tarani to one of the girls and let go of Lauren's hair.

"I can do it," whimpered Lauren, who was in obvious pain.

"Oh, now that will not do. I want you to let one of the slaves do it. Go on, girl, get her undressed," said Tarani humorously.

Lauren could feel her face burning with embarrassment as the young girl again came back over and started to remove Lauren's clothes. Then, standing there completely naked, Tarani stood next to Lauren, her face just a minuscule from touching Lauren's. Lauren could feel the woman's hot breath entering her mouth.

"Very pretty," she said as she rubbed her fingers slowly up and down Lauren's body.

Lauren knew she was taking great delight in her embarrassment, especially as she started running her finger along the side of her breasts. In a wink of an eye, Lauren tried to strike Tarani in desperation as the woman's hand moved up her inner thigh. Tarani caught hold of her wrist with ease. She gripped Lauren's wrist painfully and slowly twisted Lauren's arm until Lauren doubled over in pain.

"Now that was silly, wasn't it? I was just paying you a compliment," laughed Tarani callously. "Come on now, stand up straight......That's it,"

As Lauren gingerly returned to a standing position. She fought back the tears from the pain in her wrist and arm. Then suddenly, Lauren was a crumpled wreck on the floor as Tarani hit her with full force in the stomach. Gasping and gulping as she tried to take in a breath. Finally, she felt Tarani crouch down beside her and whisper.

"You will learn to do exactly what you are told, girl," hissed Tarani. Who rose to her feet and started making for the door.

"You have thirty minutes to be cleaned. Do not try and escape. Someone will be outside," said Tarani as she opened the door. Then turning to one of the girls, "go fetch the dress. It's on the floor in the study."

One of the girls helped her up to her feet and moved her over to the bathtub. Lauren gingerly climbed in and let the hot water cover her lower body.

"You are lucky," whispered the nearest girl. Then she looked at the other girl, who nodded and exited the room.

"She goes to get your dress. She will be back soon. You should not argue with them. Death is usually their answer. But, lucky, she did not kill you. In fact, I do not think I had seen anyone live when they tried to attack one of the masters. My name is Ruisha, but people call me Rose. What is your name?" Asked Rose.

"Hello Rose, my name is Lauren," she said as she attempted to smile against the pain in her arm.

"Hello Lauren, let's see if we can get you clean. If you are to be cleaned and given dresses. You must be special. In fact, you will probably be visited by him," said Rose as she started to apply soap to Lauren's back and chest.

Lauren thought about stopping the girl from washing her, but as embarrassing as it was for Lauren. She didn't want to get the girl in trouble. Soon, the other girl returned, placed the dress to one side, and came over to help. Both girls were scrubbing Lauren hard as they tried to get all the grime out of her skin.

After some time, the girls had finally finished and told Lauren to get out of the tub. As Lauren did so, they took her nearer to the fire and started to dry her with towels.

"Come this way. We need you to lay here," said one of the girls as they directed Lauren onto a table. They reached for bottles and started pouring liquid onto her skin. Soon both the girls were rubbing fragrance oils up and down her body.

Finally, after she had slipped on the dress, they finished preparing her face and hair and passed her a fine pair of slippers. They said she was ready. As if she knew, Tarani was entering the room.

"Ah, good, you are ready. You do not look like an elven urchin anymore. All nicely clean. You smell good enough to eat." Tarani said and licked her top teeth with a horrendous smile.

To Lauren's horror, Tarani grabbed Ruisha and, in one quick movement as she continued to look at Lauren, she pulled the girl's head sidewards and, with rapidly growing canines, sunk her teeth into Ruisha's neck. Lauren saw Ruisha grimace with pained closed eyes as blood slowly trickled down her neck as the vampiress fed. Lauren could hear the sucking noise of blood passing between the two women as Tarani, looking directly at Lauren, held Ruisha for twenty seconds, locked by her teeth. Then as quick as she pulled Ruisha's head to one side. Tarani had thrown the crying girl across the room and was delicately wiping the remaining trickle of blood from the side of her mouth.

"You look like the princess you are. Oh, I think he will be pleased, mmmm yes, very pleased. He will come soon. We need to get back to the study," smiled Tarani mockingly. Then she mocked Lauren as if she was royalty as Tarani bowed and motioned towards the door.

"After you, girl, or should I say my royal ladyship," laughed Tarani.

As they walked the short journey back to the study, Tarani told Lauren that she was about to meet the feudal Lord Magma. She would be wise to answer his questions and hold her tongue unless asked. He was not renowned for his patience, and if he ended up maiming Lauren or killing her, he would more than likely take it out on the rest of them. Tarani warned her if she only suffered maiming, she promised Lauren she would slowly skin her and then start chopping things off her, starting with her eyes, and she would have wished death had come at his hands.

"But if he finds you amusing and you please him with the truths, you might not only live, maybe you could come and live with me as my slave. It's been a long time since I have tasted one so pretty," Tarani said, laughing with real venom. She pushed the door open.

"Ah, my lover. Darius is wonderful," she said to Lauren as she roughly pushed her into the room. As Lauren flew into one of the settee's arms and nearly landed on the floor, Tarani flew into Darius and tried to kiss him with an unnatural passion.

"Tarani, be serious," snapped Darius. As he pushed Tarani backwards and held her off. "You know Magma will be angry if he sees you messing about. This is serious," he said, nearly shaking her.

"You are such a bore, Darius," she said as she threw herself into the other settee opposite Lauren and looked provocatively at Lauren. Lauren felt her skin creep under the gaze of this crazed demon Vampiri thing. Darius noticed the look Tarani gave her. He marched over to Tarani and, dragging her out of the chair, grabbed her throat and lifted her into the air.

"Be warned, Tarani, a favourite of the blood prince, you may be. But if you harm the girl, your life will be forfeit. She is for Magma. If Magma or the blood prince have any inkling, you are not focused on the cause. You will be punished with death," Darius hissed as he chucked Tarani back down. "Remember who she is."

"Yeah, yeah, I know. She is the one. I don't really care if I am honest, my love." said Tarani with a mock yawn.

"Remember though, Darius, lover you may be. But touch me again, and I might rip your throat out," warned Tarani with a wicked smile.

"You play a dangerous game, Tarani, and for nothing but fun," snapped Darius angrily. When they all heard the loud ring of a bell nearby. "He comes. Tarani, you better leave." Tarani dropped to her knees in mock servitude and then jumped up. She blew Darius a kiss and left the room.

Darius looked at Lauren and spoke to himself.

"He will be pleased."

Lauren stayed seated on the settee as Darius walked back and forth. He was obviously nervous about Lord Magma's entry. Which caused Lauren to be terrified. She couldn't think of what could unnerve Darius, she had seen him in his demon form, and he was as horrendous as anything she had seen.

The door opened. Lauren took a sharp intake of breath and

let out an involuntary little squeal as she saw the very handsome, physically imposing red-robed man in front of her. Lauren nearly passed out as the wave of unrelenting fear hit her. She was full of sheer panic. But as soon as he spoke, as quick as the fear came, she was nearly overwhelmed with a feeling of dire dread that was beyond fear.

"Hello, Lauren. Long I have searched for you, and now here you are sitting in my study and how beautiful she is, Darius, have you noticed?" the man said in a deep booming voice. Darius just nodded.

"I have been called many things over many ages. The Vampiri know me as Lord Magma. So you may just call me Magma….. do you understand?" asked Magma.

"Yes," said Lauren quietly as she stared now enthralled by this lean, beautiful muscular man.

He was so majestic standing there in his red robes, she thought. The only thing that she couldn't entirely like was his yellow eyes and red pupils. They didn't quite fit. They were somehow wrong. She looked deeper into his eyes as he looked at her, and she felt an internal battle within herself as she tried to break free from his gaze. Then going inside herself, she found an inner wall of strength. Finally, she managed to pull free, and the spell she felt she was under was broken, but the surge of fear returned.

"Do you see that, Darius? She has resisted my charm already," said Magma with his booming laughing voice. "You can now go, Darius. You are not needed."

"Yes, my lord," said Darius, who made for the door and, on leaving, he heard Magma say. "I thought this would be fun," and then Darius listened to the girl scream.

Darius smiled as he made his way up the corridor. He knew Magma was in a good mood, which would be good for the girl and good for him. As long as the girl didn't die at Magma's hands, then Darius had satisfied Magma and the blood prince. Perhaps he would have a night of passion with Tarani, he thought.

Chapter 29 - The Celtic Conclave

"Fergus, will you stop grumbling? We will arrive soon," shouted Heather from atop her snow bear, Aila.

"I told you it was a bad idea for them to take Bobster. This flee-bitten bear does nothing I bleeding tell it," spat Fergus. "I still don't understand why we must travel to the Campbells. We are the McKenzies! Damn you, woman, it's embarrassing," grumbled Fergus.

I swear to any god listening, I am going to throttle that big oaf in a minute, thought Heather.

"Fergus, how many times have we discussed this since yesterday when Berolarn left? He asked us to meet with the clans in the south. Why south, because it is nearer to where the enemy will attack, you idiot!" she shrieked the last sentence as loud as possible. Heather wanted to make sure he got the message into his thick skull.

"Bah, Berolarn, this, Berolarn that. You drive me round the twist Heather. Perhaps we should make you chieftain, or maybe we should invite Berolarn to lead our clan." Fergus shouted back.

"Fergus, if I must come over there and shut your insane nonsense, you will regret it. Trust me," snarled Heather, slightly more disinterested as she saw a snow bear in the distance. Finally, Heather motioned to Fergus and the rest of their warriors.

"A rider is coming. No one attacks. Do you hear me? I will do the speaking, you understand, Fergus," Heather said, looking at her husband with menace.

"Of course, my love," smiled Fergus through gritted teeth.

As the bear closed in on Fergus and his warriors, Heather noted the rider was someone from the Douglas clan by his colours. Great, she thought with a sigh, it was Tomas.

"Well, look who it is, boys. The great warrior himself, the flower of the Stewarts, the pet of their mighty Chieftain Willy, a Douglas half-breed who pulled himself out of the gutter by kissing the ass of the other clans," laughed Fergus.

"Shut your mouth," shrieked Heather.

"I was only playing, wasn't I, Tomas, my friend," laughed Fergus.

"Hello Heather, I see you still manage the drunken half-wit on behalf of your clan," said Tomas coldly.

"You what," shouted Fergus going purple with anger.

Fergus jumped off his snow bear and attempted to run towards Tomas but was caught with vicious certainty by Heather, who had jumped down from Aila and managed to grab Fergus by her favourite control item. Fergus's beard. With momentum stopped, Fergus landed in a heap on the floor, and Heather jumped on his back with both feet, face-planting Fergus into the snow.

"Sorry, Tomas," smiled Heather. "It has been a long time, brother." Then, as she rode on the back of the bucking Fergus, his muffled shouting caused all the warriors in their party to laugh. She continued. "What brings you north?"

"Hello, sister. It has been many years, Heather. The years

have been kind to you," smiled Tomas as he looked derisively down at Fergus. "I have been sent by William Stewart, Lord of the Stewarts and for the Douglas's….. your people."

"She ain't a Douglas no more. She is a Mackenzie," hollered Fergus as he tried to get up. But, unfortunately for Fergus, his head was pushed further into the snow by the foot of Heather. He struggled for a few seconds and then went still.

"If I let you up, Fergus, you stop with all your bravado bullshit. Do you hear!" hissed Heather as she released Fergus's head from under her boot.

"Okay, okay, will you get off me now," spluttered Fergus. Heather slowly moved off Fergus and helped the red-faced Fergus to his feet.

"Hello, Fergus," sneered Tomas. "I see you are on your travels?"

Tomas looked at hundreds of warriors on top of snow bears. Fergus was about to answer, but Heather snapped her finger in front of his face.

"Quiet a minute," hissed Heather.

"Why are you here, Tomas? You know you are not welcome in our lands without an invite," said Heather smoothly.

"War is on the march; the clans gather, Heather. I was sent to request an audience with the Chieftan of the Mackenzies …… Fergus," replied Tomas.

"Well, you found him ….. come on out with it ….. Ouch! Heather, god damn it, that hurt," shouted Fergus.

"The Mackenzies all travel for War, Tomas. Berolarn and

Luther walk our lands again. Berolarn advised that we march and gather the clans." Said Heather. "Yet you speak as if the gathering has started?" asked Heather.

"It has. We have spies at the borders of Jeliah. We have received word that thousands of the goblins now march on our lands. Alongside ogres, creochs and other beasts," said Tomas.

"You need the might of the Mackenzies," smiled Fergus.

"Indeed, Fergus. The Mackenzie's might and Heather's leadership are greatly needed," smiled Tomas.

Fergus started to redden again and was about to retort but was cut off by Heather.

"Where do the clans gather, Tomas? We were riding to the Campbell's and were about to advise the same thing. So it is excellent news that it is already in motion," said Heather.

"The Campbells, Stewarts, Macdonalds and Douglas clans are meeting within the Douglas lands. A call has gone out to some of the smaller clans. We will leave for war within the next two days. If you are of a mind, Fergus, and are willing to join with the other Clans, we will be a force to match whatever the enemy throws at us. All the other chieftains see the might of the Mackenzies being vital to our success." comforted Tomas as he tried to play on Fergus's ego. He knew Heather would know his actions. But, she would see his reasoning for it as it was also true.

"Indeed, they do right to do so. No one can match the Mackenzie's in battle," grinned Fergus with eagerness on his face.

"How many rides, Fergus?" asked Tomas.

"We have eighty snow bears and three hundred men," said Heather before Fergus could answer. "We put the word out across our lands, and this was as much as we could manage within twelve hours."

"It is similar to the others, if I am honest, Heather. But, still, our number should be around Fifteen hundred and maybe three hundred bears. If we cannot make a good day with that number. We don't deserve to be a clansman," grinned Tomas. He held out his arm to Fergus, who then gripped it.

"We should be off, Brother! What say you, do you join us," shouted Tomas at Fergus.

"The Mackenzies answer ya call Douglas," shouted Fergus to great cheers from the warriors behind them.

"Let's ride with the wind shouting behind us," cried Heather as she enthusiastically patted Fergus on the back.

All the warriors answered with a deafening shout as Heather, and even Fergus ran and jumped on their snow bears, as did Tomas.

"Ride, Mackenzies, Ride," shouted Fergus.

They all sped off as warriors in chorus started to sing the ancient song of the celts from years long forgotten.

There's a blossom that blows, that scoffs at the snow
And it faces root fast the rage of the blast
It sweetens the sod no slave ever trod
Since the mountains upreared their altars to God

The flower of the free, the Heather, the Heather

The Children of Darkness and Light

The Bretons and Scots, and Irish together
The Manx and the Welsh and Cornish forever
Six nations, are we all Celtic and free

Our blossom is red as the life's blood we shed
For Liberty's cause against alien laws
When Lochiel and O'Neill and Llewellyn drew steel
For Alba's and Erin's and Cambria's weal

The flower of the free, the Heather, the Heather
The Bretons and Scots, and Irish together
The Manx and the Welsh and Cornish forever
Six nations, are we all Celtic and free

Let the Saxon and Dane bear the rule o'er the plain
On the hem of God's robe are our sceptre and globe
For the lord of all light revealed in his height
For heaven and earth rose up in his sight

The flower of the free, the Heather, the Heather
The Bretons and Scots, and Irish together
The Manx and the Welsh and Cornish forever
Six nations, are we all Celtic and free

Over the next day, the Celts rode hard, and by midday of the following day, they had reached their destination, the home of the Dougal chieftain. The whole outside of the village stockade was alive with warriors from the various clans. Tomas indicated an area where they could make camp and advised Heather to have guards for their base as he understood blood feuds with the families ran deep. Tomas then left and would return soon after he announced their arrival.

"Angus," shouted Heather, "I need a word."

"What you want, Heather?" asked the burly red-haired warrior as he walked over.

"The Campbells, Stewarts and the Douglas's, that's what Angus. I want you to make sure nothing happens. No taunting, no fighting, no killing. Do you hear me? I want everything to remain calm while we get ready to march," said Heather sternly.

"That's no small task, Heather," replied Angus.

Looking around at the laughing and joking men as well as the snow bears. He could already see keeping his eyes on all was going to be difficult. Never mind the fact that the call of the blood ran deep across all the clans.

"I know, my friend," smiled Heather as she patted Angus on the back. "But, the other clans are under the same call. No fighting. We are here for something bigger than to settle old foolish arguments. Get some sound heads together and watch the perimeters. Maybe Elspeth, ….. Marcus and ……Caitlan," said Heather thoughtfully as she scanned the Mackenzie warriors.

"Okay, ….. Err ….. What about Fergus," said Angus with apprehension.

"Leave Fergus to me, Angus. I will deal with him. You are a good friend to Fergus, Angus," Heather smiled.

"Well, someone has to look out for the daft bugger," smiled Angus.

Looking around, she could see Fergus was already arguing

with some of the Douglas clan. Who were milling around near the Mackenzie camp. Damn his hide, she thought to herself. Though she couldn't help grinning, she ran over and dragged Fergus away.

"Heather, they were asking for it," moaned Fergus as he looked over his shoulder at the grinning Douglas warriors. "Your family think they get special treatment from me just because you are now a Mackenzie. They take liberties. No respect for a Chieftain."

Heather could feel Fergus tensing up, and she heard Douglas's laughing, and she knew he would turn any second and hit someone.

"Fergus," she said sweetly as she grabbed his face and turned it to look at her. "You know why we are here? The survival of the clans depends on it. I know the drink has not clouded your senses so much that you cannot see the words of Berolarn are true."

"I know, but Heather….." started Fergus.

"There are no buts, Fergus. Now is your time, the Mackenzies' time to stand above all others. To be the head of all clans now. But, first, you must show you are worthy, my love. Calm, thoughtful and inspiring to all you must be. Forget little slights on the Mackenzie name. Fight for glory in front of the real enemy, Fergus. You know I am right. Look at me," she said. Fergus then sighed.

"I know I am not much of husband or Chieftain, Heather. You can try and encourage me as much as you want, but I can see it in your eyes," smiled Fergus.

"But all this doesn't change the fact that they do my head in. These other clans have no respect for the Mackenzies. They think we are dung because we live in the wildest areas of Caledonia and that I am a fool. I will mind my temper and drink less whilst we secure our lands. But know this, if anyone, and I mean anyone, really oversteps the mark and takes me as this fool, I will hit them like a hurricane," insisted Fergus.

Heather studied Fergus for a minute. She loved it when he transformed back to the Fergus of old. She could see the fire in his eyes, not the drink. He had been one of the mightiest of warriors in the old days, wise and calm in all situations, and then he became this drunk slob after we lost our son. Heather continued to wish that she could reclaim the husband she loved.

"Fergus, all I ever want is for you to be what you are called. Chieftan and to be that Chieftan. You must save our people by leading our people in these troubled times. Can you do that, really?" questioned Heather. "Can you put all our petty perceived grievances aside and fight for what is ours? We don't live in servitude under another. We are not going to be enslaved or show any weakness. We're standing tall and proud. We are free. We are Celts!"

"We are Celts, bonny lassy," smiled Fergus.

He felt alive as the call to battle started pumping through his veins. Heather could see the switch happening. This might be the chance to get her husband back, she thought as she kissed him passionately and then with a grin as she pulled away. Heather patted his stomach.

"You might even lose some weight with a good war," laughed Heather.

"Indeed, I might," chortled Fergus as he grabbed the giggling Heather and attempted to kiss her again. Who proceeded to playfully slap him.

"Look," continued the laughing Heather. "Tomas returns. Best behaviour Fergus. You have now promised."

"Yeah, I know. Watch this," grinned Fergus as he marched over to Tomas, with Heather quickly following.

"Tomas," Fergus said, patting the back of Tomas and putting his arm around his shoulder.

"Brother, I did you a disservice when we met. It was the drink talking. I have now cleared my head. I apologise to you and any of the clans I may have insulted. Now, as I stand before you as the Chieftain of the Mckenzies. Do you accept my apology?"

Tomas looked at Heather, who grinned and nodded.

"Of course, Fergus. You know that you are highly regarded in the councils of the Douglas clan. That's why you hold my sister's hand," replied Tomas, who was unsure what to say to a different-sounding Fergus in front of him.

"Your words are too kind, and probably a bit of untruth lies within them," Fergus smiled. "I am sure my merit has dropped in recent years. But, the Mackenzie's are here and will take the lead in our pending victory. Have no doubt of that, Tomas. Come, brother, take me to your father." Fergus dropped his hand from Tomas's shoulder and started striding towards the stockade.

Tomas looked at Heather in shock. Heather just smiled and shrugged and started to follow her husband. These outliers are barmy, and Heather has become as much one of them as her husband, thought Tomas as he chased after them. Tomas knew Fergus was renowned for being erratic, foolish and generally incompetent in recent years. They argued for a few hours on whether to call on the McKenzies. But, they all knew this clan was not only one of the largest. They were perhaps the most frenzied in battle and would stand to the last man. In the end, they all agreed they would live with the vagaries of Fergus and the hope that Heather, a leader in her own right, would control him.

Tomas led them into the hall where his father and the other chieftains sat, waiting for their arrival.

"Fergus, ….. Heather, my daughter ….. it has been a long time since you have graced the halls of the Douglas's," beamed Gordain as he leapt out of his chair, hugged Heather, and slapped Fergus on the back.

"Gordain, I see the years sit kindly on your ugly mug," said Fergus heartedly with a smile.

"Ha, not sure about that. I have many aches and pains. Tomas is itching to be chieftain, isn't that right, lad" laughed Gordain as he looked at Tomas. "Come sit, sit. We were just discussing our plans to ride."

"You know your old friends William of the Stewarts and Jockie of the Campbells," said Gordain as both nodded at Fergus, who nodded in return. "This little angel is Bonnie of the Macdonalds, daughter of Rufus and heir to be chieftain. You know her father, Fergus?"

"Aye, I do. Well met, Bonnie. I haven't seen your father since you were a bairn. But, no offence, I am surprised to see

Macdonalds. You usually stand alone. Do you not?" asked Fergus as he sat down next to Heather as he studied the red-haired woman dressed for war.

"Different times, different needs Fergus," replied Bonnie with a nonchalant shrug. "We might be the most prominent clan, but we are not stupid either. We know from all reports the enemy is big enough to sweep us all away."

"I take it then that we are all in the same thought process as Bonnie?" asked Fergus.

"Indeed we are, Fergus," replied Gordain. "Tomas tells me you were on the road for war and have come with many warriors and bears?"

"Aye, thanks to Berolarn and Heather," said Fergus, smiling at Heather.

"Ah, Berolarn walk the lands, does he? I haven't seen that old dog for many years. In fact, I presumed he was dead. So where is he now," asked William.

"Me neither," said Gordain.

"He visited us not a day or so ago. He travels with a small party which includes the weapons master Luther. They search for something that will help the lands against the dark lord, is the best I can tell you," advised Fergus. "He took five of our Bears and made off for London."

"Well, this is a strange tale. No one goes to London. It is a place of death. Yet you know not what he seeks, Fergus? Heather?" asked Gordain.

"I would have liked to have known, but he didn't tell me anything. Heather?" asked Fergus.

"No, me neither and to be honest, I didn't feel he would tell me anyway, even if I had asked. But, yet, I trust everything Berolarn tells us," answered Heather. "He said war was coming, and we should prepare for battle."

"Yes, we set out to gather the clans, which is why Tomas met us on the road. You were in front of us, and I sit before you with much joy. Knowing that we join what has already been assembled," answered Fergus.

"You are willing to join us, Fergus and take our lead," smiled Gordain.

"Now Gordain, you know me better than that," laughed Fergus. "The Mackenzie's will be with you all the way and will fight side by side with all your clans. But, we will not follow anyone's lead. We will work out our own destiny, as will you all. A lamb to the slaughter must go willingly, not be kicked into it."

"I never had any doubt," laughed Gordain in return. "As you arrived, we talked about leaving in the morning tomorrow. We plan to hit the invaders straight in the middle with a small force whilst a large force approaches from either side." He lifted his arms and brought them together quickly, omitting a clapping noise. "Then we hit them off both sides and from the rear. So simple, except for who takes the initial hit, losses will be high. I wasn't sure if we should mix clans as none of us is willing to take the initial risk."

"The Mackenzie's will do it," said Fergus, who looked at Heather. "It is our way, we will fight whilst you surround the enemy."

"Are you sure you will not run like a coward Mackenzie," said William with a smile.

"Luckily, we do not have the Stewart blood, William. We will be fine. Let the Stewarts take the easy path. I am sure you will be capable of picking up our scraps," smiled Fergus with venom in his tone.

"Fergus," warned Heather.

"It is fine, Heather. Willy and I just jest, do we not, Willy," said Fergus, who held his hand out to William Stewart.

"Yes, Heather, we jest," said William, and he shook Fergus's hand with a sickly smile. He thought for a second or two and then continued. "It is a good plan, and we are thankful for the Mckenzies and the risk they are willing to take," finished William with a certain amount of respect in his tone.

"Good, that was easy, Fergus," smiled Gordian. "Let's get our kin ready for the march in the morning. Now, let's see about food and drink. It would be amiss not to have some hearty substance this evening before we travel."

Chapter 30 - Fergus Awakens

Fergus spent all night gently sipping at his drink. He never realised he had such disdain for water until now. Fergus was watching everybody keenly and conversing pleasantly with anyone who wished to engage with him. When he arrived with the clans, he wanted to show everyone he was still the Fergus of old, which meant banging some heads together. But Heather, God bless her, had got to him first. For some reason, Fergus actually listened to her for once. He thought it was perhaps the situation as he mulled over the day. Everyone told him the war was coming, not silly squabbles, a real war, one that would be the difference between certain death or servitude for the clans.

He craved the drink badly, and Fergus fought it with every sip of the water. The drink was the way of the Celt. As much as getting up every day. But, instead of him controlling the drink, he had allowed the drink to control him. He knew this.

Fergus realised with the dawning of what he had left of a brain that with the war, his people needed the old Fergus and with the little nudge from his beautiful wife, he would take back control. As Fergus looked around and saw Heather talking to her father, she smiled at him with such a wonderful smile. Fergus admitted to himself how lucky he was that she looked after him as Fergus constantly mourned the loss of their son. But, unfortunately, Fergus had stolen her own mourning, and that was something he couldn't give her back.

Heather had never blamed him for his death. In fact, no one had but himself. Paden had fallen as the mountain had let go of its snow. He had reached out. His hand touched the fingers of his son's outstretched hand. Fergus was so close, but the weight of the snow had taken him, and he was gone. As he reflected, this was perhaps the first time in several years that it had actually dawned on him that not only had his son fallen to his death. He had fallen and also died on that day.

Fergus continued to watch his wife.

She was definitely a firebrand and was as strong as steel. But Heather was more than this steely façade Heather showed everyone. Once you pulled back the layers, she was a kind-hearted, loving person who had everyone's interests at heart. Heather worked tirelessly to keep his clan together as he drank himself to death. She was definitely the leader he should have been. Fergus knew Heather would have been the leader of the Douglas's by birthright. It was only because she fell in love with one of the Mackenzie's and left her clan that she no longer was going to be chieftain.

Perhaps, for a time, he was that leader, but he knew he relied on her intelligence and wisdom even in the old days to make the right decisions. Although Heather should not have come, he wondered if he could convince her to stay here. Fergus knew she could fight as well as any of the warriors. Heather had trained hard to be the warrior he was. But, if he died. His people needed a leader, their leader. They would need Heather. Why was life even more complicated now he wasn't drunk?

Fergus could feel the drink depravity taking hold, he was sweating, and it was taking all his willpower not only to get a real drink. But to stop himself from shaking. Moreover, he was getting irritable, and he had a headache. So Fergus started wondering if he should just have a little drink before he went to bed. Would one hurt? Surely it wouldn't, he mulled over.

Fergus's thoughts were interrupted as he saw Heather walking over towards him. It wasn't often she was walking in his direction with a smile on her face. She waved as she saw him looking in her direction.

"Hey you, been talking to your family all evening and leaving me to my thoughts and drink," grinned Fergus as he held up his water.

"I sure have, and I've been watching you as well, Fergus," exclaimed Heather with a smile as she pushed him back slightly and sat on his lap. She threw her arms around him and looked into his eyes.

"It is time for you to come back, Fergus. It is time, our people's time, our time ….. we go to war," Heather smiled at Fergus and kissed him tenderly.

"You must let go of the ghosts. Paden awaits us both when the time is right and will take us before Dagda in all his glory, and we will sit by his side. But, we must not go until fate decides. You understand that?"

Fergus smiled.

"Heather, my love. I think you are saying to me no more drink as a first thing? Perhaps, not putting my life at risk on the field of battle by doing something stupid? Aye, lass, I do understand. When your whole clan is at risk of annihilation, all this,….." remarked Fergus as he made a hand gesture towards the other clansman in the room.

"….. started to become insignificant, as does the drink and does ….. Paden's death and my self-pity. Yes, I know I made Paden's death about me," continued Fergus as he watched

Heather study him as she was about to speak.

Fergus gently placed his finger on Heather's lips.

"Let me finish, my love. I have always known, yes always, even as I wallowed in the drink and my personal exile, ….. what was my problem? I missed Paden so much," choked Fergus. "I am not sure why, but seeing the girl Lauren and her beauty made me think much about Paden, a wife, children ….. So I just hit as low as I could, I guess," sniffled Fergus.

"Daft, really, and I was convinced no one really needed me. You were ruling my people and doing a grand job of it, Heather. Always have been better as Chieftain, Heather," grinned Fergus. "Anyway, when you said the clans' survival depends on it. When you stopped me bashing heads as we waited outside. At that moment, those words seemed to grab hold of my demons and bring me back to this world. To this day and probably onwards, I will always blame myself for Paden's death."

"But, my people need me, and I am back," insisted Fergus

"I love you, Fergus," smiled Heather as she stroked Fergus's face. "You must let go of Paden's death, mourn, grieve ….. but we remember. We remember all the good times, the joy, the laughter. His death is just a tiny part of the circle of life. Yet, that small piece is always with us as we remember the good times. It gives me solace to think back to these good times as a family. His death is nothing to me. A memory of no value, no blame, no pity. His death is nothing. It was his time, his fate. Dagda called him, and no one could stop that call. Not even you."

"I will try to let go, Heather. It is just hard," whispered Fergus.

"I know, Fergus," said Heather as she stared deep into Fergus's eyes ….. "let's leave and go back to the camp. I am bored of this place and want to spend time with my husband on his own," Heather grinned at Fergus.

Fergus laughed.

"It has been a long time since I have heard those words," Fergus grinned back as Heather held his hand and helped Fergus stand.

As they made their way back to the Mackenzie camp, they laughed and joked like they didn't have a care in the world.

"Caitlan, where is Angus?" asked Heather as she saw the female Mackenzie warrior on the outskirts of their camp.

"He is helping a few of the Stewarts back to their camp, Heather," grinned Caitlan. "You know what the Stewarts are like, a bit too much drink, and they think they can take liberties with the Mackenzies."

"Has others gone with him?" asked Fergus.

"Aye, Fergus. Angus will be fine. In fact, here he comes now," Caitlan motioned behind them.

Turning, Fergus and Heather could see Angus and a few other warriors returning from the Stewarts camp.

"Alright, Heather? Fergus? Did you have a good time while I was outside in this shitstorm?" moaned Angus sarcastically.

"Ha, I thought a Mackenzie could take a bit of snow and wind, Angus. So you are not going soft on me, eh lad?" laughed Fergus.

"I tell ya, whilst you been filling your fat belly, Fergus. It has been chuffing freezing," chortled Angus. "Damn your hide."

"Ah, well, Angus. This is the price you have to pay for the war. I am sure we are grateful, aren't we, Heather?" laughed Fergus.

"We are indeed, Angus. You and the others, go get yourself some drink and food. Have Murray and some others take watch for a while. Make sure you all get the right rest," said Heather.

"Aye, be ready, Angus, have the clan ready to ride in the morning. In fact, Caitlan, can you get the word spread before you go enjoy the drink," ordered Fergus.

Both Angus and Caitlan looked at Fergus in the darkness. They were bemused to get a proper order from him.

"Yes, Fergus. Absolutely. Will get the word moving now," said Caitlan, and she turned and started making her way through the camp, shouting at the groups.

"You alright, Fergus? You seem a bit strange this evening," probed Angus.

"You mean I am not drunk and rambling rubbish, Angus? Aye, I am fine. Heather has hit me one too many times, and I have come to my senses. Isn't that right, Heather?" laughed Fergus.

"It is. I have tried many times to knock some sense into him, Angus. But, finally, it has worked," smiled Heather.

"Angus, my friend, I am back," chuckled Fergus.

"Glad to hear it, you ol bastard. I'm tired of looking after you. About time you started doing something useful!" laughed Angus.

"Aye, well, that day is coming sooner than we think, old friend. So go get some rest, and we will see what tomorrow brings," Fergus grinned as he patted Angus on the back and led Heather onwards.

"You know Heather," said Fergus after she had tripped Fergus onto their bedding in their tent and sat on top of him. As she looked down at him and she started to undress. "I think tomorrow will be a great day ….. and tonight." He finished and pulled her down towards him as Heather giggled.

Chapter 31 - Clans Ride to War

Tomas looked out over the Horizon. They had left his homeland a day ago and had been on the road for no more than an hour this morning when he saw smoke several leagues away. But, whatever it was, it did not belong on the snow plains of Caldonia. He motioned to Fergus and William, who pulled their snow bears toward him, as did Heather.

"What is it? Tomas" asked William.

"There in the distance, do you see the smoke?" answered Tomas as he pointed in the direction of the smoke.

"Yes, I can see it," pondered Fergus.

"It is a strange sight. It looks like the war has begun. What do we know of the Hamiltons? We did not discuss them, Tomas. This is their land we now move into," asked Heather.

"We didn't have time to wait to see if they answered our call. But, their clan will know as well as we on the march of the enemy from the south. Perhaps they have ridden to engage the enemy. A foolhardy exercise if they have. They do not have the numbers without us," answered Tomas.

"They would have ridden," mused Fergus. "They are clansmen. They would not have hidden from anyone entering their lands."

"We must ride," said Tomas, who was just about to give the call when Fergus put his hand up.

"One minute, Tomas. We must follow the original plan. First, you take the Douglas and the Campbell warriors left

415

around the woods with Jockie. Then, William, Bonnie, you do the same on the right with the Stewarts and Macdonalds. I reckon if we give you both five minutes, then we all ride hard we should get to that area ….. what do you think? I reckon we will probably hit five minutes before you arrive. First, we will engage the enemy if it is them, and then you hit them on the flanks and close the circle," he grinned as he smashed his hands together as he mimicked a pincer.

"Sound good to the Douglas's," shouted Tomas.

"It is good for the Stewarts," cried William.

"The Campbells are ready," grinned Jockie.

"and the Macdonalds," shouted Bonnie

"To me, Douglas, To me, Douglas," hollered Tomas as he started to move off to the left.

"Campbell move out," yelled Jockie.

William and Bonnie did the same, going right. There were great movements of the clan's bears and warriors as they split into three groups and the Douglas, Macdonald, Campbell and Stewart clans departed into the distance. Angus made his way forward behind Fergus and Heather.

"Well, this is it, Fergus," said Angus as he looked into the distance.

"Aye, it is that," said Fergus. He turned and smiled at Heather. "Are you sure you want to ride, Heather? I would sooner see you return to the halls of your family."

"No, I am with my family," smiled Heather as she looked back at the Mackenzie clan. "You will not get rid of me that easily, Fergus."

"So be it," he smiled. He turned his snow bear around to face the clan and boomed;

Though he may die this day

He is the warrior of the McKenzie clan

None are bolder or stronger of hand than a Mckenzie

He fought and won against all of his foes

He fears no one as everyone dies on his sword

Though she may die this day

She is the warrior of the McKenzie clan

None are bolder or stronger of hand than a Mckenzie

She rides like the wind with the weapon in hand

She fights for glory. She fights for her kin

On the snow lands, we defend our homes

The battles are glorious as the Mckenzies take hold

None can stand and match our ferocity on the field

They will sing of our deeds and glory from beyond the grave

It matters not that we have fallen but how we fell.

We are Mckenzie's and our hour is now.

The clansmen started banging their swords on the shields as they screamed and hollered in salute to Fergus and the Mckenzies. The snow bears were also rearing up in excitement at the pending battle.

Fergus turned his bear back round and nodded at Heather.

"Ride like the wind," shouted Heather as she kicked off her snow bear Aila, who jumped forward and quickly ran at a ferocious pace.

The warrior's all cried in a frenzy, giving the bears their heads. Soon the Mckenzies were flying towards the smoking plains at a phenomenal rate. They would clear the distance in minutes.

Fergus caught up with Heather, turned, and grinned at her as the adrenaline took hold of him. Then, for the first time in a long time, Fergus felt really free from the guilt he had pent up over the years. He raced on with the cold force of the driving wind battering his face and pulling his hair back like trailing fire. Heather grinned back as her heart pumped faster as the rising flumes of smoke got closer.

"This is our time, Heather," shouted Fergus in her direction.

"We are one, my love," Heather shouted back as she drew her shortsword.

There were getting close now, and the lead Mckenzies could hear the shouts and screams of battle already ensuing.

"It must be the Hamiltons," shouted Angus.

"Ride," shouted Fergus.

"Ride, Ride, Ride, our clansman needs us," screamed Angus

to the warriors behind him. He pulled out a large horn and sounded it three times as they started to come over the brow of the hill and raced on to the battle ensuing in front of them.

An answer came as he saw the Hamilton's circled. Pressing forward at full pace, Fergus led his clan down the hillside.

"Mackenzies, Mackenzies," screamed Heather and Angus to have a chorus of the name returned from their clan.

Thousands of goblins screamed and started to break ranks from their current foe and surge toward them, joined by massive ogres who blundered their way forward. Fergus could feel the air alive with electricity as a storm of arrows rained down into their midsts. He realised devil magic was in the skies as they hit the first tranche of goblins as Fergus pushed his warriors on.

In slow motion, he saw some bears and their riders fall as they hit the goblins' front lines. However, they carried on with such force that they knocked hundreds of goblins out of the way before being reduced to hand-to-hand combat.

Fergus leapt off his snow bear as many of his clan did the same. The warriors and the snow bears fought better side by side rather than together. As he was about to engage a goblin, there was a flash of silver, a blur of movement and Fergus found himself flying backwards as he just managed to dodge the sweeping scimitar of one goblin as another tried to take him to the ground. He swept out wildly at the goblin who had just missed him with the slicing sword attack when another goblin joined the soldier who had attempted to tackle him. They both managed to take the giant chieftain off his feet to the ground with great effort. Fergus dug deep and, using all his strength, managed to throw one to the side as the other drove a glancing blow with a knife into his shoulder. He shouted in pain as he went berserk and rolled the attacker. Fergus managed to pin the goblin kneeling on his shoulder; he drove his sword through its chest. Fergus yelled in victory.

Heather had slain several goblins already, and her Bear Aila had slaughtered many more. Yet, there was no end to the ranks of goblins and ogres. She looked around for Fergus as she took a momentary breather. Then she spotted him. Caitlan, Angus, and others had gone berserk and were moving with such venom and ferocity through the inferior goblins towards the stricken Hamilton clan. She looked around and saw a unit of massive ogres driving towards them from the side. She quickly jumped on Aila and called out to other bears close by, and they smashed through the goblins to meet the ogres head-on. Aila jumped through the air at the lead ogre and caught him in her massive maul as his club sent Angus flying through the air. Heather had leapt off the bear as it flew towards the ogre. As she somersaulted through the air, she swung with as much might Heather could muster and nearly took another ogre's head clean off as she landed awkwardly on the ground.

Looking up, she saw the bears clearing the path of the nearby ogres. She was just about to shout for Fergus. Heather was suddenly grabbed by her shoulders and was momentarily starting to be lifted off the ground. Fergus came flying through the air and was holding …. A giant wing! Heather struggling to release herself from whatever gripped her, saw out the corner of her eye as she rose higher and higher. Fergus holding on and grappling with a red wing.

Fergus had seen the demon grab Heather and just managed to grab hold of the wing before Heather disappeared into the night. The devil struggled and was off-balance by the weight of Fergus hanging on to its wing. The Vampiri beat furiously to try and shake the infidel off her. Fergus managed to slice upwards, taking half the wing off with his blow. Heather, Fergus, and the Vampiri carrying them fell to the ground. Before both their eyes, they saw the demon transform into a female.

"You will pay for that, scum," said the Vampiri as she ran at them. Fergus rising to his feet, took an almighty swing at the head of the demon woman, who deftly avoided the death blow and smashed Fergus in the face sending him flying into the ongoing melee of the clansman and goblins.

Dragging Heather up onto her knees by the hair, the Vampiri pulled Heather's head back, canines extending much to Heather's horror. Then suddenly, the Vampiri's head flew from her shoulders, and her body slumped to the ground.

Angus dropped to his knees next to her.

"How you doing, Heather?" grinned an out-of-breath Angus.

"Okay, ….. you're alive," said a shocked Heather as she saw the blood-drenched face of Angus, who had a nasty cut along his face.

"Come to your feet. We must find Fergus, the others haven't arrived, and we are getting slaughtered…. Too many," shouted Angus over the din of the battle. Helping Heather to her feet, they caught sight of Fergus and Caitlan amid more ogres desperately trying to fend them off.

"Aila," screamed Heather. She was desperate for her bear to aid Fergus, who had dropped to one knee and struggled to get up as Caitlan valiantly tried to protect him. Heather found herself running frantically towards Fergus, as was Angus. They were slashing wildly with their swords in desperation to break through as Caitaln went down. This is where it ends, screamed in Heather's head, when finally Aila answered her call as she bound past them, taking the three ogres to the ground as she fell. She had managed to give not only Heather and Angus time to reach Fergus. He had managed to get to his feet and rejoin the melee.

"How are you, my love," shouted Fergus with an insane grin on his face.

"Been better," returned Heather as she drove a sword through the chest of one of the fallen ogres. She saw Aila trying to get up and fall back down.

"Stay down, Aila," she shouted as she fended off another blow from a goblin. As the goblin circled her, a sword flew straight through its back and out its chest. It dropped dead where it stood, and Caitlan was standing in front of her, blood spewing from her mouth. She rushed to Caitlan as she started to fall, catching her and lowering her to the ground.

"Caitlan," whispered Heather.

"It's alright, Heather. Dagda comes for me. I can see him now. ..... I go as a Mackenzie," she whispered as she took her last breath. Tears streaming from her eyes, she could see that Angus and Fergus were back in the thick of it. There was death everywhere. She could see fallen snow bears and her warriors dead strewn amongst the thousands of dead goblins. This is how it ends, she thought, as she rose to her feet, holding her sword high. Heather was just about to let out a scream of defiance as she wobbled unsteadily through the pain when she heard a horn blast and then again. The other clans, they come …… they come. She dropped to her knees, and then darkness took her.

When she came round sometime later, she was laid at the side of the battlefield. She could hear Fergus barking orders somewhere. She thought as loud as ever as she slowly opened her eyes, fearing what she would see. Instead, Heather saw Fergus talking to Angus, William and Bonnie.

"Fergus," she mumbled loud enough for him to hear her. Fergus rushed over to her side.

"Heather, my love. About time you woke up," he grinned. "We won. We drove the infidels off running."

"I heard the horns, and then everything went dark," she whispered, looking into his eyes.

"They all came, the Douglas, Macdonald, Campbell and Stewart clans. Just in the nick of time, too, we were losing badly," said Fergus.

Fergus grimaced slightly as he thought of the carnage of the Mackenzies. Though it also filled him with pride in the sacrifice of his people.

"Boom, they hit them from both sides. We had already dwindled their numbers considerably too. But they saw something we didn't. The demon who had you, the skies were filled with them. They had archers shooting them down or keeping them at bay as the bears and warriors attacked the main army from either side. Just as planned. Then it was touch and go for a bit, even then. But then something happened. There was a large boom, and suddenly the demons started to leave, flying south at speed."

"We chased the retreating army with the bears for a while and picked off hundreds more of the horde before coming back. Left you with Angus," Fergus grinned.

"Might have guessed," smiled Heather as she shook her head as Angus looked over.

"Tell you what I have learned. I do need to lose some weight. I was knackered within a few minutes," laughed Fergus.

Heather looked at his face. Same old Fergus. She would still have to live with his oddities. She smiled to herself.

"What of our people, the bears Fergus," Heather whispered. Fergus's face went dark and then was filled with sorrow.

"I am sorry, Heather. So many are now walking in the Halls of Dagda and have taken the warrior's final path. We have lost over half the bears, and now only a third of our warriors still stand. So many more are injured but are alive. We are still searching as we speak for survivors," sighed Fergus.

"So many, and the bears. So many of the bears, goblins and ogres are nothing to the bears ..... how," Heather sobbed.

"I had no idea at the time, but my understanding is that the blood-sucking vampire devils, my love," soothed Fergus as he tried to comfort Heather. "Magical attacks, specifically on the bears, concentrated on them, knowing they were our strength. As a result, many died having large burn wounds and unnatural injuries."

"Aila?" whispered Heather.

"She has many knocks and cuts, but she will be fine, Aila, a tough old girl like you," smiled Fergus. "Here, let me help you, and we can go see her."

As Heather rose unsteadily with the help of Fergus, with horror, she saw the devastation over the icy terrain. Now more red than white, stained with the blood of the fallen. There was a hive of activity amongst the carnage. The clansmen were milling about, searching the dead for any survivors. Others were stacking bodies of the fallen onto large pyres to send them on their way to Dagda.

Heather realised that they had been lucky to have won this battle. Her thoughts momentarily strayed to Berolarn, Talis, Lauren and Lilla. The Celts relied on no one for their survival. Yet, this time, she understood clearly that the Celts needed whatever quest Berolarn and the children were on to succeed. The Celts could not survive this sort of war on their own. Magic was a plaything in their eyes, but seeing the devastation wreaked on the bears, she now knew different. It was all-powerful.

"Angus," smiled Heather as she limped past Angus with the aide of Fergus.

"Bonnie..... William ..... Jockie.....where is Tomas?" croaked Heather, suddenly realising that Tomas was not here alongside the clan leaders. She turned to the sad eyes of Fergus.

"No," she whispered as the sorrow of Fergus hit her.

"I am so sorry, Heather," said Fergus sadly as he held his crying wife in his arms. "His deeds are already being spoken of between the warriors, so frenzied was his attack. Tomas drove through many, and none could stand in his path. Finally, however, his incredible skill drew the attention of some of the

Vampiri, and many swept down on him. It is said that he cut down some on his own, but they finally dragged him down."

Fergus didn't need to tell her how they ripped his throat out, and he had already ordered the horror witnesses not to reveal that one appeared to drink from his lifeless body.

"Come, my love, let's go to Aila. She awaits you," comforted Fergus as he continued leading the sobbing Heather toward Aila.

Then, as they closed in the bear, Aila, who was laid down, gave a low rumble of greeting. Heather raised her tear-streaked face, ran as best she could, flung her arms around the ginormous head of the snow bear, and buried her head in Aila's fur. Fergus watched on as his wife took solace in the bear. The only child she has thought Fergus darkly, and then he shook himself as he surveyed the lands. We must be off soon and return to the Douglas halls; Heather's father needs to have news of Tomas. Both clans were now in a tricky situation after many losses. Neither had a natural heir. There would be much to discuss as they rebuild.

Over the next few hours, the bodies of the fallen were finally on their way to Dagda as Fergus, Heather, and the others watched the raging flames of the funeral pyres.

He turned, as did the others. Fergus helped Heather onto his snow bear as Aila limped alongside, and they moved out and started the trek home.

Chapter 32 – Magma

He was ancient, had lived through many lives, and was still here. Magma was now older than any other who now walked the lands. He had left these lands long ago, and Magma had never thought he would return to them. But Magma had been forced to answer the call of the blood prince Olgrich, a pact Olgrich had made with Hel. He knew that the blood prince would stop at nothing for victory.

Magma would ensure he would pay back the self-proclaimed blood prince for this slight on his life, returning him to this monotonously dull place. He served no one but Hel. He only tolerated Hel through begrudging acceptance that he was a supreme being. Hel demanded he was to come back and help the blood prince. However, Magma had struck up a sort of peace with Olgrich. They understood each other's part in this, and the sooner he could rid the world of elves and others who followed the fool, Sol. The better this world would probably become.

Where he differed from Olgrich was on the twins and the girl. Magma knew that the blood prince feared them, and he wanted them. Olgrich saw them as either victory or defeat. Magma knew the reasons for his fear. He knew what they sort and what could happen if they acquired it. However, there was no chance of them retrieving the stone whilst under his watch.

Yes, he was Magma, and he feared nothing. Magma knew he would deal with them as he always dealt with any who crossed his path. Immense pain and death.

Chapter 33 – To Hell and Back

As Darius was leaving, Magma had walked toward Lauren and put his hand gently on Lauren's face.

"So pretty," he said as Lauren suddenly felt an excruciating burning pain explode through the skin of her face into her brain. She had never experienced pain like it. It burned deep into her soul. All she could do was scream for it to stop.

"I am sorry, Lauren. Does that hurt? I just wanted to ensure we understand each other," stated Magma as he slowly removed his hand from her face and watched with satisfaction the extreme fear and aftershocks of pain on Lauren's face.

He lazily sat down on the opposing settee and looked at Lauren, watching the rising movement of her chest in slow motion, the tiny beads of sweat on the brow of Lauren's now pale fearful face. Good, he thought she seemed to understand the meaning of pain. Perhaps he should play a bit with her before asking his questions. He slowly pushed himself up and walked back over to Lauren, who retracted back as far as she could into the corner of the settee.

"Now, Lauren. I went and sat down, thinking we had an understanding, and now I am not sure. You seemed to have an attitude buried deep in your eyes." Magma said as he kneeled in front of her. He slowly put his burning hot hands on her ankles, caressingly moved his hands upwards and delicately pulled up her dress to her knees. Then in one quick motion, he pulled her legs apart and pulled her forward. Her face was now just a few inches away from his face.

"I really thought you understood, Lauren," said Magma as he toyed with her.

"I do understand, ….. I really do, ….. I promise …..please." Lauren said nervously as she bit her lip in an attempt to stop herself from crying. She didn't understand why this man terrified her so much.

The man slowly brought his hand upwards, and as much as Lauren tried to pull away, his hands gripped her face tightly. Then, he very slowly pulled her face forward until her lips were just touching his.

"Are you sure, Lauren?" whispered Magma.

Magma felt the girl sob as he held her and her body went limp.

"Please ….. Please, do not hurt me. I have done nothing wrong," Lauren whimpered as the tears rolled down her face. Magma felt momentary happiness as some of the girl's tears entered his mouth.

"Oh, I am not sure I believe you," whispered Magma, and the room was again filled with Lauren's screams.

Her body was in spasms as he burned her brain and soul with his power, letting it course through his hands when suddenly he felt a burning in his chest, and he was thrown momentarily backwards, forcing him to let go of the girl's face.

This was interesting.

How had the girl attacked him? It was flimsy, but it had caused him a certain amount of discomfort. He looked at the crying girl's face. She probably didn't know she had done it. Perhaps this was part of what Olgrich feared. None but his own kind had ever hurt Magma. Ah, well, she must pay for that. He raised his hand and struck her hard across the face. Lauren saw his hand raise, and then the world went dark as she flew across the room and hit the wall.

Magma then sighed. Magma thought it would be a long evening as he walked across to where Lauren lay and grabbed the unconscious girl by her hair. He dragged her back to the settee and, with ease, flipped her back onto the sofa and rubbed away the hair he had pulled out with his hands. Magma then looked closely at the girl. She would be fine, he thought, noting she breathed normally, though her head was bleeding slightly, and already her face was swelling from where he had struck her.

There was something about the girl that looked vaguely familiar, he thought. He couldn't place it, but it was there. Had he met her before, perhaps? Yet she was just a child of a few summers. It would be impossible. He turned and walked over to his desk. He sat down and started to read what was happening with the war from the various pieces of correspondence.

Lauren awoke a few hours later. She stretched and thought what a strange, terrifying dream she had just had. Her face felt weird. Lauren instinctively touched her face and felt a slight tenderness. As she attempted to recall what had happened, Lauren then heard footsteps. Opening her eyes, she screamed as she saw her nightmare walking toward her.

"Hello again, Lauren. It's ok, we only just got started there is much more to come ..... what is this?" he said, looking at Lauren.

"Your face, it has healed nearly," he said curiously. "Solarian blood you may have, but no one recovers from a blow of

Magma so quickly."

Perhaps I should strike her again, maybe maim her to see what happens, he thought. But, perhaps not, he needed her to live, and he was already burning inside to kill her. He knew he would get carried away.

"Tell me what witchcraft this is, girl. What magic do you know that can heal one of my blows" whispered Magma.

"I know no magic," she said, recoiling from him.

"You see, Lauren, I thought we would be friends, you and I. Yet, you hide things from me. You do not tell me what I need to know. Is this how friends treat each over" Magma asked her questionably. "No, it is not, is it? Well, if you are not my friend, perhaps you are my enemy. Are you my enemy? Are you Lauren?"

"No, we are friends. I am not your enemy. I know no magic, I promise," cried Lauren.

"Are you sure, Lauren? I think you might be lying. Perhaps I need to remind you why you shouldn't lie." Magma said with a smile. Lauren started to speak, but the fear got the better of her, and she just looked at Magma with total dread.

He suddenly grabbed her by the back of the dress and threw her easily across the room. She somersaulted in the air and landed with a thud on her back. Winded by the hard floor, she gasped for air as Magma walked toward her again.

"I do think you are lying," whispered Magma as he knelt beside her, and he again laid his hand on her face and sent shots of agonising burning through her body. Then, finally, she couldn't stand it anymore.

"I will tell you," Lauren screamed.

"Of course you will," Magma laughed as he continued for several seconds more. He wanted to ensure that Lauren understood what the association of pain meant.

Lauren was a quivering wreck as Magma threw her onto the settee. Lauren had no idea what she was going to do. She was in so much pain that Lauren had begged him to stop. But that seemed to make him worse, as did the silence. Never had she wished more than now that her father, Berolarn, Talis or Elisha were here. They would know what to do. Her brain racing quickly, she surmised that he probably knew as much as her if Jenna was here. Jenna knew everything that was spoken at the council. Think Lauren think.

"Lauren, my dear child, are you ok? I have upset you, and that really wasn't my intention. We have much to talk about, you and I. Are you sure you are ok?" Magma said, actually sounding concerned. All Lauren could do, was nod her head, as she still hadn't worked out what to do or say.

"Good, good, I am pleased. Let us continue. Tell me instead, all you know about your quest," asked Magma.

For the next two hours, without interruption, she told of everything that had happened since her father's death that Jenna would have heard. Magma listened quietly and didn't utter another word. Occasionally, he got up and walked around as if deep in thought. When she finally finished. He thanked her for finally making an effort and was pleased Lauren had told her tale.

"I have a few questions more, Lauren. Interestingly, your brother and yourself have been in league with this Solarian

Berolarn and his pet ranger Luther. Yet neither of them has ever told you why you are so important. Is this correct?" asked Magma. His eyes were now glaring at her as if he was about to pounce and rip out her heart.

"No, honestly, I have asked many times, in different ways. Berolarn only tells you so much. He says you must walk the path to learn where the journey ends. He said all will be revealed throughout the journey. He implied there were many things he didn't understand himself," replied Lauren.

"He never told you why you seek the Dragonheart Stone? He never told you why it was you two who would be the saviours?" persisted Magma.

"No, I swear, as I said, he implied it was some prophecy he read about twins and this stone. But he said he didn't know what the stone did," said Lauren fearfully, expecting to be hit as she was running out of answers now.

Magma looked at the girl noticing her fear. She is telling the truth, I am sure of it. This Berolarn would know precisely what it does. He had heard many a tale about this powerful Solarian necromancer. But why would he think this would answer their problems of the blood prince? Would it not only make this plane of existence worse?

He was surprised that where he knew the twins and the girl's heritage. They did not. Would that not make things easier for them if they knew? It was a conundrum he would need to spend time thinking about. He decided he wouldn't speak to the blood prince until he had captured them all and played with this Berolarn. Then if it suited, Magma's purpose, the blood prince could have the children.

"Lauren, child, one more question, with an answer I feel you have omitted from telling me. The healing you experienced. You have told me you have not experienced your ancestors' thirst, rage, or hunger. Only your brother has, is this correct?" Asked Magma.

"Yes, ….. that is correct," replied Lauren.

"Can you tell me how your wound, which Magma gave you, healed so quickly? I know of the Vampiri regeneration, which needs sleep and rest. You didn't have either. Prey, do tell me, how you did it?" asked Magma.

Lauren decided she had no choice but to show him the Palantari stone. Unfortunately, he looked menacing again, and she thought he would kill her with one wrong step. Better to live and give up the stone.

"I am so sorry, Magma. I totally forgot about the Palantari stone. Berolarn said it gave me the power of healing. I haven't really thought about it since, but I guess it must have been that." Lauren replied quietly and awaited the next blow as Magma got up and came across her.

"Where is it?" he asked curiously. He had never heard of this Palantari stone.

"It's here," she said as she pulled the pendant from under her dress, took it from around her neck, and dangled it in front of Magma while taking a deep breath. Magma reached out to take it from her. But, as soon as his hand touched the stone, there was a huge bang and a massive flash of blue. Lauren saw Magma thrown across the room and smashing into the wall. Magma slowly got up, his hand smouldering as he looked at her, then his hand. Finally, he laughed aloud, which was the most unholy noise Lauren had ever heard, booming, loud and hysterical.

"I am impressed, Lauren, very impressed," Magma hissed through his laughter. "You thought you could trick me, hurt me, maybe kill me. So deceitful, yet glorious, well-done child, but I am Magma. I am unbreakable."

He went to the door and screamed for Darius several times, his voice making the room shake. It was that loud. Finally, a dishevelled and half-dressed Darius ran into the room.

"Where have you been, fool? I will kill you if I shout to you again and you take so long. Understand?" Magma shouted at Darius, who was busy looking back and forth at Magma's hand and Lauren.

"Yes, Lord Magma, A thousand apologies, it will not happen again ….. do you want me to get a healer," asked Darius, nodding at Magma's hand

"No fool, take Lauren's pendant. Hold it back up, Lauren," snarled Magma. Darius looked again at Magma's hand and then the pendant. Darius now saw the apparent connection.

"My lord, I am sure I can find someone else who can retrieve the item from the girl," said Darius with a slight bow. Magma's eyes narrowed.

"Darius, you have served me reasonably well now for months. But, in that time, you have seen others question my demands? What was their fate? Get me the pendant before I lose my patience," whispered Magma.

Darius looked at Magma and then the pendant and hesitantly went to take it off, Lauren. As soon as Darius touched the pendant, he also suffered the same fate as Magma. The crack of thunder and the flash were more minor. Yet, the throwing of Darius and the burning of the hand were the same. Except Darius was now unconscious.

"How interesting it is, as I thought. Only a god would dare to touch Magma. Only one god would strike down Darius. But, Lauren, you carry a relic of Sol. Perhaps you knew already then that you must a chosen of Sol to wield it," said Magma.

"Get up, fool," he continued, kicking Darius's comatose body. Magma sighed at the little apparent movement of Darius.

"Ok, Lauren, bring the pendant over here," requested Magma as he went towards his desk.

He picked up a box and opened the lid. "Please drop it in here," asked Magma.

Lauren complied and said farewell to the stone in her head, knowing it had probably served its purpose and saved her life. She was now more attractive to Magma.

"Thank you, Lauren. I knew that you and I could be friends," he said, smiling as he grabbed Lauren by the back of the dress and pushed her towards the doorway.

"Come, I will take you to your room," he commented as he grabbed her hair again and pulled her down the corridor.

Where Lauren went, she had no idea. But suddenly, Magma stopped, and she heard the drawing of a vast steel bar and a door being opened.

"You can stay with your old friend tonight. Garrett, make her welcome," he laughed as he threw Lauren in with such force that she landed halfway across the floor in a heap.

Quickly lifting her head as the door closed, she saw she was in a large barren room with a couple of torches lighting the room with an eerie light. She then saw a dark shadow in the corner. She squinted as she tried to determine if it was Jenna, and as the shadow leaned forward, she knew it was.

"Hello, kid, rough day for you too?" asked a subdued Jenna.

Lauren's fears had melted the moment Magma had left, and she was flowing with anger at the betrayal by Jenna and was about to run and attack her. Then Lauren saw her whole appearance. Oh, Sol, she had no arm. As quickly as her anger at Jenna arrived, it dissipated as fast. She ran over to Jenna.

"Oh, no, Jenna, what happened? Are you ok?" she asked, concerned about the pale Jenna.

"Good question, and in general, ……. I am not ok." She laughed weakly. "This is what happens when you annoy, Magma. Curse his dirty stinking hide."

"I thought you had become their spy," commented Lauren as she tried to fathom what she could do for Jenna's wounded arm. It was missing at the shoulder. It had obviously been fused together by fire. But Jenna was sweating, and obviously, the fever had her.

"I am sorry to say, Lauren, I was. ….. now do not look at me like that. You do not know what it is like being on the losing side all the time as I was all my childhood. Since then, I decided to play the game and ensure I was always on the winning side. I already knew our chances of survival were slim, and my reputation had preceded me. I was paid well and offered other opportunities for my service," said Jenna with a slow sighing tone.

"I see it got you far," sneered Lauren. She just couldn't help herself. She was annoyed at the broken woman in front of her.

"It's ok to be angry. I am mad at myself. I usually play the game far better than this. However, never have I had to deal with one such as Magma. He was annoyed that I hadn't orchestrated a situation where you all could be taken. This is punishment for not doing better," said Jenna with a laugh broken by coughing and spluttering.

"I have been with Magma. He is like a living nightmare. Who is he?" asked Lauren. Thinking back to the fear in his presence and the brutality of his actions.

"I do not know. I have never met his kind before, and trust me, I have travelled all of these lands, and I thought I had seen all. Everyone, including the Vampiri, run from his wrath." Jenna stopped speaking, closed her eyes, and tears came down her face.

Jenna said nothing more for a few seconds, then opened her eyes and made a movement with the stump of her arm as if she was trying to work out what happened as she shook her head.

"You know how he ripped my arm off? He pinned me against the wall by my neck with one hand. How I fought to try and release myself from his grip. But then his eyes, all I could do was look into those evil slitted eyes. Finally, I guess I stopped struggling, and he held me there, looking at me," said Jenna.

Jenna again stopped speaking. Lauren could see the inner battle Jenna was having, reliving the memory.

"Then his other hand came up in front of my face, and I watched it change into a claw, scaled in red, massive yellow talons grew where fingernails once were. He kept smiling as his hand transformed, turning it back and forth. His hand Lauren, his hand ….. it started to smoke, and I could feel the heat on my face. Slowly, the smoke turned to a flame that licked up and down his hand. I could see his eyes, the flaming dancing up and down his hand in his eyes."

Again, Jenna stopped speaking as she relived the memory. More tears rolled down her face, and she sobbed a little. Lauren watched her cry. She sat down at her side and put her arm around her. Jenna sat there crying for nearly five minutes as Lauren held her before Jenna continued.

"I am getting soppy in my old age," Jenna whispered, wiping the tears from her face. "Don't worry, I cry not because of fear or pain. It is more frustrating that my life will end like this…..I know my time is not long, Lauren. I feel the poison in my skin."

Jenna again closed her eyes and grimaced a while before she continued. "He said to me, this will hurt a little, Garrett. You must understand that Magma doesn't allow a hint of failure. What would everyone think if I did not punish you? They would think Magma allows failure. No, I cannot have that. You do understand, don't you? I then got annoyed, I told him I was hired by the dark lord, not him, and I answered to the dark lord only. Do you know what he did? He just smiled. Then he said, Oh Garrett, you think I care what the blood prince thinks? Do you think I am his minion, or maybe we are equal? Child, I am Magma. All bow down before me, he sneered. He then brought his flaming hand to my arm, deep he pressed, the pain ….. I have never experienced such pain ….before and the smell of your flesh, Lauren, burning. So bad it was. All I could hear through the excruciating pain was Magma laughing and asking, does it hurt."

She paused for a few seconds before turning and looking directly at Lauren.

"His hand, Lauren, burned through my skin, muscle and bone. Then, his hand took away my arm," cried Jenna.

Lauren looked at Jenna, horrified, then reached out and held her. There was nothing more to say but to give her comfort. It also, in turn, gave Lauren some comfort to know she was not alone. She wished she still had the pendant. Maybe this could help Jenna. But it was now lost.

Whilst Jenna was relaying to Lauren what had happened to her at the hands of this evil being. Magma was back in his study. He had picked up the unconscious Darius, thrown him into the corridor, and slammed the door to the room shut. He picked up the box, opened it and looked at the pendant. He carried it over to the sofa and sat down. What are we going to do now, he thought. It appears Sol is now walking the lands through the child Lauren, maybe others. This was slightly unexpected. He threw the box down and looked at his hand. In any form, Magma was not used to injury. He found the pain in his hand fascinating. Some of the blackened skin had blistered and peeled.

The others will come in search of their sister and their saviour Lauren. Magma will be ready, and he had absolutely no fear of Solarians. Who was this Berolarn to think he could come to his Lair and take what he guarded? No warlock, necromancer or whatever he was, had the power to take on the might of Magma. The Dragonheart Stone was now Magma's. He must be dealing with idiots. Yes, they must be fools.

Maybe, he should go to his lair and transform. Then, he would heal, and he would be ready. He could already feel a plan forming. He picked up the box again, snapping the lid shut and made his way to the wall, where he pushed a secret doorway open and left the room.

Chapter 34 – Old Friends or New

The companions kept moving forward but now slower than earlier. They kept the snow bears in check as Luther had a plan. At the right moment, Luther had slipped off the snow bear Bobster when they reached a suitable place of cover. He waited behind a wall as the others moved on for a few minutes. Finally, the others came to a stop and waited.

Luther could see a small individual edging their way forward. They were fast and deft of foot and movement. The way they glided across the ruins had great skill, Luther thought. The individual was garbed head to tail in black and grey, with ornate red markings. They wore the most unusual solid silver bodice in the shape of a scorpion, and their face was nearly complete masked. As they got closer, Luther could see the eyes that darted left to right and behind. Luther couldn't help thinking the eyes looked familiar and the scorpion. It couldn't be, could it, he thought.

Luther was ready to pounce. A few more steps were all that it would take. They were now in range, and Luther leapt, tackling the individual to the ground. He now held a knife at the throat of the stalker.

"Who are you? What do you want? Speak now if you value your life." Luther hissed at the person he held.

"Hello Luther, it's been a long time," said a female voice.

"Lillith," spat Luther as he pulled down the stranger's mask. He grabbed her by the throat and held the knife close to her face.

"What are you doing here, devil woman," demanded Luther as he glared at Lillith.

"Now, Luther is that any way to talk to your wife or treat her," Lillith said with a smile.

With that, Luther rolled off her and got to his feet.

"I have missed you, my love, and I have come to find you and Lilla," teased Lillith.

"I know you better than that, Lillith. You do nothing, absolutely nothing, if it doesn't benefit you. I repeat, why are you here?" snapped Luther.

With that, Lilleth, with great dexterity, flipped herself to her feet in one swift movement.

"You are as unkind as ever. Biggy sent a message saying you both were in trouble and you needed me," replied Lillith as she was rubbing the snow off her clothes.

"That stupid fool, why on earth would he think I needed you? In fact, how did he know where you were? And how did you know where we were?" asked Luther.

"It might come as a surprise to the big, high and mighty know it all that is Luther. But I occasionally meet with Biggy at pre-arranged times in the woods outside Lowedom. Remember, he was my friend, not yours. He only stayed because I asked him to look after Lilla. As for how I knew, you forget, I know these lands better than you, and I definitely have more friends. It was easy to find out your destination. It was hard work getting here. Getting through Jeliah with Biggy boy was difficult, to say the least," Lillith grinned as she turned and looked back down the road they had travelled. "But I have a few unsavoury friends in

Jeliah who helped at a price. You know what goblins are like."

"I swear I will kill that fool one of these days," snapped Luther as he saw Biggy in the distance, making his way toward them.

"Where is Lilla?" asked Lillith.

"She is with the others waiting for my return a minute or so in front. She knows nothing of you or her heritage. So you hold your tongue," snarled Luther.

"Of course, she will remember me. I'm her mother," replied Lillith coldly.

"You are not her mother, as I am not her Father. You know that as well as I. Berolarn gave her into our care as a young child and gave her a history," snapped Luther.

"Biggy," nodded Luther. "Next time, remind me not to trust a big stupid half-ogre," he said, glaring at Biggy, who just grinned.

"She is my daughter, pig, and she will remember me," shouted Lillith.

"She will not, Berolarn cast a lot of magic on her to protect her when she reached adulthood. He repeated this again when you disappeared. As a result, she remembers nothing of either of her childhoods. Instead, she thinks she banged her head and has lost her memory," replied Luther.

"You wiped her mind out of spite," said Lillith looking aghast for a second, then allowing anger to take over. She flew through the air at Luther. To find herself stopped in mid-air by the giant hand of Biggy.

"U not fight, we ageed," roared Biggy.

"Put me down, you big stupid oaf," hissed Lilleth. Then, as she struggled in his grip, she realised it was futile. Lillith stopped struggling, turned and smiled at Biggy.

"I promise! Ok?" vowed Lillith,

and with that, Biggy dropped her to the ground. Again she picked herself up and wiped off the snow again.

"My wonderful husband," Lillith commented as she looked again at Luther.

"You wiped all her memories of me. Thanks for that. You know I didn't leave her. I left you! I would have taken her, but I knew Berolarn would have hunted me down," Lillith said coldly.

"Now is not the time Lillith. We will deal with this after we have completed our quest. If you come, your life is at great risk. I would sooner you stay with Biggy and wait for our return," snarled Luther without much hope.

"No, you are not getting rid of me that easily. Not after I have trekked halfway around this godforsaken land. I am coming." Lillith replied with steel in her voice. Then, noting Luther about to speak, she continued. "Yes, I will not say anything to Lilla or Berolarn..... ok?"

"You say nothing to no one. Lilla is in love with one who travels with us. Talis. He is also Solarian. He is mighty and dangerous, as is his sister. Though they do not know it yet. Berolarn is taking them on a path of discovery. You must not, under any circumstances, interfere. Do you hear me? I am watching the situation closely, and I will be watching you. Do you understand, Lillith?" said Luther with a hardness in his conviction.

"Yes, yes, yes. Oh, how exciting, a boyfriend. Ah, young love, a life full of dreams and then you end up with crap! Oh no, I will not say anything …… I will not say a thing, OK!" said Lillith with force as she saw the look Luther gave her.

"Good, let's be off and catch up with the others. They will be waiting," replied Luther. Then, turning to Biggy as they started walking, "how is the inn, Biggy? Since you are here, can I ask who is looking after it?"

"Same old Luther", muttered Lillith before Biggy could answer.

"It tis fine, let we Charlie, she good, lok ater inn well," replied Biggy.

"Great!" said Luther in disbelief as they closed in on the rest of the companions.

Berolarn was looking back at the three figures walking down the street. He recognised Biggy ……. Who was the other one? He squinted, trying to see better when suddenly it dawned on him. It can't be ….. he thought. What in damnation is she doing here? An edge of panic hit Berolarn as he realised it was Lillith. No one more dangerous could have been walking toward him. If she told Lilla the truth before she was ready. Who knows what could happen? It could ruin everything. He cursed to himself. He hoped Luther still had sway over Lillith and convinced her to be quiet. Berolarn suddenly saw a blur of activity as Lilla dismounted Bear and ran into Biggy's arms.

"Oh, Biggy," cried Lilla as she flung herself at the giant half-ogre. "I have missed you so much."

"Missed u, Lilla," said the Biggy, clumsily patting her head.

"This is Lilla?" asked Lillith excitedly to Luther. Who looked at her with menace.

"Yes, this is Lilla," Luther replied as Lilla turned to look at the woman. "Lilla, please meet Lillith. Lillith, this is my daughter, Lilla."

Lilla continued to stare at the woman. She was middle-aged, lithe with sleek grey hair and piercing blue eyes, very unusual looking, pretty but not pretty, Lilla thought.

"You may have heard mutterings, Lilla, of a bounty hunter or assassin called the scorpion back at the Inn. Tales of heinous crimes in the hunt. All probably true as well. Lillith is the scorpion," sneered Luther.

"Thanks for such a warm introduction, Luther. I see you have not lost any of your wit or charm," Lillith said with a smile.

Talis watching the exchange, thought they both looked like they could murder each other.

"Nice to meet you, Lillith. How do you know me," enquired Lilla.

"Oh, I used to visit the inn a lot in my youth, and I remember this little scruffy urchin girl running around my feet. You have grown into a beautiful young woman Lilla, gorgeous," smiled Lillith with genuine warmth.

Lilla immediately knew she liked this woman, she looked familiar, but she couldn't picture anything about her. Lilla cursed the bang to her head that had taken her memory.

"Nice to meet you, Lillith. Come Biggy, Talis and the others are waiting," smiled Lilla.

As they arrived, Lillith was introduced to Talis and Elisha. Berolarn just nodded as he spoke her name and Lillith returned the same. Lilla noted there was a certain coldness between the two. However, they had obviously met at some time, and it looked like they had not parted on the best terms.

"Come, let's get going," said Berolarn to those on the ground. So they all mounted the snow bears except for Biggy.

"They stink," said Biggy as he got close to Bronte, who glared at him and growled. "Biggy walk."

"Biggy, you get on now, or so help me, you dung eater, I will cut you from ear to ear," cursed Luther, who was beginning to lose his patience.

Both Biggy and Bronte moaned at the situation. But, soon, Biggy was mounted, and they were back on their way.

Chapter 35 – Prepared for Visitors.

A couple of hours later, Magma returned to his study. His blackened, damaged hand had all but healed. He opened the door to his study and looked to see if Darius was still there. Then, seeing he wasn't, he started to shout his name. Darius returned within no time and was now fully garbed in battle armour.

"Magma, my lord, our spies have sent word that they will arrive soon. They have been joined by two others. One is a woman. The other they believe to be a half-ogre," said Darius.

"Good, good. Come in, Darius. How many are our forces?" asked Magma lazily.

"We have nearly one hundred goblins around the tower grounds and maybe twenty or thirty inside. We also have several ogres and a dozen Vampiri," replied Darius.

"Ok, and where is Selene," asked Magma.

"She is still confined to her room, my lord. She hasn't been allowed out since you rescued her from death," answered Darius.

"Good, have her taken to my lair now. Take the child and the spy down as well. Have them all tied to stakes at the altar. This is important, Darius, do not fail me. Are you listening?" asked Magma.

Darius nodded.

"Good ….. I want your forces to engage but to let them through," continued Magma as he paced around the study.

"My Lord?" questioned a highly puzzled Darius.

"I know it is difficult for one as dim as you, Darius," replied Magma with scorn in his voice.

"Let them through….. Kill the new ones, maybe the elven princess and the ranger too. But I want the two children and Berolarn alive. In fact, if you can capture them all, that might be better." Magma said thoughtfully. Then, shaking his head. "Either way, you will come to my lair with the children and the warlock unharmed. Do you understand?"

"Yes, my lord," replied Darius, who nodded and left the room.

Darius was angry at this situation. Magma had no idea how powerful these individuals were. Had they not lost several of his kind just to get the girl? It would be difficult enough to kill or capture them without the need to be selective about them. Why Olgrich enlisted the aid of this one, he would never be able to work out. He was more of a liability than a help.

He still couldn't work out why he never helped Selene at the inn or didn't do more at the elven outpost to capture the twins. Magma was always playing games and bringing chaos to everything he touched.

Darius decided as he started to shout orders around the tower. He would kill them all if needed and then fly to Olgrich. If Magma got in his way, Darius would also kill him. He knew his weakness was his human form, which would be his chance. Darius arrived at a door. He unlocked the magical charm holding it and kicked it open with force.

"Selene, get up. Magma wants you in his Lair," shouted

Darius.

"Hello, Darius. I see Magma has sent his little toy to get me," smiled Selene lazily.

"Shut up bitch, move your ass now, before you get what you deserve," he sneered at the Vampiri woman.

"You wouldn't be so courageous if my father was here, slime," she said, smiling still at Darius.

"You put great importance on being Olgrich's daughter, don't you, Selene? Your father already knows of your failings. They have been with you throughout your pitiful existence. The blood prince sent word for you to be executed. But, Magma keeps saving you," laughed Darius.

"You lie, Darius. I know what your problem is. You want me, and you cannot have me. I know you asked my father for me," grinned Selene.

Darius walked across to the bed. Then, dragging Selene out, he hit her across the face with the back of his hand. Selene fell to the floor and continued to laugh.

"Know this, Darius," laughed Selene, looking up at his face and wiping the blood from her mouth. "You can play the games with Magma and my father. But we all know what you are. Spineless and relatively useless. You only got to your position because of your constant whining."

"Get dressed. You have two minutes," hissed Darius as he turned and walked out the door, slamming it shut as he waited outside.

Within a minute, Selene came out, and Darius escorted her to Magma's study and pushed her through the secret door down to Magma's lair. Several minutes later, he was dragging a shouting and fighting Lauren through the secret door and carrying an unconscious Garrett over his shoulder. As he did this, he was thinking that this would end up being a bad day.

Lauren looked around the ginormous cavernous room as she was suspended by goblins to a stake driven into the stone floor. The area was of prominence in the room. Being set on a platform like a stage made for acting or a song.

Her arms and ankles were bound by a thick rope that the goblins had pulled so tight that it cut off her circulation. Then, turning her head to either side, she saw that a woman on either side was also hanging from huge wooden stakes. Jenna had been placed on her left whilst she struggled against the goblins, and a woman she didn't know was on her right. She wasn't sure, but the woman on her right also had broad iron nails driven through her hands. It looked like she had been beaten, looking at her face and unconsciousness.

The room was huge, and looking to her right, she could see it was more than a room. It was a cavern of immense scale. A tunnel nearly as tall as the giant elven trees she had seen was burrowed into its side. Lauren thought they must be deep underground, looking over at the colossal staircase she had been dragged down, which ran down the centre of the room. There must have been hundreds of steps.

All along the walls were massive tapestries depicting wars, monsters, and men, similar to what had been in Magma's study. Each one was parted by large iron fire pits suspended on the walls with flames that burned furiously from each as they lit the cavern. Two rivers also ran underneath the tapestries, one on either side. The rivers burned with flaming flickering as intensely hot lava flowed rapidly through the hall.

When the goblins had dragged her and Jenna toward the stakes. Lauren noted what looked like an altar behind them, alongside a large throne. The altar had been covered with golden objects. Lauren had also had a surge of excitement hit her as she spotted a long golden sceptre with a massive gemstone mounted in its head. It must be the Dragonheart stone by its description. The box with her pendant in it was also on the altar. Even as she fought the goblins, her mind was racing at seeing the prize they sought and the box.

Behind the altar, a large fire pit burned furiously. The heat behind Lauren was becoming unbearable on top of the heat from the Lava. She thought she might pass out as sweat started to tickle her brow. Then much to her horror, she saw Magma slowly walking down the steps. With each step, her fear and anxiety grew. Lauren watched him gliding across the floor towards them. Magma climbed the few steps to where they were and initially went to the unconscious woman on the left. He held her limp head up, looked at it, and then let it drop. Next, he walked past Lauren as she tried to shrink into the stake that held her and walked over to Jenna. He also lifted her head up. Jenna moaned as he did so. He looked at her and then let her head drop. Magma now made his way to Lauren.

"Hello again, Lauren. I come to speak to you as we decided we are friends." Magma smiled as he held her face looking at him.

Squeezing her jaw until she thought her face would implode under the pressure Magma exerted. But instead, Magma held her looking at him for several seconds until finally, Magma let go of her face. Magma turned his back on her and then started pacing back and forth in front of her, occasionally looking at Lauren as he continued talking.

"Lauren, we are finally here in the endgame. It all finishes tonight. If you are lucky, Your brother Talis, Lilla, and you, Lauren, will live to see another day. You are essential to Olgrich, or perhaps should I say the blood prince or dark lord, whatever you wish to call him. He sees you as the answer to his dominion over these lands and the legacy of his blood coming full circle. Where interestingly, your companion, Berolarn. That is the name, isn't it? The great necromancer Berolarn ...... he sees you and the kin as the world's saviour." Magma said as if bored with his words.

He then walked over to the unconscious woman, lifting her head and wobbling it like a rag doll.

"I believe the blood prince had hoped his bloodline in this one would have been enough to cement his legacy. Yet, she became a blood traitor, the worst kind of traitor to Olgrich. She married a Solarian. But, she returned, even though it took a little while for me to find out why." Magma lifted the woman's head up. "I finally convinced her to tell me why. She believed that Olgrich had learned of a child she had carried for the Solarian." He dropped her head again and walked back to Lauren.

"It is interesting what parents do for their children, is it not Lauren? Do you agree?" Lauren again nodded and answered meekly,

"Yes, Magma."

"Yes, indeed. Olgrich has never trusted that one, I think. She had pleaded youth and ignorance and had thought Olgrich was dead. So many falsehoods flowed out to him as she sought forgiveness and to walk again at his side. I understand that he constantly sent her on a quest to kill her Solarian husband, and ….. always, she has failed. Anyway, the child is now known to me, and now the child comes tonight," hummed Magma excitedly.

Lauren was perplexed about what Magma was on about. He was genuinely insane was the best she could come up with.

"When they come as they will tonight, you must be a good girl and stay very still, and no words will you speak. I wish to know more of this quest of Berolarn and why he deems you will be the saviour with the Dragonheart stone. If he doesn't answer my questions, I will cast down all who come to challenge me. You will watch the might and splendour of Magma. You understand?" asked Magma, and again Lauren nodded.

"All will burn under my wrath. Do you understand?" Magma questioned again. Lauren just nodded. She didn't have any idea what he was telling her.

"But, who knows, I think the blood prince would prize the elven princess and maybe even Berolarn. Perhaps all of you will survive this evening. But remember, Lauren, they are not my friends like you, and the only one I am probably not interested in killing is you. I like being with you. Perhaps you and I could be together for a long time," grinned Magma. "You know what that will mean."

He turned and paced again as Lauren followed him, her eyes horrified.

"Just remember if you watch them all die in pain and torment. It was because you would not answer all my questions." finished Magma, and he smiled as he stopped in front of her again.

He ran his finger down her face with a look of excitement as she started convulsing against the stake as pain flowed through her face. He held his finger against her face for a split second longer, and the pain stopped instantly as he removed his finger and started to walk off.

"Remember, Lauren. Everything that happens tonight is because of you," indicated Magma.

Chapter 36 – The Truth Starts to Emerge

Talis quickly dismounted Bear and held his arms out to grab Lilla as she jumped off.

"We are not far now. We need now to let the snow bears go. They will wait for us," said Berolarn.

"How do you know they will wait?" asked Lilla.

"I have mind merged with Bobster. He understands we need to go and that he needs to wait a few days to see if we return. Do not worry. As you know, the snow bears are more than capable of looking after themselves regardless of the foe." replied Berolarn.

Elisha, Talis and Lilla bid farewell to the snow bears and wished them safety as they returned to the others. Who was discussing the approach to the tower they could see in the distance.

"If we go to the wall next to the mountain, in that corner, there. In the darkness, we could scale the sides of the mountain and drop into an area covered by darkness," said Luther as he peered at the tower in the distance.

"To be fair, it seems a decent enough plan, even for Luther," said Lillith sarcastically.

"Ok, we wait until……" said Berolarn as he was suddenly stopped as a patrol of goblins and several ogres were now running at them. Before Talis or the others had time to react, Lillith was already running at one of the lead ogres. With the skill of a highly seasoned warrior, she slid under the ogre's

457

swinging club, and as she slid through, Lillith sliced the legs of the ogre, causing it to fall in roaring agony. The momentum took her onwards to a waiting goblin who felt the blade sweep upwards, spilling his life away as his head was nearly sliced in two. Then Luther was at her side. They both seemed to fight as one. While one ducked, the other killed. Talis and Lilla just stood there with open mouths as Berolarn flame in his hands, and Elisha joined in the melee with her long sword swinging upwards, decapitating another ogre. Biggy was going hammer and tong with another ogre as they pounded on each other.

By the time Talis had the mind to draw his bow. The battle was nearly won. He managed to kill one with his bow before it was over. Nevertheless, as Talis did a quick count, more than a score of goblins lay dead, and at least six or seven ogres were lifeless.

"Everyone ok?" asked Berolarn, looking around for more assailants. Everyone nodded. "Luther, we need to move now. They must have heard us from the Tower."

"No, not yet. It is not dark. Come over here," said Luther as he led the way to the side. He stopped outside a ruined building nearby.

"Everyone in here," ordered Luther as he pushed the door open. Once inside, Talis looked through a hole in the building wall and viewed the massive building in the distance.

They had arrived at what was left of the Tower of London. It had stood for over two thousand years, and much to his surprise, it looked in relatively good condition. The outer walls looked like they had been repaired. The only significant thing that didn't look quite right was the start of a rather large mountain on one side. On asking, Berolarn confirmed that the mountain was not there when it was built. There had been no mountains in London. It must have been a side effect of the cataclysm.

They had been there about an hour, With no further incident or sighting of the enemy. The night started to draw in, and Luther indicated they would be leaving soon. Talis sat next to Lilla and offered her some of the iron rations he was eating.

"No thanks, I couldn't stomach a thing, Talis," said Lilla as she shook her head. "I just want it over and done with now," she continued as she stared vacantly at the moon as it was making an appearance.

"Me too. I hope Lauren is ok. I am so scared for her, Lilla. In fact, I am scared for all of us," sighed Talis.

"I hate to say this, Talis, but if we die. I want you to know you are the very best thing that has ever happened to me," she said quietly as she looked at him.

"I love you," Talis replied as he took her hands and kissed them.

Lillith had overheard and seen Talis kiss Lilla's hands. She looked then at Luther. I remember when we were like that, Luther, she thought. But, you had to keep leaving us on another quest or battle. Whilst you lost the biggest fight of all, keeping your family. Well, this would not happen to these two. She would give them that chance if she could. Whatever battle was in front of them. Lillith would do everything to ensure their safety.

They continued to wait for some time as Luther continued

to peer through the hole in the wall. As much as he watched the tower, Luther had a nagging feeling something was wrong. He couldn't make out much activity on the battlements, and little noise could be heard behind the walls. It would be evident that many of their forces had not returned that night. They must know they are coming and are in the area right now. It was common sense that was the case. The goblins and ogres had been a teaser. The garrison that controlled the Tower of London was not those they killed. They were too few soldiers in view. It had to be a trap, must be. He was sure they would not walk in there with any stealth he had initially hoped. Luther was wondering if the party should separate. Perhaps they didn't know how many of them there were. In some ways, it would weaken them and give them a higher chance of capture if it came to a fight. On the other hand, it would improve their odds of getting to the stone and maybe Lauren.

"Berolarn, I think they know we are coming and have a good idea of our plans. But, unfortunately, everything feels wrong with the tower and lack of activity," Luther whispered.

"Do you think so?" asked Berolarn.

Luther explained his thoughts and the option of splitting into two groups to the companions. He surmised that if they both entered from opposing corners, one group would probably be a decoy for the other.

"I think you are right," sighed Berolarn. "Luther, Lillith, Biggy and Lilla, you go together. Elisha, Talis, you come with me."

"That is not happening. Lilla stays with me," protested Talis.

"Yes, I want to go with Talis," said Lilla with some anxiety.

"Listen, both of you," said Berolarn with kindness in his voice. "Sometimes, we must make difficult or terrible choices for the greater good. The forces of evil do not want any of us others. They want you three. ..... Lauren, they have. It would be far safer for us if you two were split for a time. If one group gets captured, it still leaves one of you free to complete the quest. Whilst one of you walks free, it might guarantee the lives of the others as they look for you."

"I do not understand why Lilla is wanted?" said Talis.

"Yes, why am I important?" asked Lilla.

"Berolarn," Luther warned. Knowing where Berolarn was going with this.

Berolarn held his hand up to Luther. "She needs to know." Berolarn said sternly. "He slowly passed his hand, which now glowed with an eerie white light across Lilla's face. A great warmth came as he did this.

"Lilla, your eyes!" said Talis in amazed wonder and excitement. "Your eyes are like mine and Lauren's."

"You are a Solarian. You are now with the last of our kind. Our legacy now lives in you three. This is why you are important to the dark lord, Lilla. He sees his victory in having you three," continued Berolarn.

"You must be mistaken," Lilla cautiously started to laugh. But seeing everyone's faces, including Talis's, she stopped laughing. "No, this cannot be true, Talis?" Then she turned to Luther. "Did you know," she sobbed though she did not know why.

Luther nodded, looking uncomfortable. "I am sorry, Lilla. It

461

was thought it was for the best. The Solarians were dwindling in number, and we foresaw that maybe there would be a time you would be sought. So, with Berolarn's guidance, we hid you as a human."

"I cannot believe this," Lilla said, turning to Talis. Who smiled, his heart still full of love, though he was not quite sure about the eyes.

"Nothing has changed, Lilla, you are who you are, and you will always be that person," said Talis with awe. "This makes sense why we are bonded as one. It makes no difference to you or us."

Lilla looked back and forth at her companions as she tried desperately to work everything out. It was a bit of a shock to find out she wasn't human. If anyone else had told her this and asked her at this moment in time what Lilla thought. Lilla knew she would have said they were crazy. But, her companions weren't anyone else, and the madness around them was always real. She breathed heavily for a few moments and quickly digested the news.

"I must admit, Berolarn," and then smiling at Talis. "This is a bit of shock you have dropped onto me, and as for you, damn your hide," she said, smiling as she turned her attention to Luther. "Had I known this earlier, perhaps I would have realised why you were such an overbearing, self-righteous pig." As her mind raced at the news, it had dawned on her that this was not the time for further in-depth soul-searching and confrontation with Berolarn. She would just go with it, for now. At this moment in time, they needed to get Lauren back.

"You both understand now?" said Berolarn.

Talis and Lilla looked at each other before Lilla replied.

"Yes, we both understand, and we will walk different paths for now," said Lilla. Then Lilla turned back to Talis and kissed him. She then turned back to the rest of the companions. "I guess we better get going then and get the stone and Lauren back."

Elisha went over to Talis and Lilla.

"Let the great god Sol bless these two," Elisha murmured, and she put a thumb on both their foreheads. "Whatever power still lays in these hands, the legacy of the Atlanteans and the elves. I will forfeit my life in protecting these two as their love will be the power to save our world." Again Lilla felt a warmth, as did Talis pass down their bodies.

"Thank you, Elisha," whispered Lilla in awe.

Elisha smiled and drew her sword from its scabbard.

"Time we went and got Lauren," Elisha said with conviction.

It was agreed that Berolarn, Elisha and Talis would take the far side of the tower. The others would follow Luther's lead and continue on the original path to the nearby mountain corner.

Chapter 37 – Captured

Luther taking the lead, led the others from the darkness to the corner wall of the ramparts. The mountain was steep, but they could scale it well enough as they managed to negotiate this first hurdle as they all dropped onto the wide rampart. Crouching down. Luther pointed to the tower at the end of the wall, some two hundred metres back along their route. The companions stealthily moved towards the building, trying to blend into the night by staying in the shadows that the moonlight had not managed to reach. They could see no activity within the inner ward of the tower as they travelled towards the building.

Luther forced the lock on the door, and they hurried down the stairs and exited. In front of them was another tower with a doorway that Luther surmised would take them into the inner courtyard. They quickly went through the building and came out on the other side to view the massive Tower of London sitting in the centre of a large yard.

As they made their way through the small passway between two inner buildings. They were hit with a massive commotion as goblins came around from either side in attack formation. Luther and Lillith were about to engage when a loud whooshing noise passed overhead, and they heard a terrible scream from Lilla. It was the vampire they had fought back at the stadium. He had swooped in overhead and grabbed the girl.

Darius landed behind the snarling baying goblins and stood with Lilla before him, holding her upright by both her arms. Next to him stood several humanoids that Luther thought must also be Vampiri. He brought his arm in front of Biggy to prevent the large half-ogre from running into melee. Luther quickly tried to devise their best action plan when the Vampiri spoke.

"We meet again, Luther. It is your name, is it not? No matter. As you can see, you are now in a predicament. Do you attack and attempt to save the girl? What do you do? You know you cannot get past our forces quickly enough." Darius laughed as he grabbed Lilla's hair and forcibly pulled her head sideward.

"Before I have my fill and rip her throat out."

"With this in mind, what are you going to do, Luther? This is the question. Are you going to attack, knowing you surely cannot win but die knowing you tried your best? Or will you be the saviour of all and lay down your weapons? Come, Luther, what are you going to do?" asked Darius with the surety of having total control of the situation.

Luther looked at Lillith, slowly put his sword down, and put his hands in the air. Lillith and Biggy did the same.

"Take them and ensure the binds are tight," Darius shouted to the goblins who had already pounced and were beating the three prisoners to the ground as they jeered and laughed.

"Bring them to me," continued Darius sounding slightly disappointed.

The prisoners were passed over to the Vampiri and they set off towards the main building, The White Tower. Darius looked over to Luther.

"It might have seemed a good decision at first, Luther. But not all is as it seems. I know you will plan to escape at some point. It is what I would have done in your situation. But, unfortunately, I have a surprise for you. You are going to meet a friend of the blood prince. I would be surprised if you managed to escape him. But it might be worth a try. I know you are well versed in the art of combat," said Darius derisively.

Luther just glared at him as he wondered who this individual was. Luther knew Darius was high ranking in the Vampiri, but it sounded like Darius bowed to another.

"Oh, by the way, he has the girl, Lauren. At times it sounded like they became quite good friends. She screamed fairly loudly. I nearly forgot myself and went in to join the fun," Darius laughed.

"Move," said another Vampiri as they pushed them violently through the doorway into the tower.

Berolarn, Talis and Elisha watched this occurring from the other side of the yard as they hid behind one of the buildings. Berolarn and Elisha spent a lot of the time holding Talis and trying to force him not only from rushing to the aid of Lilla. But, to stop him from creating so much noise, he would give away their location. They continue to watch the activity in the yard. Pulling as close to one of the buildings as possible in an attempt to remain in the shadows and away from prying eyes. They must have stood there for at least twenty minutes as the goblins milled about laughing and joking.

They noticed as the majority filtered into a large building on one side. A few goblins only remained in the yard.

This was their opportunity,

"The yard is too big for the goblins to cover the whole area effectively. But, if we wait for an opening, we can make it to the same entrance they took Lilla and the others into," whispered Berolarn.

"Berolarn, Look," whispered Elisha urgently, pointing toward two goblins coming their way.

Elisha started pulling them around the corner of the building next to her. She slowly pulled her long knife, held her finger to her mouth, and motioned Talis to do the same. They could hear the goblins getting very slowly closer and closer. They seemed to have no urgency in their movements as they laughed and joked. They could now listen to what they were saying.

"I've had enough, Shilack, enough, I'm telling ya. Dam their rotting hides. It's not what we signed up for, and all the lads think the same," said one of the goblins with a gruff, grating voice.

"You ain't wrong, Brocka. These blood-sucking scum think them know best. Oh yes, they do. Do this, Do that. It's driving me insane, Brocka," said Shilack.

"What happens to the promise, I ask? Where is the loot? The flesh, I ask. So far, we get bullshit orders of no killing, cold feet and hands. Treat us like slaves they do," growled Brocka.

"You got the point, lad. This scum thinks we don't understand. But, we know plenty, we do. Oh yeah, we will let them play their little games. Then bang, we will slit their throats and let em gurgle on their own blood for a change," cackled Shilack.

"If it wasn't for the big red. Would do it now …..."

He spoke no more words as the goblin went around the corner of the building. For a split second, the knife of Elisha entered his throat, and in one fluid movement, Elisha, with the grace of a swan, stabbed the other straight through his chest. Both goblins lay dead in a crumpled heap at their feet. When Talis forgot how good Elisha was in combat, she constantly reminded him. She had killed both before Talis had even reacted.

"Berolarn now is the time to go if we are to go at any time," urged Elisha.

Without waiting for Berolarn to answer, Elisha started moving across the yard. Following her lead, Talis and then Berolarn followed. Within seconds, they had reached the door. Elisha gently lifted the latch and pulled the door open. They entered, and the door closed behind them.

Darius, in the meantime, led the prisoners down to Magma's lair. He hated to come down here. Not only did Darius have to listen to the constant narcissistic ranting of Magma. He found the heat stifling, and the air burnt his lungs and brain. Why the fool had chosen this place as his principal residence was beyond him. Still, he was lucky that no one was allowed down there unless requested. It was infrequent that he had to visit this place.

Darius pushed Lilla a little too hard into Magma's study, and she fell. This action caused the other woman to deftly slip Jondal's grasp, and she was on Darius's back before he knew it. Lillith managed to wrap the shackles that bound her hands around his neck. Leaning back, Lillith was pulling with all her might, and Darius thought she might have ripped his head from his neck as he pushed backwards at full force into a bookcase hoping to throw her. Still, she held on, and he started to gasp for air. If Jondal hadn't recovered from the situation. Hitting

Lillith with the hilt of a sword and knocking her out, Darius might not have come away from this encounter still alive.

These prisoners were some of the most dangerous individuals he had met in a long time. Darius picked himself up. He slowly rubbed his neck and tried to let the anger subside. Darius aimed a few kicks at the stricken Lillith, then turning, he punched Lilla for causing this. He turned around and saw four of his comrades holding the enraged half-ogre, and the one called Luther was just staring at him.

"Any more, and I promise I will kill you all," Darius snarled as he dragged Lilla up by her hair. Turning to Jondal. "Pick that bitch up, and be more careful next time." He pushed Lilla towards the slight ajar entrance to Magma's lair. "Through here," he said as he pushed her roughly through the opening.

As he led them down and down the constant stairway, he heard the murmuring of the woman coming round as Jondal carried her. He stopped Lilla, turned, and spoke to Lillith as he pulled her head up.

"Know this woman if he doesn't want you anymore after he is done or if I come across you again. Then, I promise to slice you open and feast on your blood. Do you understand?" Darius hissed.

Lillith came round as he spoke, smiled and spat in Darius' face. Darius was outraged. He punched her and knocked her out of Jondal's arms. As she fell down the stairs, Darius grabbed her to stop her fall but then proceeded to smash her head multiple times against the stone floor. He would have killed her in anger if Jondal had not restrained him.

"Stop, Darius, you kill her, then Magma will surely be angry, and your life will be forfeit. Calm down!" said Jondal with urgency.

"What are you doing up there." Came a booming voice that shook the cavern as Jondal ended his sentence.

"Bringing you the prisoners down, Lord Magma," answered Jondal as he looked meaningfully at Darius. Who was letting his anger subside slowly.

"One of the prisoners had an unfortunate need to attempt escape. We had to thwart her plans." A more controlled Darius shouted down to Magma.

"Good, hurry up," returned Magma with a slight impatience in his voice.

As they started to reach the bottom of the cavern. Lilla felt nausea in the heat. It was unbearable, and she thought she had reached the belly of the earth as she saw the lava flowing on either side. Lilla could just make out figures at the far end as they started to walk across the cavern towards them. As they got closer, she realised a man clad in red was sitting on a stupendous golden throne at the side of three women tied to stakes. All appeared unconscious as they slumped forward, held only by the binds that secured them to the stakes.

It suddenly dawned with horror that the one in the middle was Lauren. The one on the left nearest to the man was Jenna. Yes, it was Jenna, she thought as she was hit by a wave of repulsion and horror as she saw Jenna was missing an arm. Lilla didn't recognise the one on the right at first, but as they arrived at the bottom of the stage, she realised it was the woman from the Inn. Did they say her name was Selene? Wife of Berolarn?

"Welcome, friends," said the man as he walked down the few steps of the staged area where the woman hung from the stakes.

"I can call us friends, can I not?" he smiled as he walked around them.

"My name is Magma, and I bid you welcome."

"What happened to this one," asked Magma curiously as he lifted Lillith's blood-soaked head up.

"She was annoying," said Darius as he felt his anger rise again.

"Annoying," laughed Magma. "Darius, my friend. One day, I can definitely see you becoming useful. Who is she? She is not expected?"

Darius shrugged.

"Ah, you, I know. Luther, the great infamous Luther. Well met, friend," said Magma as he stared at Luther. "I see you look at me as if our paths had crossed before. Is this correct?"

"I have seen you before," answered Luther curtly.

"Please, do tell Luther. Surely if we had met before, you would be dead, would you not? Not standing here before me," said Magma intrigued.

"We saw you talking in the great plains with a woman as you walked around hosts of goblins," Luther continued to be blunt in his responses.

"Ah yes, I do remember. I thought I could feel eyes on me, but something was hiding them from me. Maybe, you were with ...... your friend Berolarn? Ah, yes, it would be him. Using his little spells," replied Magma, grinning when he spoke.

"You're a big one, an ogre runt by some chance?" Magma asked Biggy.

"Biggy, no runt," said Biggy. But then, Magma suddenly hit Biggy with such unnatural force that the giant half-ogre flew through the air, landed several metres away, and did not move.

"Sorry about that," said Magma as he addressed all three companions. "He was annoyingly dim. I took him out of our discussions to talk to my best friend, Lilla. Yes, Lilla, I know your name." Magma smiled. "You look surprised. You shouldn't be surprised. You are the one I wanted to see most. You are family. You should know that we give them special attention like Selene when the family is in the room." He pointed to the woman who had attacked them at the inn. Lilla had no idea what he was talking about as she looked at him with unrelenting fear and confusion.

Magma noted the confusion with glee. Lilla doesn't know. Look at how confused she is, he thought as he beamed at her.

"I am surprised that the child doesn't know her heritage, Luther. From what I've heard, I presume you play father," Magma continued. "Not very nice to hide things from the poor child. All this deceit and lies."

"You hold your tongue," blurted out Luther angrily.

"Ah, hit a nerve, have we, Luther. I see no fear of Magma in your eyes either. Do not worry. I will bring you to fear. I will bring you pain and salvation. Yet, we will wait until the others arrive and make the family get-together complete. Darius, please have the others erect more pillars and bind these three whilst I continue to talk to my new friend Lilla," ordered Magma. "Come child, come walk with me. Darius, take off her shackles."

Darius started to undo Lilla's bindings as she looked pleadingly with fear at Luther, who shook his head as he was led off to the stage area. She was scared to death of this man and would do anything not to be in his presence. He then led Lilla down the cavern.

"You must understand, Lilla, I have lived such a long time and have seen the ages come and go from afar. I was there when we battled the forces of Sol. I was there when my kind was banished from this world. But I am back, and I am here to make this world what it always should have been. A world where the strong are the masters and the weaker pay homage through servitude. It is the natural order of things," said Magma as he strolled with Lilla, looking from her to the Lava flowing with an unquestionable certainty under the mountain.

"Why am I telling you this, you may ask? Do you know?"

"I have no idea. I am sorry," Lilla whispered apologetically, terrified that Magma would throw her into the lava.

"I do it on a whim only. Nothing more. It helps pass the time as we wait." Magma laughed as he stopped walking and reflected. He turned and looked at the terrified Lilla.

"You are still very young for your kind, and you are not yet moulded into what you can be. You are an innocent, are you not? You sit in the middle of scales, not knowing how they may tip." He continued as he started walking again. "They are finally balanced between two competing forces. I am here to disrupt that balance, a force of nature that cannot be stopped. Which side will you drop into, the path you thought you were walking or will you realise that the path is the way of your kin?" asked Magma.

"I have no idea, what to do," Lilla said as she started to cry. She couldn't understand the fear he generated inside her. She knew her destiny was at Talis's side, fighting for good and freedom. Not the path of the dark lord or this fiend. Yet she couldn't bring herself to stand on her own two feet and challenge this man. She had no idea why he kept talking about her kin and heritage. Then she recalled Luther actually telling this tyrant to shut his mouth. So what the hell is going off?

"It is alright, child. Fear is natural in front of me. Embrace it," smiled Magma. He reached out and placed his hand on her face in comfort. After a few seconds, his eyes narrowed as he looked into Lilla's eyes.

"What is this?" he said excitedly, his voice full of energy and exuberance. "It cannot be," Magma continued as he moved his hand slowly over her breast to her stomach and then pulled his hand away. "Does this change anything? I wonder what this means?" Marvelled Magma as he paced back and forth in front of Lilla. "I am sure this is a sign of the gods, should she....."

He then looked back at Lilla. "Come, Lilla. Do not be afraid. You are most precious to me." Magna put his arm around her and escorted her back towards her companions, all now hanging from stakes. Darius and the Vampiri were nowhere to be seen.

Chapter 38 – All Comes to a Head.

Walking slowly down the well-lit empty corridor, they continued to see no signs of life.

Then, finally, they could hear the odd voice in the distance, but nothing more. Elisha had been in many elvish garrisons, and it was unnerving. Something just didn't feel right.

"Something is wrong, Berolarn," she whispered. "I expected us to have encountered someone by now. These places are full of activity at all times."

"I agree, Elisha. It's some form of a trap, I think. Just not sure why they are not coming to get us now. I have no doubt it is being done for a purpose. What that purpose is, is the question we need to answer," replied Berolarn.

Darius could feel their presence and knew the three had entered. However, he couldn't understand why Magma didn't want them to engage and just take them. It seemed a risk to guide them to Magma's lair. But, he wanted no one interfering in his plans. The great Magma would see to them himself. At this moment, they were welcome to each other, he thought derisively as he grabbed hold of the human serf cleaning his room.

As his canines slowly grew, he pulled her head to one side and bit down deep, and he let the blood flow fast from her. The warmth re-exhilarated him. After a few minutes of drinking, he thought about continuing and killing her. He was enjoying her blood with an abundance of vigour and general enthusiasm. But he pushed her away and let her drop to the floor. Unconscious but alive. He would feed on her again later.

He paced around his room, Magma was unpredictable, and the enemy was strong. Darius walked out into the corridor, knowing the enemy would not come this way. He would get the other Vampiri brothers and sisters ready. Darius could see no good reason for them to get killed on Magma's whim. They must be prepared to leave if things go astray and are at risk of their own survival. They could fight another day in more significant numbers. He was also getting bored of Magma's pretending to be superior to everyone and his non-stop undertones of contempt for the blood prince and the Vampiri.

"Look, this door is ajar, and Lilla's headgear is on the floor. So it seems we are taking this way," said Berolarn as he pushed the door open slightly. He peered into the room and, seeing it was empty, walked into Magma's study. Berolarn looked around, and all three of them noted the door in the wall was open, and hot air was billowing out of the opening.

"I sense great evil, Berolarn. I have not felt such evil before," said Elisha with a visible shiver. Talis felt a certain dread, but he did not know why.

"Whatever it is, the fear is generated by magic I have never felt before. He waved his hand in a circle, and the forms of two small round silver rings appeared. Berolarn then made a fist and punched lightly at the rings. They both floated slowly now with a dot in the middle towards Talis and Elisha. They both watched each other in amazement as they landed on the brow of their heads just above their noses. The fear dissipated almost immediately, and a warmness of well-being filled their minds.

"You are not protected from the magic of fear, unlike me.

However, the spell of protection I have placed on you both will last for some time," explained Berolarn. "This way," he said as he made his way to the other doorway and started to descend the stairs as Elisha and Talis followed.

Magma thought ….. they come …... as he slowly caressed Lilla's hair as she kneeled at his feet. It would be interesting to finally meet this Berolarn. Olgrich had warned him that he had the use of the White Book of Sol. The Solarians had in their keeping all the books that Olgrich prized so highly. It would make the encounter enjoyable and bring some interest to his current mundane life.

"Stay here, child, whatever happens. I do not want you to get harmed," warned Magma speaking softly to Lilla. He could now see them entering the cavern and making their way down the steps.

"Welcome, Princess Elisha, daughter of King Ethera, child of the Atlanteans. Talis bastard child of Loran, Solarian scum and finally ….. we have the mighty Berolarn, a Solarian, a beggar in his youth. But now, I suspect, old and frail, suffering from doubt and regret," mocked Magma.

"I am Magma. I bid you welcome, friends," roared Magma.

Talis, on viewing the scene of Lilla kneeling at this man's feet, Lauren hanging, limp and possibly dead and the others hanging in various states of life. He couldn't control his anger, his thirst, his hunger.

"No, Talis," shouted Berolarn.

He heard Berolarn shout as his eyes started to fill with the red of pumping blood, and his canines began to grow. Then, before Berolarn could grab him, he flew through the air at this Magma. So it begins, thought Magma with a grin. In one perfect movement, Magma held the snarling and biting Talis flying directly at him and threw him crashing into the alter as if he was a small pebble. Then, spinning around and with a quick motion of his hand. The several arrows unleashed by Elisha turned and flew back at her at such a pace. She couldn't avoid them as the arrows smashed into her and pinned her against the wall. Berolarn could hear her groaning as he concentrated on Magma. He continued slowly descending the stairs, focusing directly on Magma.

"Well, just you and me, Berolarn. I wished it so," smiled Magma. "You are famous across the land. The blood prince even speaks of you, confident of his brother Loran. The one who ran him through with the sword held by ….. Talis," he said questionably as he flicked his hand toward the onrushing Talis. An unholy force grabbed Talis, carrying and pinning him against the stake that held Lauren. The rope that bound Lauren now bound Talis too. Berolarn stood there watching as this all unfolded, yet still to make a move.

Lauren slowly lifted her head on hearing Loran's name.

"Father," Lauren whispered from her now heat-scorched lips.

"Yes, Lauren, didn't the great Berolarn tell you any of his secrets? Your uncle is the blood prince. You are precious to him. You and your brother, he wants his family back." Magma said with glee as Berolarn continued to just watch.

"Then we have his daughter next to you, Lauren. Wife of Berolarn, cousin, the beautiful Selene. Did he not tell you?

Lauren looked slowly at Selene, as did Talis, who was now back to normal. It caused the blood prince great pain to learn his only child had run off with a half-breed and tried to forget what she was."

"So long did you manipulate her, didn't you, Berolarn? So long did the blood prince search for her? Do you remember Berolarn?" asked Magma.

"I do," said Berolarn as he started to walk down the steps.

Magma jumped off the stage area and waited for Berolarn. Magma continued once Berolarn foot left the final step.

"I am not sure, Berolarn, if you know the rest of the story, and I am sure it will pain you if you do not. I had to use all my persuasion to get it out of Selene." Magma said as he started to circle, as did Berolarn, intently viewing each other. "I am sure Lauren, Talis and especially Lilla wish to know the story."

Berolarn started to raise his hand and call the magic. But Magma was quicker, and Lilla flew through the air at speed and landed directly in front of Magma, who gripped Lilla by her throat in front of him, looking outwards at Berolarn as Magma spoke over her shoulder.

"It's a story of great unselfish love. She left Berolarn and returned to her father, begging for forgiveness. Did she not Berolarn?" asked Magma.

"She left, yes, that is true," replied Berolarn.

"How she begged for forgiveness, and you must know Berolarn she was punished, for years she was punished every day. Finally, though not trusting her, the blood prince sent her on a journey of salvation. Her task was to kill you. Yet, constantly she returned having failed," smiled Magma.

"What is your point, Magma or whatever you call yourself? Let the girl go. It is me you said you want," scowled Berolarn.

"No, No, No, Berolarn. Let me finish the story," Magma laughed as he tightened his grip around Lilla's throat, and she started to choke. Magma slowly released some pressure as Lilla spluttered and gasped for air.

"My thinking, Berolarn, is that I am not sure you know why she left you. My understanding was not because she did not love you anymore. Look over to Selene, look awake, and look at her eyes. Love pours out," teased Magma.

Berolarn quickly scanned over to Selene, who voiced "sorry" as he caught her eye.

"So why did she leave? She was fearful that her father would find you, find ...... the child ..... the daughter you both had. She went, hoping that he would not find out and that you would be the good father, would hide her daughter from harm's way. So well, did you both play this game? Though neither of you knew of each other's game. The blood prince has no idea, no idea at all. What happened to the daughter? This was more difficult to work out," grinned Magma.

"But, I pieced together that Luther was in charge of a girl called Lilla," chuckled a gloating Magma once again, holding Lilla's head up. Why did she come with you? Partner of Talis, was that the reason? A whim of her guardian or her lover? But she arrived, and I saw her face, the Solarian eyes, yet her mother's soul. Lilla, say hello to your mother and father."

"No," Lilla whispered as Berolarn started to move forward.

"Now, everyone calms down," Magma said as he squeezed Lilla's throat to make sure Berolarn understood.

"But, there is more," Magma said triumphantly as he saw Selene starting to snap the ropes that bound her and Talis struggling.

"One more movement and I will rip her beautiful throat out. ….. I promise it will be done," he said as everyone stopped moving.

Magma then continued as he held everyone still with his words.

"When you came, I didn't realise that the most important person would be the one I viewed as most insignificant. Yet when I saw her face and I learned. I must admit I was elated. The blood prince would be pleased, and his victory would probably be swift with all the children at his side. Though I must admit, I care little for Olgrich and his plans. Anyway, we talked, didn't we, Lilla? As friends do ….. Lilla, please answer the question, ….. Lilla be good now and answer," he said as he squeezed Lilla's throat.

"Yes," sobbed Lilla.

"Yes, we talked, and she was confused ….. and I tried to comfort you, didn't I, Lilla?….. Lilla, please answer. I will not keep asking," he said now menacingly.

"Yes, Magma," said Lilla as tears rolled down her face.

"Well, I have a gift. You probably have it too, Berolarn." Magma said, grinning at Berolarn. "Well, I stroked her face, and the sign hit me. I ran my hand to her womb ….. and she was carrying a child. Oh, I was so excited. Could it be? In her belly sits another child of darkness and light."

The room erupted with noise as Talis fought the bind of the stake, as did Selene and Luther."

"I will not ask again for quiet," boomed Magma, and the whole cavern shook. "I promise I will kill Lilla and her unborn bastard if I have any more disturbance." He waved his hand, and more ropes appeared around everyone tied to the stakes.

"Now, Berolarn, father, grandfather ….. is there anything I missed out on? I am sure you still have many little secrets there. I still wonder why you come for the stone?" inquired the grinning Magma.

"You know why I come ….. let the girl go. It is me you want, is it not," replied Berolarn.

"Very true, I lust for excitement," whispered Magma and as quick as the eye could see, Lilla spun across the floor into the stage with a sickening thud. Then, Magma unleashed the full force of his dark magic, which was met by Berolarn as he brought his arms together with a crash to release the intense white fire of the burning sun from his hands.

The battle raged back and forth, neither giving up any ground. Sometimes Berolarn appeared on top, then for the momentum of the struggle to turn, with Magma seeming likely to be victorious.

Berolarn dug deeper and bound his mind, body and soul together. A white energy blast that shook the whole cavern like an earthquake hit Magma full-on and lifted Magma off his feet, throwing him into the molten lava.

Berolarn looked over to the bubbling lava for a few seconds, then walked over to Lilla and helped her to her feet.

"Come, Lilla, help me release everyone," Berolarn smiled at her.

Lilla was extremely confused looking into his face, but she nodded in agreement. Then, limping as she walked up the stairs, she immediately went to Talis and Lauren and started to cut them free. Berolarn was just doing the same with Selene when Luther cried out.

"Berolarn, he rises," shouted Luther. "Lilla cut me free."

All the companions looked over to see Magma had indeed arisen from the Lava. As he returned to the stone cavern floor, Magma looked like he was walking on water. Now naked, Magma looked like he was brushing off molten lava from his arms. His body glowed red like molten steel, skin now looking scaled like a lizard. The fear he radiated hit everyone when he looked up and appeared to smile. Even Talis having Berolarn's charm, was hit with a feeling of despair, like a thunderstorm of emotions being let loose.

"I am very impressed, Berolarn, very, very impressed, but I am one of the first children born from fire. You should know the natural fire elemental has no power to hurt me," sneered Magma.

"It has been long since I had a foe worthy of my full attention. I would have to search back to the age of dreams to remember such a time. You do, unfortunately, have my attention now. I will ensure that I will make your deaths as painful as possible," threatened Magma.

Lilla ran as best she could and furiously started to cut at the binding that held Luther and Lilleth.

Magma started to transform before the eyes. It was now clear to Berolarn that the power of Magma was darkness born of another time. He was transforming into a dragon!

Everyone ran for what cover they could find on the stage as Magma was now gargantuan in size. Some hundred and twenty feet long with a tremendous yellowy red tail of nearly forty feet, covered in spikes as long as a long two-handed sword. His wings were as broad as his body was long. Magma's body was covered in deep red scales the size of cartwheels, scared and damaged from many battles. In his mouth, Lauren could see teeth that could bite buildings in half as if chewing on a piece of bread. Finally, the deep yellow eyes, set with obsidian black pupils, appear to have the flames of hell dancing inside.

Somehow, Olgrich had brought a creature of an age forgotten into this world. Berolarn thought. An ancient red dragon, the mightiest of the evil dragons and the greatest of the magic users, was walking the earth again — a rival or great alley for any demon prince. This is why everyone felt fear when around Magma, the dragon fear he had read about in legends. Berolarn now understood why he struggled against Magma using the greatest of his powers without the desired effect. He knew now he could not defeat Magma in this form. Berolarn wasn't sure he had any force that could harm an ancient red dragon.

As Berolarn's brain was scrambling, he saw Luther and Lillith running at the ginormous dragon, buying the others time. The ancient red dragon opened his mouth, and molten fire sprayed out and followed Luther, who was running at full speed to Magma's left as Lillith went right in an attempt to split

Magma's attention. Luther managed to slide under the legs of the ancient dragon as the flames fanned the back of his legs. Unfortunately, his sword bounced off as he tried to slice the front portion of Magma's leg.

Lillith, in the meantime, had managed to grab the wing of the frustrated dragon, and as Magma beat his wings, she had used the momentum to throw herself somersaulting through the air to land on the giant red-scaled back of the monster. Landing with the grace of someone who had trained for years to use her lithe form to her advantage. Lillith landed gracefully on Magma's back and was already running towards his head. As she ran up his neck, Magma gave her the advantage by lowering his head as he breathed fire at the scattering companions around the altar. Magma's wide mouth bellowed fire that fully immersed the unfortunate yet unconscious Jenna in molten flame. Disintegrating her and the stake instantaneously. Lillith used the momentum of the dragon's action to fly through the air, and she drove her sword deep into the head of Magma as she pushed off to again fly through the air, landing on the floor in front of the ancient red dragon.

For the first time in thousands of years, Magma had felt pain from steel, now, he was mad, and his anger had no bounds. As he followed the running woman with his flame. Just as he was about to immerse her in death. He felt another sharp pain. Luther had driven his sword through a joint in the scales on his back legs. Magma spun around and looked for the cause of his misery.

"I will crush you, little weapons master and chew on your dead bones," screamed Magma as he pounded his feet on the floor. He just managed to catch Luther and send him flying

485

when he was hit in the side by the burning white flame of Berolarn. Magma pulled his head back with a tremendous roar and hit Berolarn with an inferno of fire that pushed Berolarn's own flame backwards, and within seconds Berolarn was on one knee, just holding the flame from consuming him with a small circle of white flame. But, just as Berolarn thought, he could not hold it anymore. He saw Selene running towards him, and her flame hit Magma in the side. Berolarn was amazed to see it was the white flame of Sol. She could still call on Sol!

It momentarily broke Magma's concentration as she ran to Berolarn, and now together as one, they hit the ancient red with the combined power of the white flame. Magma met the white flame again with the full force of his own flame, a power as old as anything they threw at him. As he held their magic, he surveyed the room. Luther was prone. The woman who had stabbed him was now with Lilla, as was Talis. The half-ogre and the elf were both as good as dead. Magma decided his next move and he let his flame drop and took the full force of the white flame as he spun around. Though it was moderately painful, it worked as he came back around and smashed the Solarian and his Vampiri bitch square with his tail. Berolarn and Selene stood no chance as the muscular spiked tail hit them and sent them crashing into the wall near the tunnel. Neither moved. The time is now mine, thought Magma as he let the glory of the pending victory fill his body.

Then a roar that was not his filled the cavern from behind him. He knew that sound, but it could not be. Hel had only sent him.

Spinning around, he saw a majestic large golden dragon with wings speckled with silver. Nearly as big as him. It took

Magma's breath. No dragon of this multi-colouring existed. It was obviously a servant of Sol by its gold and silver markings. Magma immediately decided to take to the skies as the great gold moved towards him with snarling teeth. He would have the advantage, Magma was sure. He turned, and with a thunderous noise, he ran towards the tunnel with the golden dragon close behind him. As soon as he reached the exit, he drove into the skies, pushing off with his vast, powerful rear legs.

He could feel the golden dragon doing the same and giving chase, but he could feel the distance widening. Soon, he would be able to turn and face his attacker without fear of his weaker flanks being exposed.

Wherever Sol"s dragon came from, it carries no battle scars. This will be easy, thought Magma as his pride of his many battles with Sol's dragons and battle scars from the age of dreams fed his ego.

Talis watched in dumbfounded amazement as he watched the two dragons race for the tunnel. Then, he looked at Lilla and Lillith.

"There is nothing we can do now, Talis. We cannot help her. There are wounded. Go to Elisha, Whilst we go to help," said Lilla looking at Lillith and back to Talis ..... "Berolarn and Selene."

Talis nodded and raced up the stairs towards the elven princess, who was still pinned to the wall by four of her own elven arrows. She was soaked in blood when he reached her, head bowed, crucified against the wall. Both her arms were pinned at the shoulder by an arrow, one protruding from her chest and another in Elisha's stomach. Her breathing was weak and laboured. Talis knew Elisha was close to death as he snapped the arrows one by one and gently pulled her forward until she dropped into his arms. Gingerly he lifted her and started carrying her down the stairs.

He saw Lilla had reached Berolarn and was helping Selene to her feet, but Berolarn was not moving. As he set foot onto the cavern floor, he gently laid Elisha down and rushed onto the raised platform to find something to staunch the blood flow from Elisha's wounds. Talis ran up to the altar and pulled the red altar cloth off, sending the golden objects flying. As he turned, Talis immediately saw the pendant he had given to Lauren. Snatching it up as he ran, he jumped off the stage's apron and sped to Elisha. Dropping to his knees beside her, he gently lifted her head and placed the pendant around her neck. The pendant glowed faintly. It was not strong. But it did seem to stop the flow of blood from the wounds.

Chapter 39 – Lauren

As Lauren gave chase, pushing hard to catch Magma and end his reign of tyranny. It was still hard to believe she had transformed into a golden dragon of old. As chaos filled the cavern as the battle raged. Lilla had managed to cut her and Talis free. As Lilla ran towards Luther and Lillith, she could see Talis getting ready to use his bow. Lauren had considered using her sling, but it was too small and ineffective. Instead, she looked around for something to use as a weapon, and as her eyes surveyed the stage, her eyes saw a bright light emitting from the altar. She felt strangely drawn to the light; everything happening around her was forgotten, and the noise and melee of the raging battle were lost to her.

Lauren dreamily walked over to the altar to find the light source. It was the sceptre, the Dragonheart Stone. The stone was pulsing with a ray of brilliant light. She slowly placed her hand on the sceptre and moved her hand caressingly up the golden shaft towards the stone. As soon as her fingers touched the Dragonheart stone, the sceptre dissolved into nothing before her eyes. The whole world seemed to stop, and a soft, gentle voice greeted her.

"Hello, Lauren, daughter of Loran, daughter of Gabrielle. I am Sol Invictus, master of the unconquered sun," spoke a female voice.

The voice of Sol had told her many things. She had shown her many images of what had been and what could be. Finally, Sol revealed that she, Talis and Lilla were the chosen ones to bring balance to the world. It would be penance for their kin's sins and those of the dark lord. If they failed, the world would fall into permanent darkness.

It had been revealed that her father, Loran, had broken the laws of space and time in his quest for knowledge. As he travelled through the lands of the gods, he met Gabrielle, a golden dragon in human form who would become his wife.

When the voice had finished, Lauren knew who she was. Her mother was dominant in her as her father was dominant in Talis. Lauren knew what she needed to do, not knowing how she had transformed into her mother as she leapt off the stage towards Magma. She metamorphosised into a tremendous golden dragon from the age of dreams. Lauren felt exhilarated by the power that flowed through her veins as she chased Magma. Magma was a plague on the land, and he would pay for the suffering he caused. Lauren had no idea why, but she knew exactly how to control her mammoth dragon frame and power.

Magma was sure he had now put enough distance between them, and he turned sharply in the cold night air, opened his mouth and let forth a large blast of bellowing fire straight at the head of the chasing golden dragon. Lauren felt the heat of his attack hit the side of her neck and run down her body, causing immense pain. But she remained focused and flipped sidewards as Magma passed her, slicing his underbelly with her sharp talon feet.

Magma was enraged and flew directly at Lauren. He was going to destroy this meagre weak dragon. He would burn it alive and feast on its flesh. He roared, opening his mouth wide to grab the golden dragon by its neck. Lauren saw him coming, opened her mouth in response, and hit him with her own dragon fire blast. It hit him straight in the face. He roared in pain, unprotected from the magical fire of a dragon. Lauren then inflicted the most telling blow. As they passed each other, she whipped her tail at his face, one of her giant tail spikes punctured his eye, and he would see no more from that side.

Enraged by the new injuries, Magma lost all reason or sense of battle strategy, and he rushed again at Lauren, smashing into her side with his bulk. Both dragons fell from the skies spiralling out of control and landing heavily on the tower grounds as Magma took down one of the towers of the Tower of London and Lauren destroyed one of the outer walls of the grounds.

Magma was up first, and he ran at the golden dragon with no sense of reason remaining. Lauren reacted quickly, managing to get to her feet and sidestepping slightly as Magma hit her side with his bulk. However, as much as the pain inflicted by Magma on Lauren was costly, she had managed to grab his wing in her mouth and tear across it, using the momentum of Magma's blow. Magma screamed in agony as Lauren now took to the skies, leaving a prone Magma unable to fly. Instead, she circled, waiting for her opportunity as Magma searched for her in the heavens with sight only in one eye.

Lauren saw her chance and, seeing him prone, came at him from behind, both claws wide open, talon ready. Lauren grabbed his unguarded neck, digging in her talons as deep as her strength allowed and using the momentum of her great wings, she pulled upwards and twisted. Magma's scales and flesh gave way, and the weight of the ancient red dragon finally slipped from her grasp, and Lauren was back in the skies. She looked down, and Magma moved no more. Lauren landed and looked at the lifeless body of Magma. The golden dragon she had become had ripped Magma's throat out and drained away his life essence. She had won.

Darius and his Vampiri had silently watched this battle, and Darius turned and motioned his brethren to leave. Then, looking again over his shoulder, he took to the skies.

Lauren limped back through the tunnel, having transformed back to her usual self. She was battered and bruised, having a terrible burn on her side. But she could walk and was exhilarated at her former tormentor's death.

As she entered the cavern, she saw Talis look up, and he ran to her.

"Hello, shortcake," he smiled. "Am I glad to see you! Yeah, I know ….. I will not ask about all that dragon stuff."

"Talis," she jumped into his arms and momentarily, they were one again. Both crying in each other arms. "He has gone, dead. We have won," Lauren cried as she gripped him tighter. Slowly Talis pulled away as he remembered the injured Elisha, who he had just put the pendant onto.

"Come quickly. Elisha needs you. I have your pendant," he said urgently as he put his arm around Lauren and helped her limp across to Elisha.

She kneeled and gently took the pendant from Elisha's neck. Then, she placed the pendant back around her neck, and Talis watched in awe as some of Lauren's injuries started to heal. Talis then watched Lauren place her hand on Elisha's head and whisper a prayer to Sol, and Elisha's breathing steadied as she spoke, and slowly the wounds on Elisha were gone. Talis looked from Lauren to Elisha and back to Lauren. He noticed that though Lauren's wounds had closed, they had not healed like

Elisha's.

"Berolarn needs you, I think," said Talis. He pointed to Luther and Lillith standing with the kneeling Lilla as Selene cradled his head.

"Quickly," Lilla cried. "Please, Lauren, he is dying."

Lauren rushed over and looked at the pale, smiling face of Berolarn.

"Hush, girl." He said to Lilla, patting her hand.

Lauren placed her hand against Berolarn's head and whispered a prayer to Sol. Though Sol answered, and the pendant glowed. Berolarn did not react to her prayer and the pendant's power. His wounds remained, and he was still closing in on death. Lauren looked at Berolarn and then at Lilla.

"I ….. don't understand," said a confused Lauren.

Berolarn coughed and then spoke. "All powers have limits, Lauren, and though you bring great healing back to the land. You cannot change the predefined destiny of life. My body and mind now ebb away, and death comes for me. It has been preordained that this is my time."

He then looked at Selene and smiled at her as she cried and stroked his hair. Then turning his attention to Lilla, who was also sobbing.

"Why do you cry so badly for one who has had a full life and has done more than any who walks the lands," asked Berolarn, smiling.

"I don't know," replied Lilla, crying and laughing simultaneously. "I'm a bit overwhelmed to find out that I am pregnant," she said, looking at Talis. Who smiled, having totally forgotten this? "I have new and old parents, and one is about to leave me before I know him."

"I have two final gifts. Lean forward, Lilla. Bring your brow to my mouth," requested Berolarn weakly. Then, as she lowered her head, he whispered, "remember."

Lilla was suddenly overwhelmed with memories flooding back of her youth with her mother, Selene, and her father, Berolarn. The fun and joy of her life. Then she remembered a time with Luther and Lillith. It was all a bit disconnected as it was broken into two timelines. She shook her head and looked back at her father.

"Do not worry. The memories will fall into place soon enough, and your parents will fill in any gaps," soothed Berolarn.

"Selene, please, in my pocket," and he waited, "no, the other one," said Berolarn. Selene complied and pulled out a tiny silver charm.

"Berolarn," whispered Selene.

"This is a Celtic trinity knot and was a gift to your mother of our unity. I am sure your mother will not mind. I want you to have it, Lilla," said Berolarn with a weak smile.

"Yes, I would have gifted it to you," Selene smiled and nodded to Lilla

Luther looked on and thought he was going. It would not be long now.

"It is symbolic of your family and what we always will be. However, I used it for another purpose. It gives you access to the Solarian castle, where no other can enter, and it is also a key to the power. Call it, and it will show you the way. Talis, Lauren, you will need to go to the castle to learn for the next stage of your journey. Look for the secrets of life after death," whispered Berolarn, who struggled for breath.

Berolarn brought his hand up to Lilla's face and gently stroked it.

"Goodbye, my child, remember I am always there for you. Look deep into the knot, and you will find me." He looked up at Selene. "I always knew you would not leave me when it came to an end. Until we meet again." Berolarn whispered and closed his eyes as Selene's tears streamed down her face and dropped onto his face.

"Until we meet again," she said as he started to glow white. Selene kissed his brow and gently lowered his head to the ground. She pulled Lilla to her feet and pulled her back as a white tunnel of blinding light from the cavern's roof now engulfed Berolarn. Then the light and Berolarn were gone.

"It ends," whispered Selene.

"What has happened," sobbed Lilla. " Where is he," she shouted as she was wracked with emotion. Selene held her for a moment.

"He has gone to his father's. Sol has come and claimed him," said an emotionally drained Selene. She then slowly released Lilla. "We must go, Lilla. Our lives are forfeit if we stay here too long." As she spoke, she beckoned to Talis to come to her. Putting his arm around her, Talis led the sobbing Lilla away.

"You are right, Selene. We must leave. Hopefully, the snow

bears will still be waiting," said Luther. "Lillith, go and see if you can wake Biggy."

Lillith couldn't help but laugh as she looked over to the half-ogre, still tied up to a stake and apparently snoring as he slept.

"It will be my pleasure," she said, shaking her head still at the sight of Biggy.

"Lauren, how is Princess Elisha?" asked Luther.

"She will be fine. Let me see if I can wake her," replied Lauren.

"That is good news, Lauren. Where does the tunnel lead?" called Luther as Lauren walked over to Elisha.

"Outside the grounds of the Tower, some eight hundred yards to the east," replied Lauren as she knelt down to Elisha and started to shake her gently.

"Good. Hopefully, we can move back to where we left the bears undisturbed by the Vampiri and goblins alike," said Luther.

Biggy was awake and freed from his binds, and Elisha was not only on her feet. You would not have thought she had been mortally wounded. They hurried up the tunnel and made their escape away from the Tower. Talis was still in shock at the reality of seeing the dead shell of what had been Magma and the fact that Lauren, who was still carrying wounds, had done it by changing into a dragon. He privately mourned the loss of Berolarn, like Lilla and Selene. Berolarn was the most annoying man he had ever met, but Talis respected him as much as his father, Berolarn had been there for him over the last few months, and Talis wouldn't forget this.

The Children of Darkness and Light

As they were walking through the broken city of London. They heard a roar and thunderous feet running at them. They turned, and the three snow bears were running toward them. Never had Lauren been so pleased to see Bronte, Bobster and Bear. She ran and threw her arms around Bear as his giant head nuzzled her. The companions mounted the bears and rode away as the tower moved out of sight.

Chapter 40 – The Trip Home.

Finally, they reached the outskirts of the Mackenzie's stockade and the home of Fergus and Heather. Everything was peaceful. There was only a light breeze, and the snow fell gently on their heads. As they made their way toward the large gates of the compound. Bobster let out an enormous roar, and a scurry of activity could be heard as the gates started to open.

As the bears ran through the gates and started to make their way towards the home of Fergus, Talis noted that the villagers just stared at them, and there was a sombre mood in the air. He could feel it. He looked around at Lilla and Lauren and could tell they could also feel it by their inquisitive faces. As the bears ran towards their pen house, they all jumped off to varying degrees of success. They could see Fergus and Heather walking down the steps of their halls. They looked in the same state they did!

"Glad to see you brought my bears back. That's all five returned," grinned Fergus. So you managed to get back, though I see new faces and …… many missing," said Fergus as the smile started to drop.

"Where is Berolarn?" asked Heather sternly as she limped towards them.

"Sol came for him, Heather," said Luther. "He was happy that it was his time as he passed." Fergus and Heather looked shocked, momentarily lost for words. Then Heather beckoned them forward.

"Let's get you cleaned up and fed, and then you can tell us

your tale," smiled Heather as she tried to comprehend the news.

"This way," Heather beckoned as she turned and pulled Fergus with her.

As they entered, they heard Heather speaking to a woman and asking for water to be drawn and heated.

"Your lucky, the rooms you had are still your rooms. We left not long after you and rode to war," said Heather. "We can discuss it all. Please go to your rooms and shortly water will arrive. You can get cleaned up, and I will have the gear you still carry brought to you. If you are short of clothing, ask the woman I spoke to. Her name is Elsie." Then Heather turned to Fergus. "Fergus, go and check on the bears and see that our friend's items are brought to their rooms."

"You see, she still always ordering me about," he whispered loudly with a grin in Lauren's direction. Lauren giggled as Heather smiled and playfully slapped the departing Fergus on the back of the head.

"You will note a marked change in that one," laughed Heather.

"Please, you know the way," smiled Heather, holding her arm toward where the guest rooms were.

"But, ….. what happened to ….." said Talis.

"All in good time, Talis. Our story might be as long as yours," soothed Heather. "We will discuss all as we eat. But, now I insist, you all look like street filth, and you smell," she laughed kindly. "Though please introduce me to the two new companions," she asked.

"Oh, Yeah," said Talis, who turned towards Selene and

Lillith.

"I am Selene," smiled the woman in black.

"My name is Lillith. I was Luther's wife," said the woman in grey.

"Nice to meet both of you," nodded Heather. "Please now go and get cleaned up," she finished noting that the woman called Selene had a strange air about her. Whereas Lillith obviously was still in love with Luther. Too much hate in her eyes and sarcasm in her tone for it not to be. Nothing is ever simple, she thought to herself as they walked away from her.

Later in the day, as they all sat around the table, eating, they started to discuss the events that had led to the demise of Berolarn and the slaying of the ancient red dragon Magma.

"I would say you had been hit on the head one too many times," said Fergus as he chomped loudly on a leg of meat with the fat dribbling down his beard. "A dragon, a child's story of old, he had a magic fight with Berolarn, you say. Berolarn got smashed into a wall? With its tail. Well, I have never heard anything like it," he finished with an enormous belch.

"Fergus," warned Heather.

"What, oh sorry. I was getting carried away. Didn't mean to make light of the loss," Fergus said sheepishly. But he continued as before as he ripped the meat off the bone. "A dragon, you say. A man who landed in the fire of the mountain and turned into a dragon. Then, Lauren, you found the stone you sought, and your god stood before you? Really?" asked Fergus, looking spellbound.

"It is both our god, Fergus," said Lauren gently. Who hoped

she wasn't already overstepping by saying this. " Sol, Dagda ..... whatever name we give, she or him is one and the same."

"Well, Dagda is a man, ... well, he is Heather. If this Sol is a woman, they cannot be the same," scowled Fergus.

"Sol, or should I say Dagda, can choose any form Fergus," replied Lauren. Who was now wishing she hadn't started this? "They are celestial, divine.....they appear in whatever form they choose. It is their teachings, not the form, that matters."

"Tell me, Lauren," said Heather interrupting Fergus. "What did Sol ....."

"Dagda," interjected Fergus.

"Dagda say to you," asked Heather, glaring at Fergus, who had a smug defiant look on his face. I really wanted to talk about Berolarn, not gods, thought Heather.

"It is difficult to explain if I am honest. It was like I was floating toward a figure who was calling me. I was still in the cavern with Magma and the others...." said Lauren as she paused and thought about what had happened. "I was then shown many things, of what was, what is and what could be. Dagda told me that we, Talis, Lilla and myself, would be both the saviour and destroyer, and our decisions held the land's destiny. Our choices would be vital to overcome the dark lord and his screaming hordes. ....."

"..... Dagda then took me into the age of dreams and a different world. The images changed to my mother as a human and then as a ..... mighty golden dragon. Dagda said the gift is yours, as is the power to heal. With this comes the responsibility to make the right choices, Lauren. Suddenly I was drifting away from her….." said Lauren, who caught Fergus's eye, "Him, I mean and was coming back into the room and as I was coming back, I felt my body being torn apart and changing, though it brought no pain. I knew straight away I was now a dragon. I felt the power, the strength, the magic ….. but I was not looking in, it was me, and it was as if I had been a dragon all the time. I knew exactly what to do. My body moved seamlessly like a dragon, as did my mind. Everything was instinctive. Then as we have already told you, I battled Magma and ended up victorious and brought his reign of terror to an end."

"Can I see the stone," asked Fergus. He immediately held his hand out to Lauren. Lauren hesitated for a split second, then reached into a small bag on her side and pulled out the massive diamond, which glowed red in the middle. She passed it over to the waiting hand of Fergus. As soon as it left Lauren's hand, the red glow from the centre of the stone disappeared and became a wonderous yet clear giant diamond again.

"It is truly magic," said Fergus in awe as he held the Dragonheart stone up, looking for the red light. "If we go outside, can you transform into the dragon again?"

"Fergus," snapped Heather.

"What, I always wanted to see a dragon, and now we have one right in front of us. I might not get the chance again," protested Fergus.

"I am sorry, Fergus. I do not know how," said Lauren. Who went red with this startling admission. "It just happened. I think I need to learn and master it, Sol willing."

"Ah well, I am sure you will master it," said Fergus as he passed the stone back to Lauren.

You're a dragon and a vampire at the same time. I love that," laughed Fergus as it just dawned on him.

"Fergus, my love. You know you told me the night before the battle to tell you when you are annoying? Well, trust me, you are annoying," hissed Heather.

"Tell me what happened to Berolarn," continued Heather in a calm voice. Lilla explained his great battle with Magma, with snippets added by the others. She told Heather and Fergus of the great revelation of her heritage as she looked at Selene and Lillith. Lilla relaying her story prompted Heather to kick Fergus a few times. Especially when she saw his face after the true identity of Selene was revealed. When Lilla had finished, Heather knew there were no lies in the tale. Though she did wonder why Luther or the elven princess did not speak.

Heather mourned the loss of Berolarn and was scared for the world's fate with no Berolarn at the helm to guide the races. Instead, the clans must now rely on the children.

"What say you, vampire?" snapped Fergus. Heather could have throttled him when he spoke. Even without the drink, he was so blunt!

"You speaking to me," sneered Selene as she looked upon the fat mortal.

"Aye, you. ….." said Fergus, who was broken off from his comments by another kick from Heather.

"No, Heather, it's no good looking at me like that. If I have the daughter of our enemy in my house, I deserve to hear what she has to say," shouted Fergus.

"What would you like to know, err ….. chieftain," asked

Selene sarcastically.

"Well, one minute your bad, next minute your good….how does that work!? That would be a good start," bellowed Fergus.

"Have you loved? Do you know the happiness and pain of loving and losing a child? Do you? ….. We all have choices, chieftain. I had a love, a special love of a husband and my child, my life. I choose between the certain death of my child or the life of the child by making the child no more. My father hunted for me. He would have eventually found out about Lilla. He would have craved the child more than anything," said Selene, looking at Lilla. "I walked out of the light and back to the darkness and the hunger to save my child …. chieftain. I did this to stop him, ….. ever ….. ever ….. finding out about her, ….. Lilla. I wiped out Berolarn and Lilla from existence. I was even willing to kill Berolarn to ensure the child's safety. Do you know what that is like?" hissed Selene. "But you, sit there and look down on me as a thing of nightmare. Well, I am a nightmare for anyone who would hurt Lilla," she said as she squeezed Lilla's hand.

Lillith thought she was pretty impressed with the speech. But maybe she would be more the mother than Lillith had first considered.

Fergus got to his feet and walked around the table to Selene, who looked up at Fergus. She was ready for any attack. But then Fergus actually kneeled in front of her.

"I know your love, and I know your pain, vampire," he whispered. "Let it be known whilst I am chieftain. All of you, and you as well, Selene. You will always be welcome in my halls, even if the dark lord brings all the forces of the night to my doorstep."

Selene looked deep into his eyes to get a measure of Fergus.

"Thank you," she said quietly.

"What of you, Fergus, Heather? What of the clans? We can all clearly see your injuries," asked Luther.

"Heather, you are a better teller of tales than me," Fergus said as he got off his knees and returned to his chair.

Heather explained what happened after the companions left. How they had fought for their lives in battle on the snow plains. The horrors and deaths on that field were nothing but a mindless need to kill.

"I am sorry to hear about your brother, Heather," said Luther. "What does this mean now for the Douglas clan?"

"I am not sure," Heather said as she looked at Fergus. "We discussed it with my father as we told him the grievous news about Tomas. Unfortunately, both clans are now without an heir to take the role of chieftain. The Douglas clan line of chieftain should have been mine if I had not married Fergus. Though my father is full of grief, we talked about merging the clans as we would be stronger together than apart. Especially after the catastrophic losses we just experienced."

"Who knows, we might still have time to have another child, an heir to both clans," said Fergus in a serious tone.

"Aye, there is that punishment," said Heather rolling her eyes. Causing everyone to laugh.

"There is still life in the old dog, yet, my love," chuckled Fergus.

"I think we need to discuss more with my father and prominent members in both clans. We have much heritage that both would wish to retain, and old rivalries are hard to forget, even when we try to forge alliances through marriage. We are not renowned for ignoring the grievances of old. Even though they might have lost all meaning." said Heather, then she grinned at Fergus. "Then there would be the clan name ….. I can see it now, Mackenzie Douglas, Douglas Mackenzie, the fights and the male bravado of a name," she laughed, shaking her head as Fergus shouted.

"Mackenzie Douglas," cried Fergus laughing. Everyone else laughed at the thought of the name causing mass arguments and brawls.

The companions, Heather and Fergus, continued talking throughout the day. When it became evident that Fergus wasn't drinking, Lauren ventured to ask why.

"It makes me less compliant to the nagging of Heather," laughed Fergus, looking lovingly at Heather. Who shook her head. "To be honest, Lauren. I've been carrying my own demons. But, your visit and the battle have cleared my head for the first time in many years. It was quite evident when I was trying to hit some of the goblins I was not only slow. I was so out of breath." He patted his stomach, "something has to go, and I reckon it is this."

Everyone around the table burst out laughing at Fergus's humour, and with that, the party turned to lighter discussions.

As evening drew on, everyone finally started making excuses and retired for the night.

The next day Fergus insisted the companions stay for a while as they celebrated the passing of their kin and Berolarn. It seemed to Talis that it was another excuse for a party, but all thoroughly enjoyed the sadness and fun of the day.

Over the following days, Fergus took Elisha and Lauren out a few times with the snow bears allowing Lauren and Elisha to ride Bear each time. Fergus had been very serious most of the time as they went about the nearby lands of Caledonia. He discussed much with Elisha about the elves and Lauren about Sol/Dagda and the world's fate. Finally, Fergus promised Lauren they would only have to call, and the Celts and the snow bears would answer that call and be at their side. He made a similar promise to Elisha about a call from the elves as Elisha and Luther started to press the need to get back to Aslandure.

One evening, Fergus and Heather lay naked next to each other after what Fergus had now dubbed the baby games. Yesterday Heather had convinced him that they needed her to become pregnant again while she still had time. This was the second night they had slept with each other.

"This has not happened in years," said Fergus, out of breath.

"What hasn't happened in years," asked Heather as she turned on her side and looked at him. She then giggled as she saw the rising mound of his stomach.

"What's so funny," asked a bemused Fergus

"Look at your stomach. It is like a massive hill going up and down," grinned Heather.

"You love it," chortled Fergus as he proceeded to tickle Heather as she burst into hysterics, begging him to stop. Finally, after much protest from Heather, Fergus stopped, and they continued to talk.

"I was saying ……. You know we haven't slept with each other in all the years since Paden's death. It's been hard, you know that," said Fergus.

"Of course, we had a lot to deal with, but we move on Fergus," smiled Heather.

"It is the right thing, isn't it, Heather, to have another child?" whispered Fergus.

"We cannot replace Padan with another child Fergus. It doesn't mean we forget or lessen the pain of his loss. But, as we discussed, it will bring other joys to our life and will help cement our two clans together. Also, I am quite enjoying it," grinned Heather as she pulled him back towards her.

Twenty minutes later, as they lay there again, they continued to discuss the events of the world when Fergus offered a little thing he had noticed.

"When I have been with the Elven Princess and Lauren, there is an attraction," advanced Fergus.

"Well, it happens to you all the time, you dirty old bastard," laughed Heather as she punched Fergus.

"No, I didn't mean that!" chortled Fergus.

"I think the elven princess is in love with the child, Lauren. But, when she gets too close, she withdraws away from Lauren and its starts again. It is like watching a circle repeat itself," clarified Fergus.

"Bhah, you're just fantasising. Remembering days of your youth again, you old dog," quipped Heather.

"Well, they are stunning," laughed Fergus. "But, no, in all seriousness. The elven princess is troubled. I can see it in her words, actions and even more in her face."

"Well, it is not a problem. Love is all very natural. I see them like sisters or a young mother with her child," stated Heather. "What of Lauren? Does she give off a similar attachment or attraction?"

"No, I think she is oblivious, and obviously, she is evolving if everything they told us is true. I fear for one of them and also fear for us all. If Lauren and the elves are important to the lands, then this little thing could become a critical factor," expressed Fergus.

"Well, my love. I am sure when Dagda picked Lauren to be his chosen and placed Elisha by her side, he had his reasons. We will just have to see what fate brings," replied Heather.

The next day it was agreed it was time to leave the Celts. Fergus and Heather escorted them back through Caledonia's northern regions and arrived back at the docked elven ship. Heather pulled Lauren and Elisha to one side as the others unpacked and made their way on board the Endeavour.

"You are truly the chosen of Dagda, Lauren. Use your gifts wisely, child. Remember, you have been given much power. Much more will be demanded than you can give. Remember that some will try to manipulate such power for their desires. It is the greed of the races. Be careful and trust what is in your heart," smiled Heather, then hugged Lauren.

"Elisha, princess of the elves, I am thankful that I have met you and all that you have done for the people of Caledonia and what your people do for the lands," smiled Heather.

509

"I would say to you, trust your feelings always. It is not good to dwell on things or hide things from your heart," Heather whispered as she hugged Elisha.

Elisha just looked at Heather with bemusement and nodded.

The two women boarded Endeavour, and the ship set sail for Aslandure as Heather and Fergus waved them off.

"Let's go home, my love," said Fergus.

Chapter 41 – Questions to be Answered

They had been back at the elven city now for a few months. Princess Elisha had to demand that the king allow Selene into the city and treat her as a guest like all others. He had barked a lot about Selene being the daughter of the dark lord, and Elisha was bringing a Vampiri into their mist for the first time. But, after much argument and a guarantee from Elisha to watch her closely. Finally, Selene was allowed to reside at the palace with her other companions.

King Ethera had mourned the loss of Berolarn deeply when Elisha and the companions had told him their story. The King held a state funeral for the fallen Solarian shortly after their arrival. No one forgot the service he had done for the lands. The King informed them that a few months ago, they had received news that the attacks on the dwarves had stopped, and the armies of the goblins had withdrawn. They weren't sure why this had occurred, but perhaps it was due to the death of the ancient red dragon when he learned of the companion's quest. Either way, the elves and their allies had not marched to war, giving the humans more time to discuss their internal affairs, and the withdrawal of the dark lord's forces had allowed the dwarves to retake Heaven's Gateway.

All of the companions, except for Elisha and, to some degree Luther, spent time with Lilla and Talis. Lilla had started to dwell on everything she had learned at the time of Berolarn's death and needed advice and help to come to terms with her memories, the loss of her father and blossoming motherhood.

They had been back at the palace for nearly a month after

much prodding from Lauren. Talis finally picked up the courage to speak to Lilla.

They ate breakfast in Lilla's room and talked about Berolarn, Loran, and their childhood memories. Talis and Lauren told Lilla they had no memory of their mother, which was now Lauren's biggest regret. Lauren explained to them that she had touched the heart of a golden dragon, the outpouring of love and kindness was much a part of being a golden dragon as it was a part of her. Lauren felt they had missed this part of their lives as much as they had loved their father. The time with him had been full of fun and enjoyment, but a mother's love was missing.

Lilla agreed that this was the biggest regret drawing on her new memories. She loved her time with her mother Selene and then Lillith before that memory was also wiped. Though she had the memories, there was a disconnection from her life afterwards.

"Anyway, I need to go and find Elisha. She has lots of planning to do for a special event," commented Lauren, as she got up from the table and pushed the chair in.

"Oh, what's that? Anything interesting" asked Lilla.

"Ah, I cannot say, to be honest, Lilla. I am under strict instructions not to say anything, well, not yet anyway. I will tell you very soon, though," Lauren laughed and made her exit.

"What is all that about?" Lilla asked Talis.

"Err, I am not sure," replied Talis.

"Hmm, I am concerned about Lauren, sometimes. Have you noticed that the scars from Magma have not healed that well, even though she carries the pendant? I think they still pain her," mused Lilla as she gazed at the door that Lauren had exited.

"Lilla........Lilla," repeated Talis as he tried to break her concentration on the door.

"Sorry, Talis," she said, smiling as she turned to Talis. "What's up."

"Hmm, you know we love each other, and you are pregnant," Talis said nervously.

Lilla laughed, "Well, I noticed something strange about my stomach," she said as she gently rubbed her belly. "What are you going on about?"

"Well......er...... I have spoken to Selene, Luther, Lillith and Lauren, and they all think it's a good idea," Talis whispered.

"Talis, what is the matter with you? What are you saying?" asked Lilla, now showing concern on her face. Talis noticed the fears. This was not going as planned.

"Oh, nothing to worry about ..... I wondered if ..... err ..... we should, you know, get married," he said hastily as his face went bright red, and he looked pleadingly to a grinning Lilla.

"Well, if that is the best you can do, Talis Quicksilver, I better say yes before another girl has to suffer a similar proposal!" she laughed and kissed him passionately.

A few hours later, Lauren returned, and as soon as she walked in, unable to help herself, she spoke excitedly.

"Did you ask her? " She asked questionably to Talis. Who grinned and nodded. She swung around to Lilla. "Did you say yes?"

"I did give it some thought, Lauren," replied Lilla with a sad face.

"Oh no, you didn't ….. tell me you didn't, Lilla ….. you didn't say no," asked a gobsmacked Lauren.

"Of course, I said yes," said Lilla laughing. Lauren rushed over and started hugging them both.

Lilla and Talis found themselves trying to avoid Lauren wherever they could for the next few weeks. She was non-stop arranging their wedding and luckily spent a lot of time with Elisha. Which was probably forced. Lauren was a whirlwind setting things up and was non-stop talking about the wedding.

Finally, much to the relief of all, the wedding day came. Lilla and Talis were treated to a wedding as if they were royalty. Lilla couldn't believe the number of people in the chapel and the beautiful flowers that adorned the walls and aisles. Selene brought her up the aisle. Luther and Lillith agreed it would be what Berolarn, her father, would have wanted. As she exchanged the vows of love with Talis. Lilla was sure she heard a voice in her head; Berolarn wishing her great happiness and joy. It was as clear as if he was in the room behind her as she spun around, startled. Seeing no one but the smiling crowd, she thought it was just a dream as she smiled at a concerned Talis.

After the wedding, they had the most fantastic day partying with all the guests. They later admitted to Lauren that she had worked wonders.

As the days dreamily passed. Lilla was starting to feel the movement of the life inside her. Lilla found that her stomach was getting more prominent as she struggled to fit into her clothes.

A few weeks after the wedding, a message arrived for Talis, Lilla and Lauren. The companions were called to another meeting with the King and his closest advisors.

"It will not be long now, Lilla, until you bring life into the world," smiled the King as he spoke directly to Lilla. Then looking around the companions, he continued. "When this happens, tough choices will need to be made. We have all forgotten about the darkness in the world as we mourned the loss of our friends. But, we also witnessed the joys of love and sit awaiting the seed of this love," smiled Ethera as he nodded to Lilla and Talis.

Yet, our friend, the wisest among us, left us only at the start of this quest. We have long journeys still ahead and paths still unknown to us."

"I am not asking for any commitments from you, Lilla or Talis. But all of you ….. all of you have some tough decisions to make in the coming months.

"So who now will carry us on?" asked Ethera as he sat down and looked at the silent room.

Future Bloodline War Novels

Coming Soon

A little note: You will probably wonder why there are items that do not have as much relevance as you would think (or so it seems) in this novel. As Talis, Lilla and Lauren continue their quest to bring about the blood prince's end of tyranny. Things will become more apparent!

Printed in Great Britain
by Amazon

87061787R00301